the World

•Ironpass

•Northwarden

•Highcastle

THE BLACKWOOD

•Dolth

Rodez

Ran

Euper•

•Romney   •Tiburn

Bas-Tyra   Sadara

•Silden   Cheam

Cross   Rillanon

•Timons

Vale

THE KINGDOM SEA

THE KINGDOM OF ROLDEM

Deep Taunton•

EN REACHES

Mallow Haven

Pointer's Head•

The Peaks of Tranquility

F GREAT KESH

SHADOW

OF A

DARK QUEEN

SHADOW
OF A
DARK QUEEN

Volume I of the Serpentwar Saga

Raymond E. Feist

William Morrow and Company, Inc.

New York

It is the policy of William Morrow and Company, Inc., and its imprints and affiliates, recognizing the importance of preserving what has been written, to print the books we publish on acid-free paper, and we exert our best efforts to that end.

Library of Congress Cataloging-in-Publication Data

Feist, Raymond E.
    Shadow of a dark queen / Raymond E. Feist.
        p. cm.—(Serpentwar saga; v. 1)
    ISBN 0-688-12408-9
    I. Title. II. Series: Feist, Raymond E. Serpentwar saga; v. 1.
PS3556.E446S49 1994
813'.54—dc20   93-47455
                                                         CIP

Printed in the United States of America

First Edition

1 2 3 4 5 6 7 8 9 10

For Jonathan Matson:
more than my agent,
a good friend

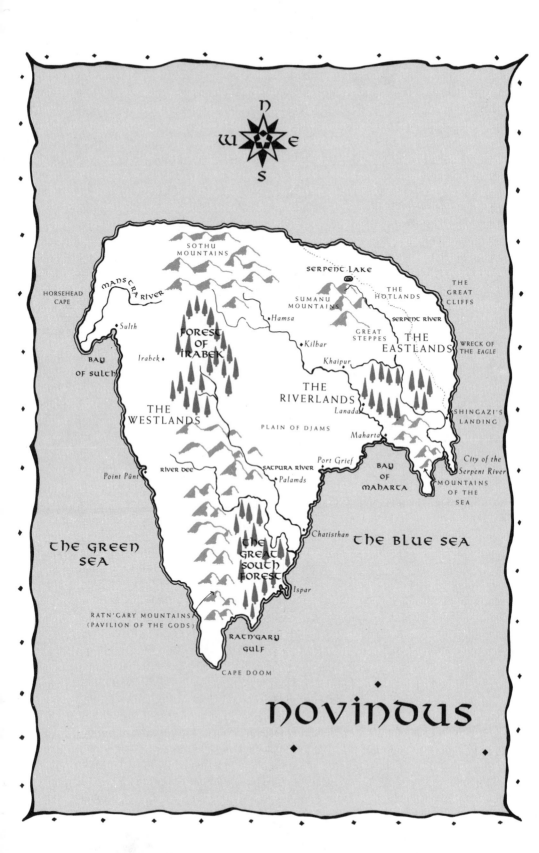

CAST OF CHARACTERS

Aglaranna—Elf Queen in Elvandar
Alika—"demon" cook at Sorcerer's Isle
Althal—elf in Elvandar
Avery, Rupert "Roo"—boy from Ravensburg, companion of Erik von Darkmoor; later prisoner; later member of Calis's company

Biggo—prisoner; later member of Erik's company

Calis—half elf, half human son of Aglaranna and Tomas; known as "The Eagle of Krondor"; leader of a military company
Culli—murdering mercenary

Dawar—mercenary in Nahoot's company
de Loungville, Robert "Bobby"—sergeant in Calis's company
de Savona, Luis—prisoner; later member of Calis's company
Durany—mercenary in Calis's company

Ellia—elven woman saved by Miranda
Embrisa—girl from Village Weanat
Esterbrook, Jacob—merchant in Krondor

Fadawah, General—Supreme Commander of the Armies of the Emerald Queen

Finia—woman at Village Weanat
Foster, Charlie—guard corporal in Calis's company
Freida—Erik's mother

Galain—elf in Elvandar
Gapi—general in Emerald Queen's army
Gert—old crone/charcoal burner met by Erik and Roo
Goodwin, Billy—prisoner; later member of Calis's company
Greylock, Owen—Swordmaster of Baron of Darkmoor; later member of Calis's company
Grindle, Helmut—merchant

Handy, Jerome—member of Calis's company

Jarwa—Sha-shahan of the Seven Nations of the Saaur
Jatuk—son of Jarwa, heir and later Sha-shahan of the surviving Saaur

Kaba—Shieldbearer to Jarwa
Kelka—corporal in Nahoot's company
Khali-shi—Novindus name for Death Goddess

Lalial—elf in Elvandar
Lender, Sebastian—Litigator and Solicitor at Barret's Coffee House in Krondor
Lims-Kragma—Death Goddess

Macros the Black—legendary sorcerer; considered the greatest practitioner of magic ever known
Marsten—sailor on *Trenchard's Revenge*
Mathilda—Baroness of Darkmoor
Milo—Innkeeper at Inn of the Pintail in Ravensburg
Miranda—mysterious friend to Calis
Monis—Jatuk's Shieldbearer
Mugaar—horse trader in Novindus
Murtag—Saaur warrior

Nakor the Isalani—strange companion of Calis
Nathan—new smith at Inn of the Pintail in Ravensburg
Notombi—former Keshian Legionary, then prisoner; later member of Calis's company

Pug—also known as Milamber; magician of great power; considered second only to Macros the Black in knowledge

Rian—one of Zila's mercenaries
Rosalyn—Milo's daughter
Ruthia—Goddess of Luck

Shati, Jadow—member of Calis's company
Shila—Saaur home world
Sho Pi—Isalani, former Monk of Dala; later prisoner; later member of Calis's company

Taber—tavern keeper in LaMut
Tarmil—villager at Weanat
Tomas—consort of Aglaranna, father of Calis; wearer of the Armor of Ashen-Shugar, last of the Dragon Lords
Tyndal—smith at Inn of the Pintail in Ravensburg

von Darkmoor, Erik—bastard son of the Baron von Darkmoor; later prisoner; later mercenary in Calis's company
von Darkmoor, Manfred—youngest son of Otto; later Baron
von Darkmoor, Otto—Baron of Darkmoor; father of Erik, Stefan, and Manfred
von Darkmoor, Stefan—Otto's eldest son

Zila—treacherous mercenary leader

BOOK I
ERIK'S TALE

Days, when the ball of our vision
Had eagles that flew unabashed to sun;
When the grasp on the bow was decision,
And arrow and hand and eye were one;
When the Pleasures, like waves to a swimmer,
Came heaving for rapture ahead!—
Invoke them, they dwindle, they glimmer
As lights over mounds of the dead.

> —George Meredith
> "Ode to Youth in Memory"

PROLOGUE

★★

DELIVERANCE

THE DRUMS THUNDERED.

Warriors of the Saaur sang their battle chants, preparing for the struggle to come. Tattered war banners hung limply from bloodied lances as thick smoke shrouded the sky from horizon to horizon. Green faces marked with yellow and red paint watched the western skies, where fires cast crimson and ocher light against the black shroud of smoke, blocking the vanishing sun and the familiar tapestry of the western evening stars.

Jarwa, Sha-shahan of the Seven Nations, Ruler of the Empire of Grass, Lord of the Nine Oceans, could not tear his gaze away from the destruction. All day he had watched the great fires burn, and even across the vast distance the howls of the victors and the cries of their victims had carried through the afternoon. Winds that once carried the sweet scent of flowers or the rich aroma of spices from the market now carried the acrid stench of charred wood and burned flesh. He knew without looking that those behind were bracing for the coming trial, resigned in their hearts that the battle was lost and the race would die.

"My lord," said Kaba, his Shieldbearer and lifelong companion.

Jarwa turned to his oldest friend and saw the concern etched faintly around his eyes. Kaba was an unreadable mask to all but Jarwa; the Sha-shahan could read him as a shaman reads a lore scroll. "What is it?"

"The Pantathian is here."

Jarwa nodded, but he remained motionless. Powerful hands closed in frustration over the hilt of his battlesword, *Tual-masok*—Blood Drinker in the ancient tongue—far more a symbol of office than the crown he had worn only on rare state occasions. He pushed its point down into the soil of his beloved Tabar, the oldest nation on the world of Shila. For seventeen years he had fought the invaders as they had driven his hordes back to the heartland of the Empire of Grass.

When he had taken the sword of the Sha-shahan while still a youth, warriors of Saaur had passed in review, filling the ancient stone causeway that spanned the Takador Narrows, the channel connecting the Takador Sea and the Castak Ocean. One hundred riders—a century—side by side, rode past, one hundred centuries to a *jatar:* ten thousand warriors. Ten jatar to a host, and ten host to a horde. At the height of his power, seven hordes answered Jarwa's battle horns, seven million warriors. Always on the move, their horses grazed the Empire of Grass, while children grew to adulthood playing and fighting among the ancient wagons and tents of the Saaur, stretching from the city of Cibul to the farthest frontier, ten thousand miles distant; it was an empire so vast that teams of horses and riders, never stopping their gallop, would take a full turning of the moon and half again to ride from the capital to the frontier, twice that from one border to the other.

Each season, one horde rested near the capital, while the others moved along the frontiers of the great nation, ensuring the peace by conquering all who refused tribute. Along the shores of the nine great oceans, a thousand cities sent food, riches, and slaves to the court of the Sha-shahan. And once a ten-year, the champions of the seven hordes gathered for the great games at Cibul, ancient capital of the Empire of Grass. Over the span of centuries, the Saaur had gathered all of Shila under the Sha-shahan's banner, all but the most distant nations on the far side of the world. It was Jarwa's dream to be the Sha-shahan who at last realized the dream of his ancestors, to bring the last city into the Empire and rule the entire world.

Four great cities had fallen to Jarwa's hordes, and another five had surrendered without a struggle, leaving fewer than a dozen outside the Empire. Then the riders of the Patha Horde had come to the gates of Ahsart, City of Priests. Soon disaster followed.

Jarwa steeled himself against the sounds of agony that carried through the twilight. The cries were of his people as they were led to the feasting pits. From what those few able to escape had said, the captives who were quickly slaughtered were perhaps the fortunate ones, along with those who had fallen in battle. The invaders, it was said, could capture the souls of the dying, to keep them as playthings, tormenting them for eternity as the shades of the slain were denied their final place among their ancestors, riding in the ranks of the Heavenly Horde.

Jarwa looked down upon the ancient home of his people from his vantage atop the plateau. Here, less than a half day's ride from Cibul, the ragged remnants of his once-mighty army camped. Even in this the darkest hour of the Empire of Grass, the presence of the Sha-shahan caused his warriors to stand tall, throw back their heads, and look toward the distant enemy with contempt. But no matter the posture of these warriors, their Sha-shahan saw something in their eyes no Lord of the Nine Oceans had ever seen before in the countenance of a Saaur warrior: fear.

Jarwa sighed, and turned without words to return to his tent. Knowing full well that no choice was left, still he hated to face the alien. Pausing before his own tent, Jarwa said, "Kaba, I have no faith in this *priest* from another world." He spit the word.

Kaba nodded, his scales gray from years of the hard life on horseback and from serving his Sha-shahan. "I know you have doubts, my lord. But your Cupbearer and your Loremaster concur. We have no choice."

"There is always a choice," whispered Jarwa. "We can choose to die like warriors!"

Softly Kaba reached out and touched Jarwa on the arm, a familiarity that would have brought instant death to any other warrior of the Saaur. "Old friend," he said softly, "this priest offers our children haven. We can fight and die, and let bitter winds sing away the memory of the Saaur. There will be no one left to chant remembrance to the Heavenly Horde of our valor, while fiends eat our flesh. Or we may send our remaining females and the young males to safety. Is there another choice?"

"But he is not like us."

Kaba sighed. "There is something . . ."

"This one's blood is cold," whispered Jarwa.

Kaba made a sign. "The cold-blooded are creatures of legend."

"And what of those?" asked Jarwa, motioning to the distant fire engulfing his capital.

Kaba could only shrug. Saying nothing more, Jarwa led his oldest friend into the Sha-shahan's tent.

The tent was larger than any other in camp, in reality a pavilion of many tents sewn together. Glancing around the interior, Jarwa felt cold grip his heart. So many of his wisest advisers and his most powerful loremasters were missing. Yet of those who remained, all looked to him with hope. He was Sha-shahan, and it was his duty to deliver the people.

Then his eyes fell upon the alien, and again he wondered which choice was wiser. The creature looked much like the Saaur, green scales covering arms and face, but he wore a deep-hooded robe that concealed the body, rather than the armor of a warrior or robes of a loremaster. He was small by Saaur standards, being less than two arms' span in height, and his snout was too long by half, and his eyes were all black, rather than red iris upon white as were the eyes of the Saaur. Where thick white nails should have been, black talons extended from his fingers. And his speech contained a sibilance, from the tongue that forked. As he removed his battered helm from his head and handed it to a servant, Jarwa voiced aloud what every warrior and loremaster in the tent thought: "Snake."

The creature bowed his head, as if this were a greeting instead of a deadly insult. "Yes, my lord," it hissed in return.

Several of Jarwa's warriors had hands upon weapons, but the old Cupbearer, second only to Kaba in importance to his lord, said, "He is our guest."

Long had the legends of the snake people been with the Saaur, the lizard people of Shila. Like the hot-blooded Saaur, yet not, they were creatures invoked by mothers to frighten naughty children at night. Eaters of their own kind, laying eggs in hot pools, the snake people were feared and hated with racial passion though none had been seen in the longest memory of the loremasters of the Saaur. In the legend it was said that both races were created by the Goddess, at the dawn of time, when the first riders of the Heavenly Horde were hatched. The servants of the Green Lady, Goddess of the Night, the snakes had remained in her mansion, while the Saaur had ridden forth with her and her god-brothers and god-sisters. Abandoned to this world by the Goddess, the Saaur had prospered, but always the memory of the others, the snakes, remained. Only the Loremaster knew which tales were history and which were myth, but one thing Jarwa knew: from birth, the Sha-shahan's heir was taught that no snake was worthy of trust.

The snake priest said, "My lord, the portal is ready. Time grows short. Those feasting upon the bodies of your countrymen will tire of their sport, and as night deepens, and their powers grow, they will be here."

Ignoring the priest for a moment, Jarwa turned to his companions and said, "How many jatar survive?"

Tasko, Shahan of the Watiri, answered. "Four and but a part of a fifth." With a note of finality in his voice, he said, "No jatar remains intact. These last are gathered from remnants of the Seven Hordes."

Jarwa resisted the impulse to surrender to despair. Forty thousand riders and part of another ten thousand. That was all that survived from the Seven Great Hordes of the Saaur.

Jarwa felt blackness grip his heart. How he remembered his outrage when word came from the Patha Horde of the priests' defiance and refusal to pay tribute. Jarwa had ridden for seven months to lead personally the final attack against Ahsart, City of Priests. For a moment he felt a stab of remorse cut deep into his soul; then he silently chided himself: could any ruler have known that the insane priests of Ahsart would destroy everything rather than let the Saaur unite the world under one ruler? It had been the mad high priest, Myta, who had unsealed the portal and let the first demon through. There was small com-

fort in knowing that the demon's first act was to capture Myta's soul for tor-
ment as he ripped his head from his body. One Ahsart survivor had claimed a
hundred warrior priests had attacked the one demon as it devoured Myta's
flesh, and none had survived.

Ten thousand priests and loremasters alongside more than seven million
warriors had died holding the foul creatures at bay as they battled from the
farthest border of the Empire to its heart, in a war spanning half a world. A
hundred thousand demons had died, but each one's destruction was paid for in
dear blood, as thousands of warriors threw themselves fearlessly at the hideous
creatures. The loremasters had used their arts to good effect at times, but always the demons returned. For years the fighting had continued, a running
battle past four of the nine oceans. Children had been born in the Sha-shahan's
camp, grown to young adulthood, and died in the fighting, and still the demons came. The loremasters looked in vain for a means of closing the portal
and turning the tide of battle to the Saaur.

From the other side of the world they had fought their way back to Cibul, as
the demon army poured through the portal between worlds, and now another
portal was being opened, offering hope for the Saaur: hope through exile.

Kaba pointedly cleared his throat, and Jarwa forced away regret. Nothing
would be gained from it; as his Shieldbearer had said, there was no choice.

"Jatuk," Jarwa said, and a young warrior stepped forward. "Of seven sons,
one to rule each horde, you are the last," he said bitterly. The young warrior
said nothing. "You are Ja-shahan," pronounced Jarwa, officially naming him
heir to the throne. The youth had joined his father but ten days before, riding
out to his father's camp accompanied by his personal retinue. He was but eighteen years of age, barely more than a year from the training grounds and a
veteran of only three battles since coming to the front. Jarwa realized that his
youngest son was a stranger, having been only a crawling infant when he had
left to bring Ahsart to her knees. "Who rides to your left?" he asked.

Jatuk said, "Monis, birth companion." He indicated a calm-looking young
man who already bore a proud scar along his left arm.

Jarwa nodded. "He shall be your Shieldbearer." To Monis he said, "Remember, it is your duty to guard your lord with your life; more: it is your duty to
guard his honor. No one will stand closer to Jatuk than you, not mate, not
child, not Loremaster. Always speak truth, even when he wishes not to hear it."

To Jatuk he added, "He is your shield; always heed his wisdom, for to ignore
your Shieldbearer is to ride into battle with an arm tied to your side, blind in
one eye, deaf in one ear."

Jatuk nodded. Monis was now granted the highest honor given to one not
born of the ruling family; he could speak his mind without fear of retribution.

Monis saluted, his balled right fist striking his left shoulder. "Sha-shahan!"
he said, then looked at the ground, the sign of complete deference and respect.

"Who guards your table?"

Jatuk said, "Chiga, birth companion."

Jarwa approved. Selected from the same birth crèche, these three would know one another as they knew themselves, a stronger tie than any other. To the named warrior Jatuk said, "You shall give up your arms and armor and you shall remain behind."

The honor was mixed with bitterness, for the honor of being Cupbearer was high, but giving up the call to battle was difficult for any warrior.

"Protect your lord from the stealthy hand, and from the cunning word whispered over too much drink by false friends."

Chiga saluted. Like Monis, he was now free to speak to his lord without fear of punishment, for in being Cupbearer he was pledged to protect Jatuk in all ways as much as the warrior who rode on the Ja-shahan's shield side.

Jarwa turned to another figure, his Loremaster surrounded by several acolytes. "Who among your company is most gifted?"

The Loremaster said, "Shadu. He remembers everything."

Jarwa addressed the young warrior priest. "Then take the tablets and the relics, for you are now chief keeper of the faith. You will be Loremaster to the People." The acolyte's eyes widened as his master handed the ancient tablets, large sheaves of parchment kept between board covers, and written upon with ink nearly faded white with age. But more, he was given the responsibility to remember the lore, the interpretations, and the traditions, a thousands words in memory for each word drawn in ink by an ancient hand.

Jarwa said, "Those who have served with me from the first, this is my final charge to you. Soon the foe comes a last time. We will not survive. Sing your death songs loudly and know that your names will live in the memory of your children, upon a distant world under an alien sky. I know not if their songs can carry across the void to keep the memory of the Heavenly Horde alive, or if they will begin a new Heavenly Horde upon this alien world, but as the demons come, let every warrior know that the flesh of our flesh shall endure safely in a distant land."

Whatever the Sha-shahan might feel was hidden behind a mask as he said, "Jatuk, attend me. The rest of you, to your appointed places." To the snake priest he said, "Go to the place where you work your magic, and know that should you play my people false, my shade shall break free from whatever pit of hell holds it and cross the gulf to hunt you down if it takes ten thousand years."

The priest bowed and hissed, "Lord, my life and honor are yours. I remain, to add my small aid to your rear guard. In this pitiful fashion I show my people's respect and wish to bring the Saaur, who are so like us in so many ways, to our home."

If Jarwa was impressed by the sacrifice, he gave no hint. He motioned his youngest son outside the great tent. The youth followed his father to the ridge and looked down upon the distant city, made hellish in the demons' fires. Faint screams, far beyond those made by mortal throat, tore the evening, and the young leader pushed back the urge to turn his face away.

"Jatuk, by this time tomorrow, on some distant world, you will be Sha-sha-han of the Saaur."

The youth knew this was true no matter how much he would wish it otherwise. He made no false protest.

"I have no trust of snake priests," whispered Jarwa. "They may seem like us, but always remember, their blood runs cold. They are without passion and their tongues are forked. Remember also the ancient lore of the last visit to us by the snakes, and remember the tales of treachery since the Mother of us all gave birth to the hot bloods and the cold bloods."

"Father."

Putting his hand, calloused with years of swordwork and scarred by age and battle, upon his son's shoulder, he gripped hard. Firm young muscle resisted under his grasp, and Jarwa felt a faint spark of hope. "I have given my oath, but you will be the one who must honor the pledge. Do nothing to disgrace your ancestors or your people, but be vigilant for betrayal. A generation of service to the snakes is our pledge: thirty turnings of this alien world. But remember: should the snakes break the oath first, you are free to do as you see fit."

Removing his hand from his son's shoulder, he motioned for Kaba to approach. The Sha-shahan's Shieldbearer approached with his lord's helm, the great fluted head covering of the Sha-shahan, while a groom brought a fresh horse. The great herds had perished, and the best of what remained would go to the new world with the Saaur's children. Jarwa and his warriors would have to make do with the lesser animals. This one was small, barely nineteen hands, hardly large enough to carry the Sha-shahan's armored weight. No matter, thought Jarwa. The fight would be a short one.

Behind them, to the east, a crackle of energy exploded, as if a thousand lightning strikes flashed, illuminating the night. A second later a loud thunder peal sounded, and all turned to see the shimmering in the sky. Jarwa said, "The way is open."

The snake priest hurried forward, pointing down the ridge. "Lord, look!"

Jarwa turned to the west. Out of the distant flames small figures could be seen flying toward them. Bitterly Jarwa knew this was a matter of perspective. The screamers were the size of an adult Saaur, and some of the other fliers were even larger. Leathery wings would make the air crack like a wagoneer's whip, and shrieks that could drive a sane warrior to madness would fill the dark. Looking at his own hand for any signs of trembling, Jarwa said to his son, "Give me your sword."

The youth did as he was bid, and Jarwa handed his son's sword to Kaba. Then he removed Tual-masok from his scabbard and gave it, hilt first, to his son. "Take your birthright and go."

The youth hesitated, then gripped the hilt. No loremaster would glean this ancient weapon from his father's body to present to the heir. It was the first time in the memory of the Saaur that a Sha-shahan had voluntarily surrendered the bloodsword while life remained in his heart.

Without another word, Jatuk saluted his father, turned, and walked to where his own companions waited. With a curt wave of his hand, he motioned for them to mount and ride to where the remaining masses of the Saaur gathered to flee to a distant world.

Four jatar would ride through the new portal, while the remaining part of the fifth, as well as all of Jarwa's old companions and loremasters, would stay behind to hold the demons at bay. Chanting filled the air while the loremasters wove their arts, and suddenly the air erupted in blue flames as a wall of energy spread across the sky. Demons flying into the trap screamed in anger and pain as blue flames seared their bodies. Those that quickly turned away were spared, but those that were too far into the energy field smoldered and burned, evil black smoke pouring from their fiery wounds. A few of the more powerful creatures managed to reach the ridge, where Saaur warriors leaped without hesitation to hack and chop at their bodies. Jarwa knew it was a faint triumph, for only those demons whom magic had seriously wounded could be so quickly dispatched.

Then the snake priest howled. "They are leaving, lord."

Jarwa glanced over his shoulder and saw the great silver portal hanging in the air, what the snake had called a rift. Through it rode the van of the Saaur youth, and for an instant Jarwa imagined he could see his son vanish from sight—though he knew it was wishful thinking. The distance was too vast to make out such detail.

Then Jarwa returned his attention to the mystic barrier that now shone white-hot where demons brought their own arts to bear. He knew the fliers were more a nuisance than a danger: their speed made them deadly for lone riders or the weak or wounded, but a strong warrior could dispatch one without difficulty. It would be those that followed the fliers who would end his life.

Rents in the energy appeared along the face of the barrier, and as they did, Jarwa could glimpse dark figures approaching from beyond it. Large demons who could not fly, save by magic, hurried over the ground, running at the best speed of a Saaur horse and rider, their evil howls adding to the sounds of battle. The snake priest put forth his hand and flames erupted where a demon attempted to pass through a rent in the barrier, and Jarwa could see the snake priest stagger with the effort.

Knowing the end was but moments away, Jarwa said, "Tell me one thing, snake: why do you chose to die here with us? We had no choice, and you were free to leave with my children. Does death at the hands of those"—he motioned toward the approaching demons—"hold no terror for you?"

With a laugh the Ruler of the Empire of Grass could only think of as mocking, the snake priest said, "No, my lord. Death is freedom, and you shall quickly learn that. We who serve in the palace of the Emerald Queen know this."

Jarwa's eyes narrowed. So the ancient legends were true! This creature *was* one of those whom the Mother Goddess had birthed. With a flash of anger, Jarwa knew that his race was betrayed and that this creature was as bitter an enemy as those who raced to eat his soul. With a cry of frustration, the Sha-shahan struck out with his son's sword and severed the head from the shoulders of the Pantathian.

Then the demons were loose among the rear guard and Jarwa could spare but a moment to think of his son and his companions' children, upon a distant world under an alien sun. As the Lord of the Nine Oceans turned to face his foe, he made a silent prayer to his ancestors, to the Riders of the Heavenly Horde, to watch over the children of the Saaur.

One form loomed above the rest, and as if sensing his approach, the lesser demons parted. A figure twice the height of the tallest Saaur, more than twenty-five feet tall, strode purposefully toward Jarwa. Powerful of form, his body looked much like that of a Saaur—broad shoulders tapering to a narrow waist, large arms and legs well fashioned—but his back bore huge wings that seemed composed of tattered black leather, and his head . . . A triangular skull, much like that of a horse, was covered by thin skin, as if leather had been stretched across bone. Teeth were exposed, fangs close together, and the eyes were pits of red fire. Around his head danced a ring of flames, and his laughter turned Jarwa's blood to ice.

The demon pushed past his lesser brethren, ignoring those who rushed forward to defend the Sha-shahan. He struck out, ripping flesh apart as easily as a Saaur tore bread. Jarwa stood ready, knowing each moment stolen before his death allowed more of his children to flee through the rift.

Then the demon reared over Jarwa as a warrior stands over a child. The Sha-shahan struck out with as much strength as he could muster, raking his son's sword across the creature's outstretched arm. The demon shrieked at the pain, but then ignored the wound, slowing for a second while black talons the size of daggers skewered Jarwa, punching through armor and body, as he gripped him around the middle.

The demon raised the ruler of the Saaur up toward his face and held him at eye level. As the light in Jarwa's eyes began to fade, the demon laughed and said, "You are the ruler of nothing, foolish mortal. Your soul is mine, little creature of flesh! And after I eat you, still shall you linger, to amuse me between feedings!"

For the first time since birth, Jarwa, Sha-shahan of the Seven Nations, Ruler of the Empire of Grass, Lord of the Nine Oceans, knew terror. And as his mind cried out, his body went limp. From a vantage above his own flesh, he felt his spirit rise, to fly to the Heavenly Horde, yet something bound him and he could not leave. He perceived his own body, being devoured by this demon, and in his spirit's mind he heard the demon say, "I am Tugor, First Servant of Great Maarg, Ruler of the Fifth Circle, and you are my plaything."

Jarwa cried, but he had no voice, and he struggled, though he had no body, and his spirit was held by mystic chains as binding as iron on flesh. Wailing spirit voices told him his companions were also falling. With what will remained he turned his perceptions toward the distant rift and saw the last of his children leaving. Taking what small comfort he could from the sight of the rift suddenly vanishing in the night, the shade of Jarwa wished his son and his people safe haven and protection from the snakes' deceit on the distant world the Pantathians called Midkemia.

1

★★

CHALLENGE

THE TRUMPET SOUNDED.

Erik wiped his hands on his apron. He was doing little real work since finishing his morning chores, merely banking the fire so he would not have to restart a cold forge should there be new work later in the day. He considered that unlikely, as everyone in the town would be lingering in the square after the Baron's arrival, but horses were perverse creatures who threw shoes at the least opportune moment, and wagons broke down at the height of inconvenience. Or so his five years of assisting the blacksmith had taught him. He glanced at where Tyndal lay sleeping, his arm wrapped lovingly around a jug of harsh brandy. He had begun drinking just after breakfast, "hoisting a few to the Baron's health," he claimed. He had fallen asleep sometime in the last hour while Erik finished the smith's work for him. Fortunately, there was little the boy couldn't do, he being large for his age and an old hand at compensating for the smith's shortcomings.

As Erik finished covering the coals with ashes, he could hear his mother calling from the kitchen. He ignored her demand that he hurry; there was more than enough time. There was no need to rush: the Baron would not have reached the edge of the town yet. The trumpet announced his approach, not his arrival.

Erik rarely considered his appearance, but he knew today was going to thrust him into the forefront of public scrutiny, and he felt he should attempt to look respectable. With that thought, he paused to remove his apron, carefully hung it on a peg, then plunged his arms into a nearby bucket of water. Rubbing furiously, he removed most of the black soot and dirt, then splashed water on his face. Grabbing a large clean cloth off a pile of rags used for polishing steel, he dried himself, removing what the water hadn't through friction.

In the dancing surface of the water barrel he considered his broken reflection: a pair of intense blue eyes under a deep brow, a high forehead from which shoulder-length blond hair swept back. No one today would doubt that he was his father's son. His nose was more his mother's, but his jaw and the broad grin that came when he smiled were the mirror image of his father's. But where his father had been a slender man, Erik was not. A narrow waist was his only heritage from his father. He had his maternal grandfather's massive shoulders and arms, built up through working at the forge since his tenth birthday. Erik's hands could bend iron or break walnuts. His legs were also powerful, from supporting plow horses who leaned on the smith while he cut, filed, and shod their hooves, or from helping to lift carts when replacing broken wheels.

Erik ran his hand over his chin, feeling the stubble. Blond as a man could get, he had to shave only every third day or so, for his beard was light. But he knew his mother would insist on him looking his best today. He quickly hurried to his pallet behind the forge, taking care not to disturb the smith, and fetched his razor and mirror. A cold shave was not his idea of pleasure, but far less irritating than his mother would be should she decide to send him back for the razor. He wet his face again and started scraping. When he was done, he looked at himself one more time in the shimmering water.

No woman would ever call Erik handsome: his features were large, almost coarse, from the lantern jaw to the broad forehead; but he possessed an open, honest look that men found reassuring and women would come to admire once they got used to his almost brutish appearance. At fifteen years of age, he was already the size of a man, and his strength was approaching the smith's; no boy could best him at wrestling, and few tried anymore. Hands that could be clumsy when helping set platters and mugs in the common room were sure and adroit when working in the forge.

Again his mother's voice cut through the otherwise quiet morning, demanding he come inside now. He rolled down his sleeves as he left the smithy, a small building placed hard against the outside rear wall of the livery. Circling the barn, he came into sight of the kitchen. As he passed the open stable door, he glanced at those horses left in his care. Three travelers were guesting with his master, and their mounts were quietly eating hay. The fourth horse was lying up from an injury and she neighed a greeting at Erik. He couldn't help but smile; in the weeks he had been tending her she had come to expect his midmorning visits, as he trotted her out to see how she mended.

"I'll be back to visit later, girl," he called softly to her.

The tone of the horse's snort revealed her less than enthusiastic response.

Despite his age, Erik was one of the best handlers of horses in the region surrounding Darkmoor, and had earned the reputation of being something of a miracle worker. Most owners would have put down the injured mare, but Owen Greylock, the Baron's Swordmaster, valued her highly. He judged it a prudent risk to put her into Erik's care, for if he could make her sound enough to breed, a fine foal or two would be worth the trouble. Erik was determined to make her sound enough to ride again.

Erik saw his mother at the rear door of the Inn of the Pintail's kitchen, her face a mask of resolve. A small woman of steely strength and determination, Freida had been pretty once, though hard work and the world's cares had taken their toll. While not yet forty years of age, she looked closer to sixty. Her hair was completely grey where it had once been a luxurious brown, and her green eyes were set in a face of lines and angles. "Quickly," she commanded.

"He'll not be here for some time," answered Erik, hiding his irritation poorly.

"There is only a moment," she replied, "and should we lose it, we shall never again have the chance. He's ill and may not return again."

Erik's brow furrowed at the unspoken implication of that statement, but his mother said nothing more. The Baron rarely visited his smaller holdings anymore, save for occasional ceremonies; at harvest it was the custom for him to visit one of the villages and towns that provided Darkmoor with most of its wealth, the finest grapes and wine in the world, but the Baron visited only a single vintners' hall, and the one in the town of Ravensburg was among the least important. Besides, Erik was convinced that for the last ten years the Baron had intentionally avoided this particular town, and knew the reason why.

Glancing at his mother, he recalled with a bitter taste in his mouth how, ten years before, she had half dragged, half led Erik through the crowd watching the Baron's arrival. Erik remembered the looks of astonishment and horror on the faces of the town officials, guildmasters, vintners, and growers when his mother had demanded that the Baron admit to Erik's paternity. What should have been a joyous celebration of the first taste of the harvest was turned into an embarrassment for all in the town, especially for little Erik. Several men of position had come to Freida several times after that, asking her forbearance in the future, a plea she politely listened to without comment or promise.

"Stop your woolgathering and come inside," Freida demanded. She turned, and he followed her inside the kitchen.

Rosalyn smiled as Erik entered, and he nodded at the serving girl. The same age and companions since babyhood, Erik and the innkeeper's daughter had been like brother and sister, confidants and best friends. Lately he had become aware that something deeper was blossoming in her, though he was unsure what to do about it. He loved her, but in a brotherly fashion, and he had never thought of her as a possible wife—his mother's obsession closed off any discussion of such mundane concerns as marriage, trade, or travel. Of all the boys his age in the town, he was the only one not officially employed at a craft. His apprenticeship to Tyndal was informal, and despite his talent for the craft, he had no established standing with the guild offices, either in the Western Capital of Krondor or in the King's city of Rillanon. Nor would his mother let him discuss having the smith live up to his oft-repeated promise of forwarding a formal petition to the guild to admit Erik as his apprentice. This should have been the end of Erik's first year as an apprentice or working at a trade. Even though he knew his way around a forge better than apprentices two or three years older, he would start two years behind others, *if* his mother let him apprentice the next spring.

His mother, whose head barely reached his chin, said, "Let me look at you." She reached up and took his chin in her hand, as if he were still a child, not nearly a man, and turned his head one way, then another. With a dissatisfied clucking sound, she said, "You're still stained with soot."

"Mother, I'm a blacksmith!" he protested.

"Clean yourself in the sink!" she commanded.

Erik knew better than to say anything. His mother was a creature of iron will and unbending certainty. Early he had learned never to argue with her; even when he was wrongly accused of some transgression, he would simply and quietly take whatever discipline was meted out, for to protest would only increase the punishment. Erik stripped off his shirt and laid it over the back of a chair next to the table used to clean and prepare meats. He saw Rosalyn's amusement at his being bullied by his small mother, and he feigned a scowl at her. Her smile only broadened as she turned away, picking up a large basket of freshly washed vegetables to carry them into the common room. Turning at the door, she bumped it open and as she backed through stuck her tongue out at him.

Erik smiled as he plunged his arms into the water she had just abandoned after cleaning the vegetables. Rosalyn could make him smile as could no other person. He might not fully understand the powerful stirrings and confusing urges that woke him late at night as he dreamed about one or another young woman in the village—he understood the specifics of mating, as any child raised around animals did, but the emotional confusion was new to him. At least Rosalyn didn't confuse him the way some of the older girls did, and of one thing he was certain: she was his best friend in the world. As he splashed water on his face again, he heard his mother say, "Use the soap."

He sighed and picked up the foul-smelling block of soap sitting on the back of the sink. A caustic mix of lye, ash, rendered tallow, and sand used to scrape clean serving platters and cooking pots, it would peel the skin from face and hands with repeated use. Erik used as little as he could get away with, but when he was done he was forced to admit that a fairly impressive amount of soot had come off into the sink.

He managed to rinse off the soap before his skin began to blister, and took a cloth handed him by his mother. He dried and put his shirt back on.

Leaving the kitchen, they entered the common room, where Rosalyn was finishing putting the vegetables into the large cauldron of stew that hung on a hook at the hearth. The mix would simmer slowly all afternoon, filling the common room with a savory smell that would have mouths watering by suppertime. Rosalyn smiled at Erik as he passed, and despite her cheerfulness, he felt his mood darkening as he anticipated the coming public scene.

Reaching the entrance to the inn, Erik and his mother discovered Milo, the innkeeper, peering through the open door. The portly man, with a nose like a squashed cabbage from years of ejecting ruffians from the common room, drew upon a long pipe as he observed the calm town. "Could be a quiet afternoon, Freida."

"But a frantic evening, Father," said Rosalyn as she came to stand at Erik's side. "Once the people tire of waiting for a glimpse of the Baron, they'll all come here."

Milo turned with a smile and winked at his daughter. "An outcome to be devoutly prayed for. I trust the Lady of Luck has no other plans."

Freida muttered, "Ruthia has better things to waste her good luck on, Milo." Taking her powerfully built son by the hand, as if he were still a baby, she led him purposefully through the door.

As Erik and his mother left the confines of the inn, Rosalyn said, "She's determined, Father."

"That she is and always has been," he said, shaking his head and puffing on his pipe. "Even as a child she was most headstrong, willful. . . ." He put his arm around his daughter's shoulder. "Nothing like your mother, I'm pleased to say."

Rosalyn said, "The gossips have it that you were one of the many seeking Freida's hand years ago."

Milo chuckled. "They do, do they?" Clucking his tongue, he added, "Well, that's the truth. Most men my age were." He smiled down at his daughter. "Best thing that happened was her saying no. And your mother saying yes." He moved away from his only child and said, "Most of the boys were after Freida. She was a rare beauty in those days. Green flashing eyes and chestnut hair, slender but ample where it counts, and a proud look that could make a man's pulse race. She moved like a racehorse and carried herself like a queen. It's why she caught the Baron's eye."

A trumpet sounded from the edge of the town square and Rosalyn said, "I'd better be back to the kitchen."

Milo nodded. "I'm going down to the square to see what happens, but I'll come straight back."

Rosalyn gripped his hand for a moment, and her father saw the concern in her eyes she had hidden from Erik. Nodding his understanding, he squeezed her hand for an instant, then released it. He turned and made his way through the street in front of the inn, following the route taken by Erik and Freida.

ERIK USED HIS bulk to ease through the crowd. Despite his strength, he was by nature a gentle youngster and would not use force, but his very presence caused others to give way. Broad of shoulders and arms, he could have been a young warrior by his looks, but he had a strong distaste for conflict. Quiet and introspective, after work he preferred a quiet cup of broth to curb his appetite while waiting for dinner, as he listened to the old men of the town tell stories, to the roughhousing and attempted girl-chasing his contemporaries saw as the height of recreation. The occasional girl who turned her attention upon him almost inevitably found his reticence daunting, but it was nothing more than his inability to think of anything clever to say. The prospect of any intimacy with a girl terrified Erik.

A familiar voice called his name, and Erik turned to see a ragged figure push through the press, using nimble quickness rather than size to navigate a path to Erik's side. "Hello," said Erik in greeting.

"Erik. Freida," said the youth in return. Rupert Avery, known by everyone in the village as Roo, was the one boy Freida had forbidden Erik to play with as a child, on many occasions, and the one boy Erik had preferred to play with. Roo's father was a teamster, a rough man who was either absent from the village—driving his team down to Krondor, Malac's Cross, or Durrony's Vale—or lying drunken in his bed. Roo had grown up wild, and there was something dangerous and unpredictable in his nature, which was why Erik had been drawn to him. If Erik had no tongue to charm the ladies, Roo was a master of seduction, at least to hear him tell it. A knave and a liar, as well as an occasional thief, Roo was Erik's closest friend after Rosalyn.

Freida nodded almost imperceptibly in return. She still didn't like the youngster after knowing him all his life; she suspected his hand in every dishonest act or criminal event that took place in Ravensburg. Truth to be told, she was more often right than not. She glanced at her son and bit back a bitter comment. Now he was fifteen years of age, Erik's willingness to be controlled by his mother was lessening. He had assumed most of the duties around the forge from Tyndal, who was drunk five days out of seven.

Roo said, "So you're going to ambush the Baron again?"

Freida threw him a black look. Erik merely looked embarrassed. Roo grinned. He had a narrow face, intelligent eyes, and a quick smile, despite uneven teeth. Even further from being handsome than Erik, he had something alive in his manner and a quick intensity that those who knew him found likable, even captivating. But Erik also knew he had a murderous temper and lost it often, which had caused him to use Erik's friendship as a shield against the other boys on more than one occasion. Few boys of the town would challenge Erik: he was too strong. While slow to anger, on the rare occasion when Erik had lost his temper, he had been a terrible sight to behold. He had once hit a boy's arm in a moment of rage. The blow propelled the lad completely across the courtyard of the inn and broke the arm.

Roo pulled aside his ragged cloak, revealing far better-looking clothing beneath, and Erik saw in his hand a long-necked green glass bottle. Clearly etched into the neck of the bottle was a baronial crest.

Erik rolled his eyes heavenward. "Anxious to lose a hand, Roo?" he said quietly in an exasperated tone.

"I helped Father unload his wagon last night."

"What is it?"

"Hand-selected berry wine," he said.

Erik grimaced. With Darkmoor being the center of the wine trade in the Kingdom of the Isles, the primary industry of Ravensburg was wine, as it was with most of the towns and villages in the barony. To the north, oak cutters and barrel makers labored to produce the fermenting vats and aging barrels for the wine, as well as corks, while to the south, glassmakers produced bottles, but the central area of the barony was dedicated to growing grapes.

While fine wines were produced in the Free Cities of Natal and Yabon province to the west, none matched the complexity, character, and age-worthiness of those produced in the Barony of Darkmoor. Even the difficult-to-grow Pinot Noir grape, originally imported from Bas-Tyra, flourished in Darkmoor as it did in no other place in the Kingdom. Lush reds and crisp whites, sparkling wines for celebration—Darkmoor's finest product brought the highest prices from the northern borders south into the heart of the Empire of Great Kesh. And few wines were as highly prized as the intensely sweet dessert wine called berry wine.

Made from grapes shriveled by a mysterious sweet rot that occasionally afflicted the grapes, it was rare and costly; the bottle Roo held under his cloak was equal in worth to a farmer's income for a half year. And from the crest on the bottle, Erik knew it was from the Baron's private stock, shipped from the baronial capital city of Darkmoor to the Ravensburg guildhall for the Baron's visit. While thieves no longer had their hands cut off, being discovered with the bottle could put Roo on the King's labor gang for five years.

Trumpets sounded again and the first of the Baron's guards rode into view, their banners snapping in the afternoon breeze, their horses' iron shoes striking sparks on the stones of the square. Reflexively, Erik looked at their legs, for signs of lameness, and saw none; whatever else could be said of the Baron's management of his estates, his cavalry always attended to their mounts.

The riders moved into the square and turned out from the small fountain that sat at its center, formed two lines, and slowly backed the commoners away.

After a few minutes, the entire area before the Growers' and Vintners' Hall had been cleared for the coach that followed.

More soldiers rode past, each wearing the grey tabard bearing the crest of Darkmoor: a red heater shield upon which stood a black raven clutching a holly branch in its beak. This group of soldiers also wore a golden circlet sewn above the crest, indicating they were the Baron's personal guards.

At last the coach rolled into view, and Erik suddenly realized he was holding his breath. Refusing to let his mother's obsession control even the air in his lungs, he quietly let out a long breath and willed himself to relax.

He heard others in the crowd commenting. Rumors regarding the Baron's failing vitality had circulated in the barony for more than a year now, and his sitting beside his wife in the coach, rather than astride his horse at the head of his guards, signaled that he must be ill in truth.

Erik's attention was drawn to two boys, riding matching chestnut horses, followed by a pair of soldiers carrying the baronial ensign of Darkmoor. The cadency mark on the left banner heralded Manfred von Darkmoor, second son to the Baron. The mark on the right-hand banner proclaimed Stefan von Darkmoor, elder son of the Baron. Alike enough to appear twins, despite a year's age difference, the boys rode with an expert ease that Erik found admirable.

Manfred scanned the crowd, and when his gaze at last fell upon Erik, he frowned. Stefan saw where Manfred stared and said something to his brother, recalling his attention to the matters at hand. The young men were dressed in similar fashion: high riding boots, tight-fitting breeches with full leather seats, long white silk shirts with a sleeveless vest of fine leather, and large berets of black felt, each adorned with a large golden baronial badge, from which rose a red-dyed eagle's feather. At their sides they wore rapiers, and each was accounted an expert in their use despite their youth.

Freida gestured with her chin at Stefan, and whispered harshly, "Your place, Erik."

Erik felt himself flush in embarrassment, but he knew the worst was yet to come. The coach stopped and coachmen leaped down to open the door as two burghers came forward to greet the Baron. First to leave the coach was a proud-looking woman, her features set in an expression of haughty disdain that detracted from her beauty. One glance at the two young men, who now dismounted their horses, confirmed that they were mother and sons. All three were dark, slender, and tall. Both youths came to stand before their mother and bowed in greeting. The Baroness scanned the crowd as her sons came to her side, and when she spied Erik looming over those around him, her expression darkened even more.

A herald called out, "His lordship, Otto, Baron of Darkmoor, Lord of Ravensburg!"

The crowd let out a respectable if not overly enthusiastic cheer; the Baron was not particularly loved by his people, but neither was he held in disregard. Taxes were high, but then taxes were always high, and whatever protection the Baron's soldiers afforded the townsfolk from bandits and raiders was barely visible; since it was far from any border or the wild lands of the Western Realm, few rogues and villains troubled honest travelers near Darkmoor. No goblin or troll had been seen in these mountains in the memory of the oldest man living in Ravensburg, so few saw much benefit in supporting soldiers who did little more than ride escort for their lord, polish armor, and eat. Still, the harvest was good, food was in bountiful supply and affordable, and order commanded gratitude from the citizens of the Barony.

When the cheer died down, the Baron turned to the notables of the town waiting to greet him and an audible gasp rang through the crowd. The man who stepped from the coach had once been equal to Erik in size, but now he stooped, as if thirty years older than his forty-five years. Though still broad of shoulder, his naturally slender build was now dramatically gaunt in contrast. His hair, once golden, was lank and grey, and his face was ashen, sunken cheeks white as bleached parchment. The square jaw and proud forehead were bony ridges that emphasized the look of illness. The Baron was helped by his younger son's firm grip on his left arm. His movements were jerky and he looked as if he might fall.

Someone near Erik said, "So then it's true about the seizure."

Erik wondered if the Baron's condition might be aggravated by his mother's plan, but as if hearing his thoughts, Freida said, "I must do this."

Pushing past those who stood before her, she moved quickly between two mounted guardsmen before they could turn her back. "As a free woman of the Kingdom, I claim my right to be heard!" she cried in a voice loud enough to carry across the square.

No one spoke. All eyes regarded the wiry woman as she pointed an accusing finger at the Baron. "Otto von Darkmoor, will you acknowledge Erik von Darkmoor as your son?"

The obviously ill Baron paused and turned to regard the woman who had asked him this question each time he had visited Ravensburg. His eyes searched past her and found her son, standing quietly behind her. Seeing his own image of younger years before him, Otto let his gaze linger upon Erik; then the Baroness came to his side and whispered quickly in his ear. With an expression of sadness on his face, the Baron shook his head slightly as he turned away from Erik's mother and, without comment, moved into the largest building in the town, the Growers' and Vintners' Hall. The Baroness fixed a hard gaze upon Freida and Erik, barely masking her anger, before she turned to follow her husband into the hall.

Roo let out a sigh, and as one the crowd seemed to exhale. "Well, that's that, then."

Erik said, "I don't think we'll do this again."

As Freida moved back toward them, Roo said, "Why? Do you think your mother's going to stop if she gets another chance?"

Erik said, "She won't get another chance. He's dying."

"How do you know?"

Erik shrugged. "The way he looked at me. He was saying good-bye."

Freida walked past her son and Roo, her expression unreadable as she said, "We have work to do."

Roo glanced back to where the two brothers, Manfred and Stefan, watched Erik closely, speaking quietly together. Manfred was restraining Stefan, who seemed eager to cross the square and confront Erik. Roo said, "Your half brothers don't care for you much, do they? Especially that Stefan."

Erik shrugged, but it was Freida who spoke. "He knows that soon he will inherit what is rightfully Erik's." Roo and Erik exchanged glances. Both knew better than to argue with Freida. She had always claimed that the Baron had wed her one spring night, in the woodland chapel, before a monk of Dala, Shield of the Weak. Then later he had requested and received an annulment so he could marry the daughter of the Duke of Ran, the records sealed by royal command for political reasons.

Roo said, "Then that is the last of it, for certain."

Erik gave him a questioning look. "What do you mean?"

"If you're right, next year Stefan will be Baron. By the look of things, he's not the sort to hesitate about publicly calling your mother a liar."

Freida stopped walking. Her face showed a hopelessness Erik had never seen before. "He wouldn't dare," she said, more a plea than a challenge. She attempted to look defiant, but her eyes showed she knew Roo was right.

"Come, Mother," said Erik softly. "Let's go home. The forge is banked, but if there's work, I'll need to get the fire hot again. Tyndal is certain to be in no condition to do it." He gently put his arm upon his mother's shoulder, astonished at how frail she suddenly felt. She quietly allowed him to guide her along.

The townspeople stepped away, giving the young smith and his mother an open passageway from the square, all sensing that somehow there would soon be an ending to this tradition, begun fifteen years earlier, when first the beautiful and fiery Freida had boldly stepped forward and held out the squalling baby, demanding that Otto von Darkmoor recognize the child as his own. Nearly every soul in the Barony knew the story. She had confronted him five years later, and again he had not rebutted her claim. His silence gave her declaration credence, and for years the tale of the bastard child of the Baron of Darkmoor had been a source of local lore, good for a drink from passing strangers bound between Eastern and Western Realms of the Kingdom.

The mystery was always in the Baron's silence, for had he denied it but once, from that day forward Freida would have had the burden of proof put squarely upon herself. The itinerant monk was never seen again in that region, and no other witness existed. And Freida had become the drudge of an innkeeper, and the boy a blacksmith's helper.

Some claimed that the Baron was merely being kind to Freida, refusing to publicly brand her a liar, for while he had obviously fathered her child, the claim of marriage was certainly the ranting of a disturbed woman or the calculated concoction of one seeking some advantage.

Others said the Baron was too much a coward to proclaim a public lie by saying Erik was not his; for anyone had merely to glance at Otto to see that Erik was his very shadow. The Baron carried shame for a badge where a better man would wear honor, for to acknowledge Erik, even as a bastard son, would cast doubt upon his own children's right to inherit, and bring down the wrath of his wife upon him.

But for whatever reason, by saying nothing, every year, he let the challenge stand unanswered. Erik could claim the name "von Darkmoor" because the Baron had never denied him the right.

Slowly they moved through the street, back toward the inn. Roo, never one to let two minutes pass in silence back to back, said, "You going to do anything special tonight, Erik?"

Erik knew what Roo referred to: the Baron's visit was an excuse for a public holiday, nothing as formal as the traditional festivals, but enough so that men would pack the little Inn of the Pintail and drink and gamble most of the night, and many of the young girls of the town would be down at the fountain, waiting for the young men to drink enough liquid courage to come pay court. There would be plenty of work to keep Erik busy. He said as much.

Roo said, "They are their mother's sons, no doubt of that."

Erik knew whom Roo meant: his half brothers. Roo glanced over his shoulder, down the street to the square, where the Growers' and Vintners' Hall and the Baron's carriage were still visible, and found that the two noble boys had returned outside, ostensibly to oversee the removal of the Baron's baggage, but both were in hushed conversation, their eyes fixed upon Erik's retreating back. Roo felt an impulse to make a rude gesture in their direction, but thought better of it. Even at this distance, he could tell their expression was of open hostility and dark anger. Turning back toward the inn, Roo hurried his step to catch up to Erik.

DARKNESS BROUGHT A lessening of the day's activities everywhere but at the Inn of the Pintail, where workers and town merchants who were not of sufficient rank to attend the dinner at the Growers' and Vintners' Hall gathered to enjoy a mug of wine or ale. A near-celebratory atmosphere gripped the inn as men told stories in loud voices, played cards and dice for copper coins, and tested their skill at a dart board.

Erik had been pressed into kitchen duty, as he often was when things got busy. While his mother was only a serving woman, Milo allowed her the position of kitchen supervisor, simply because Freida was in the habit of telling everyone what they should be doing. That she was almost always right in her estimation of everyone's duties failed to mitigate the irritation such an attitude generated. Many serving women had come and gone at the inn over the years, more than a few telling Milo the reasons for their departure. His answer was always the same: she was a longtime friend and they were not.

By any reasonable measure, they acted the family, Freida and Erik, Milo and Rosalyn, husband and wife and brother and sister. Though each slept apart from the others, Milo in his room, Rosalyn in her own, Freida in a loft over the kitchen, and Erik upon a pallet in the barn, from awakening to bedtime they played their parts naturally. Freida ran the inn as if it were her own, and Milo was unwilling to overrule her, mostly because she did a wonderful job, but also because he, more than anyone, understood the pain Freida lived with daily. Though she would never admit it to anyone, she still loved the Baron, and Milo was convinced that her demand for recognition of her son was a twisted legacy of that love, a desperate grasping at some token that for a brief time she had truly loved and been loved.

Erik pushed open the common room door and carried another cask of ordinary wine behind the bar, setting it at Milo's feet. The old man removed the empty cask from the barrel rack and moved it aside, while Erik easily lifted the new one into its place. Placing a clean tap against the bung, Milo drove it home with a single blow from a wooden mallet, then poured himself a small cup to test the content. Making a face, he said, "Why, in the midst of the finest wine in the world, do we drink this?"

Erik laughed. "Because it's all we can afford, Milo."

The innkeeper shrugged. "You have an irritating habit of being honest." Smiling, he said, "Well, it's all the same for effect, then, isn't it? Three mugs of this will get you just as tipsy as three mugs of the Baron's finest, won't they?"

At mention of the Baron, Erik's face lost its merry expression. "I wouldn't know," he said as he turned away.

Milo put his hand on Erik's shoulder, restraining him. "Sorry, lad."

Erik shrugged. "No slight intended, Milo—none taken."

"Why don't you give yourself a break," said the innkeeper. "I can sense things are quieting down."

This brought a grin from Erik, for the sound in the common room was close to deafening, with laughter, animated conversation, and general rowdiness the norm. "If you say so."

Erik moved around from behind the bar, then pushed through the common room, and as he reached the door, Rosalyn threw him an accusatory look. He mouthed, "I'll be back," and she threw her gaze heavenward a moment in feigned aggravation. Then she was again grabbing mugs off tables, heading back toward the bar.

The night was cool; fall was full upon them. At any moment it might turn bitter cold in the mountains of Darkmoor. Though they were not as high as the Calastius to the west or the Teeth of the World in the far north, still snow graced the peaks in the colder winters, and frost was a worry to growers in any season but summer.

Erik moved toward the town square, and as he anticipated, a few boys and girls still sat around the edge of the fountain before the Growers' and Vintners' Hall. Roo was speaking in low tones to a girl who managed to laugh at his suggestion while keeping an askance expression on her face. She was also employing her hands to good effect, limiting Roo's to acceptable portions of her anatomy.

Erik said, "Evening, Roo. Gwen."

The girl's expression brightened as Erik came into view. One of the prettier girls in town, with red hair and large green eyes, Gwen had attempted to catch Erik's eye on more than one occasion. She called his name as she firmly pushed Roo's hands away. A few of the other youngsters of the town greeted the blacksmith's helper, and Roo said, "Finished at the inn?"

Erik shook his head. "Just a break. I'll have to head back in a few minutes. Thought I'd get some air. Gets very smoky in there, and the noise . . ."

Gwen was about to speak when something in Roo's expression caused both her and Erik to turn. Coming into the light of the torches set around the fountain were two figures, dressed in fine clothing, swords swinging at their sides.

Gwen came to her feet and attempted an awkward curtsy. Others followed, but Erik stood silently, and Roo sat open-mouthed.

Stefan and Manfred von Darkmoor looked around the gathered boys and girls, roughly the same age as themselves, but their demeanor and finery set them apart as clearly as if they had been swans moving among geese and ducks in a pond. They had obviously been drinking from the way they moved, with the careful control of one who is masking intoxication.

As Stefan's gaze settled on Erik, his expression darkened, but Manfred put a restraining hand upon his arm. Whispering something in Stefan's ear, the younger brother maintained a tight grip. Stefan at last nodded once, his eyes heavy-lidded, and forced a cold smile to his lips. Ignoring Erik and Roo, he bowed slightly toward Gwen and said, "Miss, it seems my father and the town burghers are intent on discussing issues of wine and grapes beyond my understanding and patience. Perhaps you might care to acquaint us with some more . . . interesting diversions?"

Gwen blushed and then threw Erik a glance. He frowned at her and slightly shook his head no. As if challenging his right to advise her, she jumped lightly down from the low wall around the fountain and said, "Sir, I would be delighted." She called another girl who was sitting nearby. "Katherine, join us!"

Gwen took Stefan's extended arm like a lady of the court, and Katherine awkwardly followed her example with Manfred. They strolled away from the fountain, Gwen exaggerating the sway of her hips as they vanished into the darkness.

After a moment, Erik said, "We'd better follow."

Roo came to stand directly in front of his friend. "Looking for a fight?"

"No, but those two won't take no for an answer and the girls—"

Roo put his hand firmly on Erik's chest, as if to prevent his moving forward. ". . . know what they're getting into with noble sons," he finished. "Gwen's no baby. And Stefan won't be the first to get her to pull up her skirts. And you're about the only boy in town who hasn't bedded Katherine." Looking over his shoulder to where the four had vanished into the night, he added, "Though I thought the girls had better taste than that."

Roo lowered his voice so that only Erik could hear, and his tone took on a harshness that his friend recognized. Roo used it only when he was deadly serious about a topic. "Erik, the day may come when you will have to face your swine of a brother. And when it does, you will probably have to kill him." Erik's brow furrowed at Roo's tone and words. "But not tonight. And not over Gwen. Now, don't you have to get back to the inn?"

Erik nodded, gently removing Roo's hand from his chest. He stood motionless for a second, trying to digest what his friend had just said. Then, shaking his head, he turned and walked back toward the inn.

2

★★

DEATHS

TYNDAL WAS DEAD.

Erik still couldn't believe it. Each time he came into the forge during the last two months he had expected to see the burly smith either asleep on his pallet at the rear of the forge or hard at work. The man's sense of humor when he wasn't sober, or his dark moodiness when he was—everything about him was etched in every corner of this place where Erik had learned his craft for the previous six years.

Erik inspected the coals from the previous night's fire and judged how much wood to add to bring it back to life. A miller's wagon had lurched into the courtyard the night before with a broken axle, and there would be ample work to fill his day. He still couldn't get over Tyndal's not being there.

Two months previously, Erik had climbed down from his loft expecting the events of the morning to be as usual, but one glance at Tyndal's regular resting place had sent the hairs on Erik's neck straight up. Erik had seen the smith drunk to a stupor, but this was something else. There was a stillness to the old man that Erik instinctively recognized. He had never seen a dead man before, but he had seen many animals dead in the fields, and there was something eerily familiar in the smith's attitude. Erik touched Tyndal to assure himself the old blacksmith was truly dead, and when he touched cold skin he jerked his hand away as if from a burn.

The local priest of Killian, who acted as a healer for most of the poor in the town, quickly confirmed that Tyndal had indeed drunk his last bottle of wine.

Since he had no family, it was left to Milo to dispose of the corpse, and he arranged a hasty funeral, with a quick pyre. The ashes were scattered, and a prayer was said to the Singer of Green Silence by her priest, though smiths were more correctly considered the province of Tith-Onanka, the god of war. Erik felt that somehow the prayer to Killian, the goddess of the forest and field, was appropriate: Tyndal had repaired perhaps one sword in the six years Erik had been around the forge, but countless plows, tillers, and other implements of farming.

A sound in the distance caught Erik's ear. A midday coach was coming along the western road from Krondor, the Prince's City. Erik knew that the chances were excellent it was Percy of Rimmerton at the reins, and if so, he would be putting in to the Pintail for refreshments for his horses and passengers. The driver was a rail-thin man of enormous appetite who loved Freida's cooking.

As Erik had anticipated, within minutes the sounds of iron-shod wheels and hooves echoed loudly as the commercial coach approached the courtyard. Then it turned in and with a loud "Whoa!" Percy reined in his team of four. The commercial coaches had begun their travel between Salador and Krondor five years previously and had proved a great success for their innovator, a wealthy merchant in Krondor named Jacob Esterbrook, who was now planning a coach line from Salador to Bas-Tyra, according to gossip. Each coach was essentially a wagon, with a covered roof and sides, and a small tailgate that when lowered provided a step into the wagon. A pair of planks along the sides provided indifferent seating, and the ride was lacking any pretense to comfort, as the wagons were rudely sprung. But the journey was swift compared to that by caravan, and for those unable to secure their own mounts to ride, almost as rapid as horseback.

"Ho, Percy," said Erik.

"Erik!" replied the coachman, whose long thin face appeared to have been frozen in a grin surrounded by road dirt. He turned to his two passengers, a man dressed well and another in plain garments. "Ravensburg, sirs."

The plainly dressed man nodded and moved to the rear of the coach as Erik obliged Percy by unlatching the tailgate. "Are you lying over?" he asked the driver.

"No," answered Percy. "We go on to Wolverton, where this other gentleman is bound; then we are done with this run." Wolverton was the next town in the direction of Darkmoor, and less than an hour away by fast coach. Erik knew that the passenger would be unlikely to welcome a meal stop this close to his destination. "From there I'm going empty to Darkmoor, so there's ample time and no hurry. Tell your mother I'll be back in a few days, gods willing, and I'll have an extra of her best meat pie." Percy's grin continued to split his thin face as he patted his stomach, miming hunger.

Erik nodded as the driver turned his team and quickly had them up to a trot and out of the courtyard. Erik turned to the man who had dismounted the coach, to ask if he required lodging, and found him vanishing around the corner of the barn.

"Sir!" Erik called, and hurried after.

He circled the barn and reached the forge, finding that the stranger had set down his bag and was removing his travel cloak. The man was as broad of shoulder and thick of arm as Erik, though he was a full head shorter. He had a fringe of long grey hair receding from his bald pate, and a thoughtful, almost scholarly expression. His brows were bushy and black, and his face was clean-shaven, though the stubble grown while traveling was almost white.

And he inspected everything carefully. He turned to see the young man standing at the door and said, "You must be the apprentice. You keep an orderly forge, youngster. That is good." He spoke with the odd flat twang typical of those from the Far Coast or the Sunset Islands.

"Who are you?" asked Erik.

"Nathan is my name. I'm the new smith sent up from Krondor."

"From Krondor? New smith?" Erik's expression showed his confusion.

The large man shrugged as he hung his travel cloak on a wall peg. "The guild asked if I wished this forge. I said yes, and here I am."

"But it's my smithy," said Erik.

"It's a baronial charge, boy," said Nathan, his tone turning firm. "You might be competent in most things—you might even be talented—but in time of war you'd be mending armor and tending the barony's mounts, as well as taking care of farmers' draft horses."

"War!" exclaimed Erik. "War hasn't touched Darkmoor since it was conquered!"

The man took a quick step forward and put his hand on Erik's shoulder, gripping him firmly. "I think I know how you feel. But law is law. You're a guild apprentice—"

"No."

The smith's brows lowered. "No? Didn't your master register you with the guild?"

With conflicting emotions, anger and ironic amusement, Erik said, "My former master was drunk most of the time. I've conducted the business of this forge since I was ten years of age, Master Smith. For years he promised to take the journey to Krondor or to Rillanon, to register my apprenticeship with the guild office. For the first three years I begged him to send a message by Kingdom Post, but after that . . . I was too busy to continue begging. He's been dead for two months now, and I've done well enough tending the barony's needs."

The man stroked his chin and then shook his head. "This is a problem,

youngster. You're three years older than most who begin their apprenticeship—"

"Begin!" said Erik, his anger now coming to the fore. "I can match skills
with any guild smith—"

Nathan's expression darkened. "That's not the point!" he roared, his own
anger at being interrupted giving him volume enough to silence Erik. "That's
not the point," he repeated more quietly when he saw that Erik was listening.
"You may be the finest smith in the Kingdom, in all of Midkemia, but no one
at the guild knows this. You have not been listed on the roster of apprentices,
and no one with a guildmaster's rank has vouched for your work. So you must
begin—"

"I will not apprentice for seven more years!" said Erik, his temper threatening to get the better of him.

Nathan said, "Interrupt me again, boy, and I'll cease being civil with you."

Erik's expression showed he was not in the least bit apologetic, but he stayed
silent.

Nathan said, "You can go to Krondor or Rillanon and petition the guild.
You'll be tested and evaluated. If you show you know enough, you'll be allowed
to apprentice, or perhaps you'll even get journeyman's rank, though I doubt
that seriously; even if you're the best they've ever seen, there's still the politics of
it. Few men are willing to grant to another rank without the sweat to have
earned it. And there's always the possibility they'll call you a presumptuous lout
and throw you into the street." The last came with a hard tone, and suddenly
Erik realized that this man had spent at least seven years as an apprentice and
perhaps twice that as a journeyman before gaining his master's badge—and to
him Erik must sound a whining child.

"Or you can apprentice here, in your hometown with your family and
friends, and be patient. If you are indeed as well taught as you claim, I'll certify
you as quickly as I can, so you can petition for a forge of your own."

Erik looked as if he was again going to object that this was his forge, but he
said nothing. Nathan continued, "Or you can set out today, on your own, and
become an independent smith. With your talent you'll make a living. But without a guild badge you'll never set up shop in any but the rudest villages, unless
you wish to travel to the frontier. For no noble will trust his horses and armor
to any but a guildmaster, and the rich common folk to no less than a guild
journeyman. And that means, no matter how gifted you are, you'll always be
nothing more than a common tinker."

Erik remained silent, and after a moment Nathan said, "Thoughtful, is it?
That's good. Now, here's the choice of it: you can stay and learn and perfect
your skills and I'll count myself a lucky sod for having a second pair of trained
hands around, belonging to someone I don't have to teach every tiny thing. Or
you can brood and be resentful, and think you know as much as I, and be useless to us both. There's only room for one master in this forge, boy, and I am

he. So there's the end of it, and there's the choice. Do you need time to think on this?"

Erik paused, then said, "No. I need no time to think about it, Master Nathan." Sighing, he added, "You are correct. There is only one master in a forge. I . . ."

"Spit it out, boy."

"I have been responsible around here for so long I feel as if it is my forge, and that I should have been given it by the guild."

Nathan nodded once. "That's understandable."

"But it's not your fault Tyndal was a slacker and my time here counts for nothing."

"None of that, boy—"

"Erik. My name is Erik."

"None of that, Erik," said Nathan; then suddenly he swung hard and connected a roundhouse right that knocked Erik onto his backside. "And I told you, interrupt me again and I'd cease being civil. I am a man of my word."

Erik sat rubbing his jaw, astonishment on his face. He knew the smith had pulled the blow, but he could feel the sting of it anyway. After a moment he said, "Yes, sir."

Nathan put out his hand and Erik took it. The smith pulled Erik to his feet. "I was about to say that any time spent learning a craft counts. You only lack credentials. If you're as good as you think you are, you'll be certified in the minimum seven years. You'll be older than most journeymen when you seek your own forge, but you'll be younger than some, trust me on that. There are slower lads that don't leave their master's forge until they are in their late twenties. Remember this: you may be coming late to your office, but your learning started four years earlier than most boys' as well. Knowledge is knowledge, and experience is experience, so you should have a far shorter time of it from journeyman to master. In the end, it will all work out."

Turning slowly, as if examining the smithy once again, he said, "And from what I see here, if you can keep your head right, we'll get along fine."

There was an open friendliness in that remark which caused Erik to forget his stinging jaw. He nodded. "Yes, sir."

"Now, show me where I sleep."

Without being told, Erik picked up the smith's travel bag and cloak, and motioned. "Tyndal had no family, so he slept here. There's a small room around back, and I sleep in the loft up there." Erik pointed to the only place he'd called his own for the last six years. "I never thought about moving into Tyndal's room—habit, I guess." He led the smith out the rear door and to the shed that Tyndal had used for his bedroom.

"My former master was drunk most of the time, so I fear this room is likely to be . . ." He opened the door.

The smell that greeted them almost made Erik gag. Nathan only stood a moment, then stepped away as he said, "I've worked with drunkards before, lad, and that's the smell of sour sickness. Never seek to hide in a wine bottle, Erik. It's a slow and painful death. Meet your sorrows head on, and after you've wrestled with them, put them behind."

Something in his tone told Erik that Nathan wasn't simply repeating an aphorism but was speaking from belief. "I can put this room right, sir, while you take your ease at the inn."

"I'd best make myself known to the innkeeper; he is to be my landlord, after all. And I could use something to eat."

Erik realized he hadn't thought of that. The office of guild smith might be granted by the guild and a patent for a town might be exclusive, but otherwise the smith was like any other tradesman, forced to make a profit the best he knew how, and responsible for setting up his own place of business. Erik said, "Sir, Tyndal had no family. Who . . ."

Nathan put his hand on Erik's shoulder. "Who should I be paying for all these tools?"

Erik nodded.

Nathan said, "My own tools will be coming by freight hauler any day now. I have no desire to take what is not rightfully mine, Erik." He scratched his day's growth of whiskers as he thought. "When you're ready to leave Ravensburg and begin your own forge, let us assume they go with you. You were his last apprentice, and tradition has it that you are to pay the widow for the tools. As he had no family, there's no one to pay, is there?"

Erik realized what an incredibly generous offer he was being made. An apprentice was expected somehow to supplement his earnings so that by the time he reached journeyman's rank he could purchase a complete set of tools, and an anvil, and have the money to pay for the construction of a forge if needed. Most young journeymen were able to begin modestly, but Tyndal, for all his sloth in his last years, had been a master smith for seventeen years and had every conceivable tool of the trade, two and three of some. With proper care and cleaning, Erik would be set up for life!

Erik said, "If you would like, I can show you to the kitchen."

"I'll find my way. Just come get me when this room is cleaned up."

Erik nodded, and as Nathan moved off toward the rear of the inn, the boy held his breath and went into Tyndal's room. Throwing open the single window didn't help, and Erik hurried back outside because of the stench. Unpleasant odors bothered Erik, strong as he was in most ways, and he confessed to a weak stomach. Though he was used to the smell of the barn and forge, nevertheless the odor of human illness and waste caused the bile to rise in his gorge, and he had tears in his eyes from the reek by the time he got Tyndal's bedding outside the hut.

Breathing through his mouth and turning his head away, he hurried to the large iron tub his mother used for washing and threw the filthy linens into it. As he was building up the fire beneath, his mother approached.

"Who is this man claiming to be the new smith?" she demanded.

Erik was in no mood to battle his mother, so he calmly said, "Not claiming; is. The guild sent him."

"Well, did you tell him there already was a smith here?"

Erik got the fire under the tub going and stood up. As calmly as he could manage, he said, "No. This is a guild forge. And I have no standing with the guild." Thinking of Tyndal's tools, he added, "Nathan's being very generous and is keeping me on. He'll apprentice me to the guild and . . ."

Erik expected an argument, but instead his mother only nodded once and left without further comment. Puzzled by her lack of outburst, Erik stood a moment until the crackling of the fire under the tub reminded him he had a still-unfinished task. He took one of the hard cakes of soap used to wash the inn's bedding and broke it in half. Tossing the hard soap into the tub, he began stirring with a paddle. As the water turned a deep brown, he thought: why no argument from his mother? There was an air of resignation from her that he had never seen before.

Leaving the sheets to simmer in the tub, Erik hurried back to the smith's room, grabbing some rags and a mineral oil cleaner he used on especially filthy tack and tools. He removed the balance of Tyndal's possessions, a single large chest and a sack of personal items. A rickety wooden wardrobe he left inside, in case Nathan choose to hang his cloaks and shirts there; he could always haul it away later if the new smith didn't care for it.

When he had the last of Tyndal's possessions outside, Erik regarded the meager pile. "Not a lot to show for a lifetime," he muttered. He picked up the chest and hauled it over to one corner of the small yard behind the barn, and picked up the sack and placed it on top. He'd go through them later to see what Tyndal had left that might be of use. There were always poor farmers on the outskirts of the vineyards who grew other than grapes, and they always could use serviceable clothing.

Then Erik took the rags and cleaner and began scrubbing years of accumulated grime off the walls.

ERIK ENTERED THE kitchen to find Milo sitting at the big table, staring across at Nathan, who was finishing a large bowl of stew. Milo was nodding at something the smith had just said, while Freida and Rosalyn both made busy preparing vegetables for the evening meal.

Erik glanced at his mother, who stood expressionless at the sink, listening to the men speak. Rosalyn inclined her head toward Erik's mother, indicating concern. Erik nodded briefly, then moved beside his mother, indicating he wished to wash up. She nodded curtly and moved toward the oven, where the bread purchased that morning from the baker was being kept warm.

Nathan continued what he had been saying when Erik entered. "While I have the knack with iron, I'm indifferent with horses, truth to tell, above the legs. I can adjust a shoe to balance a lameness, or to compensate for some other problem, but when it comes to the rest, I'm as simple as anyone."

"Then you've chosen wisely to keep Erik on," said Milo, showing an almost fatherly pride. "He's a wonder with horses."

Rosalyn asked, "Master Smith, from what you've said, you could have had any number of large baronial forges, or even a ducal charge. Why did you pick our small town?"

Nathan pushed away the bowl of stew he had finished, and smiled. "I'm a lover of wine, truth to tell, and this is a great change from my former home."

Freida turned and blurted, "We're scant weeks past burying one smith for the love of too much wine, and now we've another! The gods must hate Ravensburg indeed!"

Nathan looked at Freida and spoke. His tone was measured, but it was clear he was not far from anger. "Good woman, I love the wine, but I'm no mean drunkard. I was a father and husband who took care of his own for many years. If I drink more than a glass in a day, it's a festival. I'll thank you to pass no judgment on matters you know nothing about. Smiths are no more cut from the same bolt of cloth as all men of any other trade are alike in all ways."

Freida turned away, her color rising slightly, but she said nothing save, "The fire is too warm. This bread will be dry before supper." She made a show of turning the coals, though everyone knew it was unnecessary.

Erik watched his mother for a moment, then turned toward Nathan. "The room is clean, sir."

Freida snapped, "Will you all be sharing that one tiny room?"

Nathan rose, picking up his cloak and leaning over to retrieve his bag. As he hoisted his possessions, he said, "All?"

"These children and your wife you spoke so tenderly of?"

Nathan's tone was calm when he replied, "All dead. Killed by raiders in the sacking of the Far Coast. I was senior journeyman to Baron Tolburt's Master Smith at Tulan." The room was still as he continued. "I was asleep, but the sound of fighting woke me. I told my Martha to see to the children as I ran to the forge. I took no more than two steps out the door of the servants' quarters when I was struck twice by arrows"—he touched his shoulder, then his left thigh—"here and here. I fainted. Another man fell on top of me, I think. Anyway, my wife and children were already dead when I awoke the next day." He glanced around the room. "We had four children, three boys and a girl." He sighed. "Little Sarah was special." He fell silent for a long moment, and his face took on a reflective expression. Then he said, "Damn me. It's nearly twenty-five years now." Without another word he rose, and nodded his head once to Milo, then moved to the door.

Freida looked as if she had been struck. She turned toward Nathan, her eyes brimming with moisture, and looked as if she were about to speak, but as the smith left the kitchen she was unable to find the words.

Erik looked after the departing smith, and then back toward his mother. For the first time in his life he felt embarrassed for her and he found the feeling unpleasant. He glanced around the kitchen and noticed Rosalyn looking at Freida with an expression of irritation and regret. Milo made a show of ignoring everyone as he rose from the table to move to the tap room.

Erik said at last, "I'd better see if he's settled in. Then I'll be seeing to the horses."

Erik left and Rosalyn moved around the kitchen in silence, trying to spare Freida any more embarrassment. After a moment she realized the older woman was silently weeping. Caught in an impasse as to what to do, she hesitated, then at last said, "Freida?"

The older woman turned toward the younger, her cheeks damp from her tears. Her face was a mask of conflict, as if she wished to vent some deeply buried pain but couldn't let it surface past a sharp retort. Rosalyn said, "Can I do anything?"

Freida remained motionless for long seconds, then said, "The berries need washing." Her tone was hoarse, and she spoke softly. Rosalyn moved toward the sink and began working the hand pump her father and Erik had installed only the year before so she and Freida wouldn't have to carry water from the well behind the inn anymore. As cold water filled the wooden sink, Freida said, "And stay the sweet child you are, Rosalyn. There's too much pain in the world already."

The older woman hurried from the kitchen on some imagined errand, and Rosalyn knew she just wished to be alone for a while. The exchange with the new smith had released something Freida had buried and Rosalyn didn't understand, but in her sixteen years the girl had never seen Erik's mother cry. As she cleaned the fruit for the evening's pies, she wondered if this was a good thing or not.

THE EVENING WAS quiet, with only a few locals calling in at the Pintail for a quick drink, and only one seeking a meal. Erik finished cleaning the kettle as a favor to Rosalyn, and hauled it back to the hook over the fire, now low-glowing embers.

He waved good night to Rosalyn, who was carrying four flagons of ale to a table occupied by four of the town's more eligible young journeymen, all of whom were flirting with the innkeeper's daughter, more to keep some sort of status with one another than out of any real interest in the young girl.

Passing through the kitchen, Erik found his mother standing by the door, looking at the night sky, ablaze with stars. All three moons were down this night, a rare occurrence, and the display was always worth a moment to observe.

"Mother," said Erik quietly as he started to move away.

"Stay awhile," she said softly, a request and not an order. "It was a night like this I met your father."

Erik had heard the story before but knew his mother was struggling with something that had occurred while she spoke to the smith. He still didn't fully understand what had happened in his mother, but he knew she needed to speak. He sat down on the steps beside where his mother stood.

"Otto had come to Ravensburg for the first time as Baron, after his father's death two years before. He had attended the Vintners' and Growers' reception for him, and after drinking with the town leaders, he had gone for a walk to clear his head. He was brash and quick to dispense with protocol, and had ordered his servants and guards to leave him alone."

She stared into the night, calling up memories. "I had come down to the fountain with the other girls, to flirt with the boys." Erik recalled his own last visit to the fountain with Roo and realized the practice was long established. "The Baron came into the lantern light and suddenly we were a bunch of awkward children." Then Erik saw a spark in his mother's eyes, and heard an echo of the spirit that had captivated men's hearts before he was born. "I was as awed as the rest, but I was too proud to show it," she said with a rueful smile, and years dropped away from her. Erik could imagine the impact such a sight after an evening spent drinking must have had on the Baron as he spied the beautiful Freida at the fountain.

"He had court manners, and rank, and riches, and yet there was something honest in him, Erik: a little boy who was as afraid of being sent away as any other boy. He was twenty-five, and young for that age. But he swept me off my feet, with sweet words and a wicked humor in them. Less than an hour later he had bedded me under a tree in an apple orchard." She sighed, and again Erik was put in mind of a young girl, not this woman of iron he had known all his life.

"I had a terrible reputation, but I had never known another man. He had known other women, for he was sure, but he was also tender and gentle and loving." She glanced at her son. "In the dark, under the stars, he spoke of love, but the next day I thought I'd never see him again and counted myself just another foolish girl taken in by a nobleman's charms.

"But against any hope of mine, he came to me a month later, in the late afternoon, alone, astride a horse flecked with foam from a hard ride from his castle. Hidden by a large cloak, he had slipped into the inn as we were readying for the night's trade, and there he sought me out and revealed himself. To my astonishment, he professed love and asked for my hand." She gave a bittersweet laugh. "I called him mad and ran from the inn.

"Later that night, I returned to find him waiting at this very spot, like a common farmhand. He again told of his love for me, and again I told him he was bereft of sense." Tears gathered in her eyes. "He laughed and said he knew it seemed that way, but after taking my hand and gazing into my eyes, he kissed me once and convinced me. This time I knew why I had gone with him the first time—not because of his rank and station, but because I loved him as well.

"He cautioned me that none must know of our love for each other until he had journeyed to Rillanon to petition King Lyam for my hand, for tradition bound him to his liege lord's pleasure. But to seal our love, and to provide me with a claim, we spoke our vows in a small chapel used during the harvest, with an itinerant monk who had been in town less than a day, conducting the ceremony. The monk made a pledge not to speak of the vows until Otto gave him leave, and left us alone, for the next morning Otto planned to leave to see the King."

Freida was silent a moment; then her tone took on a familiar bitterness. "Otto never returned. He sent a messenger, your friend Owen Greylock, with news that the King had denied his petition and had instructed him to wed the daughter of the Duke of Ran. 'For the good of the Kingdom,' Greylock said. Then he said the King had ordered the Great Temple of Dala in Rillanon to declare the wedding annulled, and had the order placed under Royal Seal, so as not to embarrass Mathilda or any sons she might bear. I was advised to find a good man and forget Otto." Tears ran down her cheeks as she said, "What a shock good Master Greylock got then when I told him I was with child."

She sighed and reached over and gripped her son's arm. "As my time neared, rumors circulated about who was your father, this merchant or that grower. But when you were born, and quickly became the image of your father in his youth, no one denied you were Otto's boy. Not even your father will deny it publicly."

Erik had heard the story a dozen times before, but never told quite this way. Never before had he thought of his mother as a young girl in love or of the bitter rejection she must have felt when news of Otto's marriage to Mathilda had come. Still, there was no profit in living for yesterday. "But he never acknowledged me, either," said Erik.

"True," agreed his mother. "Yet he left you this much: you have a name, von Darkmoor. You may use it with pride, and should any man challenge your right you may look him in the eye and say, 'Not even Otto, Baron von Darkmoor, denies me my right to this name.'"

Erik reached up and awkwardly took his mother's hand. She glanced at him and smiled her stiff, unforgiving smile, but there was a hint of warmth in it as she squeezed his huge hand, then released it. "This Nathan: I think he may be a good man. Learn what you can from him, for you'll never have your birthright."

Erik said, "That was your dream, Mother. I know little of politics, but what I have heard in the taproom leads me to believe that should you have had the High Priest of Dala himself as witness in the chapel that night, it would count for little. The King, for reasons known best to him, wished my father married to the daughter of the Duke of Ran, and thus it was, and thus it would always have been."

Erik stood. "I will need to spend some extra time with Nathan, letting him know what I can do, and finding out what he wishes me to do. I think you're right: he's a good man. He could have sent me packing, but he's trying to do right by me, I think."

Impulsively, Freida threw her arms around her son's neck, hugging him closely. "I love you, my son," she whispered.

Erik stood motionless, uncertain how to respond. She spared him the need by letting go and turning quickly into the kitchen, shutting the door behind her.

Erik stood a moment, then slowly turned and moved toward the barn.

As THE MONTHS passed, things fell into a routine at the Inn of the Pintail. Nathan blended in quickly, and after a while it was hard to recall what the inn had been like with Tyndal as smith. Erik found his new master a fount of information, as much of what Tyndal had taught him had been basic, solid smithing but Nathan knew much that made the work above-average, even exceptional. His knowledge of the different requirements for weapons and armor opened a new area for Erik, for Nathan had been the Baron Tolburt's own armorer in Tulan at one time.

One day the sound of hooves upon cobbles caused Erik to look up from where he held a hot plow blade Nathan was hammering for a local farmer. The slender figure of Owen Greylock, the Baron's Swordmaster, appeared as he rode his mount around the barn from the rear court of the inn.

Nathan took away the blade and plunged it into water, then set it aside as Erik came to stand next to the horse, holding her bridle as Greylock dismounted.

"Swordmaster!" said Erik. "She's not lame again, is she?"

"No," said Owen, indicating that Erik should see for himself.

Erik ran his hand along the horse's left foreleg as Nathan approached, then motioned the youngster to stand aside. Nathan examined the horse's leg. "This is the horse you told me of?"

Erik nodded.

"You say it was this suspensor tendon, was it?"

Greylock looked on with approval as Erik said, "Yes, Master Smith. She had pulled it slightly."

"Slightly!" said Greylock. He had an angular face, made even more stern by a severe hairstyle—high bangs, with most of the rest cut straight around the nape of his neck—which split into a smile, serving to make him even more unattractive, for his teeth were uneven and yellowing. "Totally blown, I should say, Master Smith. Puffed up to the size of my thigh, and the mare could barely stand to put weight on it. I thought I'd have to send for the knackers, for certain. But Erik had a way, and I'd seen his work before, so I gave him the chance and he didn't disappoint." Shaking his head in mock astonishment, he said, " 'Slightly.' The lad's too modest for his own good."

"What did you do?" Nathan asked Erik.

"I wrapped her leg in hot compresses at first. There's a drawing salve the healing priest at the Temple of Killian makes that makes your skin feel hot. I used that on her leg. I hand-walked her and wouldn't let her pull again, even if she got rammy. She's spirited and wanted to bolt more than once, but I put a stud chain over her nose and let her know I'd have none of it." Erik reached over and patted the mare on the nose. "We became pretty fair friends."

Nathan stood and shook his head, obviously impressed. "For the four months I've been here, Swordmaster, I've been hearing of this lad's skill with horses. Some of it I took to be local pride felt by his friends." Turning to Erik, he smiled and put a hand on his shoulder. "I don't say this lightly, lad. Perhaps you should put aside your apprenticeship as a smith and turn your hand to healing horses. I am self-admitted indifferent in healing animals, though I will put my shoeing work up against any man's, but even I can see this horse is completely sound, as if she had never been injured."

Erik said, "It's a useful skill, and I like to see the horses healthy, but there's no guild. . . ."

Nathan was forced to agree. "True enough. A guild is a mighty fortress and can shelter you when no amount of skill can save you from"—he suddenly remembered the Baron's Swordmaster was standing a few feet away—"many unexpected ends."

Erik smiled. He knew what the smith had been about to say had to do with the long-standing rivalry between the nobility and the guilds. Started as a means to certify workmen and guarantee a certain minimum standard of skill, the guilds had become a political force in the Kingdom over the last century, to the point of having their own courts to adjudicate matters within each guild, much to the irritation of the King's courts and the courts of the other nobles. But the nobles were too dependent upon the quality assurance of the many guilds to do more than grumble about flouting authority. But often one of the craft guilds had saved a member from some injustice at the hands of a noble.

Despite a long tradition of responsible nobility in the Kingdom, there were always one or two minor earls or barons who thought they could simply ignore a debt. Having a patent of arms from the King did not ensure wealth, and more than one noble had attempted to use rank and position rather than coin of the realm to settle his debts.

Erik distracted Greylock. "Swordmaster, what cause brings you to Ravensburg this day?"

The usually serious Swordmaster's face returned to its usual dour expression. "You, Erik. Your father rides to Krondor on state business. He'll be here this evening. I came early to see if . . ."

"If I could prevail upon my mother to let him alone?"

Greylock nodded. "He's not well, Erik. He shouldn't be making the journey and . . ."

"I'll do what I can." He knew promising was vain should his mother take it into her head to repeat her performance of the last time Otto came through the town. "She may have finally gotten over making me the next Baron."

Greylock made a sour face. "I would be out of place to comment on that." Then he softened his expression. "Trust me on this. If you can, stand by the corner of the town road where the sheep meadow ends and the first vineyard begins, on the east side of the town, before sunset."

"Why?"

"I can't say, but it's important."

"If my father is so ill, Owen, what cause has he to ride to Krondor?"

Greylock mounted his horse. "Ill news, I'm afraid. The Prince is dead. It will be announced to the populace by royal messenger later this week."

Erik said, "Arutha is dead?"

Greylock nodded. "He fell and broke his hip, I've been told, and died of complications. He was an aging man, nearly eighty if I have it right."

Prince Arutha had been a fixture in Krondor all of Erik's life and his mother's before him. Father to the King, Borric, who had succeeded Arutha's brother Lyam only five years earlier, he had been the man most responsible for peace in the Kingdom, by all accounts.

To Erik he was a distant figure; certainly, Erik had never seen the Prince, but he felt a small stab of regret. By anyone's measure he was a good ruler and a hero in his youth. As Greylock turned the mare around, Erik said, "Tell my father I will stand where he asked."

Greylock saluted and lightly touched spurs to the mare's flanks, and she trotted out of the inn courtyard.

Nathan, who had come to understand a great deal of Erik's history in the months he had been living at the Pintail, said, "You'll want some extra time to clean up."

Erik said, "I hadn't thought of that. I was just going to leave at suppertime."

It was late spring, and sunset came close to an hour after supper. Erik would need most of the hour to make it to the other side of Ravensburg, and through the vineyards to the sheep meadow, but only if he went in his dirty clothing.

Nathan playfully hit Erik on the back of the head with his open hand. "Dolt. Get yourself cleaned up. Sounds important."

Erik thanked Nathan and hurried to the forge. Below the pallet in the loft where he slept, behind the ladder, sat a trunk with all of Erik's belongings. He took out his one good shirt and carried it over to the washbasin. Removing his dirty shirt, he took the harsh soap and some clean rags and worked feverishly to rid himself of as much dirt as possible. At last he felt presentable and put on his good shirt.

He hurried out of the barn and went to the kitchen, where food was being placed upon the table as he entered. Sitting down, he drew a suspicious look from his mother. "Why are you wearing your good shirt?" she asked.

Not willing to share his father's request for a meeting with his mother, lest she demand to accompany him and force a confrontation, he muttered, "I'm meeting someone after supper," then started noisily eating the stew placed before him.

Milo, who was sitting at the head of the table, laughed. "One of the town girls, is it?"

This brought an alarmed look from Rosalyn, the color rising in her cheeks as Erik said, "Something like that."

Erik continued to eat in silence, while Milo and Nathan spoke of the day's events, and the women joined Erik in silence.

Nathan had a dry sense of humor that made it difficult at first to know if he was being mocking or merely amusing. This had resulted in Freida and Milo both treating him with some coolness at first.

But his warm nature and clear appreciation of life's little moments had won over even Erik's mother, who could often be seen trying to fight back a smile at some quip of Nathan's. Erik had once asked him how he kept so even a disposition, and the answer had surprised him. "When you lose everything," Nathan had said, "you've nothing left to lose. You've got two choices then: either kill yourself or start building a new life. When I started this new life, without my family, I decided the only sensible thing in it was to live for the small rewards: a job well done, a beautiful sunrise, the sound of children laughing at play, a good cup of wine. Makes it easy to deal with the harsher side of life.

"Kings and marshals can look back and relive their triumphs, their great victories. We common folk must take what pleasure we can from life's little victories."

Erik hardly touched his food, and at last bade everyone excuse him as he almost jumped up from the table and hurried out through the common room, Milo's laughter following after. He almost ran through the door of the inn and barely avoided knocking Roo down as the youngster was about to enter the inn.

"Wait a minute!" cried Roo as he fell in beside his larger friend.

"Can't. I have to meet someone."

Roo grabbed the larger youth by the arm and was almost dragged along a step or two before Erik stopped. "What?" he asked Roo impatiently.

"Did your father send for you?"

Erik had long since stopped being amazed at the town gossip Roo was able to ferret out, but this had him stunned. "Why do you ask that?"

"Because since late yesterday the road has been thick with Kingdom Post riders, sometimes as many as three in a bunch, and a company of the Baron's horse, followed by two companies of foot soldiers, passed by the eastern boundary of the town this morning, heading south, and the Baron's own personal guards showed up an hour ago at the Growers' and Vintners' Hall. That's what I was coming to tell you. And you're wearing your best shirt."

Not wishing to have Roo along, Erik said, "The Prince of Krondor is dead. That's why . . ." He was about to say that was why his father was coming to the town, on his way to Krondor, but instead said, "all the fuss."

Roo said, "So those soldiers are heading south to support the garrisons along the Keshian border, in case the Emperor gets ambitious now that Arutha's dead." Now suddenly an expert in military matters, Roo was left standing by Erik, who had resumed his hurried march.

Seeing he was suddenly alone, Roo yelled, "Hey!" and chased after his friend, catching up with him as Erik left the street of the Pintail and entered the main square of the town.

"Where are you going?"

Erik stopped. "I have to meet someone."

"Who?"

"It's personal."

"It's not a girl, or you'd be heading north to the fountain, not east toward the baronial road." Roo's eyes widened. "You are meeting your father! I was just joking before."

Erik said, "I don't want anyone to say anything, especially not to my mother."

"I'll keep this to myself."

"Good," said Erik, turning Roo around with two large and powerful hands on narrow shoulders. "Go find something amusing to do, and not too illegal, and I'll talk to you later tonight. Meet me at the inn."

Roo frowned, but sauntered off as if he had intended to leave Erik alone anyway. Erik resumed his journey.

He hurried through the businesses clustered around the town square, two- and three-story edifices overhanging the narrow streets, then moved between the modest homes owned by the higher-ranking members of the various crafts and guilds, then the ramshackle houses used by workers, married apprentices, and traders without storefronts.

Leaving the town proper, he hurried along the east road, past small vegetable gardens where pushcart traders grew their wares to sell in the town market, and the large eastern vineyards. Reaching the point where the baronial road leading to Darkmoor intercepted the main east–west road through Ravensburg, he waited.

He mulled over what possible reason he could have been asked to meet his father at this relatively remote location, dismissing the most fanciful of all, that his mother's dream would somehow be realized and his father would acknowledge him.

His musing was interrupted by the sound of an approaching company of horsemen. Soon he could see them crest a distant hill, a company of riders appearing out of the evening's gloom to the northeast. As they neared, he could see they were the Baron's own, leading the same carriage Erik had seen the last time the Baron had paid the town a visit. He felt a tightening in his chest as they neared, and no small apprehension, for his two half brothers could be seen riding beside the carriage. The first riders hurried past, but Stefan and Manfred reined in.

Stefan shouted, "What! You again?"

He made a threatening gesture as if to draw his sword, but his younger brother shouted, "Stefan! Keep up! Leave him alone!"

The younger brother set heels to his mount and moved to keep up with the vanguard, but his older brother hesitated.

As more soldiers rode past, Stefan shouted, "I warn you now, *brother:* when I ascend to the Baron's office, I'll be nowhere near as tolerant as our father. If I catch a glimpse of you or your mother at any public function, I'll have you arrested so quickly your shadow will have to search to find you." Without waiting for a reply, he viciously dug his spurs into his horse's flank, causing the high-spirited gelding to leap forward into a fast canter, then a gallop, so he could overtake his younger brother.

Then the main detachment of soldiers approached, followed by the Baron's carriage. As they passed, the riders moved at a steady canter, but the carriage slowed. When it was almost upon Erik, the curtain of the carriage closest to him was pulled back, and he could glimpse a white face peering through the gloom at him. For a moment, father and son locked gazes, and Erik felt a sudden rush of confused feelings. Then all too suddenly the instant passed, and the carriage rolled away, the driver using the reins to urge his team of four ahead, to overtake the escort.

Erik stood puzzled and angered as the following troop of soldiers approached. He had expected to speak at last to his father, not merely share a momentary glimpse.

As he turned to leave, the last rider reined in and said, "Erik!"

He turned to see Owen Greylock dismounting. Forgetting courtesy, Erik vented his anger. "I thought we were friends, Master Greylock, at least as much as rank permitted. But you had me traipse through the town to this place so that Stefan could insult and threaten me, and my father peek out from his warm carriage at me!"

Greylock said, "Erik, it was your father's request."

Erik put hands on hips and took a deep breath. "So it was his idea to have Stefan as much as tell me to leave the barony?"

Greylock led his treasured mare to where Erik stood, and put his hand on the younger man's arm. "No, that was Stefan's impromptu performance. Your father wished to see you one last time. He's dying."

Erik felt unexpected emotions break to the surface, panic and regret, all viewed somehow at a distance, as if the warring emotions were taking place within someone else's breast. "Dying?"

"His chirurgeon warned against this, but with the Prince's death, he felt the need to attempt the journey. Borric has named his youngest brother, Nicholas, to succeed his father, until his own son, Patrick, is of an age to rule the Western Realm. Nicholas is an unknown; everyone expected Erland to take the post. It could be a fair political bloodbath in Krondor this week."

Erik knew the names: Borric, the King, and Erland, his younger twin brother. Patrick was the King's eldest son, and by tradition one of the two should have taken the office of Prince of Krondor, but the intrigues of the court meant little to Erik.

"He asked me here so he could catch a glimpse of me as his carriage sped by?"

Greylock squeezed Erik's arm for emphasis. "His *last* glimpse of you." He removed something from his tunic. "And to give you this."

Erik beheld a folded parchment being handed him by Greylock. He took it and noticed it was free of any stamp or seal. He unfolded it and began to read. " 'My son—' "

Greylock interrupted. "No one is to know the contents but you, and once you are done, I am to burn this. I will stand away while you read this to yourself."

He led the horse away, while Erik read:

My son, If I am not yet dead when you read this, I soon shall be. I know you have many questions, and no doubt your mother has answered some. I am sorry to say that I can give you little more than that, and less satisfaction.

When we are young, we feel passions that are but faint memories when we are not very many years older. I think I did love your mother, when I was very young. But if so, then that love, like memories, faded.

If I have any regrets, it is that I could not know you. You were innocent of your mother's and my indulgences, but I have responsibilities that cannot be set aside because of my regret over a youthful indiscretion. I hope you understand and realize that whatever life we might have imagined as father and son was an impossible illusion. I hope you are a good man, for I am proud of the blood that flows in both our veins, and would hope you honor it as well. I have never publicly denied your mother, because at least I can allow you a name. But beyond this I can do little else.

Your brother Stefan will be set against you in every way. My wife fears any threat to her son's patrimony, and if it is any comfort to you, I have paid a price for remaining silent before your mother's accusations. I have shielded you and your mother more than you might know, but once I am gone, that protection will vanish. I urge you to take your mother from the barony. There is a growing frontier along the Far Coast and in the Sunset Islands, and opportunities for a young man of ability. You could make something of yourself there.

Leave Ravensburg and Darkmoor, and make yourself known to one Sebastian Lender, a solicitor and litigator with an office at Barret's Coffee House, on Regal Street in Krondor. He will have something there for you.

I can do no more. Life is often unfair, and while we might wish for justice, it is usually an illusion. For what it is worth, you have my blessing and my wish for a happy life.

Your Father

Erik held it in his hands a few moments after he had finished, and at last he held it out to Greylock. Owen took the parchment and produced one of the elegant flint and spring-loaded igniters that were all the rage among those who smoked tabac. He struck a series of sparks until one lodged in the parchment, and blew it to a flame. Holding the parchment by the edge, he let the flame grow until it engulfed the document. Just before his fingers would be burned, he let the parchment float away, rising on its own heat as it was consumed.

Erik felt empty. He now realized that whatever he had expected when summoned to this lonely spot, it had been something more than this. His attention returned to Greylock as the Baron's Swordmaster mounted. "Was there anything else?"

Owen said, "Only this: he urged you to count the threat as dire and take the warning with the most gravity."

"Do you know what that means?"

"Not by his words, Erik, but I'd be a fool not to guess. It might be considered a wise thing if you were on your way to a new home when we return from Krondor. Stefan has a temper that blinds him and a dangerous nature."

"Owen?" Erik said as Greylock made ready to ride on.

"What?"

"Do you think he ever really loved my mother?"

Greylock looked startled by the question. He paused, then said, "To that I cannot speak. Your father was a man to hide much within. But this I can tell you: whatever you read in that missive take to heart and count an honest telling, for there is no deceit in the man's nature."

He rode off, and Erik found himself alone. Then he began to laugh. Everything in his life had stemmed from a deceit. Either Greylock was a poor judge of his lord's nature, or Otto had reformed his ways after deceiving Erik's mother. But to Erik it was of little significance which was the case.

Unsure of his own feelings, he began the trek home. But one thing he knew: Greylock would not take the time to underscore his father's warning if it wasn't real and deadly. For the first time in his life, Erik considered leaving Ravensburg. He laughed again at the irony of no more than a month's having passed since word returned from the guild that it had approved Nathan's registration of Erik as apprentice.

A bitter taste of tin filled Erik's mouth, and his stomach knotted as he moved through the twilight. His desires were few and his needs simple, yet it seemed fate had decreed them to be impossible.

Not knowing what he could possibly say to his mother, he walked like a man three times his age, each step slow and deliberate, his shoulders bent under an incredible weight.

3

★★

MURDER

ERIK HALTED.

The sound of so many horses' hooves pounding on the cobbles nearby was unusual in Ravensburg. He put down the bundle of clothing he had tied a moment before, and set it upon the trunk containing his mother's personal belongings.

The sound was definitely louder now, and Erik knew a group of riders was heading for the inn. He glanced at Milo, who was speaking softly to Freida on the other side of the kitchen. The decision to leave Ravensburg had been difficult, and to Erik's surprise it had not been his mother who objected. She seemed resigned to never realizing her girlhood dream of her son's being legitimized by his father. It was Nathan who had been the most vociferous in urging them to stay. When it was clear they were leaving, he bade them travel to the Far Coast. He spoke in almost reverent terms of the nobles of the Far Coast, Duke Marcus, cousin to the King, and his own Baron of Tulan, who had done everything in his power to aid those who had suffered in the massive destruction of the Far Coast at the hands of pirates a quarter century earlier. Stefan's threats were repulsive to Nathan, whose view of the responsibilities of the nobility to the commons was at odds with the experience of most of those at the inn. All Milo would say was that nobility in the West was vastly different to that in Darkmoor.

Erik and Freida had been gathering up their belongings, making ready for the morning coach that would take them west to Krondor. Erik was to call at the Hall of the Guild of Smiths with a letter from Nathan, explaining that his leaving the forge at Ravensburg had nothing whatsoever to do with his skills. It explained more of the situation than Erik was comfortable with having known by strangers, but Nathan had assured him the guild was like a family. The letter urged the guild to find Erik a position somewhere on the Far Coast or in the Sunset Islands.

The sound of horses entering the courtyard of the inn caused Freida to cast a worried look Erik's way. It was only two days since Greylock had burned Otto's message, but still she was worried that Stefan might act prematurely to harm her son.

Erik opened the door to the rear courtyard and found twenty men in the baronial livery dismounting, Owen Greylock at their head. "Master Greylock, what is it?"

Erik half expected to hear Owen say they had come to arrest him, but instead the Baron's Swordmaster took Erik by the arm and steered him away from the soldiers. "Your father. He suffered another seizure. We turned around yesterday afternoon, and now we must stop. His chirurgeon says he will not live to reach Darkmoor. He's being taken to the Peacock's Tail"—the most lavish inn in Ravensburg—"and the rest of the men will be quartered in the other inns around the town. Another company rides all night to Darkmoor to fetch the Baroness. Your father will not live more than a few days."

Erik felt surprisingly devoid of any feeling at the news of his father's impending death. The message from him had made whatever childish fantasies about the man evaporate, to be replaced by a distant image of a man unable to do the right thing by a common woman and his own child. The closest feeling Erik could muster was pity. At last he spoke. "I don't know what to say, Owen."

"Have you given thought to our last conversation?"

"Mother and I are leaving tomorrow morning."

"Good. Keep out of the town square tonight, and see you are on the coach when it leaves. Stefan and Manfred are understandably distressed, and there's no telling what that hothead Stefan's capable of doing. As long as the Baron's alive, he'll probably remain close at hand, so if he doesn't catch sight of you, all should be well." Glancing at the soldiers, he said, "I will stay here, with this guard, until I'm summoned to the Baron's side."

Erik knew that Greylock had intentionally chosen to bring his own contingency of guards to the Inn of the Pintail, against the possibility of trouble, and he said, "Thank you, Owen."

"Just doing as my lord would want, Erik. Now go inside and tell Milo I need all his rooms."

Erik did as he was asked, and soon the inn was busy, with Rosalyn, Freida, and Milo all hurrying to get every room ready for guests. Each soldier saw to his own mount, but Erik and Nathan had plenty to do fetching fodder into the barn and the large corral on the north side of the barn where twelve of the twenty mounts were herded.

Erik finished bringing in the last bale of hay for the horses, and washed up in the forge. Nathan came to stand behind him and said, "I am sorry to hear about your father, Erik."

Erik shrugged. "I don't have much feeling about this, Nathan. Milo's been the only father I've ever known, though he acts more like an uncle. You've treated me more like a son in the last five months than Otto did my entire life. I don't know what I should be feeling."

Nathan put his hand on Erik's shoulder and gave it a firm squeeze. "There is no 'should' to it, lad. You feel what you feel, and there's no right or wrong. Otto was your father, but you never knew him."

His voice was quiet and calm as he went on, "It's changing diapers when the wife's too busy with another child's illness, or listening to the child prattle after a long tiring day because it's *your child's* prattle, that makes a father, not getting a girl pregnant. Any fool can do that. It's holding a child who's frightened at night, or tossing one in the air to make her giggle. You've had none of that from Otto. I can understand how you could feel little at his passing."

Erik turned to regard the burly smith. "I shall miss you, Nathan. I mean what I said. You helped me understand what a father should be like."

He embraced the older man, and they hugged for a long moment. Nathan said, "And you've given me a chance to imagine what it would have been like had my sons lived, Erik. I'll treasure that." Then, with a harsh barking laugh: "And you've made it hell to be my next apprentice, lad. You're a talent and you've got years of experience under your belt. I may be short-tempered with some tangle-footed boy of fourteen who has never stepped inside a forge before."

Erik shook his head. "I somehow doubt that, Nathan. You'll be fair with him."

"Well, let's not dwell on partings. Let's go inside and grab some food before those soldiers eat everything in sight."

Erik laughed at that and realized he was hungry, despite the prospect of leaving the place of his birth and never returning, and the specter of his father's death at any hour.

They entered the kitchen to find Freida busy preparing food, as if it were just another night at the inn, and Rosalyn hurrying between the kitchen and the common room, while Milo fetched ale and wine from the taproom.

Erik and Nathan washed up and entered the commons. Instead of the usual loud talk, the soldiers were quietly eating and drinking, keeping their voices low. Owen sat alone at a corner table and motioned Erik and Nathan to join him.

They did, and Milo brought over three large glass goblets of wine. When he had left, Owen said, "Where are you bound for tomorrow, Erik?"

"Krondor," he said. "To the guild office for another apprenticeship."

"So it's west, then?"

"Yes. The Far Coast or the Sunset Islands."

Nathan said, "They've found gems and gold in the mountains near Jonril, so the rush is on. The trading houses from the Free Cities, as well as every adventurer, thief, and swindler, have descended there. But it also means a good opportunity, because the Duke of Crydee has asked for additional smiths, as well as other Craftmasters, to be sent there."

Owen nodded. "This place changes little, and most of us are born into our lives with small chance of making them different. Out there, with some ambition, some thought, and a touch of luck, a common man can rise to riches or even to the nobility."

Erik said, "Riches, with luck, I guess. But a commoner become a noble?"

Owen smiled his crooked smile. "It's not common knowledge, but the King's adviser, the Duke of Rillanon, was common-born."

"Truth?" said Nathan.

"He did some favor or another for the late Prince of Krondor, and was given a squire's rank when he was but a lad. His wit and service to the Kingdom earned him a rapid rise, and now he is second only to royalty in power." He lowered his voice to a near whisper. "There are those who claim he was not only a common boy, but a thief as well."

Erik said, "That is impossible."

Owen shrugged. "Nothing is truly impossible, I think."

Erik said, "Well, maybe when he was a boy, but that was fifty years ago."

Owen nodded. "Things change. Once, centuries ago, this was the frontier, Erik."

Erik's brow furrowed as if he didn't understand.

Nathan said, "I grew up on the Far Coast, Erik. I think what friend Greylock means is that you'll find a different stripe out there, men who are concerned more with what you know and can do than with who you are, or who your father was. Too many things going on to worry about rank; you've got to depend upon your neighbors. Goblins, dark elves, bandits, and other problems constantly coming at you—those make a man glad for help close by. You don't have time to worry about a lot of the things that make life here in the Kingdom the way it is."

Greylock nodded. Erik said nothing for a moment, thinking about the possibility things might turn out right after all, when the front door of the inn opened, and Roo hurried in.

He saw Erik from across the room and quickly came through the crowded commons to where his friend sat. Nodding with as much deference as he could muster to the Baron's Swordmaster, he said, "Master Greylock, they need you over at the Peacock, sir."

Owen threw a quick glance at Erik. His expression betrayed his worry. It couldn't be good news. He stood, said a quick good-bye, and left. Roo took his place. Nathan said, "You a squire these days, Roo?"

Roo made a face as if that remark put a bad taste in his mouth. "I was hanging around the fountain by the Growers' and Vintners' Hall and a soldier came out and told all of us to spread out and look for the Swordmaster and fetch him to the Peacock's Tail. So I told the other lads I'd come here."

Erik smiled. "I was hoping you'd come by tonight."

"I would have been here sooner, but Gwen was at the fountain and . . ."

Erik shook his head. "So you're back in her favor once again?"

"Trying to be," said Roo.

Nathan said, "How'd you like to apprentice at the forge, Roo?"

It was a joke, and they all knew it, but Roo still said, "What, me get all dirty and grimy? You get your hands calloused, and the horses step on your feet! Not on your life. I have plans."

Erik smiled, but Nathan said, "Really? What sort of plans?"

Roo glanced around the room, as if fearing to be overheard. "There are ways to make a living that have nothing to do with guilds and apprenticeships, friend smith."

Nathan's brow furrowed. "You're going to end up in jail, Roo."

Roo put up his hands as if protesting innocence. "No, nothing dodgy, I swear. It's just my father has been hauling enough from Krondor up to here that I'm getting pretty good at nosing out what the markets are for different things. I've saved a little money, and I'm going to invest it in a cargo one of these days."

Nathan appeared impressed. "A shipping concern?"

"There are syndicates in Krondor and Salador that routinely underwrite the cost of freight hauls from one city to another, or cargoes for ships bound to distant ports. They have subscribers and return nice profits on their investments."

Nathan nodded. "True, but there's risk as well. If a cargo isn't delivered on time, your profit can vanish. Worse, if bandits take the caravan, or the ship sinks, you lose everything."

Roo looked as if this would never happen. "I plan on starting small and building up my capital for a few years."

"What do you plan on doing to eat and put a roof over your head while you invest in these ventures?" asked Nathan.

Roo said, "Well, I haven't quite worked that out, but—"

"How much capital have you, Roo?" interrupted Nathan.

"On to thirty golden sovereigns," he said proudly.

Nathan was impressed. "Quite a beginning. I think I'll forbear asking how you've managed to amass such a young fortune, and"—he turned to Erik—"I suggest you get back to the forge and keep out of sight. When the coach comes in the morning is time enough for your good-byes. If Master Greylock needs another word with you, I'll send him to you."

Erik nodded and rose. Roo followed him. The two youngsters passed from the crowded common room to the kitchen, where Rosalyn was hurrying to carry a large platter of steaming greens out to the soldiers. Freida worked feverishly over her stew as if it were just another busy night at the inn and not her last in the home of her birth.

Erik walked outside with Roo, and as he passed the corral, the horses there wandered over to investigate the two boys. Erik inspected their legs out of habit. "Milo will need to order up hay tomorrow," he muttered to Roo as he slowly walked along the fence. "This lot will have eaten the entire contents of the loft by the time they've gone."

Roo turned and faced Erik while they were walking. He seemed to half skip, half dance to keep from tripping while walking backwards. "Erik, let me come with you."

Erik said, "Why would you want to come with me?"

"Look, you're the only real friend I've got here, and I've got no trade. I wasn't joking about joining a syndicate. I can get a job in Krondor and invest my money until I'm rich. Once you get to Krondor, you'll see there are better things to do than return to apprenticeship."

Erik laughed, and stopped, so Roo wouldn't have to continue his backward walk. "What about your father?"

"He'd just as soon be rid of me as not," Roo said with bitterness. "The bastard hasn't had a kind word for me since Mum died." Suddenly, as if by magic, a dagger appeared in Roo's hand, then equally suddenly he returned it to inside his loose shirt. "I can take care of myself if I need to. Now, let me come along."

Erik said, "I'll talk to Mother. She's not likely to offer any encouragement."

"You'll talk her into it."

"Well, assume I do, you need to get your things together and have some copper to pay the coach."

"Everything I have is in a bundle at my father's. I'll run and get it."

Erik shook his head and watched Roo run off into the night. He glanced around, suddenly feeling melancholy. This would be his last night under the barn roof. It was a poor lodging by any measure; occasionally leaky, drafty, and offering too little protection from winter's cold and summer's heat, but it was home. And he'd miss Milo and Rosalyn.

As he returned to his place in the loft, Erik thought of Rosalyn, pretty, but not teasing as Gwen and some of the other girls were. His feelings for her were often tempered by his sense of family. She was the sister of his heart, if not by blood, and while he was as interested in girls as any boy his age, something about Rosalyn made him uneasy. In many ways he'd miss her most of all.

Tired from the long day's work and from worry, Erik quickly dozed off, only to be startled awake by a sudden feeling of panic. He sat up and looked around the dark barn loft. Unseen enemies were hovering nearby. The sound of men talking carried from the inn, and the horses in the corral and barn snorted. Erik rolled over on his side, head on his arm, thinking about the strange feeling of danger that had suddenly come upon him.

He closed his eyes and again saw Rosalyn's face. He would miss her, and Milo, and Nathan. Soon he was dozing again. Before he lapsed into a deep sleep, he dreamed he heard Rosalyn gently calling his name.

"ERIK!"

Erik came awake with a start as a hand shook his shoulder. He had been hard asleep, in a deep numbing slumber of emotional exhaustion, and he couldn't quite get his bearings.

"Erik!" Roo's voice cut through the gloom, and Erik looked up into his friend's face. Roo was dressed as he had been earlier, but he wore a travel bundle tied around one shoulder, slung over his back.

"What is it?"

"You'd better come quick. Down by the fountain. Rosalyn."

Erik half leaped down the ladder, Roo scampering down after him as fast as he could. Erik sprinted past the corral of horses and, as he approached the inn, could hear the voices from within. "What time is it?"

"Nine of the clock was the last call. Half past that, I think."

Erik knew that with this many soldiers in town, some of the town girls would be down at the fountain. But Rosalyn was certainly not likely to be one of them.

"What happened?"

"I don't know," answered Roo. "Gwen can tell you."

Erik ran through the streets until he came to the fountain, where a group of three young off-duty soldiers were attempting to impress the local girls with tales of their heroics. But the expression on Gwen's face as he saw it in the lantern light showed that all thoughts of harmless flirtation were gone. She looked very worried.

"What is it?" demanded Erik.

"Rosalyn came here, looking for you."

"I was in the loft," said Erik.

Gwen said, "She said she called for you there, but you didn't answer."

Erik cursed his sound sleep and said, "Where is she now?"

Roo said, "They say she went off with Stefan."

"What?" Erik turned at his half brother's name and gripped Gwen by the arm. "Tell me what happened."

Gwen motioned for Erik to follow her, out of hearing of the soldiers. "She was going back to the inn when the Baron's sons came. Stefan started saying sweet things to her, but there was something about his manner she didn't like. She tried to leave, but didn't know how to say no to someone of his rank, and when he took her by the arm, she went along. But he didn't lead her back to the inn; they went off toward the old orchard." She pointed off in the general direction. "He was more dragging her along than escorting her, Erik."

Erik had taken one step after them when Gwen held his arm. "Erik, I've been with Stefan. The last time he was here I went to his rooms at the Peacock. . . ." Her voice lowered as if she was ashamed to speak. "He left marks on me, Erik. He likes to hit while he's having you, and when I cried, it made him laugh."

Roo had been standing beside Erik. As Erik turned away toward the apple grove, Roo saw an expression on Erik's face that caused him to hesitate an instant. While Erik moved away with purposeful steps, Roo grabbed Gwen by the arm. "Go to the Pintail and find Nathan. Tell him what happened and to come to the orchard!"

Roo hurried over to where the three soldiers watched Erik disappear into the night. One looked at Roo with an open expression of curiosity on his face, and Roo said, "If you don't want bloodshed, run and find Owen Greylock and tell him to come to the old orchard."

Roo then ran as fast as he could after the rapidly receding figure of Erik. The slender boy was one of the fastest runners in town, but Erik had already moved out of the lantern light of the square and had vanished down the street leading to the old apple orchard at the edge of town.

Roo hurried through the streets, his footfalls slapping the stones with a sound that seemed to evoke the anger and outrage in the night. Each step sounded like a hand striking a face, and with the sound, Roo felt his blood rise. Quick to anger, slow to release a grudge, Roo knew a fight was coming and was composing himself to help his friend. He didn't like Stefan, anyway, from what he had seen of him, but as each stride took him closer to confrontation, it was turning into a serious hatred. As he left the last buildings behind, he caught a glimpse of Erik at the far edge of his vision, before he faded into the darkness.

Roo hurried after, but Erik was possessed with an outrage that lent his feet wings. Roo had never seen Erik run so swiftly.

Roo crossed the low pasture and jumped the fence that brought him to the edge of the old orchard, a favored meeting place for young lovers on warm nights. Reaching the edge of the trees, cloaked in threatening darkness after the brightly lit town square and lantern-dressed streets, Roo was forced to slow to a walk. He moved between the dark boles, then suddenly was upon Erik, who turned at his approach. Erik made a motion for silence, then whispered, "Over there, I think," as he tried to catch his breath.

Roo listened and was about to say he heard nothing over the pounding of his own heart when a faint movement, as if someone shifted his weight, could be heard, the softest rustle of cloth upon cloth. It was in the general direction Erik indicated. Roo nodded.

Erik moved like a hunter stalking prey. There was something very wrong in all of this. Rosalyn would never have come away with any boy to the orchard, for there was only one reason to be here. Rosalyn was still a virgin, of that Erik was certain, still too young to have a lover. Some girls, like Gwen, matured early and enjoyed the company of older boys, while others were shy. Rosalyn was not only shy; once outside her father's inn she was intimidated by the company of any boys besides Erik and Roo. Even the most innocent compliment would bring a blush to her cheeks, and when the other girls started talking about the town boys, she would excuse herself in embarrassment. Erik knew in his heart she was in danger, and the silence of the orchard frightened him. If another couple had been making love anywhere within this grove, sounds would carry this quiet night.

Abruptly, both boys heard a sound that made their hair stand on end. A girl's cry split the night, followed by the sound of a fist striking flesh, then silence. Erik leaped toward the sound. Roo hesitated an instant, then followed.

Erik ran without thought toward where the sound had come from. Then he saw Rosalyn, and his world froze for an instant. The girl lay back against the bole of a tree, her face bruised and her dress in tatters. Her blouse was torn from her, exposing her breasts, and her skirt was ripped away, with only a tattered rag around her waist. Erik could see blood running from her nose and she was without motion. Erik felt something hot and blinding rise up within him.

A sense of movement, rather than anything really seen, caused Erik to move to his right, saving his life. A searing pain erupted in his left shoulder as Stefan's sword point pierced it. With a cry of agony, Erik felt his knees go weak from the unexpected shock. Then Roo flew past his friend, driving his head into Stefan's stomach. Erik almost fainted when the sword point was wrenched from his shoulder. His vision swam and his stomach knotted, and he had to force himself not to lose consciousness. He forced himself back to his feet as he shook his head to clear it. The sound of Roo's panic-stricken plea for help brought him back to alertness.

In the dark, with only the middle moon shining through the branches, he could see Roo wrestling Stefan on the ground. The smaller lad had surprised Stefan, but that advantage was now gone. Stefan was using his superior strength and size to force himself atop Roo. Only the fact his sword was designed for fighting at arm's length saved Roo's life. Had Stefan held a dagger, the boy would surely be dead.

As Roo called his name, Erik ignored the terrible pain in his left shoulder and with a single step came up behind Stefan. He grabbed his half brother around the waist and yanked him up in a massive bear hug, a primitive cry erupting from his own throat. Stefan's breath exploded from his lungs as the young smith's powerful arms closed hard around his chest; the sword fell from Stefan's hand as he was lifted abruptly off Roo. Held above the ground, all he could do was kick helplessly backwards at Erik and claw at his hands.

Erik stood like a man possessed by an avenging spirit as he attempted to crush the life from Stefan. He couldn't take his eyes from Rosalyn, who lay in mute tableau, a testimony to Stefan's cruelty. Erik had seen her naked as a child, for they had bathed together, but not since they had grown. The sight of her breasts, her own blood dripping between them, was something obscene to Erik. Lover, husband, child should have touched that flesh, with nurturing love. His Rosalyn deserved better than the rough handling of a jaded and cruel noble.

Roo rolled to his feet, his dagger pulled from within his shirt. Murderous anger flashed in his eyes as he stepped forward. Stefan struggled with hysterical strength and Erik felt his grip loosen. As Roo reached them, Erik heard a distant voice shout, "Kill him!" and as Roo drove home the blade, Erik realized the voice commanding Stefan's death was his own.

Stefan stiffened and bucked once, then went limp, and even when Roo yanked free his blade, the son of the Baron did not twitch. Erik felt his skin crawl with an otherworldly sense of disgust, as if he were holding something profoundly unclean, and he let go. Stefan fell limply to the ground.

Roo stood over him, holding the still-bloody dagger, and Erik saw rage was still in his friend's expression. He said, "Roo?"

Roo blinked and looked down at his blade, then at Stefan. He wiped the blade on Stefan's shirt and put it away. Frustration and anger still pumped through Roo's mind and body; in need of another target to vent them on, he aimed a vicious kick at Stefan's body. The toe of his boot struck ribs, breaking them. With a final gesture of contempt, he spit on the corpse.

Suddenly the anger drained out of Erik. "Roo?" he repeated, and his friend turned to face him.

Erik's expression was one of confusion and Roo's a mask of equally confused anger; a third time Erik said his friend's name. Roo finally answered, his own voice hoarse with excitement and fear. "What?"

"What have we done?"

Roo looked blankly at Erik a moment, then looked down at Stefan. Instantly what had just occurred registered on him. He rolled his eyes heavenward and said, "Oh, gods, Erik. They're going to hang us."

Erik glanced around, and the sight of Rosalyn shook him back to more pressing needs than concern over his own fate. He crossed the distance between Stefan's body and hers and knelt beside her. She lived, but her breath was shallow and labored, and he moved her to a more upright position. He watched helplessly, not knowing if he should cover her up, or see if he could stop the bleeding from her nose, or what. Then she moaned slightly.

Roo appeared with a fancy cloak, obviously Stefan's, and covered her. "She's in danger," said Erik.

"So are we," answered Roo. "If we stay, they will arrest us and hang us, Erik."

Erik looked as if he were about to pick up Rosalyn, but Roo said, "We must get away!"

Erik said, "What do you mean?"

Roo said, "We've killed the Baron's son, you idiot."

"But he abused Rosalyn!"

"That doesn't give us a warrant to execute him, Erik. Do you want to go into court and swear that this was only about Rosalyn? If it had been anyone else in the entire world but your own half brother . . ." He left the thought unfinished.

"We can't leave her here," said Erik.

The sounds of men shouting echoed through the night. "She won't be un-discovered for long. This orchard is going to be swarming with the Baron's soldiers in a few minutes." As if to punctuate the observation, Erik could now hear distinct voices as the men advanced toward the orchard.

Roo looked ready to run at a moment's notice as he looked around the glade. "We didn't have to kill him, Erik. If we are put in the dock and made to testify, we can't honestly say we had to kill him." Roo put his hand on Erik's arm as if to drag him from the scene. "I wanted him dead, Erik. You did, too. We mur-dered him."

Erik found it almost impossible to keep events clear in his head. He knew he had felt something close to murder in his heart as he wrestled with Stefan, but now that was a distant memory, and events were jumbled.

"I've got my money, here"—he indicated his travel bundle—"so we can make for Krondor and buy passage to the Sunset Islands."

"Why there?"

"Because if a man lives for a year and a day in the islands and commits no crime, he's pardoned for whatever he did before he came there. It's an old law from when the islands came into the Kingdom."

"But they'll be looking for us."

Rosalyn stirred, with a faint moan of discomfort. Roo leaned down and asked, "Can you hear me?"

The girl didn't answer. Roo said, "They'll probably think we're going to Kesh. A man can hide in the Vale of Dreams and get across the border without much trouble." The vale, the border between Great Kesh and the Kingdom, was a no-man's-land of smugglers, bandits, and garrisons along both sides of the frontier. Men came and went and few questions were asked.

Erik moved his shoulder experimentally and felt light-headed when a stabbing pain answered his movement. "This isn't right," he said.

Roo shook his head. "If we stay here, we will be hung. Even if we had twenty witnesses, Manfred would make sure we were found guilty." Roo looked around as a distant shout split the night. "Someone's coming. We have to go *now!*"

Erik nodded. "I should go back to the inn—"

"No," said Roo. "They'll expect that. We must go down the old western trail. We'll go all night and cut into the woodlands at daybreak. If they send the dogs after us, we had better be across a dozen streams or more before noon."

"Mother—" began Erik.

"She'll be safe," Roo interrupted. "Manfred has no reason to trouble her. You were always the threat, not your mother." A shout from the far side of the orchard caused Roo to swear. "They're on the other side already. We're trapped!"

Erik said, "There!" He pointed to an old tree both had played in over the years. The centerpiece of the old orchard, the tree was heavily shrouded in leaves and might offer possible haven.

They crossed the short distance to the tree and Roo said, "How's your shoulder?"

"Hurts like blazes, but I can move it."

Roo didn't hesitate but scampered up the tree. He moved as high as he could, leaving the slightly heavier lower branches for Erik. By the time Erik was out of sight, torchlight and lanterns could be seen coming close.

Roo shook for a moment as he lost balance, then regained it, and Erik was now almost sick with pain, fear, and disgust. Stefan's death was still unreal to him; he could see the dark shape of his body on the ground and expected him to rise up in a moment, as if this were all some mummery put on at a festival.

Then a soldier with a lantern saw Rosalyn. "Master Greylock! Over here!"

Through the leaves, Erik could barely make out the figures that rushed to where Rosalyn and Stefan lay a few yards apart. Then he heard Owen Greylock's voice. "He's dead."

Another voice asked, "How is the girl?"

A third said, "She's in a bad way, Swordmaster. We should get her to the chirurgeon."

Then Erik heard Manfred's shout of rage. "They've killed my brother!" An almost inaudible oath and a sobbing cry was followed by "I'll kill him myself."

Erik caught a glimpse of Owen Greylock's slender form between the nearby leaves and heard the Baron's Swordmaster say, "We'll find those who did this, Manfred."

Erik shook his head. The three soldiers who had seen him and Roo run after

Stefan and Rosalyn would certainly place them at the scene. A soldier said, "I know there was bad blood between the bastard and your brother, but why did they beat the girl?" Erik knew then that they had already been identified.

Erik felt his anger rise again. A familiar voice said, "Erik wouldn't harm Rosalyn." Nathan was there!

"Are you saying my brother did this, Master Smith?"

"Young sir, I only know that this girl is as gentle a soul as the gods have placed upon this world. She was a sister to Erik and one of Roo's few friends. Neither boy would harm her." Then he pointedly added, "But I can certainly imagine them killing anyone who did."

Manfred's voice rose in anger. "I'll have no excuse for black murder, Master Smith. No member of my family would do this." Manfred raised his voice to a shout of command: "I want every man on his horse and combing the country-side, Swordmaster. If those two murderous dogs are found, I want them held until I can join whichever soldiers find them. I don't want them hung until I'm there to watch."

Nathan's voice cut through the muttering of the gathered soldiers. "There will be no hanging them out of hand, young lord. That's the law. And as you are a member of the family that is wronged, neither you nor your father can sit in judgment; when caught, Erik and Roo are to be bound over to a King's justice or magistrate." Then Nathan's tone became warning. "Erik is a guild apprentice, so if you really want troubles, young sir, try to put my apprentice into a noose without due writ."

"You'd bring the guild into this?" asked Manfred.

"I would," answered Nathan. Erik felt tears gather in his eyes. Nathan, at least, understood why this had happened. "I suggest the young lord returns to his father's side. Someone needs to break this grave news to him, and it should be someone he loves." To drive the point into the ground, he said, "It should be you, young sir."

There was a stirring and a weak cry from Rosalyn, and Nathan took command. "Master Greylock, would you ask two of your lads to carry the girl back to the inn?"

Greylock gave instructions and began issuing commands to search for Erik and Roo.

They remained in the tree while soldiers fanned out in all directions, and said nothing to each other until it had been quiet for some time.

Then slowly they dropped to the ground, and crouched, ready to bolt should any noise indicate they were discovered. At last Roo said, "For a while we have luck on our side."

"Why?"

"They don't think we're behind them. As they widen the circle to find us, there'll be more places we can slip through. Any local farmer would think of the old western trail, but Greylock's probably never heard of it; all his trips west have been by the King's Highway. For a while we can worry about soldiers in front of us, not behind us."

Erik said, "I think maybe we should give ourselves up."

Roo said, "You may have Nathan and the guild to protect you, *maybe*, but I don't. Manfred will get me hung before the sun sets on the day they find me. And don't think he's likely to worry about the law much if it dawns on him that you're now a threat to his inheritance, not Stefan's."

Erik felt a sinking in his stomach. Roo whispered, "You've made him Baron next, and I don't think he's going to want you around to thank you, Erik. We're dead men if we can't make straight to the Sunset Islands."

Erik nodded. He was still light-headed and in pain, but he rose to unsteady feet. Without another word he followed Roo into the darkness.

4

★★

FUGITIVES

ERIK FELL.

Roo turned and helped his friend back to his feet. In the distance, the baying of hounds could be heard, accompanied by the clatter of horses.

The boys had been running on and off since leaving the orchard the night before, with no more than a few minutes' rest at any one time. Erik's wound refused to stop bleeding, though the flow was slight. Still, it throbbed and burned with heat and he felt himself grow weaker by the hour as they worked their way down out of the low mountains of Darkmoor.

The area west of Darkmoor and north of the King's Highway was still fairly underpopulated. Rocky terrain with little to recommend itself to farmers, much of the land had been timbered out but left unplowed. Thick stands of trees gave way to a sea of stumps, only to be replaced by unexpected rocky ridges. This region was rich with gullies, ravines, dead-end canyons, and low, flat meadows. Despite their having run down any number of streams, the sound of the dogs had been carrying on the wind for hours. And as Erik weakened, the sound was getting closer.

As the morning sun crested the peaks behind them, Erik said, "Where are we?"

Roo said, "I'm not sure. When we left the old wagon trail, I think we turned around a bit. The sun's in the right place, so we're still heading west."

Erik looked around, perspiration streaming off his forehead. He wiped it away and said, "We'd better keep going."

Roo nodded, but after three or four fumbling footsteps, Erik collapsed. Roo tried to help his friend up. "Why'd you have to be so damn big?"

Erik gasped for air and said, "Go on without me."

Roo felt the hair rise upon his neck and felt panic slash through his stomach. Finding strength he didn't know he had, he forced Erik to his feet. "And have to explain to your mother how I lost you? I don't think so."

Roo silently prayed that Erik could hold on long enough for them to find shelter and hide from the dogs. Roo was terrified. One of the heartiest lads in Ravensburg, Erik had stamina almost as legendary as his strength among the boys he grew up with. His ability to work from dawn to dusk since the age of ten, his ability to carry iron ingots to the forge, his ability to withstand the constant weight of draft horses leaning on him while being shod—all had given Erik an almost superhuman stature among the townspeople. His weakness was as alien to Roo as it was to Erik himself. Roo found it far more frightening than anything else that confronted them. With Erik at his side, he felt he had a fighting chance to survive. Without Erik, he was helpless.

Roo sniffed the air. "Do you smell something?"

Erik said, "Only the stink of my own sweat."

"Over there." Roo motioned with his chin.

Erik put his hand against his friend's shoulder and rested a moment as he sniffed the air. "Charcoal."

"That's it!"

"There must be a charcoal burner's hut upwind."

"It might mask our scent," said Roo. "I know we can't go much farther. You've got to rest, get your strength back."

Erik only nodded, and Roo assisted him as they moved toward the source of the smoke. Through light woods they stumbled as the sound of the dogs grew louder by the minute. Erik and Roo were not woodsmen, but as boys they had played in the woodlands near Ravensburg enough to know those searching for them were less than a couple of miles behind and coming fast.

The woods thickened and grew more difficult to navigate, darker shadows confusing their sense of direction, but the smell of burning wood grew stronger. By the time they reached the hut, their eyes stung from it.

An old woman, ugly beyond belief, stood tending a charcoal kiln, feeding small cuts of wood into it, banking flames as she ensured the wood burned down properly; too hot, and she'd have ashes.

Seeing the two young men suddenly appear out of the gloom, she shrieked and almost dove inside the rude hut beside which her kiln rested. The shrieking continued and Roo said, "She'll bring them down on us if this keeps up."

Erik tried to raise his voice over her shouting. "We mean you no harm."

The shrieking continued, and Roo added his protestation of no evil intent to Erik's. The woman continued to shriek. Finally Erik said, "We had best leave."

"We can't," answered Roo. "You're on your last legs now." He said nothing about the wound, which continued to weep blood, despite the rags pressed against it.

Stumbling down a small incline to the charcoal burner's hut, they confronted a simple piece of hide that served as a door.

Erik leaned his weight against the mud-covered wall and pulled aside the leather door. The woman huddled back against the bale of rags that served as her bedding, shrieking all the more.

Erik finally shouted, "Woman! We mean you no harm!"

Instantly the shouting ceased. "Well," she answered, her voice as raspy as a wire brush on metal, "why didn't you say something?"

Erik almost laughed, he felt so light-headed and giddy. Roo said, "We were trying to, but you kept screaming."

Getting up off the rags, showing a surprising nimbleness for her age and weight—easily as much as Erik's and he stood a good foot and a half taller than she—the woman stepped out of the hut.

Roo reflexively stepped back. She was the ugliest human being he had ever encountered, if indeed she was human. From her appearance, she could possibly be one of those trolls he had heard about that haunted the woodlands of the Far Coast. Her nose was a lumpy red protrusion, resembling a large tuber, with one big wart on the tip of it, from which several long hairs grew. Her eyes could only be called piggish, and they wept from some sort of inflammation. Her teeth were blackened stumps with green edges, and her breath was as foul as anything Roo had remembered smelling that wasn't dead. Her skin looked like dried leather, and he shuddered to consider what her body under that assortment of filthy rags might resemble.

Then she smiled and the effect was heightened. "Come to pay old Gert a visit, have you?" She tried to be girlish as she combed her fingers through grey hair tangled with straw and dirt, and had the boys not been so tired and frightened, they would have laughed. "Well, my man is gone to the city, so maybe—"

"My friend is hurt," interrupted Roo.

Suddenly the old woman's manner changed again as she caught the sound of the dogs on the wind. "King's men are hunting you?"

Roo thought about lying, but Erik said, "Yes."

Roo said, "Baron's men, really."

"Same thing. Soldiers." She spat the last word. "Well, you'd better hide." She motioned for them to enter the tiny hut. "They won't find you in there."

Roo helped Erik into the hut and gagged at the stench. Erik's eyes watered and he gasped, "I thought Tyndal's room was bad."

Roo said, "Try breathing through your mouth."

Gert knelt down next to Erik and said, "Let me look at that," motioning to his bloodstained shoulder.

Erik pulled aside his tunic and the rags. The rags pulled the skin where blood had dried and he gasped in pain. Gert probed at the wound with a filthy finger and said, "Sword wound. Seen a hundred of them. Swollen around it. Got the hot sickness in it. Going to kill you, boy, if we don't clean it out. You got a strong stomach?" she asked Roo.

He nodded, swallowing hard. "I'm here and haven't thrown up yet, haven't I?"

"Ha!" She almost cackled as she laughed. "There's more to you than meets the eye, Roo Avery." She rose up as high as the low floor permitted and said, "I have just the thing to put you right. Be back in a jiffy."

Roo lay back, glad to be resting despite the stench of the hut. He glanced around; enough gaps in the wall permitted light to enter, and he saw what looked to be a water jar with a long neck. He moved the clay vessel and heard a promising sound of liquid. Pulling the cork, he sniffed and got no odor. He sipped and was rewarded with fresh water. Drinking a huge mouthful, he suddenly realized he was ignoring his sick friend.

He put the neck of the jar to Erik's lips and he drank several mouthfuls, then sank back into the pile of rags. A fly began to buzz around Roo's head and he absently swatted at it.

Erik drifted off into a difficult slumber, his fatigue overwhelming his fear. His breathing came heavily, and perspiration continued to pour off his brow.

Roo tried to relax, wondering if they could trust this strange old woman but knowing that further flight was next to hopeless. Then suddenly there was the sound of barking nearby, and Gert's shriek cut the air.

Erik came awake with a start at the sound. "What . . . ?" he began, but Roo grabbed his arm.

Dogs could be heard barking nearby and Gert shouted, "Shoo! Away with you!"

Then horses approached and the boys heard Gert shout, "Get these miserable curs away! They'll be bitin' old Gert in a minute."

A commanding voice said, "Have you seen two men, one large and blond, the other short and dark?"

"And if I did, what's it to you?"

"They're wanted for murder."

"Murder, is it?" There was a long pause, punctuated by the sounds of the dogs sniffing the area and the occasional odd yelp of inquiry. "What's the reward?"

Erik felt Roo's hand tighten on his arm at that, and the answer was, "The Baron's offered one hundred golden sovereigns for their arrest."

"That's a tidy bit, isn't it?" said Gert. "Well, I haven't seen them, but if I do, I'll want the gold."

"Check inside the hut," ordered the leader.

"Here, now!" Gert began to protest.

"Stand aside, old woman."

Erik backed away, trying as hard as he could to push himself backward through the dirt wall, while Roo drew the ragged, filthy blankets up below his chin.

The leather door was swept aside, and the light was almost blinding after the darkness. "What a stench!" said the soldier, drawing back.

"Go on," commanded the leader of the troop.

The soldier stuck his head back inside and blinked against the darkness, then looked directly at Roo and Erik. He looked to one side and then the other, and at last pulled his head back out. "Nothing in there but filthy rags and some pots, Captain."

Roo and Erik exchanged glances of wonder in the gloom. What magic was this?

"What's the matter with the dogs?" asked the captain.

The man who must have been the Houndmaster said, "They seem to have lost the scent. The charcoal must be confusing them."

"Then let us go back to the last place you know they had it, and begin again. Lord Manfred will have our ears if those murderers escape."

The dogs began to bark as the Houndmaster blew his whistle, commanding them to follow. The horses rode away, and Roo let out his breath, held since the soldier stuck his face into the hut.

"What caused that?" asked Roo.

Erik said, "I don't know. Maybe it was too dark to see."

"No, it was a spell. This Gert is a witch of some sort."

Erik said, "The captain said 'Lord Manfred.' My father is dead."

Roo didn't know what to say. He glanced at his friend; in the gloom he saw that Erik had leaned back and closed his eyes.

After a few moments, the leather door was pulled back. Instead of Gert, a young woman appeared before them, tall enough to have to lean forward to enter. Her hair was dark, black in the gloom of the hut, and her features were masked, as she was silhouetted against the daylight.

"What . . . ?" began Roo.

"Say nothing," she replied, then turned to Erik. "Let me examine that wound."

Something in her manner caused Roo to feel uncertain. Her clothing was nondescript, at least what he could see of it: a simple dress of some middling color, perhaps grey, perhaps green or blue; it was difficult to tell in the dark hut. Her features were partially visible now that the door was again shut. She had a high forehead and regal nose, fine features that would have looked pretty had they not been set in an expression of concentration.

She pulled back Erik's tunic and glanced at the wound. "This will have to come off. Help me," she ordered Roo.

He helped Erik stay upright as the woman gathered up the bottom of the tunic and pulled it up and over Erik's head, causing him no little pain. He lay back, perspiration running off his body, panting as if he had exerted himself in hard work for hours. She touched the wound and he grunted in pain, teeth clenching.

"You're a fool, Erik von Darkmoor. Two, three more days, and you'd be dead from blood poison."

Roo got a good look at the woman and thought she was beautiful, but something very offputting in her manner made him view it as a distant, unobtainable sort of beauty.

"Where's Gert?" asked Roo softly.

"Off on some business for me," came the answer.

"Who are you?"

"I told you to say nothing, Roo Avery. You need to learn there are times to speak and times to listen, and which time is which. When you have need to speak, you may call me Miranda."

She set about tending Erik's wound. From somewhere in the cluttered hut she produced a bag from which she fetched a small vial. Opening it, she poured the contents over the wound, and Erik gasped at the pain. Then he relaxed. She next pulled the cork from a flask of liquid and said, "Drink this."

Erik obeyed and made a face. "It's bitter."

"Not as bitter as untimely death," said Miranda.

She quickly finished tending Erik's wound, placing a poultice over it and then bandaging it. By the time she was finished, Erik was asleep. Without another word she rose and left the hut.

Roo watched Erik sleep for a minute, then got to his feet and peeked outside. There was no sign of another person and he left the hut.

Looking around, he saw only the charcoal kiln smoldering and a pile of dog droppings from when the pack had been nearby, but otherwise the area was deserted.

"Hello there, love!" came a cheerful voice behind him, and Roo jumped. He turned to find Gert approaching with a pile of wood in her arms.

"Where is she?" asked Roo.

"Where is who?"

"Miranda."

Gert stopped and made a face. "Miranda? Can't say as I know any Miranda. When the soldiers left, I went to get more wood to burn, and haven't seen any Miranda."

"A young woman, about this tall"—he held his hand up a bit higher than his own head—"with dark hair, very pretty, came into the hut and tended Erik's wound."

"Pretty, you say?" Gert scratched her chin. "I think you must have been dreaming, boy."

Roo took a step toward the hut, drew aside the hide door, and said, "Did I dream that?" He pointed to the fresh bandage on Erik's shoulder.

Gert stared at it. "That's a puzzler, now, isn't it, dearie?" She stood there a minute. "All manner of queer folk in the woods, though. Perhaps she was one of those elf creatures you hear of, or a ghost."

Roo said, "She was the most flesh-and-blood ghost you'll ever see. And she looked nothing like any elf I've heard of."

He looked at Gert and saw her smiling; then her expression turned somber. "Well, some mysteries are best left alone. I've got wood to burn, so get back in there and take a rest. I have something to eat around here somewhere."

Roo felt fatigue wash over him. "Rest is good," he muttered, suddenly tired beyond belief. The thought of sharing a meal with Gert did nothing for his sense of well-being, but sleep was welcome. Reentering the hut, he was surprised he didn't notice the stench this time. Must have gotten use to it, he thought.

Quickly he felt a heavy lethargy sweep over him. Odd sounds intruded, but he found them difficult to identify. He lapsed into a deep sleep, ignoring the very busy sounds of preparation from outside.

A CHATTERING FROM above caused Roo to sit upright, brushing leaves from his face. He looked around, then up, and saw the author of the scolding racket, a red squirrel defiantly challenging their right to be camped under his tree. Before Roo could clearly focus on the creature, it vanished around the bole.

Then he realized he was outside. He turned and saw Erik sleeping soundly, under a clean blanket, his chest rising and falling evenly, his color good. Roo looked down and saw he was likewise bundled against the night's chill in another heavy blanket, and he felt behind him, to where his head had rested.

Like Erik's, his head had rested on a travel bundle. His own was missing. He opened the new one, fearing he had been robbed. Inside, he discovered a clean tunic and trousers, a fresh pair of underdrawers and stockings, and at the bottom he found his money pouch. He quickly counted and was pleased to find his twenty-seven golden sovereigns and sixteen silver royals all there.

Roo stood, and found himself remarkably rested. Of the charcoal burner's hut there was no sign, not even ashes from the kiln. Roo felt he should have been alarmed by this, but he found himself amused and close to happy.

He knelt beside Erik and tried to examine the bandage. It was still clean and, if anything, looked as if someone had just changed it. He gently reached out and touched his friend on the arm. "Erik," he said.

Erik came awake, blinking for a moment, then sat up. "What?"

"I wanted to see how you felt."

Erik looked around. "Where are we? Last thing I remember . . ."

"A hut and an old woman?"

Erik nodded. "And someone else, too. But I can't recall who."

"Miranda," said Roo. "She said that was her name, but old Gert said she knew nothing of her."

Roo stood and extended his hand to Erik. Erik took it and let his friend pull him to his feet. Expecting to be the worse for wear, Erik discovered he felt fairly fit.

"How's the shoulder?"

"Stiff," he answered as he moved it experimentally. "But better than I thought it would be."

Roo looked around. "There's no hut, no kiln, no Gert, no nothing."

Erik said, "And what are these?" He pointed to the two blankets and bundles on the ground.

"Someone was taking great pains to see we don't freeze in the night, and they've given us clean clothing."

Erik suddenly looked at the clothing he was wearing, and then pulled away his tunic and sniffed. "I should smell like a horse after a day in the field, but I don't. And this shirt feels clean."

Roo examined his own clothing. "You don't suppose old Gert gave us a bath?" He found fear rising up rather than humor.

Erik shook his head. "I don't know what to think." Then he glanced around. "It's about nine of the clock from the angle of the sun, so this day is a quarter over. We'd better get moving again; I don't know why the soldiers didn't find us in the hut, but they'll come back and check again, I'm certain."

"Check your bundle," said Roo. "See what's in it."

Erik did as he was bidden and found his was packed much the same as Roo's: fresh shirt and trousers, underdrawers, and stockings. Also there was a small loaf of hard bread, and a note.

He unrolled the tiny parchment and read aloud: "You lads are safe for the time being. Make straight for Krondor and Barret's Coffee Shop, Erik. You are now in our debt, Gert's and mine. Miranda."

Roo shook his head. "Running from the King's justice and now we're in debt to a pair of witches."

"Witches?"

"What else do you think?" said Roo, looking as if a demon were about to leap up from the earth and snatch him to hell. He glanced around, the color gone from his face. "Look at that! That's the same low ridge we had to come down to reach the hut! There was a hut, and a kiln—now there's no sign that anyone has ever been here." He walked over to where the kiln had been. "There's no soot, no ashes. Even if you moved the bloody damn thing, you couldn't clean up this much." He got down on one knee. "There's got to be something!" His voice was growing loud, as if he was becoming angry at discovering the hut and kiln missing. "Damn it, Erik! Someone stripped us, bathed us, cleaned our clothing, and dressed us again, and we never woke up. What else could it be but magic!" He rose and went over to Erik. He put his hands on his friend's arms, and said, "We're trapped by a debt to two evil black witches." His voice continued to get louder, and Erik realized anger was quickly turning into hysteria.

"Easy," said Erik as he placed his hands on Roo's shoulders and squeezed reassuringly. Moving to where the kiln had been, he looked quickly around. "There's nothing left to show we were ever here, that's for certain." He rubbed his chin. "Gert was no beauty, but I don't remember anything about her that smacked of evil, Roo."

"No one that ugly could be good, believe me," said Roo, his tone showing he was obviously not reassured by Erik's judgment.

Erik smiled. "It's a mystery and it makes my flesh crawl, too, but we were not harmed and I seen no way anyone, witch or not, could force us to serve without our consent. I know little of this, but the priests claim you can only enter the service of dark powers willingly. I'll not be obliged for a favor unasked for, should the price be a black deed."

"Fine, you can sound like a litigation solicitor all you wish while demons are carrying you off to the Seven Lower Hells, but I'm making straight for a temple when we reach Krondor and asking for a protection!"

Erik shook Roo gently by the arm. "Take a breath and let's be off. If you're right, and we need protection, we still must reach Krondor first. They may think it likely we're striking for the Vale of Dreams, but that patrol last night means they're looking everywhere."

Roo bent down to pick up the bundle and blanket, and as he folded the blanket, he noticed something. "Erik?"

"Yes, Roo."

"See that dog dung over there?"

Erik looked over, partly amused, and said, "What about it?"

"I noticed that last night when I went out to talk to Gert, but look at it now."

Erik knelt and saw the dried droppings. "These are days old." He started searching around and found a place where one of the horses had also relieved himself not too far away. "Three or four days, from the look of it," he said after causing the horse dung to fall apart with a touch of his boot toe.

"We slept three or four days?"

"From the look of it," Erik repeated.

"Can we leave now?"

Erik smiled, but there was no humor in it. He picked up his blanket, folded it, and tucked it inside the bundle. Then he swung it over his shoulder, saying, "I think we'd best do so."

Roo gathered together his new bundle, shoved the blanket inside in a haphazard fashion, and swung it over his back. Without another word, the two lads headed west.

ERIK HELD UP his hand. They had been traveling for three days, moving steadily westward through the woodland north of the King's Highway. They avoided the occasional farm they encountered and lived off wild berries and the bread they had found in their bundles. Hard and chewy, it nevertheless provided surprising nourishment and kept them going. Erik's shoulder was healing rapidly, far sooner than either young man thought possible.

They spoke little, fearing discovery, and fearing also to delve into the mystery of the charcoal burner's hut. It had been the second day after leaving that they realized that both Gert and Miranda had known their names without either young man's having mentioned them.

Toward sundown, a distant voice cried out, a wordless sound of pain. Erik and Roo exchanged glances and moved away from the narrow path they had followed.

Whispering, Roo said, "What's that?"

"Someone's hurt," said Erik, his voice as low as his friend's.

"What should we do?"

"Avoid trouble," answered Erik. "That may be miles away. Sound carries funny out here." Neither of them had been too far from their hometown as boys, so there was always some background sound of civilization, no matter how faintly heard: a voice calling across the vineyards, the sound of a wagon caravan moving down the distant King's Highway, a woman singing while she washed clothing in a stream.

These woodlands were hardly wild, having been heavily forested over the years for lumber, but they were infrequently traveled and were therefore dangerous. Other lawbreakers besides Erik and Roo were likely to be hiding in the forest.

Erik and Roo moved along at a slow pace, reluctant to rush into danger. Near sunset they found a man lying on his back below a tree, a crossbow bolt in his chest. His eyes were rolled back into his head and his skin was cold.

Roo said, "It's funny."

"What's funny?"

He looked at Erik. "We killed Stefan, but I never got a good look at him. This is the first dead man I've had a chance to look at."

"Tyndal was the first for me," said Erik. "Who do you think this is?"

"Was, you mean," said Roo. "Soldier of some sort." He indicated the sword held in loose fingers, and the small round shield still on the left arm. A simple conical helm with a bar-nasal lay a short distance away, having rolled off his head when the man fell.

Roo said, "There might be something useful here."

"Stripping the dead is not to my liking," answered Erik.

Roo knelt next to the man and investigated the contents of a small pouch. "He won't mind, and we can certainly use that sword."

In the pouch he found six copper coins and a ring of gold. "This will be worth a bit," he said.

"Looks like a wedding band," observed Erik. The dead man was young, only a few years older than himself. "I wonder if it was intended for his sweetheart. Perhaps he was going to ask her to wed."

Roo pocketed the ring. "We'll never know. One thing for certain, he's never going to get the chance to ask." Roo took the sword and handed it hilt first to Erik.

"Why me?"

"Because I have my knife and I've never used a sword in my life."

"Neither have I," protested Erik.

"Well, if you need to, just swing it like your hammer and hope you hit someone. You're strong enough, you should be able to do a lot of damage if you connect."

Erik picked up the sword, then pulled the shield off the man's arm and put it experimentally on his own. It felt alien, but he felt better for having it there.

Roo put the helm on his own head, and when Erik looked at him with a questioning expression, he said, "You've got the shield."

Erik nodded, as if this made sense, and the two set off, leaving the nameless man to the scavengers of the forest. The idea of burial was ignored, as they had no shovel and were concerned that whoever killed the man might still be around.

A short time later they heard movement in the brush ahead. Erik signaled Roo for silence, then motioned that they should circle off to the right. Roo nodded and began walking with a tiptoed exaggeration that would have been comic if Erik hadn't been as badly frightened as his friend.

They almost walked past the man, but he shifted his weight and they heard the brush he hid in rustle. Then a dull thud sounded as a crossbow bolt sped through the air and struck a tree nearby.

From a short distance away, a fearful voice shouted with false bravado, "I have enough bolts to fell an army, you bastard! You had better leave me alone, or I'll do to you what I did to your friend."

Then, from what seemed almost within touching distance, a voice shouted, "Leave your wagon and run, old man. I'll not bother you, but I mean to have your cargo. You can't stay awake forever, and if I set eyes on you again, I'll cut your throat for what you did to Jamie."

Erik could hardly act, he was so startled by the sound of the man's voice so close. Roo looked at his friend, eyes wide in fright, and motioned that they should move away. Erik was about to nod agreement when a voice shouted, "Hey!"

Suddenly a man with a sword and shield stood up, less than six feet ahead of them. He saw Erik and Roo and leaped toward them, brandishing his sword as another bolt flew through the air, missing all three of them. Erik reacted. He blindly thrust with the sword, not intending to do more than push the fighter away. The man tried to parry, but he was expecting a feint, not a blind thrust, and Erik's sword slipped along the man's blade and the point took him in the stomach.

Both Erik and the man stared at each other with astonishment on their faces, then with what sounded like a faint "Damn" the man collapsed at Erik's feet.

Erik was rooted in shock, but Roo leaped away and for his trouble was almost impaled by another bolt. "Hey!" he yelped.

"Who is that?" asked a voice from beyond the brush.

Erik hazarded a look through the brush beyond the man he had just killed and saw a wagon sitting in a small clearing. Two horses stood in traces beyond it, and behind it a crouching figure waited.

"We're not bandits!" cried Roo. "We just killed the man you were shooting at."

"I'll shoot you, too, if you come closer," cried the man behind the wagon.

"We won't come closer," shouted Erik, a note of desperation in his voice. "We just blundered into this mess and we don't want any trouble."

"Who are you?"

Roo pulled on Erik's sleeve. "We're on our way to Krondor, looking for work. Who are you?"

"Who I am is no one's business but my own."

Roo got a familiar look, one Erik knew meant Roo was planning something that usually got both of them in trouble. "Look, if you're a merchant traveling alone, you're an idiot," shouted Roo. He spoke now in a voice forced to ease. He looked green at the sight of the dead man. "If you're out here, you must be a smuggler."

"I am no damn smuggler! I'm an honest trader!"

"Who's avoiding paying toll on the King's Highway," replied Roo.

"There's no law against that," came the answer.

Roo grinned at Erik. "True, but it's certainly a hard way to save some copper. Look, if we come out slowly, will you promise not to shoot?"

There was silence, then: "Come ahead. But I've got a bolt pointed at you."

Roo and Erik moved slowly out of the woods into the clearing, hands held where they could be seen. Erik held the sword point down, because he had no scabbard in which to sheathe it, and he had the shield back on his arm so the man could see he was not hiding a weapon in the other hand.

"You're a couple of boys!" said the man. He stepped out from behind the wagon, holding an old but obviously useful crossbow leveled at them. The man was gaunt and looked older than his years. Long dark hair fell to his shoulders, from beneath a felt cap with a tarnished badge on it. His clothing was old, and oft-mended, and he obviously cared nothing for fashion; his tunic was green, his leggings red, his boots brown, and his belt black. He wore a yellow scarf, and nothing about him was remotely appealing. His beard was grey, and his eyes were black.

Roo said, "Master merchant, you chose a brave course, but it almost proved your undoing."

"Likely you're bandits like those other two," he answered, making a threatening gesture with the crossbow. "I should put a bolt through you just to be safe."

Erik was out of patience with this talk and queasy from the bloodshed. "Well, shoot one of us, damn it! And the other will cut you in two!"

The man almost jumped back, but seeing Erik plant his sword point first in the dirt, he lowered his crossbow slightly. Roo said, "You've no driver?"

"Drive myself," said the merchant.

"You really keep your overhead down," observed Roo.

"What do you know about overhead?" asked the man.

"I know a thing or two about business," said Roo in the insouciant tone Erik knew well: it meant Roo had almost no idea what he was talking about.

"Who are you?" repeated the man.

"I am Rupert," answered Roo, "and my big friend's name is—"

"Karl," interrupted Erik, not wishing his identity known. Roo winced, as if he should have thought of that himself.

"Rupert? Karl? Sounds Advarian to me."

"We're from Darkmoor," said Roo, then winced again. "Lots of Advarian stock in Darkmoor. Rupert and Karl are common enough names."

"I'm Advarian," said the man, putting away his crossbow. "Helmut Grindle, merchant."

"Are you going west?" asked Erik.

"No," snapped Helmut. "I've just got the horses facing west for my amusement. They're trained to walk backwards."

Erik flushed. "Look, we're bound for Krondor if you don't mind company."

"I do mind," snapped the merchant. "I was doing fine until those two murderers tried to boost my cargo, and I would have killed the second one—I was just about to let fly into that brush when you killed him for me."

Erik said, "I'm sure. Look, we're going to Krondor, and it would profit us all if we stayed together."

"I don't need guards and I won't pay for mercenaries."

Erik said, "Oh, wait. I don't mean you need to pay us—"

Roo leaped in. "We'll share guard duty with you for food. Besides, I can drive your team."

"You're a teamster?"

"I can drive up to six horses without a problem," Roo lied. His father had taught him to handle four.

Helmut thought about it. "Very well. I'll feed you, but you're standing night watch, and I sleep with my crossbow."

Erik laughed. "No need to fear, Master Merchant. We may be murderers, but we're not thieves." His bitter irony was lost on the man, who, grumbling, motioned for them to approach the wagon.

"We've still got the better part of an hour's light left, so there's no sense in dawdling. Let's get moving."

Roo said, "Get started and I'll catch up. That second man had another sword."

"See if he has any gold!" shouted Helmut after him. Bending over, he said to Erik, "He'll probably lie to us both if he finds any. It's what I would do." Not waiting for a reply, he clambered up on the seat of the wagon and shouted at the horses as he shook the reins. Erik watched as the overworked and underfed animals pulled into the traces, and the wagon lurched forward.

5

★★

KRONDOR

THE WAGON HALTED.

Helmut Grindle pointed. "Krondor."

Erik, sitting in the back of the wagon, turned and looked over the shoulders of Grindle and Roo, who had been driving. Erik had been impressed to discover that for once his friend really could back up his claim. He drove the team like an experienced teamster; obviously, Roo's father had been good for something besides getting drunk and beating up on him.

Erik looked down the long winding road known as the King's Highway. They had turned south after Grindle had passed the last toll station, entering the road near a town called Haverford. Twice before that patrols of armed soldiers had ridden past, but at no time did they even pause to look at Roo or Erik.

As Roo snapped the reins and the wagon started down the road toward the city, a patrol of city guardsmen rode toward them. Erik sat as calmly as he could in the rear, attempting to look as much like just another wagon guard as possible. Roo's hands knotted on the reins and the rear left horse snorted at the tension in the line, not sure if she was asked to change pace or direction. Roo forced himself to relax and the two of them watched as the soldiers approached. Then, abruptly, the guards pulled up. "There's a long wait," said the guard sergeant.

Grindle asked, "What's the holdup?"

"The King has entered the city. South gate by the palace is sealed off for his retinue. Everyone else is forced to use the north gates," he said, waving in the

general direction Grindle's wagon was headed. "And the gate watch is searching the wagons."

Grindle swore as the guards rode off.

Roo and Erik exchanged glances. Roo shook his head slightly, indicating
Erik should say nothing about the wagon search. In conversational tones, he
said, "That's some city."

"That she is," replied Grindle.

Krondor sprawled at the head of a large bay, beyond which an expanse of
blue stretched off to the horizon: the Bitter Sea. The old city was walled, but an
extensive foulburg—the part of the city outside the walls—had grown up over
the years, until now it was much larger than the inner city. Inside the walls, the
view was dominated by the palace of the Prince of Krondor, which sat atop a
hill hard against the south side of the bay. Ships, looking like tiny white slips of
paper, rested at anchor or sailed in and out of the bay.

Roo said, "Master Grindle, what do you think are the best commodities to
ship from this city?" Erik suppressed a groan as the merchant began his long
answer. In the days since joining up with Grindle, Roo had been pestering the
merchant for ideas on making money. At first the man was reluctant, as if Roo
would somehow steal a thought from him and he'd be the poorer for it. Roo
made several statements as if they were fact that got the old merchant going,
telling the youth he was an idiot and would end up ruined before he was twenty
years old. When challenged as to why, he'd open up with a sound argument. By
cleverly asking questions, Roo would turn the conversation into an ongoing
lecture on how to conduct business.

"Rare, that's the thing," said Grindle. "You can hear there's a shortage of
hides for making boots in Ylith. So corner all the hides in Krondor you can. By
the time you reach Ylith, you find some lad from the Free Cities has already
imported ten wagonloads of hides and you're ruined. But rarities! There are
always rich men looking for fine cloth, precious gems, exotic spices, and the
like." Glancing around to see he was not overheard, he continued. "You can
build volume in commodities. You can be the largest wool shipper in the West,
but one plague of anthrax on the sheep herds, one ship sunk on its way to the
Far Coast, and bang!" He slapped his hands together for emphasis. One of the
horses cocked an ear at the noise. "You're ruined."

"I don't know," said Roo. "People may not have money to buy luxuries, but
they have to eat."

"Bah!" said Grindle. "Rich people always have money to buy luxuries. Poor
people often don't have money to buy food. And rich people may eat better
than poor, but one man can only eat so much, no matter how rich."

"What about wine?"

Grindle launched into a discussion, and Erik sat back, turning his mind to
the last few days. At first bored by the chatter, Erik discovered there was a lot
about the business world that was interesting, especially in terms of risk versus

reward. Grindle claimed he was only a modest merchant, but Erik was beginning to believe that was intentional understatement. The cargo in the wagon was an odd mix, a half-dozen bolts of embroidered silk, a dozen small jars carefully lashed together with huge amounts of cotton wadding for protection, some wooden boxes with heavy cord tied around them, and some odd sacks. The boys never asked what was in the packages and Grindle never volunteered. From the course of the recent discussion, Erik assumed the man traded in precious goods, small but of high value, and wore poor clothing and drove a modest-appearing wagon to throw off suspicion. Erik suspected Grindle might have gems or some other cargo of small bulk and large value there.

The first night together, Erik had noticed that while the wagon was dirty on the outside it was clean in the back where the cargo lay, and it was very well repaired. The wheels had recently been reset and the work had been first-rate, with the hubs properly packed and the iron bands on the wheels carefully attached with more than the minimum number of nails. The horses were likewise more than they seemed. Grindle kept them modestly dirty, though not enough to pose a health problem, but they were scruffy-looking animals until you examined them closely. Their hooves were trimmed at the proper angle and the shoeing was absolutely masterful, as good as any Erik had seen. The animals were more than sound, they were fit and well cared for; every night Grindle supplemented their roadside grazing with fresh grain from a bag he stored under the wagon seat.

Roo clucked and rustled the reins and the wagon rolled forward again, moving in behind a long line of wagons that were stretching along the highway toward the city. Grindle said, "This is the longest damn wait I've seen in my life!"

"It doesn't look like we're moving any time soon. I'll go look." Roo handed the reins to Grindle.

Erik said, "I'll go with you," and leaped down off the wagon, following after Roo.

As they moved along, several wagon drivers were standing up in their seats, attempting to see what the delay ahead might be. Ten or so wagons ahead of Grindle's, they encountered a teamster heading back toward the end of the line, muttering curses.

"What's the holdup?" asked Roo.

The man didn't even look at them as he said, "Some damn nonsense if you ask me. They're searching the wagons before they even reach the outer edge of the foulburg. Couldn't do it at the city gate, proper like. No, they set up a second search point down at the creek bridge. I guess they just have to ruin a man's chances of a hot dinner. It'll be hours before we get through." The man reached his own wagon, five ahead of Grindle's, and swung up to take the reins from his apprentice. "Prince's funeral—every noble in the West and half from the East in town—and market day, yet they're climbing through every wagon and looking at every man coming in like they were on the hunt for the King's own murderer." The man's comments descended into general muttering, peppered by some colorful obscenities, as Erik motioned for Roo to come away.

Out of earshot of anyone in the waiting line of wagons, Roo said, "What do we do?"

Erik said, "I don't know. With all this funeral stuff going on, it may be something else they're on the watch for, but it could be our necks if they are looking for us." He thought a minute. "Maybe we wait until dark, circle away from this road, and see if there's another way into town less watched. And there's still the problem of getting into the city proper behind the wall."

"One at a time. If we can get into the foulburg, we can find a way through the walls, I'm certain. There's always a way in and out of a city for folks who don't want too much attention drawn to themselves."

"Thieves and smugglers?"

"Yes."

"What if we circle the city and strike out for another port?"

"Too far," said Roo. "I don't know how far Land's End is to the west, but I remember my father swearing a blue streak when he had to go there. Almost half again as far, he'd say. And I don't know what sort of ports there are to the north.

"Besides, on the road, without Grindle's wagon, we'd stand out like we were painted red."

Erik nodded. "Well, we'd better go back and say something to Grindle so he doesn't get suspicious."

"He's suspicious already, but he's not overly curious, which is better," answered Roo. Then, with his infectious grin, he added, "Besides, I think he likes me. He says he has a daughter I should meet, and I'll bet you she's as ugly as he is."

Erik had to laugh. "Going to marry for money?"

As they approached Grindle's wagon, Roo said, "Only if I get the chance."

Grindle listened as they explained the delay, then said, "Are you going on ahead?"

Roo said, "I think so. We can get through the gate faster if we go now, and you're safe from any marauders, so you don't need our company any longer, Master Merchant. We've got business near the port, and the sooner we can get there the better."

"Well then, the gods' speed to you, and if you ever return to Krondor, drop by and tell me how you're doing." To Roo he said, "You're a rogue and a liar, boy, but you have the makings of a good merchant if you'd just stop thinking everyone else around you is slower than yourself. That will be your undoing, you mark my words."

Roo laughed and waved good-bye to Grindle as Erik shouldered his travel bag. They walked down the line of wagons until they were sure they were out of sight of the merchant, and then they angled off, away from the King's Highway and toward a small farm to the north.

Erik swatted a persistent fly that refused to stay away from his face. "Got the little bastard!" he said with satisfaction.

Roo waved away several others and said, "Now, if you could manage to kill all his little brothers and sisters, as well . . ."

Erik lay back on a bale of straw. The farm was deserted, looking as if the entire household had gone into the city for some reason. It was a well-tended smallholding with a house, two outbuildings—one a privy and the other a root cellar—and a barn. They had found the barn unlocked and wagon tracks leading away, so Erik supposed the farmer and his family had been stuck somewhere in that long line of people waiting to get into the city or had gotten there earlier in the day.

Erik and Roo were waiting for sundown before attempting to cross the open fields to the east of the city and make their way into the foulburg. Roo was confident that once they found a likely inn he could find someone to show them the way into the city for a small fee. Erik wasn't as certain of the plan, but had nothing to offer by way of an alternative, so he said nothing. They sat at the rear of the barn, beneath the hayloft.

"Erik?"

"Yes?"

"How do you feel?"

"Not bad. My shoulder feels like new."

"No, I don't mean that," said Roo, nibbling on a long straw. "I mean about everything—killing Stefan and the rest."

Erik said nothing for a long while; at last he said, "He needed killing, I guess. I don't feel much of anything. I felt very strange when he went all limp after you stuck him. I felt a lot worse when that bandit got in the way of my sword point. That made me feel sick." He was quiet for a minute. "It's odd, isn't it? I hold my own half brother so you can kill him and don't feel much—not even relief because of the way he abused Rosalyn—but a complete stranger, a murderer probably, and I feel almost like vomiting."

Roo said, "Don't be so hard on murderers. That's us, remember?" He yawned. "Maybe you have to be holding the blade; that robber dying didn't bother me, but I can still feel the way it was when I stuck my dagger into Stefan. I was sure mad at him then."

Erik let out a long sigh. "It doesn't do to dwell on this, I think. We're outlaws and there's nothing to do for it but try to get to the Sunset Islands. There's a legacy of some sort waiting for me at Barret's Coffee House, and I mean to go there, then find the first ship heading west."

"What legacy?" Roo sounded intrigued. "You never mentioned it before."

"Well, 'legacy' may be too big a word. My father left something for me with a solicitor and litigator at Barret's Coffee House."

The sound of a wagon in the distance brought both young men to their feet. Roo peered out the door. "Either the farmer got tired of waiting in the line or he's back from morning market in the city, but either way the entire family seems to be riding in the wagon and we can't get out without being seen."

"Come on," said Erik, climbing the ladder to the hayloft. Roo followed and found what Erik had been looking for, a door outside. He knelt and said, "Stay back against the wall until they've unhitched the wagons and gone inside. Then we'll jump down from here and head into the city. It should be about time, anyway."

Just then the door to the barn was heaved open, and a child's voice shouted above the loud creaking, "Papa! I didn't get to see the Prince."

A woman's voice said, "If you hadn't been hitting your sister, you would have seen him ride by."

Another male voice, an adult's, said, "Papa, why do you think the king named Nicholas Prince instead of Erland?"

"That's the business of the Crown, and none of mine," came the answer as the wagon rolled into the barn, backed in by the farmer. Erik peeked over the edge of the loft and saw the farmer sitting in the wagon seat, letting his eldest son push the horses backwards as he kept an eye on things. They had obviously done this hundreds of times, and Erik appreciated the ease with which they ensured the horses did exactly what was asked, keeping the wagon intact and those riding in it safe. They continued to talk.

The son said, "Father, what's it going to be like with a new Prince?"

"Don't know," said the farmer. "Seems like Arutha was ruling there long as I can remember. Back to before I can remember. Fifty-three years on the throne of the West. Well, Nicholas is the son said to be the most like his father, so maybe things won't change much." The wagon stopped rolling. "Get Davy out of his traces first and put him away. I want you to take Brownie outside and walk her so I can see if she's really lame on her left front or just acting lazy, like usual."

The elder boy did as he was instructed while from the house the distant shouts of the younger boy and a girl could be heard, followed almost instantly by a scolding from their mother. The farmer dismounted from the wagon and removed some grain sacks from the back, loading them into a pile below the hayloft.

When the second horse was out of her traces, father and son left the barn, and Erik said, "We'd better clear out. If they need fodder for the animals, the boy will be up here in a few minutes."

"It's still light out," Roo complained.

"It's almost sundown. We'll just keep the barn between us and the house for a bit. If anyone sees us we'll be two travelers walking across the field, heading for town."

Roo said, "I hope you know what the hell you're talking about."

Erik pushed open the door to the outside through which hay was hoisted into the loft, and looked down. "It's only a bit of a jump, but be careful not to twist your ankle. I don't want to have to carry you."

"Right," said Roo with thinly disguised concern. He looked down to the ground below and found the distance far greater than he had remembered. "Can't we climb back down the ladder and sneak out?"

"One door, remember? And they're exercising a horse right in front of it."

The creak from out front told Erik and Roo the farmer was returning. "Lazy creature. Why should I feed you if you're pretending to be lame to get out of work?" asked the farmer with affection.

His son's voice carried to the loft as Erik lowered himself to hang from the edge, then let go. "I like the way that lameness moves from foreleg to back, then from right to left, depending on which way she's going." His laughter showed his genuine amusement.

Roo repeated Erik's movements, hanging for what seemed the longest moment before he let go, expecting to slam hard into the ground and break both legs. Erik's powerful hands closed around his waist and slowed him just enough so that he landed lightly on his feet. Roo turned and whispered, "See, nothing to it."

"Did you hear something out back?" came the voice of the son.

Erik motioned for silence and they hurried away from the barn.

Whatever curiosity the farmer's eldest son might have had, the requirements of caring for the animals must have displaced it, for no one came to investigate the sound. Erik and Roo hastened along, until they were a quarter mile across the field, then slowed to a casual walk.

They plodded down the rolling hillside, approaching the outer buildings of the city as the sun went down. Erik looked at the foulburg as they neared it, and said, "Keep an eye out for guards."

They reached a low row of huts and simple gardens, with no clear passage between the buildings. In the evening light they could see a few hundred yards to the north of them that another road entered the city. They made out movement along the road, but neither Roo nor Erik could tell if it was field hands returning to the city or soldiers on patrol using the thoroughfare.

Roo said, "Look," and pointed to what was little more than a clear space between two houses, but through which they could reach the first north–south street in town without having to use the main roads. They stepped over a low fence, carefully avoiding the rows of vegetables planted there, and made their way to the back of the hut. Ducking low so as not to be seen through the single window, they skirted away from the rear door and moved between the buildings. Obviously in one of the poorer sections of town, this little alleyway was heavily littered with trash. They picked their way along, trying to be as quiet as possible.

Reaching the street, Roo peered out and pulled back, hugging the wall. "It's pretty empty."

"Do you think we're beyond where the guards are?"

"I don't know. But at least we're in Krondor."

Roo moved out into the street, then strolled along, as Erik caught up. They glanced right and left and saw only a few locals, some of whom paused to study the two young men. Roo started to feel self-conscious about the attention and motioned for Erik to follow him into a small neighborhood tavern.

They entered a dingy, smoke-filled common room, populated by only two other men and a barkeep, who looked at them with suspicion. "Help you?" he asked with a tone that indicated help was far down his list of priorities.

Roo removed his travel bag and said, "Two ales."

The man didn't move, continuing to stare at Roo. After a moment, Roo dug into his belt pouch and pulled out a pair of copper coins. The man took the money, inspected it, and then put it in his own belt pouch. He reached under the bar and produced two empty flagons, which he carried halfway down the bar to a large tap. He pulled it twice, filling each flagon with a frothy brew. Returning to where Roo and Erik waited, he put them down before the two young men. "Anything else?"

Erik said, "Anything to eat?"

The man indicated a kettle hanging before the fireplace on the other side of the room. "Stew's done. Two coppers a bowl, three if you want bread."

The smell wasn't promising, but Erik and Roo were both hungry, having had nothing to eat all day. Erik said, "We'll take the stew and the bread."

The man still didn't move, until Roo put more money on the bar. Then he went and filled two wooden bowls with stew and carried them back. He produced a couple of small loaves of bread and set them down on the dirty bar next to the bowls, then produced two almost clean wooden spoons and put them in the bowls before Erik or Roo could intercept them.

Roo was too hungry to notice, and seeing his friend not suffering from eating the stew, Erik tried his own bowl. It was nothing like his mother's, but it was hot and filling, and the bread was acceptable, if a little coarse.

As casually as he could, Roo said, "What's all the fuss about?"

"What fuss?" asked the barkeep.

"Outside, at the gate," replied Roo.

"Didn't know there was a fuss."

Erik said, "We just got to Krondor and didn't feel like waiting in that long line to eat."

The barkeep was silent until Roo put money on the bar and signaled for two more ales, even though the first were only half-drunk. The barkeep produced another set of flagons and said, "Prince of Krondor died."

"We heard that," said Roo.

"Well, his son is being installed in the office tomorrow. His brothers are here."

"The King's in Krondor?" said Erik, feigning surprise, even though he had heard that earlier.

"That's why there's so much security at the gates," said the barkeep. "There's a pair of murderers they're looking for; did in some noble east of here, if you believe the story. Of course, everyone and his uncle's pet dog is in town for the festival. Funeral parade was today, which is why everyone took the day off to gawk at the King. Tomorrow they have this ceremony, then another parade, so those that couldn't see anything will get their chance. After that, the King will take his father back to Rillanon for burial in the family vault. And Prince Nicholas will come back as the new Prince of Krondor. Then we'll have another festival, and everyone will drink too much and nothing will get done. Then all the visiting nobles will go home."

"You don't sound very impressed," said Erik.

The front door opened and two more rough-looking men entered, sitting down at the table occupied by the first two.

The barman shrugged. "Why should I? Old Prince, new Prince, the taxes are the same."

Roo continued to sound matter-of-fact. "Well, now that we're getting some food in us, I guess we'll just have to go stand in line like everyone else."

The barkeep said, "Not, I should think."

Roo tried to look uninterested and said, "You know another way into Krondor?"

At this the barkeep's expression changed to one of surprise. "No, just that they close the gate in an hour and you won't be able to get in tonight."

"They close the gate?"

"With the King in the city, of course," answered the barman, now interested. "You have a problem?"

Erik was about to say nothing at all was the matter, but Roo quickly said, "We have to find a ship and be on it at first light tomorrow."

"Plan on taking another, then," said the barkeep. "For many of those waiting to get into the city will simply sleep before the gate, so even were you to leave now and take a place outside, you'll be hours getting through tomorrow. It will be like that every day until the King and his family leave next week."

Narrowing his gaze, Roo said, "I don't suppose you know of another way into the inner city? Say, perhaps, one used by locals and not widely talked about?"

The barman glanced around the room as if fearing being overheard—highly unlikely, given that the other four men in the room were lost in their own conversation—and said, "I might. But it would cost you."

"How much?"

"How much do you have?"

Before Erik could plead poverty, Roo said, "My friend and I can pay ten gold pieces."

The barman looked surprised at the amount, but only said, "Let's see your gold."

As Roo made to undo his backpack, Erik placed a restraining hand on his shoulder. "Ten gold pieces is all we have in the world. It's taken us months to scrounge it together. We were going to purchase passage with it."

"You're young and strong. You can work your passage. There are ships leaving for Queg, the Free Cities, Kesh, every port you might wish to reach. They are always looking for deckhands."

The barman nodded, and the sound of chairs being pushed away from the table caused Erik to turn. The two men who had just entered were already closing, billy clubs held high. Roo tried to duck under a blow and for his trouble caught the strike on his shoulder instead of his head. His knees went loose from the pain and he fell.

Erik tried to draw his sword, but the nearest man was upon him. Letting go of the hilt, Erik unloaded a backhand blow that sent the man flying into the one coming behind him.

The man who was clubbing Roo turned and shouted, "Get him!"

Erik was starting to draw his sword when a blow to the back of the head stunned him. He felt his legs go out from under him and his vision swam.

Two men grabbed him and hoisted him up, and before he could resist he was tied like a fatted calf. The barman came around, holding the lead-filled club he had struck Erik with from behind, and said, "The little one is probably worthless, but the big fellow will bring a good price as a galley slave, or maybe even as a fighter in the arena. Get them to the Quegan buyer before midnight. The envoy's escort galleys leave tomorrow on the evening tide, after the festivities at the palace."

Erik tried to say something, and for his troubles caught another blow to the head. He slumped down, unconscious.

ERIK'S EYES OPENED. He sat up. His head throbbed and his vision went in and out of focus, as his stomach knotted. He swallowed hard, closed his eyes, discovered that made his nausea worse, and opened them again. He found his hands were restrained by heavy iron bracelets and his legs by even heavier shackles. He looked around, expecting to be in the bottom of a ship bound for Queg. Instead he found himself in a cell.

A groan from close by caused him to turn around. Erik found Roo likewise shackled and trying to sit up. Erik gave him a hand and the smaller youngster tried to clear his head.

"Sort of a bad day for you two, wasn't it?" said a voice from behind them.

Erik turned to find a man leaning back against a window ledge, bars behind him, his body silhouetted against daylight, the small aperture being the sole source of light. He moved away from the window, coming to squat down before Erik. Erik could make out his features in the dimly lit room. He was a broad-shouldered, bull-necked man of middle years, with dark receding hair, cut close, and deep blue eyes. There was something odd about his manner and expression, but Erik couldn't put his finger upon it. He needed a shave and was dressed in plain tunic and trousers. High boots, well cared for but old and worn, and a wide belt were his only other garments.

"Where are we? I . . ." He closed his eyes as his head swam a minute. "We were struck from behind."

"Some of the locals trying to sell you to Quegan slavers," said the man. His voice was slightly raspy and his manner of speech common. Erik wasn't sure, but there was something about his accent that reminded him of Nathan's, so he assumed the man was from the Far Coast.

The man smiled, but there was a hint of meanness behind the smile. "You were on your way to a less than pleasant ocean voyage. With the emissary from Queg in the city, along with several of his King's galleys, the Duke of Krondor thought there might be something like this going on."

"You're not with them?"

"Ha! I'd as soon kiss a goblin as leave a Quegan slaver alive." He glanced at Roo, who was regaining his wits. The man continued, "The Duke's men intercepted the slavers on their way to the docks. He was both surprised and pleased to discover that you two were among those heading out of the city. There's been quite a search on for you, my friends."

"Then you know who we are?" said Erik with resignation. "Who are you?"

"You've heard of the man they call the Eagle of Krondor?"

Erik nodded. Who that man was and why he was called that wasn't widely known, but that he existed was common knowledge. "Is that you?"

"Ha!" The man gave a harsh bark of laughter. "Hardly. But I work for him. You might call me the Dog of Krondor. I bite, so don't irritate me." He made a growling noise and snarled in a fair imitation of a dog. "My name is Robert de Loungville. My friends call me Bobby. You call me sir."

Roo said, "What have you to do with us?"

"I just wanted to see if you had any serious wounds."

"Why?" asked Roo. "Can't hang an injured man?"

Bobby smiled at this. "Not my concern. The Prince needs desperate men, and by all reports you two are about as desperate as they get. But from what I see, that's all you are. Well, pitiful, too. The Prince may have to look elsewhere for his desperate men."

"We're just going to be hung?" asked Erik.

"Hardly," said the man. He got up from his squatting position, groaning theatrically as he did so. "Knees aren't what they used to be." He moved to the cell door and motioned for the jailer to open it. "The new Prince of Krondor, like his father, is a very particular man when it comes to observing the law. We will have a trial; then we will hang you." He passed through the door and it closed behind him.

A short time later the door opened again and an old man entered. He was dressed in richly fashioned clothing, but of plain cut, as if designed for one who was active despite his rank and years. The man's hair was silver, he wore a closely trimmed beard, and his eyes were dark and penetrating. He studied the two prisoners carefully.

Kneeling before Erik, he said, "Tell me your name."

"Erik von Darkmoor . . . sir."

Then he turned to Roo. "You are Rupert Avery?"

Roo said, "Yes. And who are you?" His manner showed he took exception to being treated so roughly, and if he was going to be hung he might as well vent his temper on whoever was nearby, irrespective of rank.

The man smiled, amused by Roo's sharp manner. "You may call me Lord James."

Roo sat up and moved, as far as the length of chain that bound his leg shackles to the wall permitted, and peered upward through the small window. "Well, Lord James, how long do we rot here in the Krondor jail before we're tried and hung?"

"You're not in the Krondor jail, my abrupt young friend," answered James. "You're in the Prince's palace and your trial will commence the day after tomorrow, as soon as Nicholas has taken his office. Unless you're in a particular hurry, in which case I could ask the King to preside this afternoon."

"Well, by all means," snapped Roo. "If His Majesty isn't too busy, I'm sure we'd all just as soon get this over with. And he'd drop everything else just because you asked."

James smiled and there was a dangerous quality to it. "I'm sure he would; I'm something of an uncle to the King," he said. "I'm also the new Duke of Krondor."

Standing, the Duke said, "Have you anyone to speak on your behalf?"

Erik said, "There is one man, at Barret's Coffee House, by name Sebastian Lender. He might speak for me."

The Duke nodded. "I know him by reputation. Tricky bastard. He may keep you from being hung. I'll send for him and have him speak with you about your defense." He moved toward the door. "Then I'll see if the King's free tomorrow," he said pointedly to Roo. "But if I were you, I'd wait until Nicholas sits the Western Throne. He's of more even temper than his brother, and His Majesty doesn't take kindly to those who go around murdering his nobles."

"Nobles?" said Roo. "Stefan may have had a father of rank, but he was still a swine."

James smiled, again without humor. "Perhaps, but as his father had died less than an hour before him, for a very short time he was Baron of Darkmoor."

The door was opened and Duke James left. Erik looked at Roo and said, "So much for the Sunset Islands."

Roo sat back down, unable to see anything through the small window. "Yes, so much for the Sunset Islands."

ERIK AND ROO were moved the next morning, without being told why. A squad of soldiers wearing the livery of the Prince of Krondor's own Household Guards arrived and unchained Erik and Roo from the wall, leaving the shackles and cuffs on. They were escorted to a large cell with a long, barred wall, through which other cells with wooden doors could be seen. The cell was partially belowground. At head height, a long window, less than one foot high, ran the length of the cell, and both prisoners could see it allowed a view of a long gibbet erected at the far side of a large courtyard. A half-dozen nooses hung from a single long crossbeam, supported by heavy timbers between each noose.

Erik studied it briefly; it would be a simple enough execution. The prisoners would be marched up several steps at one end and made to step up on three-foot-high wooden boxes, which were kicked out from under their feet once the nooses were around their neck.

Erik and Roo took up places alongside the bars and sat in silence. Erik glanced around the cell. Seven other men were likewise manacled and shackled, awaiting whatever fate held in store. All looked rough and dangerous, some more than others. Erik was used to being the largest boy in his town, and had grown to be one of the strongest men, but at least two of the men in the cell were his equal in size, perhaps in strength as well.

At midday another pair of prisoners were admitted to the cell, these looking as if they had been severely beaten after being apprehended. One of the men, a hulking brute being dragged by three guards, had obviously put up a struggle, as he was barely conscious, but the other kept up a steady stream of invective as the guards threw him roughly into the cell, then left. He called after them, "When I'm out of here, my lads, you can bet we'll be settlin' accounts! I have your names! Every one of you." He spoke with an affected speech, trying to sound educated while being betrayed by his lower-class accent. Sitting down, he added, "You bloody bastards."

Looking at Erik, who sat across from him, then at his nearly unconscious companion, he said, "Old Biggo don't look so good, does he?"

From a corner of the cell another man said, "Better for him if he stays out on his feet. Won't feel his neck getting stretched."

"We're not for the gallows, old Biggo and I!" said the other man with fear in his voice. "We're well connected, we are. Friends to the Sagacious Man himself!"

"Who is the Sagacious Man?" asked Roo.

From across the cell another man said, "The leader of the Mockers. And this liar has been about as close to the Sagacious Man as I have been to the King's mother."

"You watch!" said the man who had been boasting. "We'll be out of here soon!"

The door at the end of the hallway opened and a man entered, flanked by two guards. He wore a finely made robe, and upon his head was a hat Erik found comical—a short brim around a circular crown, fashioned from purple felt. A whipcord tie under his chin held it in place on his head. He had the face of a scholar or priest, thin and pale, with a long nose and square jaw. But his eyes were alive and seemed to miss nothing as they swept around the room.

The guards did not open the cell, but stood away. The man came and stood at the bars. "Who here is Erik?"

Erik stood up and moved to stand opposite the stranger, and Roo came to his side. "I'm Erik."

"What is your surname?"

"I am called von Darkmoor."

The man nodded. "I am Sebastian Lender, from Barret's Coffee House." He studied Erik and Roo for a long minute, as if memorizing every aspect of their appearance. Then at last he said, "And you two are in a great deal of trouble."

"So we gathered," answered Roo.

"I may be able to save your lives," said Lender. "But you must tell me exactly what occurred. Don't leave out anything and don't lie to me."

Erik told him exactly how he recalled things, and Roo added what he knew. Afterward Lender said, "With what Baron Manfred has testified and the girl, Rosalyn, has said, it's clear that Stefan was hoping to lure you into a trap where he could kill you."

"When do we stand trial?" asked Erik.

"Two days from now. As it's a capital case and one of the King's nobles was the victim, you're being tried in Royal Court, here at the palace." He was thoughtful. "The Prince is likely to be hard, but fair. The Court of Common Pleas tends to breed a more cynical justice. Everyone brought before the justices there is innocent."

Erik said, "My father said to find you—"

"Yes. I was to give you something."

"What?"

"An odd legacy, I'm afraid. A small amount of gold, which will be barely sufficient to pay my fees, I'm sorry to say. And a pair of boots; the boots were your grandfather's, according to what Otto told me, and as you were of a size, your father supposed they might fit you. Also there was a fine dagger, which I obviously can't give to you here."

"A dagger?" asked Roo.

Lender put up his hand. "Over the years I have managed many stranger legacies. In any event, it is moot until the trial. We shall see if that goes as we wish; if so, we can move on from there."

"What are our chances?" asked Erik.

"Thin," answered Lender frankly. "Had you stayed, you might have built a persuasive brief that you killed Stefan in self-defense. Manfred admits that he went seeking his father to gain an order from him telling Stefan to leave off some hot-blooded plot or another. He will not tell what that was, claiming only that Stefan was looking for trouble."

"Will he testify to this?"

"He already has," said Lender. "He'll be on his way back to Darkmoor, after Nicholas takes office tomorrow, and I have a copy of his deposition before the King's Magistrate. It's very noncommittal in places, and had I known I was to be arguing on your behalf, I would have been a lot more probing than was the King's man."

"Can't you ask him more questions?" asked Roo.

"Not unless he's compelled by King's warrant," answered Lender, "and I suspect the King won't be inclined to agree."

"Why not?" asked Roo, not entirely sure what was being said. "The King wants justice, doesn't he?"

Lender smiled, and it was the indulgent look of a master being asked something obvious by a gifted but untutored apprentice. "Our King, more than most, seems interested in justice; something to do with some time he spent in Great Kesh as a youngster, I believe. But he's also interested in not making it look too easy to kill a nobleman and avoid hanging. There's justice, and then there's justice."

Erik sighed. "And we did kill Stefan."

Lowering his voice, Lender said, "Did you go to find him with murder in your heart?"

Erik was silent a minute, then said, "Yes, I guess I did. I knew he was going to try something with Rosalyn; I knew what I would find and I knew I'd end up killing Stefan. I can't even say I just went to protect her."

Lender glanced at Roo. The slight boy nodded and Lender let out a long sigh. "If that's true, I doubt any power can save you from that." He pointed out the high window at the gibbet.

Erik nodded, and Lender left without further comment.

6
★★
DISCOVERY

THE CREATURE STIRRED.

The woman stood patiently as the creature's companions moved to one side. Several others huddled in distant corners of the immense hall, speaking quietly to one another, while those who had been attending the sleeping monster crossed to join them. The woman ignored them and studied the waking creature. To the mortal eye, the beast appeared to be the grandmother of all dragonkind, a gigantic being whose bulk massed high above her servants. She loomed enormous even in the vast hall that served as her home. In distant sconces, oil lamps flickered, but both the dragon and the woman needed little natural light to navigate the gloom. A faint scent of spice hung on the air, perhaps as an artifact of the making of the oil, perhaps to sweeten the air; the woman didn't know.

At last the dragon opened eyes the size of palace windows and blinked. She stretched, and lowered her head as she yawned, displaying ivory teeth the size of flashers, the giant two-handed scimitars used in Great Kesh. Her skin was the reason for the absence of more illumination, for it consisted of gems, fused over plates once golden in color. Brighter illumination caused a riot of rainbow light throughout the hall and while capable of arts beyond most human understanding, the dragon found the constantly dancing reflections gave her a headache.

The woman had met dragons before, though nothing quite like this one, and while little could impress her, she conceded to herself that this was indeed an impressive-looking being. They had "spoken" to each other using magic arts, but this was their first true meeting in the flesh. Despite attempts at keeping the identity of this creature hidden over the last half century, legends of the "great jeweled dragon" had already surfaced in various parts of the Kingdom.

But the woman knew this was no true dragon, despite being the get of dragons at birth. The spirit of the original dragon had perished in the great battle that had climaxed in this very hall almost fifty years before. Inhabiting the vessel that had once known the mind of Ryath, daughter of Rhuagh—perhaps the greatest of all golden dragons—was a consciousness alien and ancient: the Oracle of Aal.

A great rumbling voice issued from within the throat of the creature. "Greetings, Miranda. How fare you?"

The woman nodded as she said, "I am well. The travel from the statue at Malac's Cross is disorienting."

"It was designed to be so. Only those with a certain gift may trigger it, and I wish to ensure that whatever talents they possess, they are vague about the true location of this hall."

Miranda nodded in agreement. "Understood. How fare you?"

"Time grows short. The heat tires me and I sleep more each day. Soon I shall enter the birth sleep and then shall I end this phase of existence."

"Time grows short indeed. How much longer will we have your guidance?"

"Already the future grows clouded and dim to me. My daughter will not have the gift for the first twenty years of her life, so soon, for five years of my birth sleep and twenty years of my daughter's infancy, you will be as you were before I came to this world. There is more."

"What?"

"Much of what I should see I cannot, which means only that my own future is involved; for to all creatures, even me, knowledge of their own future is denied."

The Oracle of Aal was considered the oldest being in the universe, ancient when the Valheru rose to challenge the gods during the Chaos Wars. Thinking of that, Miranda turned to look at a dais behind the oracle. Willing a shift in her perception, the woman saw the stone flick into existence. A fey green in color, it pulsed with an inner light. She stared at its hypnotic rhythms for a moment, then said, "Are they stirring again?"

"They are always stirring," said the oracle. "Now they move with more vigor. Somehow they still have influence with those outside who are receptive to their call."

"They" were the Valheru, the ancient beings known as the Dragon Lords to most inhabitants of the world. Trapped by forces even beyond their own ability to understand, they were bound in the stone by a mysterious agent. From the stone rose a golden sword with an ivory pommel. The woman named Miranda knew that a half century before, a great battle had raged in the city above, called Sethanon, and in this chamber a battle of equal proportion took place. The strange half-man, half-Valheru Tomas, inheritor of the mantle and power of Ashen-Shugar, the Ruler of the Eagles' Reaches, battled a creature of spirit in the form of his ancient kinsman Draken-Koren, the Lord of Tigers. At that time, Pug of Stardock, magician of two worlds, and Macros the Black, sorcerer nonpareil, battled to hold closed a tear between two universes, aided by two Tsurani Great Ones, magicians from the world of Kelewan. And the dragon, Ryath, battled a Dread Lord, a creature from an alien space-time, whose very touch drained life.

In the end, the Valheru had been trapped within the stone, the Dread Lord vanquished at the cost of Ryath's life, and all the forces supporting the false prophet Murmandamus vanquished. Not one soldier on either side, in the Kingdom or serving the moredhel chieftain, knew what the war had been about. No one among the highest-ranking chieftains of the Nations of the North—as the dark elves and goblins were called—knew that Murmandamus had been a Pantathian serpent priest magically transformed to resemble their legendary leader. Only the King's family and a few trusted friends knew of the Lifestone and the presence of the Oracle.

And now the primary defender of the Lifestone, the magic and physical entity of the oracle dragon, was dying.

"How will this change take place?" asked Miranda.

The dragon lifted her head and nodded slightly to the right, where six robed figures stood speaking softly to one another. "These, my husband servants, they are already making their transformation."

The figures removed their hoods and Miranda could see faces that were little more than those of boys. The dragon continued, "When the heat began to rise, I made the call, and youths from around the area, those with a certain gift, answered. They wandered from their homes and came to Malac's Cross, to where the statue stands, and then I brought them here. Those that were lacking the true gifts needed were sent away, and thought only that they had been dreaming. Those who chose to stay were allowed to test, and those who failed were also sent away, with little memory of their time here. But these six are the first of the youths who have proven worthy to stand at my daughter's side."

Six elderly men came to stand next to the six youths. "These, who are their teachers, will join with me to create that which will be my daughter, and when they are done, these bodies will die. Then will the remaining spirit and knowledge enter these six young men." To another group on the other side of the hall the dragon motioned, and another six older men came forth. "I hope more of the young who have come to us prove worthy, for those who have no successor when it comes time to die . . . their knowledge is lost forever."

Miranda said, "Only twelve of you?"

"Had Pug not fetched us from our dying world, there would be none of us.

And should a thirteenth worthy child come to us before the birthing, he, too, can become one with us. If a girl child comes, then another daughter, to serve with the first daughter. We may yet grow in number, we of the Aal."

Miranda hid her impatience. She had other concerns at present. "Then you birth your daughter?"

"Then my spirit joins with the spirits of my husband servants and we meld entirely, all memory and feeling, all pain and joy, to one consciousness, and that is split again, and those boys will be our sons, and my daughter shall be formed."

"The new Oracle?"

"She shall be."

"And what body will she inhabit? I see no young girl here."

"This dragon's body is magic; it is strong beyond any that the Oracle has used since our oldest memory. It shall be used again."

"So this is why you will not be with us for twenty-five years?"

"Yes. She will be a child, even though she will have my powers eventually."

Miranda sighed audibly. "At least she'll be a large enough girl to give anyone pause should they break in." For a moment she considered. "Do you know where Pug is?"

The Oracle closed her eyes and considered. "He is absent from his island. I sense him out there"—she made a vague gesture with her head—"among the worlds."

"Damn," Miranda swore. "I think we will need him here before your daughter is strong enough to defend this hall." She considered something in silence a while. "How long before you enter the final heat?"

"We join in less than a year, Miranda. Then I shall be gone, for with the re-forming, something is always lost. This is why we, who were old when the stars were new, why we remember little of our own beginning. But in that rebirth, more strength and knowledge come, and she who follows after me shall be eventually my equal, then at last my better."

Miranda muttered, "If we live that long."

"Dark tides are forming. They rise against distant shores but shall reach even here, eventually."

"I must be gone. There is little time and much to be done. I fear a great many foolish choices have already been made and that we depend too much on auguries and portents."

"You chose a strange audience for that argument," answered the Oracle.

"That you've been useful is without question," said the young woman. "But fate is not immutable, I believe. I think one can seize destiny if one is but willing to make the attempt."

"So believe those who oppose you," said the Oracle. "This is the root of the problem."

"Those are deluded fanatics, who live in a mad dream that has no basis in reality. They bring death and pain for no cause whatsoever."

"True, but they share your sense of self-determination."

"On that note," Miranda said dryly, "I bid you farewell. Are you sufficiently protected here?"

"Our arts are sufficient for all but the most powerful."

"Then I shall be gone. Will we meet again?"

"I do not know," said the Oracle. "Too many possible endings appear to my mind, and none clearly marked as likely."

"Then fare you well on your journey to immortality, and pray that we lesser beings live long enough to greet your daughter when she comes into her own."

"You have my wishes for success," said the dragon.

Then the young woman was gone, vanished from before their eyes with little more than a gust of wind filling the empty place where she had stood.

To the one most senior among her companions the dragon said with a chuckle, "She is much like her father, don't you think? That touch of the cynical in her nature could be the weak spot that undoes her. I hope fate is kind to her."

The seniormost companion said, "Very much like her father."

WINDS SWEPT THE figure atop the hill, blowing her cloak and robes in billowing wings behind her. Smoke from distant fires stung her eyes as she beheld the carnage below. Riders were hunting down stragglers, raping and killing for sport. Using her arts, she studied in detail one scene after another. Men made like animals in the fury of battle now visited pain and destruction on helpless men, women, and children. She balled her fists in rage, but stayed her hand. Those who commanded the riders would descend upon her in an instant if she revealed her presence magically. While fear was not her companion, prudence was, and she understood her worth lay in being able to accomplish many things between now and the time of true battle. When that issue was decided, the fate of a world and more would hang in the balance, not the lives of these pitiful wretches.

Even at this distance, the cries of pain carried on the wind, and Miranda turned away from them as she moved down the hillside. For the time being she willed her heart to stone, for while she ached to help these few survivors, she knew that far more critical issues demanded her attention.

As she approached the scene of battle, she crouched low. Ducking behind low rocks, she waited as a company of drunken warriors wearing emerald armbands rode by, a screaming woman held across the neck of one man's horse. Miranda felt her face flush in rage. She willed herself to calmness; losing her head now would help no one.

Skirting the action, she came to a village in ruin. No building had been left standing—a solitary wall here, a charred doorframe there, but nothing that could be remotely called shelter. Acrid smoke stung Miranda's eyes as she searched for any signs of life.

Seeing none, she ventured deeper into the village, seeking any information that would prove useful. In the distance, she saw movement, and ducking behind a section of wall, she waited. Another company of horsemen rode by, less vigilant than they should have been, but not the drunken roisterers she had seen earlier. These were seasoned soldiers, Miranda calculated. These men were not mere mercenaries but those posted to the central companies of the invaders' forces. By being at this location, she now had a fair estimate of the invaders' rate of march. Cursing quietly, for it was faster than she had suspected, she moved away from the center of the village. She could will herself away at any time, but she was tired, and the effort to cloak her presence from her enemies was taking its toll. A little undisturbed rest in a quiet place would be needed for her to leave this area and not let her enemy know she had observed.

Miranda ducked through a burned doorframe, between two still-standing sections of wall, and even her iron-willed composure cracked at the sight that greeted her. Gasping, she had to put her hand out and grip the doorjamb, for her knees went weak as the sight of dead children greeted her. Tiny bodies charred to blackness were piled in the center of the fire-gutted building. Miranda felt a low animal growl of pain and wrath building in her throat and bit it back as rage threatened to overwhelm her composure. She knew well that should any of the monsters who had visited this horror on the children blunder within her sight, she would destroy him without thought, without regard for the consequences to her or her mission.

Forcing herself to calm, she took two deep breaths and fought back tears of anguish. Babies with smashed heads were placed upon older children with charred arrows still protruding from them. At least, thought Miranda, the children had been killed before the building had been set alight. Bitterly she wondered if death from a blade or arrow was, in truth, kinder than dying in flames. Bidding peace to the souls of those tormented tiny bodies, she left the building.

She picked her way amid the rubble to the outskirts of the village farthest from where she had last seen the raiders. She peered around the corner of what had once been an inn and saw nothing. Dashing from the village across a rivulet running down from the hills, she made it to a copse of trees. There she almost died.

The woman was terrified and so her knife slash went wide, but Miranda still took a cut along her left forearm. Biting back a cry of pain, Miranda reached out and gripped the woman's wrist with her right hand. A quick twist and the woman was forced to release the blade.

Hissing in pain and anger, Miranda said softly, "Silence, fool! I'll not hurt you." Then she saw the two cowering children behind the woman. "Or your babies." Her tone softened a bit. She released the woman's wrist and inspected the damage done to her arm. Miranda saw a shallow wound, and she closed her right hand over it.

"Who are you?" said the woman.

"I am called Miranda."

The woman's eyes welled with tears and she said, "They . . . they're killing the children."

Miranda closed her eyes a moment, then nodded. Women the raiders could use awhile along the line of march before they finally killed them, but children would be useless. Slavers following the main army might take them, but out here at the leading edge of battle, all little ones could do was inform enemies of what they had seen.

Gasping through the tears, the woman said, "They picked up the babies and swung them by the heels—"

Miranda said, "Enough," but her tone, while firm, was also pained. "Enough," she repeated softly, ignoring the wetness gathering in her own eyes. She had seen the tiny crushed skulls. "I know."

Then she took account of who stood before her. The woman's eyes were wide with terror, but would be judged large under normal conditions. Her ears were upswept beneath blond locks and possessed no lobes.

Miranda glanced down at the children: they were twins. Miranda's own eyes widened in disbelief as she asked, "You are what they call 'of the long-lived'?"

The woman nodded. "We are."

Miranda closed her eyes and shook her head. No wonder the woman was nearly beside herself. Those beings known through most of the world of men as elves gave birth rarely, and children usually grew up to adulthood decades apart from their siblings. Some elves lived to see centuries pass, and the death of one child was more terrible than humans could imagine, but twins were almost unheard of among the eledhel, as they called themselves. For these two little boys to be lost would be a tragedy beyond human imagining for an elf.

Miranda said, "I know what's at risk."

"The entire village was slaughtered," said the woman. "I took the boys into the woods to forage for food; we were to leave tonight. We were going to seek out the Jeshandi and ask for shelter there." Miranda nodded. The Jeshandi numbered a high percentage of the long-lived among them and would likely have taken in this woman and her children. "We didn't think the raiders would be here for another few days." Her eyes filled again and she said, "My man . . ."

Miranda removed her hand from the cut on her arm and inspected it. The cut had ceased bleeding and now a pink scar was the only sign of damage. She said, "If he was in the village he is dead. I'm sorry." She knew how hollow that sounded.

Suddenly the elven woman regained her composure, and she said, "Then I must protect the children alone."

"Damn," said Miranda. "If we can get clear of this murderous mob, I may be able to help." She glanced down at the two boys and saw enormous eyes staring up at her from tiny faces. No older than four or five years of age, they would be counted children for nearly another three decades by their race, and would not be considered mature for a century. But by either standard, human or elven, they were beautiful children. Sighing in resignation, Miranda said, "I will save your children."

"How?"

"Come with me and be silent."

Miranda moved away. The woman and the two boys followed, and while Miranda could have wished they had the legendary wood skills lore gave to their race—these three were villagers and were not adept at moving through the heavy undergrowth—at least these three were far quieter than a like trio of humans would have been.

Wending their way up the path from the village that they must have used to enter the forest, Miranda led the fugitives. After nearly an hour, Miranda said, "Is there any place near here where I might rest?"

The woman said, "There is a small clearing ahead, and on the other side the entrance to a cave."

Miranda nodded and returned her attention ahead. The raiders might be combing the area for survivors or they might be enjoying the fruits of their looting. Small villages like this yielded little by way of valuables, and if there were few women of suitable age for the men's amusement, the captains might have sent men out on patrol simply to avoid conflicts over who could be among the first to rape the women.

The elven woman tried to lead onward the two silent boys, and after a moment, Miranda picked up one of the two. The woman nodded and picked up the other and they carried them. Miranda knew that any child frightened enough will go silent, instead of crying, and these babies were severely frightened. Without conscious thought, she kissed the child on the temple and stroked his hair before starting to walk.

Making their way through the trees, they stopped once at the sound of distant horses and waited. When the sound receded, they continued. Reaching a heavy growth, they moved through the underbrush to a clearing, on the other side of which stood a cave. "It's safe here," said the woman.

Miranda put down the child and said, "Wait." She advanced into the darkness, using her magic arts to see in the gloom. The cave was indeed empty, and showed enough signs of human use that it was unlikely any animal would attempt to use it as a den. She went back outside and said, "Come—"

Before she could finish, a man crashed through the brush, shouting, "I told you I saw tracks!"

Pulling a long knife from his belt, he said, "A couple of brats! But the women are young!"

Another man answered from behind, but whatever he said was lost as Miranda shouted, "Get inside!"

The woman grabbed her two children, each by one arm, and hurried inside the cave. Miranda pulled a long dagger out of her belt and waited. Another man followed the first into the clearing.

Both looked like common mercenaries. The first wore a ragged tabard over rusty ring mail, the design faded and unknown to Miranda. The second was a tall man, wearing a heavy gambeson cut off at the shoulders, for it was obviously a size too small and would have confined his ability to fight otherwise.

Miranda waited as the two advanced. "What are you going to do with that?" snarled the second man, pointing at the dagger. He glanced at his companion.

"Put that away, girl," said the first with a nervous smile. "We'll treat you good if you don't cause problems. Give us trouble and we'll make it rough for you."

Miranda waited, and when the first man stepped close enough to attempt to reach for her, she took a quick step forward, faster than either man expected, and stuck the dagger into his throat.

She wrenched the dagger out as the second man jumped back in shock and the first died, his life gurgling out of his gashed throat. "Hey!" cried the second man, his quick moves marking him a dangerous foe, no matter his ragged attire. His sword hissed from its scabbard and he was ready for any attack before she could close, so she moved back.

A distant clatter of hooves, and the man shouted, "Here! Over here!"

Miranda cursed as answering calls rang through the air. While he warily observed her, she feigned an attack. His sword lashed out and he briefly exposed his arm to her. She flicked out with her blade, but it slid off the ring mail protecting his shoulder.

He laughed as he unleashed a powerful backhanded blow designed to remove her head from her shoulders, but she merely squatted. As the blade cleaved air, she thrust upward with her dagger, taking him in his unprotected groin.

A shriek of pain and he doubled up as Miranda yanked free her blade. A cascade of crimson told her she had reached the artery deep in the groin and the mercenary was doomed to death in moments.

The sound of approaching hooves signaled that Miranda also had but a few minutes to live if she did not act quickly. Hurrying into the cave, she knelt before the elven woman. "What is your name?"

The woman, crouching before the two boys, replied, "Ellia."

"I can save you and the children, but I cannot take you to the Jeshandi. Will you come away with me?"

Hearing the riders entering the glade, she said, "What choice have I?"

"None," said Miranda. She leaned across Ellia, as if embracing her, and put her hands upon the boys' heads, then suddenly everything around them spun into darkness.

A moment later, the air shifted, and it was warm night. The woman gasped, and said, "What . . . ?"

Miranda fell backwards awkwardly and sat hard upon damp soil. "We are . . ." she began, and it was clear she was disoriented.

Ellia glanced around as Miranda fought the confusion of the transition. They were in a large clearing surrounded by thick forest, with a broad stream or small river hurrying through it. The merry sound of water splashing over rocks was a startling alternative to the sound of men dying.

Ellia stood and took a step to Miranda's side, bending to help her to her feet. The dark-haired woman shook her head to clear it.

A sizzling sound in the distance caught their attention, and both looked for its source. A faint glow of green appeared in the night sky; then it turned into a point of light.

"Quickly, into the water!" commanded Miranda, and without hesitation, Ellia turned and scooped up her two children, carrying one under each arm. The river was shallow but running rapidly, and the elven woman had to struggle to keep her feet on the slippery rocks. "Don't look back!" shouted Miranda, and Ellia obeyed silently as she waded hip-deep in the stream. The two boys clung tightly to their mother, remaining silent despite the sudden darkness and the cold of the river.

The searing sound grew louder and soon the boys had their faces buried against their mother's bosom, as if in refuge against the harsh sound. Ellia thought her ears would begin to bleed, and the children finally could endure it no longer and began to wail.

A shattering explosion hurled Ellia forward, and for a panic-stricken moment she thought she would lose the children. Water closed over their heads, but she rolled to her backside and forced herself to her knees, holding her children close the entire time. The boys sputtered and coughed as their heads came out of the icy water, but neither had let go.

The stumble and fall had turned Ellia around and she couldn't help but look where Miranda stood. A brilliant orange light fired down from the heavens, a long line of energy that engulfed the young woman. Miranda raised her arms as if warding off the harsh energies. A sudden blast of hot air struck at Ellia, hot enough to dry much of her head and shoulders above water. Miranda moved her hands suddenly, and a latticework of purple-tinged white energy appeared and began to spread along the column of orange light, racing back toward its source. As it passed up the length of orange energy, it burned brilliant white, too brilliant to watch. Ellia turned as rapidly as she could in the water, shielding the boys as much as possible from the heat.

Wading forward, she reached the far bank and half lifted, half pushed the boys up onto the grass. Then she struggled to get herself out of the waist-deep water. Suddenly strong hands reached down and lifted her easily out of the river.

Three men in green leather watched the fierce display across the water. One leaned upon a longbow and spoke to Ellia in a language alien to her. She placed reassuring hands upon her boys' shoulders and said, "I don't understand."

The man glanced at the other two and raised an eyebrow in surprise, then looked back at Ellia. "You speak Keshian, but not your own tongue?"

His accent sounded odd to Ellia, but she could understand him. "I speak the language taught to me by my parents."

The harsh light suddenly vanished, leaving the clearing suddenly inky in contrast. Miranda swayed in the darkness, as if drunk, then she steadied herself and turned. Across the river, she saw Ellia and the boys standing with three elven warriors. "May I enter?" she called weakly in the King's tongue.

"Who seeks Elvandar?" answered one of the warriors.

"One in need of counsel with Lord Tomas."

"Cross if you are able."

Dryly Miranda said, "I think I can manage."

She waded to the far side and the elven woman said, "What magic is this?"

"These are your people, Ellia. These are the eledhel, and this is the boundary of Elvandar."

"*Elvandar?*" She looked confused. "That is a legend, a tale told by old ones to children."

The leader of the three warriors said, "I judge there are many questions to be answered, but this is not the place, nor is it the time. Come, we have two days of travel to reach the Queen's court."

"The little ones are tired," said Miranda, "and they are frightened."

The elf looked down and saw the boys. His eyes widened slightly, a gesture that would have been lost on most humans, though Miranda marked his surprise. "Twins?"

Ellia looked at Miranda, who answered, "They are."

Another elf warrior said, "I shall go now and carry word to the court." He turned and vanished into the woods.

The first elf made a gesture and the remaining elf nodded once and followed after his companion. To Miranda the first said, "I am called Galain. My companions are Althal, who is returning to our campsite to prepare food for you, and the other is Lalial, who will take word to the Queen and her consort."

He shouldered his bow, then, without asking leave, knelt and picked up the two boys as easily as he might have picked up two kittens. The boys looked at their mother, but neither child voiced protest. Miranda touched Ellia's shoulder, then motioned with her head that they should follow their guide.

Miranda used her natural sight to keep the others in view. Her arts were depleted by the battle on the riverbank. It had been a short struggle, but no less vicious for its brevity. Through her exhaustion, Miranda felt the satisfaction of knowing that on the other side of the world the Pantathian magician who had thrown that tracking energy after her had not expected her counterspell. With grim pleasure, she knew he was now a smoldering corpse.

THEY REACHED CAMP without having spoken a word. The fire was burning brightly as Althal placed more wood on it, and rich smells of smoke and crisping game reached Miranda's nose.

The boys were now asleep and Galain gently set them down upon the ground. Softly he said, "It will be light in a few hours. They can eat when they awake."

The elven woman sat heavily upon the ground, and Miranda knew she was exhausted, emotionally as well as physically. Her home had been destroyed and certainly her husband was dead, and suddenly she was in a strange place with people she didn't know, without even the most basic personal possessions to call her own. In the language of her homeland, she said, "Who are you?"

Switching into Yabonese, the language of the neighboring Kingdom province, and related to the ancient language of Kesh, the common ancestor of the language spoken by Ellia, Galain said, "I am named Galain. We are of the eledhel—as are you."

"I do not know this word eledhel," said Ellia, outwardly calm, though Miranda knew she must be terribly frightened.

"It means 'the light people,' in our own language. There is much you will need to know. But to begin, ages ago our race was divided into four tribes, for want of a better term. Those who are eldest among us, the eldar, are the keepers of wisdom. Those who live here in Elvandar and serve Queen Aglaranna are called eledhel. There are others: glamredhel, the wild ones, and moredhel, the dark ones. Some years ago we learned of your people, whom we call ocedhel, 'people from across the sea.' We are not sure if you are properly glamredhel or eledhel who have lost knowledge of their own race. But either way, you are welcome to Elvandar. We live here." He smiled. "We are like you. Here you will be safe."

Ellia looked pointedly at his face, studying his eyes. As if reading her thoughts, he pushed back his long hair to show her the upswept, lobeless ears that marked elvenkind. She sighed in relief. "Safe . . ." she repeated. Her tone showed she scarcely believed.

Miranda said, "You will learn that you are as safe here as anyplace on this world."

Ellia nodded, hugging her knees to her chin as she closed her eyes. After a moment, a tear appeared upon her cheek and she sighed.

Galain left her to her memories, and spoke to Miranda. "You make an impressive entrance."

Spitting the word, Miranda said, "Snakes."

Galain's eyes narrowed. "The serpent men?"

Miranda nodded.

Galain said, "We will leave as soon as the boys awake and eat. Sleep now if you can."

Miranda didn't need convincing. She lay upon the damp ground where she sat, and within moments was fast asleep.

THE BOYS RODE upon the shoulders of Galain and Althal, while Ellia and Miranda hurried along. Miranda knew they were not moving as quickly as they would have been able to unburdened, but she had to struggle to keep pace. Only Ellia's awkwardness gave her some small comfort, for it was a lifetime living in the woodlands that gave these elves their surefooted passage in the undergrowth, not their race.

The boys had awakened and eaten, and without discussion the party had left the campsite near the river. They had moved for the better part of the day, and had paused only long enough to eat some dried meat and fruit at midday. Then they had moved steadily though the trees until an hour before dusk.

Galain had gone hunting while Althal made a fire. Within the hour, Galain had returned with a brace of rabbits. While not sumptuous fare for four adults and two children, there was enough so that no one slept with hunger pangs.

Morning came too quickly for exhausted children and two tired women, but they were again on the trail as the sun rose in the east. By noon they encountered a patrol of hunters who quickly exchanged information with Galain and Althal. The conversation was lost upon Ellia, who was ignorant of the subtleties of elven communications, and Miranda missed a great deal.

Near midafternoon, they came to an enormous clearing. Ellia stumbled, her mouth opening in awe, and even Miranda was impressed.

Across the clearing rose a mighty city of trees. Boles to dwarf the mightiest oak rose high above them, blotting out the sky. A canopy of leaves formed a massive roof above the trunks that stretched away beyond sight. Dark green, the awning of treetops was punctuated by an occasional tree of a different color, some golden, others white, a few sparkling with emerald or azure lights. A soft glow seemed to tease the limits of vision, as if a magic haze enveloped the entire area.

Galain said, "Elvandar."

They crossed the clearing, and as they approached the nearest trees, Miranda could see figures moving. Workmen labored, curing hides, fashioning weapons in forges, and carving wooden implements. Others fletched arrows, worked stones, or prepared food. But the common nature of these tasks took nothing from the impact of the city itself; Elvandar was perhaps the most magical place upon the world. Soothing sounds, rather than the loud noise of workers, filled the air, and voices were musical rather than harsh.

Reaching a giant tree, Miranda saw stairs had been cut from the living wood of the huge trunk.

"If you have a fear of heights, say now, Miranda."

Miranda came out of her revery and saw Galain studying her and Ellia. She said nothing, shaking her head, and Galain led them upward.

As they climbed, Miranda saw that some of the larger branches were flat on top, forming narrow roadways upon which elves walked, moving from tree to tree. Many of the trees were hollow, and what seemed to be small dwellings were fashioned inside.

The elves who passed smiled in greeting, and several were openly delighted upon seeing the twin boys. Most wore leather, brown or green in color, but others wore soft robes, decorated with gems or beads. All were uniformly tall; some were fair, but others were as dark of hair as was Miranda.

A few wore furs and carried weapons, with metal-studded armbands and necklaces of gold set with precious stones. These looked openly at the women in curiosity, and their expressions were less friendly when turned upon Galain.

As they passed, Althal spoke. "The glamredhel are still not completely at ease here. But then they've been with us but a short time."

"How long?" asked Miranda.

"Those two who passed, not yet thirty years."

Miranda had to suppress a laugh. "Barely a long visit."

Galain turned and smiled, showing he understood her humor. She wasn't sure if Althal shared his understanding.

To the back of a large branch a platform was anchored, and from it rose a stairway of wood and rope. Mounting it, the two elves escorted Miranda and Ellia to another, larger platform, and along a broad thoroughfare. This led to a maze of platforms, small markets, and meeting areas, and at last they reached a gigantic platform, dominating the very heart of Elvandar.

Entering, Galain led them to the center, where he faced two figures sitting upon a dais. He and Althal gently put the boys down and bowed. "My Queen," Galain said, "and Tomas."

The woman was impressive, a regal-looking elf with golden-red hair and eyes the color of ice-blue glaciers. Hundreds of years old, she looked much as a human would in the prime of youth, her face unlined and her body still straight and limber. Her features were chiseled and delicate, but there was strength in her bearing.

The man at her side was even more striking, for he was not quite human or elven in appearance. Six inches over six feet in height, he was broad of shoulder and deep in the chest without looking bulky. His eyes were an even paler blue than his companion's, and his hair was sun-streaked yellow. His features were human: even brow with straight nose, full but not soft mouth. Yet somehow an agency had molded those features, casting an alien image over them. He was too regal to be handsome, yet when he smiled, a boy's charm appeared.

The woman rose and Miranda bowed, and Ellia looked confused. At last she curtsied clumsily, while the boys clung to her.

Ignoring formalities, the Elf Queen came up to Ellia and gently took her in her arms and embraced her. Then she knelt before the boys and touched each upon the cheek. She said something softly, and Ellia said, "I don't understand."

Galain said, "Our Queen speaks to your companion."

In the Keshian dialect most like Ellia's, Aglaranna said, "I said, 'You bring us treasure.' Your sons are beautiful. We are so much the richer for their joining us."

Ellia's eyes welled with tears as she said, "They look like their father."

Tomas rose, and as he crossed to stand before Ellia, he said, "It is not the way of my wife's people to speak the name of those who have traveled to the Blessed Isles. In his sons he lives on. You are more than welcome here." To Althal he said, "Take these newly come to us and find them a home. See to their needs." Then he addressed Ellia. "You are safe here, and under my protection. No harm will come to you or your sons in Elvandar. At first our ways will seem strange to you, but you will come to know that they are your ways, truly, and that your fathers' fathers had been apart from us too long. Welcome to your true home."

Weak with relief, Ellia allowed herself to be led away, one child holding fast to each of her hands. When they had left, Tomas said, "And who are you?"

"A friend of your son's," answered Miranda.

Galain leaned upon his bow and said, "I thought your name familiar."

Tomas's expression remained neutral. He motioned for Miranda to come away from the dais and led her over to a table, where several elves had placed refreshments. Motioning for a few members of the Queen's court to attend, he said, "How is Calis?"

"Disturbed," answered Miranda. "Has he told you his mad plan?"

By the fearful expression on Aglaranna's face, she could see he had. Tomas nodded.

"Well, for better or worse, I'm helping him." Then she shook her head. "Though how much good I'm doing is . . ." She picked up a pear and bit into it, chewed, and swallowed. "Now, the snakes know someone with some talent was snooping around their army." She explained what had happened: her scouting the advancing army across the sea, the encounter with Ellia and the boys, her escape, and the final attack at the bank of the river.

After she was finished, Aglaranna said, "It was unlikely they'd think their mad campaign would escape the notice of those with power for long. It may be they think you one of any number of magicians or priests."

Miranda nodded. "And they have no way of knowing where I am. The one who found me is in no condition to tell them. The others might suspect I'm here, but they won't attempt to breech your defenses . . . yet."

Tomas said, "We can speak more of these matters in the morning. You should rest. Night is almost upon us and you look fatigued."

"Oh, that's what I am," agreed Miranda, "but by morning I plan on being a great distance from here. There is much to be done and little time in which to do it. I must seek out your son and confer with him, and next convince some otherwise reasonable men to agree to a most foolish and dangerous undertaking. Then I can be about other business. I hadn't planned on coming here straight away, but now that I'm here, can you tell me something?"

"What?"

"Where I can find Pug?"

Tomas glanced at his wife and said, "We've not seen him for years. The last message I had from him was seven years ago. He said he was concerned over the reports my son brought back from his last voyage to Novindus. He had consulted with the Oracle of Aal, and . . ."

"And what?" prodded Miranda.

Tomas's blue eyes regarded Miranda for a moment, as if measuring her. He said at last, "He said he feared that his own powers would be lacking in the coming battle and he needed to seek allies."

Miranda smiled and there was nothing of humor in that smile. "His powers were lacking." She shook her head. "Who else on this world matches him in power, save you?"

"Even my powers pale compared to what Pug can do if need be," answered Tomas. "My arts are set by my heritage, and are as they were at the end of the Riftwar, fifty years ago. But Pug, he studies and learns and masters new things yearly, and it may be no one since Macros the Black can approach his might."

At the mention of Macros, Miranda made a sour expression. "Much of what is alleged about his prowess was based upon his listeners being gullible, by all reports."

Tomas shook his head. "I have been places you could only imagine, woman. And I stood at Macros's side in the Garden of the City Forever, and I saw the creation of this universe. He may have been a man given to overboasting at times, but not by any great margin, I will avow. His powers approached the gods', and his skills would be welcome in the coming fray."

Miranda said, "Still, by all reports the Black Sorcerer is fifty years vanished from his realm. So then, whom could Pug be seeking?"

Aglaranna said, "Find the where, and that may tell you who."

Tomas said, "If he is not upon this world, then I suspect you must go to other worlds. Have you the arts?"

Miranda said, "If I don't, I can find those to help me who do. But where to begin the search?" She looked at Tomas. "Reputedly, you and Pug were as brothers. You would know where to begin the search."

Tomas said, "I can think of only one place, but it is much as if I said search the sea for a particular fish. For the place to begin searching is as vast as any place in all the myriad possible universes."

Miranda nodded, saying, "The Hall of Worlds."

Tomas nodded, too. "The Hall of Worlds."

7

★★

TRIAL

ROO STIRRED.

He felt a hand on his leg, and in his sleepy state he brushed at it weakly. He felt it clamp down and suddenly he was wide awake.

An ugly face loomed over his, leering and grinning. "You're an ugly sod, boy, but you're young." It was the nervous man with affected speech of the day before who was now fondling Roo's leg.

"Ah!" shouted Roo. "Keep away from me!"

The man laughed. "Just having a joke, me lad." He shivered. "Damn cell will give a man his death. Now shut up and go back to sleep, and we can both get warm." The man turned over, back to back with Roo, and closed his eyes.

The brute called Biggo, who had regained consciousness an hour after being tossed into the cell, said, "Don't terrorize the lad, Slippery Tom. This is the death room. He's too much on his mind to be thinkin' of romance." His speech had the lilt of Kornachmen of Deep Taunton, rarely heard in the West.

Slippery Tom, ignoring the jape and the accompanying laughter, said, "It's a cold morning, Biggo."

Seeing Erik now awake, Biggo said, "He's not a bad sort for a liar and murderer, is Slippery Tom; he's just scared."

Roo's eyes widened. "Who isn't?" he said with a frantic note in his voice. He closed his eyes tight, as if to shut out everything by force of will.

Erik sat back against the unyielding stone wall. He knew Roo had spent a fitful night, awakening several times shouting in his sleep as he wrestled with personal demons. Erik glanced around the cell. Other men slept or sat quietly in their place as the night wore on. Erik knew that the bravado Roo had exhibited since awakening in the cell the day before had been some sort of madness: he couldn't accept the inevitability of his own death.

Biggo said, "Spanking young bottoms is common enough in the prison gangs, but Slippery is just looking for someone warm to cozy up to, lad."

Roo opened his eyes. "Well, he smells like something died in his shirt last week."

Tom said, "And you don't exactly remind me of flowers, youngster. Now shut up and go back to sleep."

Biggo grinned, and his bearlike face looked nothing so much as that of an overgrown child, one with broken and crooked teeth. The beating administered by the guards the day before had done nothing to enhance his appearance; blue, purple, and red lumps decorated his visage. "I like to sleep cuddled with someone warm. Like me Elsmie. She was sweet." He sighed as he closed his eyes. "Too bad I'll never see her again."

"You talk like we're all going to be convicted," said Roo.

"This is the death cell, me lad. You're here because you're going to be tried for your life, and not one in a hundred who has sat here lived two days past his trial. You think you got a way to beat the King's justice, boyo?" asked Biggo with a laugh. "Well, good on you if you do. But none here are babes, and we all knew what the deal was when we took to the dodgy path: 'get caught, take your punishment.' That's the way of it, for a fact." He closed his eyes, leaving the two young men to their own thoughts.

Erik had been awake most of the night, falling asleep only a few hours before, wrestling with the same questions. He had never been a religious sort, going to temple on the festival days, joining the vineyard workers in the blessing of the vineyards every year. But he hadn't given much thought to what it would be like to face Lims-Kragma in her hall. He vaguely knew that every man came to stand before her, to account for his deeds, but he always thought of that as some sort of priest talk, what Owen Greylock had called a "metaphor" where one thing said stood for another. Now he wondered: Would he simply end? When the box was kicked out from under his feet and the rope either snapped his neck or choked the life from him, would it turn all dark and meaningless? Or would he awake in the Hall of the Dead, as the priests claimed, joining the long line of those waiting for Lims-Kragma's judgment? Those found worthy were sent on to a better life, they said, while those found wanting were sent back to learn those lessons that had eluded them while living. There was talk that at some point those who lived pure lives of harmony and grace were elevated somehow, beyond human understanding, to a higher existence.

Erik turned his mind away from the question, again; there was no answer he knew, until he actually faced death. Either way, he thought with a silent shrug, it'll be something interesting or I'll not mind. He closed his eyes on this thought, finding it strangely comforting.

THE DOOR AT the far end of the hall clanked open, iron bands striking cold stone. Two guards with drawn swords led a prisoner into the hallway. Another two guards walked before and after him, holding wooden poles looped through iron rings on a wooden yoke set around his neck. The pressure on the yoke kept the man from being able to reach either guard, and the awkward procession made its way to the door of the death cell.

The prisoner was otherwise undistinguished. He seemed a young man, little older than Erik or Roo, though this was hard to determine, as his race was alien to the two young men from Ravensburg. He was one of the yellow-skinned men from Kesh, from a province called Isalani. A few had passed through Ravensburg from time to time, but they were still the object of interest to the provincial residence of that town.

This man was plainly dressed, in a simple robe, with an empty carry-cloth—a large cloth used to carry belongings, in place of a backpack—hung around his neck. His feet were bare, and his head was uncovered, showing a thatch of thick black hair roughly cut above the ears, but falling long in back. Black eyes regarded the unfolding events without expression.

When the door was reached, the first guard unlocked it and ordered the prisoners to move to the far end of the long cell. Once they had obliged him, he opened the door and the two men with the poles steered the prisoner to the opening. With practiced dexterity, the lead guard unfastened the neck yoke and the two guards slipped the poles out. The collar was removed, and with unnecessary force the remaining guard put his boot to the prisoner's back and shoved him into the cell.

The prisoner stumbled one step, but caught himself and stood motionless. The others looked on in curiosity.

"What was that all about?" asked one man.

The new prisoner shrugged. "I disarmed a few of their guards when they tried to arrest me. They objected to that."

"You disarmed them?" said another prisoner. "How did you do that?"

The young man sat down on the vacant stone bench. "I took their weapons from them. How else would you imagine I did it?"

A few of the prisoners asked the newcomer his name, but no conversation was forthcoming, as the new prisoner closed his eyes while remaining seated upright. He crossed his legs before him, each foot resting upon the opposite thigh, and put his hands, palms upward, on his knees.

The other prisoners looked at him for a few minutes, then returned to sitting and waiting for whatever fate would bring them next.

An hour later the hall door opened again and a company of soldiers entered. The man Erik had met before, Lord James, walked in. Then the men in the cell began to mutter as a woman entered, followed in turn by a pair of guardsmen. The woman was old, or at least she appeared that way to Erik. Older than his mother, at any rate. Her hair was a startling white and her brows were pale enough for him to think her hair had always been this color. The lines in her face notwithstanding, Erik thought she was nice to look at, and she must have been beautiful when young. Her eyes were an odd blue, almost violet in the darkness of the cell, and she carried herself with the bearing of nobility, despite an expression of sadness on her face.

Erik wondered what could be the cause of this expression of regret: could she have some sort of feeling about the men who would be tried in the Prince's chamber this day? She stopped before the bars, and the sullen prisoners were completely silent. For some reason, Erik found himself standing, feeling the urge to touch his forelock, as he would to any lady of quality who passed on the road in her carriage. Roo followed his example and soon the other men were standing as well.

The woman ignored the filth and wretched stench of the cell as her hands closed upon the bars. She was silent while her eyes searched out every face, and when her gaze at last turned upon Erik, he found himself suddenly afraid. He thought of his mother and Rosalyn, and thinking of Rosalyn made him think of Stefan, and suddenly he was ashamed of himself. He couldn't look at the lady any longer and lowered his eyes.

For long minutes the woman stood silently, her rich gown becoming dirtied by contact with the rusty iron of the bars as she leaned against them. Erik glanced up and found that as she looked from man to man, only the new prisoner could return her gaze, and at one point he even smiled slightly. But for several of the men her penetrating gaze was too much, and they began to weep. Then at last her own eyes began to fill with tears and she said, "Enough."

Lord James nodded curtly once and motioned for the two guards to escort her out of the cell. When they were gone, he said, "You men will face trial this afternoon. Kingdom justice is swift; those of you found guilty of capital crimes will be brought back to this cell and in the morning we will hang you. You'll be given one last meal and time to make your peace with the gods. Priests of the twelve orders will come for those who ask for shriving, and for the rest of you who don't wish to speak with a priest, well, you can spend time contemplating your sins. If you have an advocate, he will be allowed to speak for you before Prince Nicholas; if you don't, you must speak for yourself or the Crown will convict you by default. There is no appeal, so make your brief persuasive. The King is the only man who can overrule the Prince, and he's busy."

Without another word, the Duke of Krondor turned and left the cell block.

A guard waiting in the connecting hall reached in and pulled the door shut behind him.

The men stood silently for a long minute, then one, the man called Slippery Tom, said, "Something about that witch gave me a chill."

"It was like having me mum finding me with my brother's sweets on festival day," said another.

Slowly they sat, and when every man was back in his place, Roo turned to Erik and asked, "What was that all about?"

Erik shrugged. "You know as much as I do."

"She read your minds," said the newcomer as he returned to his contemplative pose.

"What?" came from several of the men. "She read our minds?"

Without opening his eyes, but with a very faint smile, the newcomer said, "She was looking for some men." Then suddenly his eyes opened and he glanced from face to face. "I think she may have found them."

His eyes lingered on Erik and he said, "Yes, I think she has."

THE MIDDAY MEAL was plain but filling. The guards brought in a platter of bread loaves and a round of hard cheese, as well as a bucket of a vegetable stew. No knives, forks, or other potential weapons were permitted, but dull-edged wooden bowls were provided for the stew. Finding himself suddenly hungry, Erik shouldered through the press at the bars as the guards handed out the food.

"Here, now!" shouted a guard. "There's enough for all of you, though why you'd have any appetite when you're going to hang tomorrow is beyond me."

Erik took a bowl and grabbed a loaf of bread, broke off a hunk of cheese, and returned to where Roo sat. "Aren't you going to eat anything?"

Roo said, "If the guard's not lying, there will be more when I get to the bars." He rose slowly and moved to where the press of prisoners was lessening, then took his bowl and held it close to the bars as the guard filled it with a metal ladle. Then a loaf of bread and some cheese was given to him, and he returned to Erik's side.

One of the prisoners said, "The food's better here than at me mum's!"

That brought a weak laugh from two of the men, but the rest ate in silence.

SHORTLY AFTER THE meal, the guards came to escort the prisoners to the Prince's court. Each man's leg irons and shackles, wrist irons and collars, and all the chains were inspected. The newest prisoner, the Isalani, stood silently as the wooden collar was presented to him. He said, "I will cause you no difficulty." Then with an enigmatic smile he said, "I am interested in what is about to occur."

The guard sergeant seemed to think about it, but the man walked quietly out of the cell and stood in place behind the man who had been led out before him. The guard sergeant made a curt nod, indicating it was all right, and the other prisoners were put in the line.

"All right, any of you makes a break, we shoot you down and that's the end of it. So if you prefer a crossbow bolt to the rope, now's your chance. But be warned, if the bolt doesn't kill you outright, it's a messy, pitiful way to go. Saw a man with his lung punched out of him; that was a sight. Now, move the prisoners along!" The company of crossbowmen lined the hallway where they marched, and the prisoners, now numbering twelve, were led through the palace, up to the Prince's hall.

Dirty, poor, and miserable, these men were ushered into the presence of the second most powerful man in the Kingdom, Nicholas, Prince of the Western Realm of the Kingdom of the Isles, brother to King Borric, Heir Apparent to the Crown. The Prince was a man of forty-some years of age, and his dark hair was still almost entirely without grey. His eyes were dark brown and deeply shadowed; the stress of burying his father was obvious, etching deep lines on his face.

He wore mourning black, and his only badge of office was his royal ring. He sat in the large chair at the end of the hall, raised upon a dais. The chair next to his, used by his mother when his father ruled only days before, was empty. The Dowager Princess Anita was in seclusion in her quarters.

Standing beside the throne was the Duke of Krondor, Lord James, and beside him, the mysterious lady who the Isalani said read minds.

The prisoners were ushered into the Prince's presence and the guard sergeant had to order them to bow. The men made an awkward attempt, and at last the court was called to order.

Several onlookers lined the sides of the halls, and Erik noticed Sebastian Lender among them. That made him feel slightly better than he had in days.

The first prisoner was called before the Prince, a man named Thomas Reed, and to Erik's surprise, the man called Slippery Tom moved before Nicholas.

Nicholas looked down on Slippery Tom. "What are the charges, James?"

The Duke of Krondor nodded to a scribe, who said, "Thomas Reed stands accused of theft and aiding and abetting in the murder of the victim, a spice merchant named John Corwin, late of Krondor."

"How do you plead?" asked James.

Slippery Tom glanced around the room and tried to present as pleasant an expression as possible to Nicholas. "You Majesty—" he began.

" 'Highness,' " interrupted James. "Not 'You Majesty,' 'Your Highness.' "

Grinning as if this social gaffe were his worst offense, he said, "You Highness, it were this way—"

James interrupted, "How do you plead?"

Suddenly angry eyes regarded the Duke as he said, "I was attemptin' to explain this to His Highness, sir."

"Plead first, then explain," said Prince Nicholas.

Tom seemed to think of his options a moment. "Well, strictly speaking, I guess I would have to say I was guilty, but only in a sense of it."

"Enter the plea," said James. "Do you have anyone to speak on your behalf?"

"Just Biggo," said Tom.

"Biggo?" said Nicholas.

James said, "The next defendant."

"Oh, well, then tell me your story."

Tom began to spin an improbable tale of two poor workmen attempting to do the right thing in a bargain gone sour with a spice merchant of dubious character who cheated the two basically honest workers. When confronted with his perfidious acts, the spice merchant had pulled a knife and in the ensuing struggle had fallen on his own blade. The two wronged men, regretting the malefactor's death, had taken his gold only in the amount they were owed, which happened to be all he was carrying. "And that's not all he owed us," said Tom.

Nicholas looked at James. "Corwin?"

"Honest, for the most part," said James. "What I could find out tells me he occasionally received some Keshian spices without benefit of duty, but that's not unusual."

Nicholas said, "Why did John Corwin owe you money?"

With a feral light in his eyes, Tom said, "Well, truth to tell, You Highness, we was bringing the merchant some Keshian spice, without bothering to call it to the attention of the duty office at the Port Authority, if you see. We was only doing it to support our families."

Nicholas glanced at the woman who had remained silent, and Erik followed his gaze. She looked at Tom for a moment, then briefly shook her head no.

Nicholas said, "What's the state's request?"

James said, "Thomas Reed is a habitual criminal, a self-confessed member of the Guild of Thieves—"

"Wait a minute, lord!" shouted Thomas. "I was just making some idle boasts, trying to get some respect from the guards—"

James ignored the interruption. "The state asks for death."

"Granted."

With that single word, Slippery Tom was sentenced to die the next morning.

Erik looked at Roo and wondered if the terror he saw in his friend's eyes was as apparent in his own.

★★

SLOWLY EACH MAN was brought before the bar of justice, and each time at the end of the plea, Erik saw the Prince look at the woman. Each time she shook her head no, save for once, when Biggo was on trial, when she nodded yes slightly. But it seemed to make no difference, for Biggo was condemned to the gallows with the others.

When there were fewer than half to be tried, the scribe called, "Sho Pi!"

The Isalani was brought before the Prince, and James recited the charges: "Sho Pi, a citizen of Kesh, Highness. Arrested for brawling. He killed a guard."

"Your plea?" asked the Prince.

The Isalani smiled. "Plea? I have none, Highness. The facts are as recited."

"Then enter the plea as guilty," said Nicholas. "Have you anything to say before sentencing?"

The smile broadened, and the Isalani said, "Only that facts and truth are not interchangeable. I am but a poor student, formerly a monk of the order of Dala. I was sent to find my master."

"Your master?" asked Nicholas, seemingly interested in the story, decidedly different than the run-of-the-mill pleas heard so far today. "Who is he?"

"This I do not know. I was an indifferent student at the monastery where I was trained, save in the art of fighting. I admit to being unworthy of the calling; the Abbot sent me out, telling me that if I had a master he was outside the order, and to seek him in a city where men brawl daily." The man shrugged. "Often in jest, truth is revealed, and I meditated for days upon what my former Abbot said. Given some insight by hunger, I decided to seek my master in your city, though it was far from my own land. I traveled and worked, and found myself in Krondor but a week ago."

"Since then he's been arrested three times," said James.

The man named Sho Pi shrugged. "Unfortunately, this is true. I have many flaws, and a temper is among them. I was being cheated at cards, and when I objected, a struggle ensued, and when I pleaded my innocence to your city watch, I was attacked. I merely defended myself."

"During the struggle he killed a guardsman," said James.

"Is this true?" said Arutha.

"Regrettably, but in my defense may I say that it was never my intent to kill the man. I was merely trying to disarm him. I had taken his sword from him when he unexpectedly twisted away from me, pushing himself into his companion, who threw him forward upon the sword I was now holding. It is very sad, but it happened." He spoke as if he were reciting a lesson, without emotion, not pleading for his life.

The Prince looked at the woman, who nodded slightly. Then he said, "What is the state's request?"

"The state requests thirty years' labor in the prison gang."

"Granted," said Nicholas.

For reasons Erik couldn't understand, Sho Pi seemed amused at this as the guard escorted him back to the prisoners' dock.

Two more men were ordered to their death; then, when Erik and Roo were all that were left, their names were called. Sebastian Lender stepped forward with Erik, and James said, "Your Highness, we have a special case here. Erik von Darkmoor and Rupert Avery are charged with the murder of Stefan, Baron von Darkmoor."

"How do you plead?" asked Nicholas.

Before either young man could speak, Lender said, "If it pleases Your Highness, I would ask that it be recorded that the two youths before you plead not guilty."

Nicholas smiled and leaned back in his throne. "Lender, isn't it? You used to cause my father no end of irritation. Now I see why. Very well." He looked at Erik and Rupert. "Do you have something to say?"

Again, before either young man could speak, Lender said, "I have here, Highness, documents sworn before the High Constable in Darkmoor and two priests of local temples, under oath, on behalf of these young men." He opened a large leather document case and pulled from it a copious sheaf of papers. "Not only do we have the sworn testimony of one Rosalyn, daughter of Milo, owner of the Inn of the Pintail; I have a testimony from several guardsmen who were witness to events leading to the conflict, and from Baron Manfred von Darkmoor as to his brother Stefan's state of mind before the incident." He handed them to James, who looked irritated at the need to peruse such a large amount of information in a short time.

"While my Duke of Krondor looks over these documents, Master Lender, I would be pleased to hear the young men tell what happened."

Erik looked at Roo and, with a nod, indicated he should begin. "It started at the fountain, Your Highness, the one before the Growers' and Vintners' Hall in Ravensburg. I was there with some others, just talking, when Rosalyn came looking for Erik. While I was talking to her, Stefan and Manfred, the Baron's sons, come—came up to us and began talking to Rosalyn. Manfred kept telling Stefan they needed to get back to their father, Otto, who was dying at the time, but Stefan kept talking about 'Erik's girl,' and how she was too sweet to waste on a bastard blacksmith, and things like that."

Nicholas sat back and seemed intent on the story as Roo recounted all he could remember up to where Erik took off after Stefan, and the ensuing fight. When he was done, Nicholas asked Erik for his story. Erik told it calmly and without any attempt to avoid responsibility for his taking his half brother's life.

When the story was told, Nicholas said, "Why did you run?"

Erik shrugged. "I don't know. It seemed . . ." He looked down a moment, then back up, locking gazes with Nicholas. "It seemed impossible that I could kill the swine and not be hung for it."

"Did you hate him that much?"

Erik said, "More than I thought, Highness." Inclining his head at his friend, he said, "Roo saw it coming long before I did. He told me once that I might have to kill Stefan someday. Stefan and I met only three times before that night, and all three times he sought me out to cause problems, calling me names, insulting my mother, claiming I wanted his inheritance."

"Was there any truth to it?"

Erik shrugged. "I don't think so. I never thought much about being noble, or having office. I'm a smith, and I'm the best horse man in Darkmoor—ask Owen Greylock, the Baron's Swordmaster, if you doubt me. I only wanted a guild badge and my own forge, no more than that. My mother only wanted me to have a proper name. It was her passion that made Stefan fearful. But even if she dreamed I might someday be a noble, it was never any dream of mine. I had the name already." His voice lowered, and his tone became almost defiant. "That was, at least, one thing my father did allow me. He never publicly denied me the name von Darkmoor, and I'll take that to the grave with me."

Roo visibly winced at the phrase. Nicholas sighed. "This is very convoluted. Lord James, have you a suggestion?"

James was still leafing through the papers given to him by Lender. "Highness, may I suggest you take this case under advisement, and after supper I'll have the state's recommendation for you."

"Granted," said Nicholas. "Court is adjourned." Guards motioned for the prisoners already in the dock to leave, and Erik and Roo found themselves being marched back to join the others.

Erik looked at Lender. "What happened?" he asked.

Lender didn't look hopeful. "He'll think about it. You should know after supper." Watching the Prince rise from his throne and leave the hall to enter his private chamber, Lender said, "It will be decided by morning, either way."

Guards moved them into line behind Sho Pi, and Roo said, "What do you think is going to happen?"

"If you had not run, and had told this story at once, I think Nicholas would have been inclined to believe you, but you ran, and that counts against you." He was silent as the guards chained the prisoners into line, and Lender said, "If it goes badly, the gallows. If it goes better, thirty years on the work gang. The best I can imagine is service in the Royal Navy for ten years."

The guards ordered them to move out, and suddenly Sho Pi looked over his shoulder at Erik. "Or something else." He smiled enigmatically at the remark. Erik thought his behavior odd for someone facing thirty years of hard labor.

The prisoners marched out of the hall, back to the death cell.

Those who had been condemned to die alternated between numb despair and frantic rage. Slippery Tom was the most antic with fear; he paced the long death cell concocting plan after plan to overpower the guards and escape the palace. He was convinced the Mockers were waiting for any sign of revolt to launch a raid into the palace to set their captured brethren free.

After a hour, Biggo stood up and said, "Give it a rest, lad. You're going to hang."

Slippery Tom's eyes widened and with a scream he lunged at his friend, grabbing him around the throat. Biggo gripped hard on Tom's wrists and forced the hands away from his throat, and as he spread his hands, Tom's face came close to his own. Suddenly Biggo head-butted Tom, whose eyes rolled up into his head as he lost consciousness.

Biggo deposited the limp form of Slippery Tom in a hay-strewn corner. "That should quiet things down for a while," he said.

Another man said, "Is that what you want? Peace? Well, you'll have all the peace you'll ever need come tomorrow morning, Biggo. Maybe Tom's right and we should die fighting guards."

Biggo laughed. "With what? Wooden bowls?"

"You anxious to die?" demanded the man.

Biggo rubbed his chin. "Everyone dies, laddie; it's just a question of when. As soon as you took to the dodgy path you were doomed to the gibbet, like it or not." He sighed and looked reflective. "Doesn't seem right to be killing guards for doing their job. We're going to die anyway, so why spread the misery? Some of them have wives and children." He leaned back, resting his elbows on a ledge behind the stone bench he sat upon. "Hanging may not be so bad. Either your neck's cracked"—he snapped his fingers—"and you're gone, or it chokes you. Choking's not so bad, I'm thinking. I was choked once in a fight. You get sort of light-headed and everything collapses around your vision, and there's this bright light. . . . No, me boyo, it'll be over quickly."

Another man said, "Give it a rest, Biggo. We're not temple-goers like you."

"It was that very choking I spoke of that made me a religious man, Aaron. Why, if Shaky Jake hadn't busted a chair over Billy the Sly's head, I'd have died right there. I decided then it was high time I got righteous with the gods, I did. So I went off to Lims-Kragma's temple and talked to a priest, and gave an offering, and I don't miss a holy day unless I'm too sick to walk." He sat back and crossed his arms. "Tomorrow, when I'm in the Death Goddess's hall, and she says to me, 'Biggo, you're a liar and a thief and a murderer, even if you didn't mean to be one, but at least you're a pious bastard,' I'll smile at her and say, 'That's right, Your Goddessness.' That should count for something."

Erik found it hard to find anything amusing in his present circumstances, and Roo was close to tears for fear they would be joining those sentenced to die. The only three men not under the death mark were Sho Pi, Erik, and Roo. Sho Pi would be transferred to the work gang after the hanging, which he would watch as a lesson. He seemed unfazed by the prospect of spending the next thirty years hauling rocks out of the royal quarry or dredging out the royal harbor. It was rumored some young men had survived their thirty years, so it was possible he might emerge alive, someday, a broken man in his fifties who might somehow forge a life. For most men it only put off death.

The door at the far end of the cell opened, and Erik jerked around to see who was there, half hoping, half fearing it would be Lender. Instead it was guards with the evening meal. More bread and cheese, but this time the stew had beef in it, and there was a cup of wine for each prisoner.

Erik found himself hungry, despite his worry, but Roo simply ignored the food, curling up and falling into a sleep of emotional exhaustion. Most of the men ate in silence, save the Isalani, who came to sit next to Erik. He said, "You think you will go free?"

Erik looked off into space for a minute. "No, I think had we stayed and faced down our accusers, maybe. Had they seen the blood flowing from my shoulder from Stefan's sword, maybe then.

"As it is now, I think we are probably going either to be hung or to spend out our lives working next to you on the labor gang."

The Isalani said, "I don't think so."

"What makes you say that?"

"That woman. I don't know why, but it was important that she see what we were thinking when we were before the Prince."

"If she was reading minds, like you claim, then it was to see if we were telling the truth."

"No, something else."

"What?"

"I'm not sure. Maybe what kind of men we are."

Erik finished his meal, and when Roo offered no protest, he drank his wine as well. The evening stretched on, and the door opened again.

Erik turned and was astonished to see Manfred von Darkmoor enter, flanked by two guards wearing the livery of Darkmoor and two others wearing the Prince's colors. Manfred motioned with his head to Erik to come to the far end of the cell where they could speak privately.

Erik got up slowly, and the guards stood away as the two half brothers reached the far end of the cell. Erik said nothing, waiting for Manfred to speak.

After looking at Erik a moment, Manfred said, "Well, I suspect you wonder why I'm here."

"I would think that was obvious," said Erik.

"I'm not entirely sure why I'm here, truth be told. Perhaps it's because I have lost one brother and am about to lose another, whom I don't know."

"I may not be lost, *brother,*" said Erik dryly. "The Prince has taken the evidence under advisement, and I have a very gifted solicitor arguing on my behalf."

"So I have heard." Manfred looked Erik up and down. "You do look a great deal like Father, you know. But I suspect you have your mother's steel in you."

"Why do you say that?"

"You never knew our father; he was a weak man in many ways," Manfred said. "I loved him, of course, but it was difficult to admire him. He avoided fights, mostly with Mother, and he hated being in the public eye." With an ironic smile, he added, "I, on the other hand, find that I rather like it." Picking an imagined speck from his sleeve, he said, "I don't know if I should hate you for killing Stefan or thank you for making me Baron. But either way, Mother is up talking to the Prince right now, ensuring you go to the gallows."

Erik said, "Why does she hate me so?"

Manfred said, "I don't think she hates you, really. Fears you is more like it. It was our father she hated."

Erik looked surprised. "Why?"

"Father liked the ladies, and Mother always knew he had been forced into marrying her. From what I gathered, after I was born they were man and wife in name only. It was Mother who ensured we had only male servants or ugly women working in our castle; Father had an eye for pretty young girls. Even with Mother's precautions, Father found every pretty woman within a day's ride of the castle. Stefan was a lot like him in that respect. He really thought he'd hurt you if he took your girl and had his way with her."

"Rosalyn wasn't my girl," said Erik. "She was more like a sister."

"Even better," said Manfred. "He would have delighted in knowing that. If he could have taken your mother while you watched, he'd have liked that even more." His voice lowered. "Stefan was an evil bastard, Erik, a mean-spirited pig who delighted in causing pain. I should know, because I was on the receiving end of it most of the time. It was only when I caught up with him in size and could defend myself that he left me alone." Almost whispering, he said, "When I first saw him dead, I was angry enough to have killed you myself that minute. After the shock wore off, I realized I felt relief that he was gone. You did the world a favor by killing him, but I'm afraid that fact won't help you at all. Mother's going to see you hung. I guess I'm here to tell you that at least one of your brothers doesn't hate you."

"Brothers?"

"You're not father's only bastard, Erik. You may have a score of brothers and sisters out there. But you were the oldest, and your mother made sure the world knew it. I guess that's really the reason you are going to hang tomorrow."

Erik tried to muster as much courage as he could. "We'll still see what the Prince has to say."

"Of course," said Manfred. "If you do somehow come out of this without being hung, and after you've spent your time on the prison gang, send me a letter." He turned and walked away, then turned to look back at Erik. "But don't enter Darkmoor if you wish to stay alive."

Erik stood alone for a minute after Manfred left, then returned to his place next to the sleeping Roo.

TIME DRAGGED ON and Erik found himself unable to sleep. Several others fell into fitful dozes, and only Biggo and the Isalani seemed able to sleep comfortably. A couple of the men sat in silent prayer.

At midnight, the door opened and a handful of priests entered, from various orders, and each stood across from the prisoner who wished to take comfort. This continued for an hour or more; then the priests left, and still no word from Lender.

Erik at last fell into a half-sleep, with panic waking him up several times, his heart pounding and his chest constricted, as he fought against the rising terror.

Suddenly a loud clang echoed in the otherwise silent cell block and Erik was on his feet as Sebastian Lender entered the room. Erik lightly kicked Roo awake, and the two hurried to the far end of the cell.

Erik looked at what Lender carried and his chest constricted in terror. A pair of boots, fashioned out of soft leather, with high tops that folded down, were clutched in the old man's hands. They were a horseman's boots, well made and artfully crafted, and Erik knew why Lender carried them.

Erik said, "We're to die?"

Lender said, "Yes. The Prince gave the order less than an hour ago." Lender handed the boots through the bars to Erik. "I'm sorry. I thought I had built a persuasive brief, but the mother of the man you killed is the daughter of the Duke of Ran and has much influence in this court as well as the King's. The King himself was consulted, and in the end you were both sentenced to death. There is nothing that can be done." He pointed to the boots that Erik now clutched before him. "These were your father's last gift to you; I thought it would be unfitting for you not to have them at least for a few hours before . . ."

"They hang us," whispered Roo.

Erik pushed the boots back through the bars. "Sell them, Master Lender. You said the gold he left me wouldn't cover your fees."

Lender pushed them back toward Erik. "No, I failed and I will give your gold to whoever you instruct me to. There is no fee, Erik."

Erik said, "Then send the gold to my mother, at Ravensburg. She's at the Inn of the Pintail and she has no one to care for her. Tell her to use the gold wisely, for it is all I will ever be able to give her."

Lender nodded and said, "I pray the gods will be gentle with you, Erik, and you as well, Rupert. You have no evil in your hearts, even if you have done this violent thing."

Lender looked close to tears as he turned away, leaving the two young men from Darkmoor alone in the far corner of the death cell.

Erik looked at his boyhood friend and said nothing. There was nothing to say. He sat and stripped off his common boots, and pulled on the rider's boots. They fit as if they had been fashioned for him. High, to mid-calf, they were soft and clung like soft velvet instead of harsh hides. Erik knew that if he worked for a lifetime he would not have been able to afford their like.

He sighed. He would at least wear them for part of one day, from the cell to the gallows. He only regretted he didn't have at least one opportunity to test them on horseback.

Roo sat on the floor, back against the bars. He looked at Erik, his eyes wide with fear, and whispered, "What do we do now?"

Erik tried to smile reassuringly at his friend, but the best he could manage was a crooked grimace. "We wait."

Nothing more was said.

8

★★

CHOICE

THE DOOR OPENED.

Erik blinked, surprised to discover he had dozed, in a numb, emotionally exhausted sleep. Guards, heavily armed against the possible rebellion of the condemned, entered. Last through the door was the strange man Robert de Loungville.

"Listen, you dogs!" he shouted, his gravelly voice striking them like a leather glove. With a twisted smile he said, "You come when bidden and die like men!" He called six names, and the last of the six was Slippery Tom. Tom held back, as if somehow he could hide among the group who would be hung second. "Thomas Reed! Get out here!" commanded de Loungville.

When Slippery Tom only crouched lower behind his friend Biggo, de Loungville sent in a pair of guards, swords drawn. The other prisoners stepped aside, and the two grappled with Tom a moment, then dragged him from the cell. He started to cry out for mercy and wailed the entire way to the gallows.

No one in the cell spoke. They all listened to the sound of Tom's screaming as he was carried farther and farther from them, then turned as one to look out the cell window as the screaming grew again in volume. The first six prisoners were marched in line, save for Tom, who was still being dragged; his voice reached a near shriek in terror. Repeated cuffing from the guards who carried him only seemed to increase his panic, and short of knocking him senseless, they had no way to shut him up. If they were put off by the screaming, they showed no sign; Tom obviously wasn't the first man they had dragged shrieking to his death; he would be silent soon enough.

Through the bars, Erik watched with a mixture of revulsion and fascination as the first five men plodded up the six wooden steps that led to the gallows. In some distant corner of his mind he knew he would soon be following them, but he couldn't bring himself to accept that reality in his heart. This was all happening to someone else, not to him.

The men stepped up on the high boxes placed under the nooses, and Tom was carried up to where he would die. He kicked and spit and tried to bite the guards, who held on to him tightly. Then they lifted him up to the box, while another jumped up beside him and quickly placed the rope around his neck. Two more guards held him in place lest he kick the box over and die before the order was given.

Erik didn't know what to expect—an announcement of some sort or reading of a formal verdict—but without ceremony Robert de Loungville came to stand directly in front of the condemned, his back to the men still in the cell. His voice carried across the yard as he said, "Hang them!"

Guards kicked hard at the boxes under the men's feet, in one case twice to move it from under the man who slumped down in a faint at de Loungville's command. Slippery Tom's screaming was choked off abruptly.

Erik felt his stomach knot at the sight before him; three men went limp, a sign their necks had snapped; one jerked twice, then died; but the last two kicked as they were slowly choked to death. Slippery Tom was one of the two, and it seemed to Erik he took an impossibly long time to die. The slender thief kicked, striking one of his guards with a heel, and Biggo said, "Should tie a man's legs, you'd think. Robs him of dignity, kicking around like that."

Roo stood next to Erik, tears of terror streaming down his face as he said, "Dignity?"

Biggo said, "Not much else left to a man now, laddie. Man comes into the world naked, and leaves the same way. Clothes on his body don't mean anything. He's naked in his soul. But bravery and dignity, that counts for something, I'm thinking. Maybe nothing to anyone, but someday, you never know, one of these guards might be telling his wife, 'I remember this big fellow we hung once; he knew how to die.'"

Erik watched as Slippery Tom kicked, then twitched, then at last ceased moving. Robert de Loungville waited for what seemed a long time to Erik before, with a motion of his hand, he shouted, "Cut them down!"

The soldiers cut the dead men from the gibbet, and while they were being carried down to be placed on the ground, other soldiers hurried with fresh nooses and put them in place.

Suddenly Erik realized they were coming to get him. His knees began to shake and he put out a hand to steady himself, pressing his palm against the rough stone. *This is the last time I'll feel stone against my hand,* crossed his mind. Robert de Loungville motioned for a company of guards to form up, and they marched out of sight of the waiting prisoners.

Through the walls they could hear the tread of boots upon stone as the guards marched from the yard to the death cell. Closer and closer they came, and Erik alternately wished that they were here and it was over and that they would never reach the death cell. He pressed his hand hard against the wall as if the rough feel of it against his flesh somehow denied the approaching end of his life.

Then the door at the end of the hall opened and the guards marched through. The cell door was opened and de Loungville was calling their names. Roo was called fourth, Erik fifth, and Sho Pi, as the only one who would not be hung, was last.

Roo got into line and looked around, panic on his face. "Wait, can't we . . . isn't there . . ."

One of the guards put a firm hand on his shoulder. "Stay in line, lad. That's a good fellow."

Roo stopped moving, but his eyes were wide, with tears running down his face, while his mouth moved, saying nothing that Erik could understand.

Erik glanced around and felt a sick numbness in his stomach, as if he had been poisoned. Then his bowel tightened and he felt the need to relieve himself and was suddenly fearful he would fill his pants when he died. He found his chest tight and had to will himself to breathe. Sweat dripped down his face and ran from his armpits and groin. *He was going to die.*

"I didn't mean it . . ." said Roo, pleading with men who had no power to save him.

The sergeant in command gave the order. The prisoners were marched from the cell, and Erik wondered how he was managing to keep in step, for his feet were leaden and his knees trembled. Roo shivered visibly and Erik wished he could have touched his friend's shoulder, but the shackles and manacles prevented such movement. They left the long hall next to the death cell.

The condemned moved down a long corridor, to another that led to a short flight of steps. They walked up them, turned another corner, and out through a door into daylight. The sun was still not above the walls, so they moved through shadow, but above them a blue sky promised a beautiful day. Erik's heart almost broke wishing he could see that day.

Roo cried openly, making inarticulate noises punctuated by a single word, "Please," but he managed to walk. They moved past where the first six bodies lay in the yard, as a charnel wagon was being drawn close enough for the dead to be loaded into it. Erik glanced down at the dead men.

He almost stumbled. He had seen death before, having found Tyndal and having looked at Stefan and the nameless bandit after he killed them, but he had never seen this. The men's faces were contorted, especially those of Tom and the other man who had strangled, their eyes bulging from their sockets. The other four whose necks had broken still looked ghastly, with eyes staring lifelessly at the sky. Flies were already gathering on the corpses, and no one was bothering to shoo them away.

All at once Erik was being moved up the steps and he felt his bladder weaken. He had not needed to relieve himself, and suddenly he felt an overwhelming urge to ask for permission to do so before he was hung. A wave of childish embarrassment swept up from some deep well of memory and he felt tears coursing down his cheeks. His mother had scolded him at an early age for messing his bed during the night, and for reasons beyond his ability to understand, the thought of messing himself now was the worst fate he could imagine. From the reek of urine and excrement, others had already lost control; he didn't know if it was those ahead of him or those who had already died. He felt a desperate need not to lose control and have his mother get mad.

He tried to look at Roo, but suddenly he was stepping up on the box, a guard stepping up next to him to place the noose expertly around Erik's neck without hesitation, then step down without upsetting the box below Erik's feet. He tried to look over, but for some reason, he couldn't see Roo.

Erik felt himself tremble. He couldn't make his eyes work, and images of bright sky overhead and dark shadows under the walls made no sense. He heard a few mumbled prayers and what he thought was Roo's softly pleading ". . . No . . . please . . . no . . . please," over and over.

He wondered if he should say something at the end to his friend, but before he could think of anything to say, Robert de Loungville came to stand before the condemned men. With astonishing clarity, Erik could see every detail of this man who was to order his death. He had shaved in a hurry that morning, for a slight stubble had turned his cheeks dark, and there was a slight scar above his right eye Erik hadn't noticed before. He wore a fine red tunic, with a badge that Erik could now see depicted the Seal of Krondor, an eagle soaring over a peak above the sea. He had blue eyes and dark brows, and his hair needed to be trimmed. Erik wondered how he could see so much so quickly, and felt his stomach rebel. He was about to be sick from fear.

The only prisoner not slated to die was brought to stand beside de Loungville, who turned to him and said, "Watch this and learn something, Keshian."

Nodding once to the men on the gibbet, he ordered, "Hang them!"

Erik sucked in his breath in terror as he felt a powerful blow knock the box from beneath his feet. He heard Roo's shriek of terror, and then he fell.

The sky spun for Erik as he moved through the air. His only thought was of the blue above, and he heard himself cry, "Mommy!" as he felt his body hit the end of the rope. A sudden jerk made his skin burn as the rope tightened around his neck, then with another jerk he continued to fall. Instead of the expected crack of his own neck or the sudden choking as his windpipe was crushed, he felt a numbing slam along his face and body as he fell hard against the wooden floor of the gibbet.

Suddenly Robert de Loungville was shouting, "Get them to their feet!"

Rough hands dragged Erik upright, and with a half-dazed sense of being somewhere else, he looked around and saw stunned men returning his confused expression. Roo gaped like a just-landed fish and his face was sporting a red mark from where it had struck the boards. His eyes were puffy and red, and snot ran down from his nose as he cried like a baby.

Biggo glanced around, blood running from a cut on his forehead, as if trying to understand this evil prank that robbed him of his meeting with the Goddess of Death. The man next to him, Billy Goodwin, closed his eyes and sucked in breath as if he were still choking. Erik didn't know the name of the man at the far end of the gibbet, but he stood silently, his expression as stunned as the others'.

"Now listen, you swine!" commanded Robert de Loungville. "You are *dead men*!" He glanced from face to face. He raised his voice, "Do you understand me?"

They nodded, but it was clear none of them did.

"You are officially dead. I can have anyone who doubts my word hauled up again, and this time we'll tie the rope to the crosspiece of the gibbet. Or if you'd prefer, I will happily cut your throat."

Turning to the Keshian prisoner, he said, "Get over there with the others." The shackled men were being pulled roughly down the steps to stand next to the bodies of the dead.

Soldiers cut short the rope hanging from each of the five men, and two placed a similar noose around Sho Pi's neck. "You'll leave those on until I tell you to take them off," shouted de Loungville.

He came up to the five still-stunned men and looked each in the eyes as he walked slowly before them. "I own you! You're not even slaves! Slaves have rights! You have no rights. From now on, you will draw each breath at my whim. If I decide I don't want you breathing my air any longer, I'll have the guards close that noose around your neck and you will stop breathing. Do you understand me?"

Some of the men nodded, and Erik said, "Yes," softly.

De Loungville nearly roared when he said, "When I ask you a question, you will answer loudly so I can hear you! Do you understand me?"

This time all six men said, "Yes!"

De Loungville turned and began walking along before the men again. "I am waiting!"

It was Erik who said, "Yes, sir!"

Coming to stand before Erik, de Loungville put his face before Erik's, so their noses were less than an inch apart. "Sir! I am more than a sir, you toads! I am more than your mothers, your wives, your fathers, and your brothers! I am your god from this moment on! If I snap my fingers, you're dead men in truth.

Now, when I ask you a question, you will answer, 'Yes, Sergeant de Loung-ville!' *Is that clear!*"

"Yes, Sergeant de Loungville!" they said, almost shouting, despite raw throats from the mock hanging.

"Now load those men into the wagon, you swine," de Loungville commanded. "Each of you take one."

Biggo stepped forward, picked up the body of Slippery Tom, and carried him as a man might a child, loading him into the wagon. Two gravediggers stood in the charnel wagon and dragged the corpse deeper into the wagon bed to make room for the next.

Erik picked up a body, not sure what the man's name or crime had been, and carried it to the wagon, placing it where the gravediggers could grab it. He looked at the man's face and didn't recognize him. He knew it was one of six men he had seen for two days and probably spoken to, but he couldn't recall who this man was.

Roo looked down at the man at his feet, then tried to pick up the body. He struggled, tears from an apparently inexhaustible fount streaming down his face. Erik hesitated, then moved to help him.

"Get back there, von Darkmoor," commanded de Loungville.

"He can't do it," said Erik, discovering his voice still hoarse and his neck sore from the rope burn. De Loungville's eyes narrowed menacingly, and Erik quickly added, "Sergeant de Loungville!"

"Well, he'd better," said de Loungville, "or he'll be the first one of you sent back to hang." He pointed back up the steps with a dagger he now held.

Erik watched as Roo struggled to find strength enough to drag the corpse to the wagon. The ten feet must have looked like a mile. Erik knew Roo had never been a strong boy, and whatever vitality was usual, his had fled days before. He looked as if his arms were damp rope, and he had no power in his legs as he dragged hopelessly on the corpse.

Finally it moved, first a foot, then two, and after a moment more, another. Grunting as if he were carrying suits of armor up a mountain, Roo pulled until he got the body to the foot of the wagon. Then he collapsed.

De Loungville came to stand over him, crouching down so his face was level with Roo's. He shouted so loud he nearly screamed, "What? Do you expect those honest workmen to climb down from there and finish your job for you?" Roo looked up at the short man, silently pleading to die.

De Loungville reached down and gripped Roo by the hair, pulling him to his feet, holding the dagger to his throat. "You're not going to die, you useless piece of pig snot," he said, as if reading the boy's mind. "You're mine, and you will die when I tell you it is my pleasure that you die. Not before. If you die before I tell you, I will reach into the Death Goddess's hall and yank you back to life, and then *I* will kill you. I will cut your belly open and eat your liver for dinner if you don't do as I tell you. *Now get that dead meat into that wagon!*"

Roo fell backwards, hard against the wagon's tailgate, and barely kept himself from falling. He leaned down, got his arms under the body's arms, and heaved.

"You're no good to me, boy!" bellowed de Loungville. "If you don't get him in that wagon by the time I count to ten, you worthless slug, I'll cut your heart out before your eyes! One!"

Roo heaved and his face betrayed panic. "Two!" He forced his own weight forward, and got the corpse sitting up. "Three!"

He lifted with his legs and somehow got himself half turned around, so that the dead man rested against the tailgate. "Four!" Roo took a breath and heaved again, and suddenly the man was halfway into the wagon. "Five!" Roo let the body go and reached down quickly, gripping the corpse around the hips. He ignored the reek of urine and feces as he heaved with his last reserve of strength. Then he collapsed.

"Six!" screamed de Loungville, leaning over the boy, who sat at the base of the wagon.

Roo looked up and saw the man's legs were hanging over the end of the tailgate. He struggled to his feet as de Loungville shouted, "Seven!" and pushed as hard on the legs as he could.

They bent and he half pushed, half rolled the dead man all the way into the wagon as de Loungville reached the count of eight.

Then he fainted.

Erik took a step forward. De Loungville turned, took a single step, and delivered a backhanded blow to Erik that brought him to his knees. Lowering his head to lock gazes with the stunned Erik, Robert de Loungville said, "You will learn, dog meat, that no matter what happens to your friends, you will do what you're told when you are told and nothing else. If that's not the first thing you learn, you'll be crow bait before the sun sets."

Straightening up, he shouted, "Get them back to their cell!"

The still-stunned men moved raggedly along, not certain what had happened. Erik's ears rang from the blow to his head, but he risked a glance back at Roo and saw that two guards had picked him up and were bringing him along.

In silence the men were taken back to the death cell and herded in. Roo was unceremoniously tossed in, and the door slammed shut behind.

The man from Kesh, Sho Pi, came to look at Roo and said, "He'll recover. It is mostly shock and fear."

Then he turned to Erik and smiled, a dangerous look around his eyes. "Didn't I tell you it might be something else?"

"But what?" asked Biggo. "What was all this vicious mummery?"

The Keshian sat down, crossing his legs before him. "It was what is called an object lesson. This man de Loungville, who works, I imagine, for the Prince, he wishes you to know something without any doubt whatsoever."

"Know what?" asked Billy Goodwin, a slender fellow with curly brown hair.

"He wants you to know that he will kill you without hesitation if you do not do what he wants."

"But what does he want?" asked the man whose name Erik didn't know, a thin man with a grey beard and red hair.

Closing his eyes as if he were about to take a rest, Sho Pi said, "I do not know, but I think it will be interesting."

Erik sat back and suddenly giggled.

Biggo said, "What is it?"

Finding himself embarrassed before these men, he said, "I loaded my pants." Then he started to laugh, and the laughter had a hysterical edge to it.

Billy Goodwin said, "I dirtied myself, too."

Erik nodded, and suddenly the laughter was gone and he found to his amazement he was crying. His mother would be so angry with him if she found out.

Roo ROUSED WHEN food appeared, and to their astonishment it was not only abundant but good. Before, they had gotten a vegetable stew in a heavy beef stock, but now they were served steaming vegetables and slabs of bread, heavy with butter, and cheese and meat. Rather than the usual bucket of water, there were cold pewter mugs, and a large pitcher of chilled white wine—enough to slake thirst and ease the tension, but not enough to get anyone drunk.

They ate and considered their fortune.

"Do you think this is some cruel thing the Prince is doing to us?" asked the grey-bearded man, a Rodezian named Luis de Savona.

Biggo shook his head. "I'm a fair judge of men. That Robert de Loungville could be cruel like this if it suited his needs, but the Prince isn't that sort of man, I'm thinking. No, like our Keshian friend here says—"

"Isalani," corrected Sho Pi. "We live in the Empire, but we are not Keshian."

"Whatever," said Biggo. "What he said about this being a lesson is right. That's why we still have these on." He flipped the length of rope that still hung from around his neck. "To remind us we're officially dead. So that whatever happens next, we know that we're living on sufferance."

Billy Goodwin said, "I don't think they'll have to remind me anytime soon." He shook his head. "Gods, I can't remember what I was thinking when they kicked the box from under me. I was a baby again and waiting for my mum to come fetch me from some difficulty. I don't think I can tell what I felt like."

The others nodded. Erik felt tears start to gather as he remembered his own feelings as he fell. Pushing that aside, he turned to Roo. "How are you doing?"

Roo said nothing, only nodded as he ate.

Erik knew he was looking at something powerful changing in his friend, something was marking him and making him different from what he had known all his life in Ravensburg. He wondered if he was changing as much as his friend.

Guards arrived later to remove the trays and pitchers, and no one spoke. Soon the cells fell into darkness, and the single torch that illuminated the hall outside remained unlit.

"I think it's de Loungville's way of telling us to sleep as soon as we can," said Biggo.

Sho Pi nodded. "We will get an early start on whatever it is we do tomorrow, then." He curled up on the stone shelf and closed his eyes.

Erik said, "I'm not sleeping in my own filth." He removed his boots and trousers, then took them to the slops bucket and did his best to shake loose the dirt there, using a bit of the drinking water to clean them as best he could. It was a gesture, nothing more, and the pants were still dirty and again wet when he put them back on, but he felt better for trying.

Some others followed his example, as Erik nodded at Roo, who sank back into a corner with his arms wrapped around him, despite the fact it wasn't at all cold that night. But Erik knew his friend felt a chill inside that no fire would ever drive out.

Erik lay back, and to his astonishment felt a warm fatigue sink into his bones, and before he could ponder the amazing events of the day he was asleep.

"GET UP, YOU scum!" shouted de Loungville, and the prisoners stirred. Suddenly the cell erupted in a cacophony of sound as guards slammed shields against the iron bars and began to shout.

"Get up!"

"On your feet!"

Erik was standing before he was fully awake. He looked at Roo, who blinked like an owl caught in a lantern's light.

The door to the cell was opened and the men ordered out. They came to stand in the same order they had marched to the gibbet in, and waited without comment.

"When I give you the command to right turn, you will all turn as one and face that door. Understand?" The last word wasn't a question but a harsh command.

"Right turn!"

The men turned, feet shuffling, the shackles making any quick movement difficult. The door at the end of the cell block opened, and de Loungville said, "When I give the order, you will start forward, with your left foot, and you will march behind that soldier there." He pointed to a guardsman with the chevron of a corporal on his helm. "You will follow him in order, and any man who fails to keep his place will be back on the gallows within one minute. Are we clear on that?"

The men shouted, "Yes, Sergeant de Loungville!"

"March!"

The first man in line, Billy Goodwin, moved out, but it was obvious that Biggo and Luis didn't know their left from their right, and it was a ragged group that set out after the corporal. They followed through a long corridor, away from the courtyard where they had endured the false hanging the day before. They climbed a long flight of stairs and were taken into what appeared to be the palace proper. Their chains clanked as they moved quickly, and suddenly Erik was self-conscious, as they were hurried past some court officials who glanced at them and returned to whatever discussion they were having.

Erik realized he was still filthy, as were all the other five men, though Sho Pi was only in need of a bath. The rest had soiled their clothing and had infused it with the reek of terror. The bit of cleaning the night before had done nothing to rid the clothing of the stink. Usually untroubled by the smell of honest sweat, a constant companion to a blacksmith, Erik was now repulsed by the stench that intruded on his nose.

"In there," said de Loungville, and Erik realized it was the first time he had spoken in a calm voice in two days.

They entered a large chamber, with six steaming tubs of water, each as high as a man. The door was closed and Erik heard it bolted from outside. Guards came and unlocked the manacles and shackles. "Strip off those rags!" said the corporal.

Biggo started to remove the rope from around his neck, but de Loungville shouted, "Leave that there, swine! You're dead men and that's to remind you. Strip off the rest!"

The men removed their clothing. Erik put his boots in a corner, and watched as a serving boy gathered up the ragged, stinking clothing.

"You're going to meet someone very important," said de Loungville. "We can't have you stinking the place to high heaven. I don't mind, but I'm lowborn like you swine and have no tender ways; others aren't so tolerant." He motioned, and other boys, dressed in the livery of palace squires, carried buckets of soapy water. Without warning, they lifted the hot soapy water and poured it over Biggo and Billy Goodwin, and then returned to the tubs for more. "Wash down!" shouted de Loungville. "I want you as clean as you've ever been in your life!"

The men began to clean away weeks of grime, body filth, and stench. Harsh salves were brought to rub into their hair to rid them of any lice, and Erik thought he'd have no hair left, yet by the time they were done, he stood shivering but revived. He hadn't felt this clean since the night before he and Roo had killed Stefan.

He looked at Roo, who nodded and gave a pale imitation of his former smile. He hugged himself as water dripped off the only thing he wore, the noose around his neck. He had scant body hair, and Erik was astonished how much he looked like a little boy.

Clothing was produced, plain grey tunic and trousers, and Erik was allowed to reclaim his boots, as the others with footgear were. Biggo and Billy went barefoot.

They were lined up and inspected by Robert de Loungville, who said, "You will be allowed to go without chains for a while; the noise and sight of them might be offputting to some of the more tender-natured of those we are about to meet. But first you will follow me."

The corporal ordered them to return to line and they did so, falling in raggedly in the same order they had entered the bathing room.

They were marched to a small courtyard and there brought to a halt. Along the top of the wall, guards with crossbows were stationed, while every fifth man held a longbow. "Those fellows up there with the big bows are Pathfinders," said de Loungville. "They can hit a sparrow at a hundred yards. They're up there to keep any of you from becoming inspired during our next little demonstration."

He motioned and a guard handed him a sword. "Any one of you scum think they know how to use this?"

The prisoners looked at one another, saying nothing.

"Do you!" bellowed de Loungville into the face of Luis de Savona.

"I'm a fair hand with the sword, Sergeant," he said softly.

De Loungville reversed the sword and handed it to de Savona. "Then here's the deal. Run me through with this and you can walk out of the palace a free man."

De Savona looked around and, after a long moment, shook his head, throwing the sword to the ground.

"Pick that up!" raged de Loungville. "I'll tell you when to put something down! You pick up that sword and run me through with it, or I'll have that man up there"—he pointed to one of the Pathfinders—"put a clothyard shaft through your thick skull. Is that clear?"

De Savona said, "Either way I'm a dead man."

De Loungville came up to the taller Rodezian and shouted into his face, "Do you doubt my word? I said if you killed me you would be a free man! Are you saying I would lie to you?"

When de Savona said nothing, Robert de Loungville struck him across the face. "Are you calling me a liar?"

Luis bent, grabbed the sword, and as he came up, he moved forward. Lunging, he abruptly found de Loungville had easily sidestepped the sword, and suddenly he was on his knees, with de Loungville behind him, the noose now pulled tightly around his neck. As he struggled for air, de Loungville said, "I want you all to listen.

"Every man you meet from now on is your better. Each of them can take any weapon you have away from you like you were a baby. Each of them has proved himself a hundred times over to me, and I will grant any and all of them permission to cut your throat, strangle you, bludgeon you with a club, kick you to death, or whatever else they feel like if you so much as fart without my permission. Is that clear?"

The men mumbled something and he yelled, "I can't hear you!" De Savona was beginning to turn crimson from lack of air. "If he dies before I can hear you, you'll all hang."

"Yes, Sergeant de Loungville!" shouted the men, and de Loungville let go of the noose around de Savona's neck. The Rodezian lay gasping for breath, and after a moment he got to his feet and staggered into his place in line.

"Remember, *every* man you meet from now on is your better."

He motioned for the guards to move the men out, and the corporal let them back into the palace. They moved quickly through a long passage, and abruptly they were in what appeared to be a private quarter of the palace.

They were led into a good-size chamber, one far smaller than the grand hall where the court had been conducted, and there they saw the Prince of Krondor, Duke James, the strange woman who had come to see them and who had been at their trial, and other nobles of the court.

The woman stood stiffly, as if this was a difficult place for her to be, and she looked from face to face, and jerked slightly when she looked at Sho Pi. Some silent communication seemed to pass between them, and at last she turned to Lord James and the Prince and said, "I think they will do as you wish. May I be excused now, Sire?"

The Prince of Krondor said, "I can only imagine how difficult this was for you, my lady. You have my thanks. You may withdraw."

The Duke whispered to the woman a moment and she nodded and left the hall. De Loungville said, "Sire, the dead men are here."

The Prince said, "What you started was with my father's knowledge and permission, Bobby. I am still trying to make sense of it all."

James said, "Nicky, you've seen what the snakes can do with your own eyes. You were at sea when Arutha agreed to Calis and Bobby's plan. You'd still be at sea if we hadn't sent for you when your father died. Don't doubt for a moment it's necessary."

The Prince sat, took off the circlet of office he wore, and studied the prisoners, who waited silently. After studying them for a long moment, he said, "Was all *this* really necessary?"

James said, "It was. Every condemned man would lie to you about his willingness to serve. They'd give up their mothers when the box was being kicked from under their feet. No, these men are the six who could be trusted the most among those condemned to die."

Nicholas looked from face to face and said, "I still don't see the need for the charade at the gallows. Certainly that was cruel beyond reason."

De Loungville said, "Excuse me, Sire, but these men are now officially dead. I have made that abundantly clear to them all. They know that we can execute them at whim and they are to a man desperate to stay alive."

"What about the Keshian?" asked the Prince.

James answered. "He's something of a special case, but my wife feels he will be needed."

The Prince sat back and let out a long sigh. "Coming to this office wasn't easy. Borric agonized long hours about who should sit this throne until Prince Patrick is old enough to come take my place and I can return to the sea. That's three years of this.

"I'm a sailor, damn it. I haven't spent more than a month in port in twenty years. This administering . . ."

James smiled, the light in his eyes making him look far younger than his years. "You sound like Amos."

The Prince shook his head as a faint smile graced his lips. "I guess I do. He taught me all there was to know about the sea." He looked at the men. "Have they been told yet?"

Robert de Loungville said, "That's why they're here, Sire."

The Prince nodded to Lord James, who said, "Each of you men is being given a choice. Listen carefully, so you'll understand what is at stake."

Robert de Loungville said, "By the grace and generosity of His Highness, execution of your sentence has been postponed. You have not been pardoned, nor have you had your sentence commuted. Are you clear on this?"

The men glanced at one another, then several nodded.

James said, "You men will all die. The only question is how and when."

Robert de Loungville said, "The Kingdom needs something done. And we need desperate men who are willing to do it. To this end we have pulled you from the brink of death and we offer you this choice:

"Any man who is enough at peace in his conscience to face the Death Goddess can ask and we will take him from this hall to the gallows and execute him. That ends his worries in this lifetime."

He glanced around the room and no one said anything, not even the previously pious Biggo. "Good. You are going to be trained for this job that needs to be done, and when we are finished we are going to sail halfway around the world, and we are going to go places few men of the Kingdom have ever gone before and lived to tell about. And while we are going and while we are there, you may bloody well wish you had elected to go to the gallows this afternoon.

"But if we somehow get through it all and get back to Krondor . . ."

Nicholas said, "Your sentences will be reviewed and you will be paroled or pardoned, depending upon whatever recommendation Lord James makes to me."

"And that will depend on what recommendation is made by those who lead you," said James. "So if you have any hope in you that someday you might again be free, do as you are told."

The Prince nodded and de Loungville said, "Turn around!"

The prisoners did as they were commanded, and they were marched out of the hall. Instead of being returned to the prison block, they were taken to a small courtyard where a wagon waited. It was a shallow-bed affair with a buckboard, two drivers, and two benches in back where the men could sit three to a side, with a guard at the rear. A company of horse soldiers moved in to flank the wagon, and de Loungville shouted, "Get in that wagon!"

The men did as commanded, and soldiers quickly chained each prisoner's right ankle to an iron ring under the small seat. De Loungville mounted a horse brought to him by a groom and gave the order for the company to move out. The gates to the courtyard were opened, and as the wagon rolled through, Erik could see they were leaving by a gate that led to a small road. At the far end of the road they could see a private dock, which must be for the palace. They turned away from the dock and moved toward the city itself.

They reached a second gate, and guards swung this wide, letting the procession leave the palace grounds. The hooves of the horses beat a loud clang as iron struck paving stone, and the horses snorted to be outside and moving. Erik looked around. It was barely past noon. So much had passed since that first glimpse of sky at dawn.

The sun had burned off whatever morning fog and low clouds had gripped the city, and now a glorious fall day was upon them. Warm sunlight caressed his face as cool ocean breezes carried the sound of gulls and the tang of salt.

He remembered the stab of pain he had felt when he had thought he would not see the day, and the terror and panic that had gripped him as rough hands had placed him upon the gallows returned. Erik felt a choking sensation in his own chest, and suddenly, without any ability to control it, he began to weep.

Roo looked over and nodded, and tears began to run down his face, too, but no man in the wagon said anything, soldier or prisoner. After a few minutes, Erik got himself under control and he sat back, feeling the breeze cool him, and vowing to never again be that afraid.

9

★★

BREAKDOWN

ERIK GROANED.

He struggled to carry the bag of rocks up the hill, his feet slipping on the treacherous mound of stone. The hill was formed by the rocks being hauled by the six prisoners up its unstable side.

Reaching the top, Erik paused, took a deep breath as sweat poured down his face, and swung the heavy bag off his shoulder. He upended it and rocks went cascading down the side of the mound, causing those behind to curse as they were forced to dodge the stones. He knew the guards would allow him a moment to catch his breath before he negotiated his way down the dangerous stone mound to continue this pointless task.

He let his vision sweep the vista below. The mound of rocks rose up in the midst of a military camp. He had never seen a soldiers' compound, but he guessed this was unlike any other such installation in the world. A huge square, it was surrounded by wooden walls upon which sentries patrolled, as much to ensure no one approached from outside as to keep prisoners inside. A good three hundred yards of woodlands had been cleared around all sides, providing that no one could get close enough to the camp to witness what occurred inside.

In the midst of the camp were three large buildings, also fashioned from logs. Ten large tents, each designed for six men, were arrayed along the north wall of the compound. A familiar sound carried through the morning air, and Erik looked toward the southern wall, where stood an armory, leather shop, and cook shed.

"Von Darkmoor!" shouted a guard, and Erik realized he had lapsed into daydream. The next warning would be followed by a fowling blunt, an arrow with a hard ball of lead covered with leather that could break a man's arm if it struck there. Usually it just knocked the hapless target from the peak of the hill, followed by a rough ride down the rocky slope. That would be followed in turn by an equally rocky berating from Robert de Loungville.

The sergeant stood a short distance away, watching as the men moved slowly up the rock pile, trying not to dislodge stones onto the men behind. He spoke softly to the corporal, whose name was Foster. They pointed at various men as they struggled to get the rocks up the hill.

Roo moved toward Erik and he puffed mightily as he said, "Only two or three more trips, I figure."

The scrawny boy from Darkmoor had never been one for labor, Erik knew, but over the last week he had managed to keep up with the others. Part of it, Erik knew, was the food. None of them had ever eaten that well in their lives. And while they were roused from sleep at dawn, they turned in early enough so they were sufficiently rested.

Erik had felt his old strength return, and if anything he was even more fit than before. He and Biggo loaded up more than the others, because they could carry more, but every man pulled his share of rocks up that slope.

Erik made one more transit from the small mounds dumped by the wagon to the growing hill. When he got to the bottom, he saw Robert de Loungville wave him to stand near by. When all six prisoners were finished, standing in ragged line, de Loungville came up to them.

"Tired?" he asked, his face set in a friendly smile.

The men muttered they were and he nodded in understanding. "I bet," he said. "Could be you're as tired as you've ever been in your life?"

The men muttered agreement. He rocked back and forth a little on his feet, then shouted, "And what do you do when your enemy hits you when you're tired?"

Suddenly Erik was slammed into from behind, his assailant taking him down. A man in black moved away as Erik rolled over on his back, out of breath and heart pounding.

The others were likewise on the ground, save Sho Pi, who danced nimbly away as a black-clad man lay facedown in the dirt.

De Loungville said, "Here, now? How did you manage that?"

Sho Pi said, "By never for a moment assuming I'm safe, Sergeant."

De Loungville raised his brows and, with eyes wide with respect, nodded. "That is an attitude I can appreciate." He moved with almost a saunter as he approached Sho Pi. "You would do well," he said to the others, "to follow this man's example." Without warning he leveled a flying kick at Sho Pi's knees, which the Isalani deftly avoided.

Suddenly the Isalani was a blur of motion as he sidestepped the smaller but solid man. He kicked out with his right leg, and tattooed de Loungville with a series of kicks to the face and chest, then he swept with his leg, coming full circle, and took de Loungville's feet out from under him.

The men who were still on the ground laughed at the sight of their tormentor humbled, but that laughter turned to silence as two guards ran up pointing crossbows at Sho Pi, forcing him away from de Loungville.

Robert de Loungville sat up, shaking his head, and then jumped to his feet. "Did you think that was funny?"

None of the men spoke.

"I said, 'Did you think that was funny?' "

The men shouted, "No, Sergeant!"

De Loungville turned and said, "I'll show you something funny." His voice rose to the near shriek the men had become used to over the last week. "That pile of rocks is in the wrong place!"

Erik bit back a groan as he knew what was coming next. "You will take that pile apart and move it over there." De Loungville pointed to a place where the wagon, now empty, stood. "Then when I've decided exactly where I want the rocks, I'll have you move them again. Is that clear?"

Without thought Erik shouted, "Yes, sir!"

"Now get started."

Erik didn't look to see what the others were doing. He stood, shouldered his sack, and started to the pile of rocks. He reached the edge and bent over to pick up rocks, but de Loungville's voice cut the air. "From the top down, von Darkmoor! I want it moved from the top down!"

Erik winced, and without comment started the dangerous climb to the top of the rock pile. Halfway up the slope, Erik heard Billy Goodwin say, "I'd like one good shot at that bastard."

From even farther down the slope, Erik heard Biggo say, "With your luck you'd probably kick him in the heart and break your foot." Erik couldn't help but laugh, and suddenly he realized it was the first laugh he had experienced since Stefan had died. Suddenly his foot slipped and he half fell, slamming both knees into the rocks. As he winced in pain and regained his feet, he cursed the day he had first seen this camp, a week earlier.

Five miles to the east of Krondor, the wagon he had ridden in had turned south, leaving the heavily traveled road from Krondor to Darkmoor. But it wasn't the main road southeast that headed toward the Vale of Dreams and the border with Kesh. Rather, they had followed an old wagon trail to what looked to Erik to have once been a farming village near a small lake, surrounded on three sides by sheltering hills. The Crown had obviously taken over this area, for several guard posts had been erected along the way and three times they had been forced to stop while Robert de Loungville had shown proper passes. Erik had been curious, for with all the guards riding with them, and the tabards of the Prince's own Household Guard, the guards along the way had still appeared cautious.

The other thing that had piqued Erik's interest had been how veteran those soldiers guarding the way to this camp had appeared. All the men had been older; not one smooth cheek in the crew, and many had borne scars. And most wore differing tabards, some the black with the golden eagle of Bas-Tyra, others the golden gull on brown of Crydee.

A guard sergeant at the gate had greeted de Loungville by name, many calling him Bobby, but still looked over his pass. Once inside the compound, Erik and the others had their first glimpse of the camp. A dozen men, all wearing black tunics and trousers, had been practicing with bows in a corner of the compound as the wagon had rolled through the gate, and as the large doors were swung shut, Erik caught sight of a dozen more practicing their horsemanship. He had gawked as the wagon had ground to a halt and the prisoners had been unchained.

The men had been forced to run from the wagon to stand in front of the main building for over an hour, toward what end Erik had never understood.

As he had waited, he had reveled in the simple fact of still being alive. His experience on the gallows had left him alternating between black depression and giddy elation. He had entered the compound in good spirits, which hadn't worn off as he had waited before the nameless building.

De Loungville had gone inside for over an hour and had returned with a man who appeared to be some sort of chirurgeon, who had examined all the prisoners and had made several comments on their condition Erik hadn't understood. For the first time in his life he had some sense of how horses felt when he examined them for fitness.

The prisoners had been run through some strange drills and asked to march around. This had brought rude comments and mocking observations from those men in black who were standing around while the prisoners drilled.

At the end of the day, they had been ordered to the second large building, the mess. Fully half the tables were unoccupied after the men in black were seated. Young boys in the livery of squires of the Prince's court in Krondor raced between the tables heaping abundance beyond Erik's dreams on them. Breads, hot and slathered with butter, pitchers of cow's milk, cooled by ice brought down by riders from the nearby mountains. Meats—chicken, beef, and pork—surrounded by vegetables of every description were set down next to platters of cheese and fruit.

Erik was suddenly hungry beyond belief and ate.

He lay almost comatose in a tent next to Roo that night.

The next morning, training had begun, and they had been ordered to build the mountain. Robert de Loungville had ordered them to pick up seemingly endless piles of rocks and move them half the distance across the compound to build this hill.

His reverie was broken by Sho Pi saying, "I apologize."

Erik reached the peak and, as he knelt and started filling the bag with rocks, said, "For what?"

"My temper got the best of me. Had I let him knock me down, we would not have to do this over."

Erik finished loading up his sack. "Oh, I think he'd have found a reason. You just provided a convenient excuse."

Moving carefully down the hill as Sho Pi took his place at the summit, Erik said, "It was worth it to see him dumped on his prat."

"I trust you feel that way tomorrow, friend Erik."

Despite aching shoulders and legs and black-and-blue marks all over his body from the constantly rolling rocks, Erik knew he would.

"GET OUT OF there, you dogs!"

Erik and Roo were out of their bedding and on their feet before they were fully awake. Corporal Foster looked at the six men. Billy Goodwin, Biggo, and Luis were on one side of the large tent, while Erik and Roo were on the other with Sho Pi. All six stood at what they had come to learn was the approved stance, what the soldiers called "at attention," head back, eyes forward, hands to either side of them, palms in, feet at an angle together at the heels, each man before the foot of his wood and straw bed.

If this morning was like the others, they would be working for an hour or so before the morning meal, when they would be required to sit in silence at a table removed from the forty or so men who occupied the compound. They had been forbidden to speak to the other men, and those black-clad soldiers had shown no inclination to speak to the prisoners.

That they were soldiers was beyond doubt to Erik. They spent long hours drilling, climbing the wooden walls, jumping barricades, riding horseback, practicing with all manner of weapons.

Instead of being returned to the rock hill, for their third day of moving the rocks to Robert de Loungville's newly chosen location, they were marched before the big building where Erik was now convinced the officers lived. They were told to stand at attention and wait, while de Loungville entered the building.

A few minutes later he reemerged with another man behind. The second man struck Erik as looking somewhat odd, though he couldn't place why. He was slender, blond, and youthful—no more than twenty or twenty-five years of age—but de Loungville showed obvious deference to him as they spoke.

"These are the last six," he said. The blond-haired man nodded, saying nothing. "I don't like this," de Loungville continued. "We planned for sixty men, not thirty-six."

The other man spoke at last, and there was something strange in his speech: soft and well mannered, yet different from what Erik had heard among the nobles and wealthy merchants of Darkmoor and Ravensburg. Erik had heard a lot of foreign accents in his day, but he couldn't place this one. "Agreed, but conditions force us to make do with what we have. What about these?"

"They have promise, Calis, but we've months of training ahead."

"Who are they?" asked the man called Calis.

Robert de Loungville moved before Biggo. "This one's called Biggo. Strong as an ox and almost as intelligent. Quicker than he looks. Calm—doesn't rattle easily."

He stepped before the next. "Luis de Savona. Rodezian cutthroat. Likes to use a knife. Handy where we're going."

Then he said, "Billy Goodwin. Looks like a simple lad, but he'd cut your throat for the fun of it. Too mean when angered, but he can be broken."

He came to stand before Erik. "This is von Darkmoor's bastard. Probably too stupid to live, but he's almost as strong as Biggo and he'll do as he's told."

Then he was before Roo. "Rupert Avery. He's a sneaky little rodent, but he's got potential." He then grabbed Roo's ever-present noose and pulled him forward, almost off balance, as he shouted into his face, "If I don't kill him first for being so damned ugly!"

Then he let go and Roo almost fell backwards overcompensating, as de Loungville stepped before Sho Pi. "This is the Keshian I told you about. Could be very useful to us if he can learn to keep his temper. More dangerous than Goodwin; this one doesn't show it when he's getting angry."

Then he turned to the six prisoners. "Do you see this man, here?" asked de Loungville.

The prisoners said, "Yes, Sergeant!"

De Loungville said, "Be afraid of him. Be very afraid." He looked from face to face. "He is not what he seems. He is the Eagle of Krondor, and wise men keep out of sight when he flies above."

Calis indulged himself in a slight smile at the rhetoric, nodded, and said, "You men will live or die as the Kingdom requires. I will see you dead before I will let you jeopardize the mission we will be upon. Is this understood?"

The men nodded. They had no idea what mission they were to be a part of, but it had been driven home daily that it was vital to the interests of the Kingdom and that each of them would instantly be killed if they appeared in any way to threaten its success. Erik was certain he had never been more convinced of any single fact in his life than he was of this.

Calis studied each face, then said, "You have two weeks, Bobby."

"Two weeks! I was to have three more months!"

With a hint of a distant sadness, Calis said, "Arutha is dead. Nicholas was not told of his father's plan until the day after hearing of his death. It was a shock. He's not convinced of the wisdom of what we do." He turned and looked at de Loungville. "Two weeks, and any man who isn't reliable, hang him." Without another word he returned inside the building.

De Loungville glanced from face to face one more time, then said, "Be very afraid."

THE NEXT MORNING, the hill of rocks was gone. The men in black had been ordered to remove it, and thirty of them had made quick work of the pile. Erik and the others had been taken to another part of the compound by Corporal Foster.

He had stood before them and said, "Any of you murdering mother-lovers think you know how to handle a sword?"

The men glanced at one another, but no one spoke. They had learned within a few hours of arriving at camp that when Foster or de Loungville asked a question, you had better be absolutely sure of the right answer if you opened your mouth.

"I thought so," said Foster. "Easy enough to club a man from behind in an alley, eh, Biggo?" He grinned without humor.

Foster moved down the line. "Or slip a dagger into a man's back when he's drunk in a tavern, eh, Luis?"

When he got to Erik he said, "Or you can just hold him from behind while your little rat-faced sweetheart sticks a knife into his gut."

Erik said nothing. De Loungville had a harsh nature and was a tyrant, but didn't seem to find particular pleasure in his work. Corporal Foster seemed to enjoy insulting the prisoners. Billy Goodwin had lost his temper with Foster the second day and had endured the humiliation of being soundly drubbed by the experienced soldier before the entire company in the compound. The men in black had gathered to laugh at the thrashing.

Two soldiers approached, each carrying three swords. "Well," said Foster, "these two lads and myself are going to attempt to show you a thing or two about using this weapon, so you don't hurt yourself if you happen to find one in your hand someday." Taking out his own sword, he said, "Better men than you have managed to cut off their own foot."

The soldiers passed out a blade to each man. Erik held his awkwardly. It was a common Kingdom shortsword, heavier than the fast rapier, shorter than the broad-, bastard-, and greatswords used by some fighters. It was, he had been told as a boy, the simplest weapon to train with.

"Pay attention," said de Loungville. "Your life will certainly depend on it."

So began an intensive week of arms study. For a half day they stood in the yard, slamming away at one another with wooden practice weapons, until every one of them was covered in black-and-blue welts. Then, after the midday meal, they were taken to the stable area.

"Who's a rider here?" asked de Loungville.

Erik and Luis raised their hands. Two horses were led toward them, and de Loungville said, "Get aboard and let's see what you know."

Luis quickly mounted, but Erik walked around his horse and inspected the animal.

De Loungville said, "Waiting for him to invite you up, von Darkmoor?"

Ignoring the sarcasm, Erik said, "This animal isn't sound."

"What?" asked Robert de Loungville. "He looks sound enough to me."

"He's off in the left rear." Erik reached down and ran his hand along the animal's left rear leg, and the gelding obligingly raised his foot. A thick mat of dirt, hay, and dung was packed in the hoof. Erik reached for a pick that hadn't been on his belt for a month, and smiled to himself ruefully. "Old habits." He looked up. Without a word one of the two grooms handed Erik a hoof pick and he pulled the mass loose. Even standing a few feet back, de Loungville could smell the stink.

Erik held the hoof, inspecting it. "Thrush. That won't make him lame until the hoof rots off, but there's certainly something else here." Erik dug into the frog and the horse protested and began to pull away. "Hold!" shouted Erik and gave the horse a backward slap with his hand, more an admonishment than any real punishment. Sensing he was being treated by someone who knew what he was doing, the horse quieted, though he obviously wasn't pleased. "Got a rock here, small one, but in there good." Suddenly it popped out and blood and pus oozed after it. "A couple of days of soaking that hoof a time or two in hot salty water should fix him right up. Just needs to be packed with poultice to keep it from festering." He let go of the leg. "Someone's not taking proper care of these horses, Sergeant."

De Loungville said, "Someone is going to find himself shipped back to the Shamata garrison at first light tomorrow if there's one other lame horse in that stable tonight!" To one of the grooms he shouted, "Bring another mount."

As the horse was led away, de Loungville asked, "How did you know?"

Erik shrugged. "It's what I do. I'm a blacksmith. I can see little things most don't notice."

De Loungville rubbed his chin as he thought, then softly he said, "Get back in line."

While waiting for a fresh mount to be brought, de Loungville said, "Let me see you take the yard at a trot, de Savona!"

Luis moved the horse easily forward and Erik nodded slightly in approval. The Rodezian had a good seat and didn't saw at the horse's mouth. He overbalanced a little and his legs were somewhat out of position, but overall he was a fair rider.

The afternoon wore on, with each of the men taking a turn at riding. Roo sat well enough, despite his having little experience, and Sho Pi seemed to have a natural aptitude—good balance and a relaxed seat. Biggo and William were both tossed before they made it halfway around the compound, and by the end of the day, every man but Erik and Luis was complaining of muscles in his legs he never knew existed now stretched and beaten.

FOR THE FIRST three days after meeting Calis, Erik and the other five prisoners were put through intensive weapons training as well as at least two hours of riding each day. Erik was developing a fair sense of how to use a sword, as was Roo, who used his quickness to good advantage.

No one asked, but it was clear that they were being trained for combat and that their ability to prove something to Robert de Loungville was critical to their future survival. No one spoke of Calis's final instruction to de Loungville, that any man found unreliable was to be hung.

No one cared to speculate on what would constitute reliability in two weeks' time.

Each man's strengths and weaknesses began to emerge as the week wore on. Biggo was fine as long as he had clear instructions, but when something unexpected arose, he was indecisive. Roo was daring, and took chances, and as often as not received lumps and bruises for his troubles.

Billy Goodwin lost his temper in a blind rage, while Sho Pi lost his temper and became intensely focused, in a fashion that made Erik consider him the most deadly of the company.

Luis de Savona was a fair swordsman—though he claimed he excelled with the dagger—and a decent horseman, but his vulnerability was his vanity. He could not say no to any challenge.

Sho Pi was naturally gifted and never repeated a lesson. He sat effortlessly in the saddle and used a sword easily mere hours after having been shown what to do.

Five days after Calis had inspected them, training in the camp changed. The six prisoners were ordered out with an equal number of men in black, and the dozen of them were marched to a distant area of the compound, where two soldiers waited, wearing the brown and gold tabard of the Duchy of Crydee. On the ground before them lay a host of strange-looking objects, some which appeared to be weapons, others which were incomprehensible.

The two soldiers, a captain and a sergeant, began a lecture on these alien weapons, quickly demonstrating what each was capable of doing. After that demonstration was over, the men were marched to another area, where a man who appeared to be a priest of Dala began to instruct them in the basics of caring for wounds.

By the end of the day, Erik had a firm picture in his mind of one thing: they were going to war. But from the unspoken urgency of each man's instruction this day, they were going into war with a dearth of preparation.

THE SOUND OF horses whinnying in greeting brought Erik awake. He rolled from his bunk and moved aside the door flap of the tent. Looking out, he saw a company of Royal Krondorian Lancers entering the compound, some distance away. He glanced toward the east and saw the sky already lightening. They would be roused from sleep in another hour.

He started to return to bed, but something caught his attention. For a moment he stared at it without recognition, then it struck him. He watched until he was almost sure of what he saw, then moved to Roo's bunk. Kneeling, he shook his friend awake, covering his mouth to keep him from waking the others. In the gloom he made a motion for his friend to follow him.

They crept out of the tent, and then Roo said, "What?"

"Miranda. She just rode in with a company of Royal Lancers."

"Are you certain?" said Roo.

"No—that's why I'm going to get a closer look."

Erik turned and, hunkering down so those marching post on the wall wouldn't notice him, moved off. The sentries weren't there to keep Erik and the others inside, he was now certain, but to ensure no one outside got close.

The two young men circled around to the far side of what Erik had come to think of as the officers' quarters; at least, that was where de Loungville retired every night, and where Calis seemed to reside. They ducked along, keeping away from the line of lancers, who sat their horses easily as they turned their mounts around and began riding back toward the gate. Erik glanced at them long enough to realize they weren't heading out again, merely moving away from the command building. Erik had a suspicion but said nothing to Roo.

The two of them darted along behind the building, and crept under a window. Faint voices carried. Erik motioned for Roo to remain silent and moved to another window. Here he could barely make out the sound of conversation.

". . . need to be gone before the camp rises. Every man here has seen me at least once. It would not do for my presence to be detected. Too many questions."

A man's voice—Erik thought it sounded like Calis—answered: "I agree. Something urgent must have brought you here. What is it?"

"Nicholas received a warning from the Oracle. She begins her mating with the eldest of her attendants, and the new Oracle will be conceived this summer."

Calis was silent a moment, then said, "I know as much about the Lifestone as any living, Miranda, save those who saw it at Sethanon. I'm not certain I appreciate the significance of what you tell me, though."

Miranda laughed, and Erik thought it a sound without humor. "It seems that as we embark on this dangerous course, the Oracle of Aal begins a mating, birth, and death cycle that will take the better part of five years. In other words, just as we seek to end the danger to the Lifestone, the Oracle is going to mate, give birth to her successor, and die. We will be without the oracle's visions for the next twenty-five years, until the daughter reaches maturity."

Calis said, "I know little of the Ancients of Aal, save the legends about them. I take it this mating is a surprise to you?"

Miranda mumbled something Erik couldn't hear, then said, ". . . the limit of seeing one's own future, I suppose. A rebirth that limits the Oracle's abilities for a twenty-five-year period once every thousand years is little more than an inconvenience, from that perspective, but it's certainly ill timed from ours."

"Is Nicholas thinking of canceling our plans?"

Miranda said, "I don't know. I can't read him as I could his father. He's so much like him in some ways, yet so different in others. I've only met him twice before, and I have no doubt he would have little trust for me were it not for you and James vouching for me."

"You've convinced us of your sincerity and commitment to stop the enemy, even if you're damn unbending in revealing much about yourself." He paused a moment. "What's the upshot of all of this?" asked Calis.

"It means we need to move even sooner than we thought. It means you should dismantle this camp starting today and have your ships ready to depart next week."

Calis was silent. Then he said, "I have six men who are not trained, and we're barely half the number we had planned on. I cannot depend on hired mercenaries. Too many good men died last time because I made that mistake. I need—" He stopped himself. "You know all the arguments. Bobby and I made them to Arutha three years ago. If we must go with only thirty-six men, I will take the next nine days to evaluate the last six. I'll hang them myself before I'll let them become a weak link in the chain we're forming, but I'll at least give them that little bit of time to prove themselves."

Miranda's voice rose. "I have been through a great deal to select these men, Calis. I think I know each one well. I think you have only two who might break, Goodwin and de Savona. The others will do as we need."

"Might break," he repeated. "That's the problem. You think. If I knew they would break, I'd execute them tonight. If I knew they would stand fast, I would leave tomorrow. But if we judge wrong, and if one of them breaks at the wrong time . . ."

"Nothing is certain."

There was a dry chuckle and Calis said, "Working with an oracle has given us something of a false illusion of certainty, I'm afraid. If we return to the certainty that nothing is clear before it happens, we might survive this venture."

"I'm leaving. If you insist on lingering the next nine days, so be it, but Nicholas is adamant we should move as soon as possible. We've captured two agents and they know we're up to something."

"Dead?"

"Now they are. Gamina read both men before they died and found out little we didn't already know, but it's clear the snakes are closing in on this facility. You've done well covering your tracks for the last year, but now they know something unusual is happening outside of Krondor. The next bunch of spies they send won't be sniffing around the palace, they'll be out here in the woods looking for this encampment. Once they discover it was here—"

"We've taken every precaution."

"Someone who loaded a wagon of beef will say something in an inn. Someone at the palace will let a list of prisoners be seen while he's out of an office. It will take time, but within a year, not only will the snakes know you're in their way again, they'll have the name of every man with you."

Calis was silent, then said something Erik couldn't make out. Suddenly there was a sound of a door opening and closing, and Erik motioned for Roo to follow him in a hurry. They returned the way they went and made it back to their tent. Moving back to their bunks, Erik was silent for a moment as he caught his breath; then he woke Biggo. "Quiet. Wake the others."

When Luis, Sho Pi, and Billy were awake, Erik said, "Some time before you were caught, did you run into a woman named Miranda?"

The four looked at one another, and it was Sho Pi who spoke first. "Dark of hair and with intense green eyes?" Erik nodded. "She spoke to me outside of Shamata, while I was on the road to Krondor. There was something about her that I noticed at once. She has power."

"What did she tell you?"

Sho Pi shrugged. "We talked of things of little importance. I found her very beautiful and was flattered at the attention, but her interests seemed more abstract than carnal. And I was curious why I sensed she was so much more than she seemed."

"Was there anything she said that got you tossed into jail?"

Sho Pi said, "Nothing I can remember."

The others talked about their encounters, Billy and Luis saying she had used a different name, but it was clear that all six men had encountered the woman at some point, less than a month prior to being arrested.

Biggo said, "That girl gets around, if she was talking to you"—he pointed at Sho Pi—"at Shamata the week before running into Erik and Roo near Darkmoor."

"How does she know us?" asked Luis.

Erik said, "It has something to do with an oracle who reads the future. We're important in some way, but only if we survive the next nine days. I don't know why we were saved from the gallows, and I don't know what we might be to these people if we continue to live, but I have no doubt of this: if Calis thinks we're dangerous to his plans, he'll hang us all before he breaks camp in nine days. If he thinks we're trustworthy, he'll keep us alive. It's that simple."

Billy said, "It means we've got to work hard."

"We've been breaking our backs!" complained Luis.

"I mean work hard at being what they want."

Sho Pi said, "Billy is right; he and I must stem our temper." He rose and returned to his own bunk, where he sat back, resting on his elbows. "Biggo must begin to show he can think for himself."

"What of me?" said Luis, obviously fearful of not being judged trustworthy in nine days' time.

"You must put aside your pride. You must stop acting as if every order is an insult, and every task beneath you. Your arrogance will get you hung."

"I am not arrogant!" demanded Luis, obviously ready to take offense.

Erik saw a fight coming and, thinking quickly to stem it, he said, "There's more!"

"What?" said Biggo.

"If one of us fails, we all fail."

"What!" said Billy.

"If one of us is judged unworthy, they're going to hang all six of us."

Roo looked at Erik a moment, then nodded. "We're a team. We live or die as one."

Luis glanced around the tent and saw all eyes upon him. "I . . . will work on humility. When that little *cabrone* tells me to shovel dung, I will cheerfully say, *Sí, me comandante.* How high?"

Biggo grinned. "If there's a stiffer-necked bunch around than you bloody Rodezians, it's them Tsurani up in LaMut, but not by much." Looking at Sho Pi, he said, "I've gotten by for years playing dumb so that folks won't expect much of me. I guess it's a habit now. I'll try to look a little brighter."

Sho Pi said, "And you, Rupert. You must stop trying to be so clever. It will get you killed. You are not as clever as you think, nor are others as stupid."

Erik said, "What of me?"

Sho Pi said, "I do not know, Erik von Darkmoor. There is nothing you do that is obviously wrong. Yet . . . there is something. I do not know. A hesitancy, perhaps. You need to be more decisive."

Further discussion was halted by the arrival of Corporal Foster, and the men leaped up to stand before their beds. The corporal looked around, for obviously something had been occurring just before he arrived, but nothing was obvious, so after a moment he shouted, "All right. Outside and fall in, you worms! We don't have all morning!"

★★

FOSTER STOOD OVER Billy, screaming insults at him. The prisoner looked as if he was about to leap to his feet and attack the corporal. A man in black stood not ten feet away puffing heavily from the exertion of the recently ended combat. They had been dueling, with Billy getting the upper hand, when suddenly Foster had tripped Goodwin. Then, before he could react, the corporal was standing over him as if it were Billy's fault.

Then Foster said, "And your mother was a whore!"

As he turned away, Billy leaped to his feet. Before he could charge Foster, Erik hit him with a tackle, driving his shoulder into Billy's waist. They went to the ground and rolled, Erik using his strength and weight to keep Billy under him.

Suddenly soldiers were hauling them apart and Foster was shouting, "Here, now! What's this about?"

Erik, blood running from his nose from one of Billy's elbows, said, "Keeping him from doing something stupid, Corporal."

Foster regarded Erik a moment, then said, "Right." Turning to Billy, he said, "Going to jump me from behind, you swine? Well, how'd you like to try it from in front?" He backed away, pulling his own sword. "Let him go."

The soldiers obeyed and Billy stood with his own weapon ready. Then Biggo stepped between him and the corporal. "Wouldn't be smart for Billy, would it, Corporal, what with those lads on the wall unlimbering their bows, and all, would it?"

Billy glanced up and saw that a pair of longbowmen had strung their weapons and nocked arrows, and were watching closely.

"Stand away, Biggo, you overblown pile of cow dung!" commanded Foster. "I'm going to cut a few pieces off this dogmeat."

Luis came over to stand next to Biggo, with Sho Pi a step behind. Roo joined them, and Erik shook off the two soldiers who held him and joined the other five.

"What's this—mutiny?" shouted Foster.

"No," answered Sho Pi. "Just trying to keep the situation from becoming dangerous."

"I'll have that man hung!" shouted Foster as Robert de Loungville approached to see what was occurring.

Biggo said, "Then I think you should hang us all."

Robert de Loungville said, "What's this, then? Volunteering to go back to the gibbet?"

Biggo turned and with an affable smile said, "Sergeant, if one of us is to be hung for thinking we'd like to murder the good corporal, then you'd better hang us all, because we all think it at least a dozen times a day. And I'd rather you get it over with now than make us work for another week at this soldier drilling; I'm kind of tired of it. With all respect, Sergeant."

De Loungville raised his eyebrows in surprise. "This man speaking for you all?"

They looked from one to another. Then Erik said, "I think that's the way it is, sir."

Suddenly de Loungville was standing nose to nose with Biggo, having to rise up on his toes to accomplish the feat. "You're not being told to think! What makes you imagine we care what you think? If you're thinking, that means you have *too much time on your hands*. I can fix that."

Turning to the two guards who had held Erik a moment before, he said, "We need the stables swept. Get these murderous dogs down there and have them pick up everything they find! And I don't want them dirtying perfectly good brooms and pitchforks! They can pick everything up by hand! Now move them out!"

The two soldiers motioned for the prisoners to fall in and quick-marched them out of sight. As they vanished, Foster looked at de Loungville and said, "I think it's starting to work, Bobby."

De Loungville scratched his chin as he pondered. "I don't know. We'll see. But it had better. We're going south short-handed and I'd hate to have to hang this lot the day before we sail."

Foster said, "If Billy Goodwin didn't cut my throat for calling his mother a whore—she was, but he's touchy about it—then I think he's learning. And the way they stuck up for him."

De Loungville nodded. "Maybe you're right. Or maybe they're being clever. We'll have to see, won't we?"

Without waiting for an answer, he turned and headed back to the command building.

10

★★

TRANSITION

THE ALARM SOUNDED.

Drums beat as the camp turned out. It had been three days since Erik had overheard the discussion in Calis's office, and the six prisoners had been training hard, focusing their attentions on doing whatever was necessary to remain alive. Foster became even more of a tyrant, abusing the men at every turn, and de Loungville studied them closely, looking for any sign they might fail to meet his demands.

Now a new day began with an unexpected twist. The prisoners moved out of their tent a good half hour earlier than usual and saw that the other men who lived in the compound were all hurrying to the command building. As they followed, they were intercepted by a guard, a soldier named Perry of Witcomb, who said, "Fall in behind me, and stay together. No talking!"

The six fell into their usual order, with Biggo at the lead and Sho Pi at the rear, Billy, Luis, Roo, and Erik in between. They reached the building as the door opened and Calis and de Loungville emerged.

De Loungville held his hand up for silence and said, "Listen up!"

Calis said, "We've been discovered. Two of our sentries were killed last night."

A muttering broke out among the men in black, and de Loungville had to call for quiet again. Calis continued, "You all know what to do; we break camp now."

Instantly the thirty men in black raced to their tents and the majority of soldiers began hurrying to their assigned places. Foster turned to Perry of Wit-comb and gave instructions. The soldier gestured to the six prisoners and said, "You lot, come with me."

They followed the soldier through the frantic but organized activity, and he led them to a large tent not far from the blacksmith's shop. "Find clothing that fits," he ordered, "and put it on."

The six entered and in the gloom saw a pile of common clothing. Erik stripped off his boots and then his tunic and trousers, throwing the ragged grey garments into the corner. He joined the others in rummaging through the pile, picking up tunics and judging their size, casting aside those that were obviously too small. Luis and Billy as well as Sho Pi found clothing quickly, being of more average size. But Roo, because of his diminutive stature, and Biggo and Erik, because of their bulk, took longer to find clothing that fit. Eventually, all six stood wearing fresh garments. Erik had found a dark blue tunic with an open collar and long sleeves. A pair of sailor's trousers were the only pair of pants he could find that fit. He gave up trying to push the flared legs into the top of his boots, and let them fall outside.

Laughter caused Erik to turn and there he saw Roo with an angry expression. "It's the only one that fits!" he said as Billy and Luis made rude observations. The shirt was open to the waist, and a lurid purple color. Making matters worse, the only pair of trousers small enough were a bright crimson.

"Then pick one that doesn't fit," said Erik, trying hard not to laugh.

Roo peeled off the offending shirt and looked some more, finding a plain white tunic that was only slightly too large. He tucked the voluminous tails of the shirt into his loud red waistband and Erik nodded. "Now you look only slightly ridiculous instead of completely ridiculous."

Roo grimace, then smiled. "Red's my lucky color."

"Get out of there!" called Perry and the prisoners came out of the tent. "Get to the smithy, and get aboard the last wagon in line. There will be two mounted crossbowmen behind you, so don't imagine you'll get a chance to go for a stroll."

He started to move away, then turned and said, "And tuck those nooses out of sight."

The six prisoners had grown used to being required to wear the nooses at all times, outside their tunics. They had put them back on after changing. Now they tucked them inside, so they wouldn't be seen.

Biggo had to quickly strip off his tunic and put on the noose, then put the tunic on, as the neck of his shirt was close-fitting. Luis said, "A bit lumpy for high fashion, my friend, but it will do."

Since coming to the compound from the prison, Erik had noticed Luis was vain—in addition to having a temper and being arrogant—but he still found himself liking the Rodezian knife man. He had shaved off his grey beard, but let his mustache grow, as well as keeping his shoulder-length hair neatly trimmed. Luis was becoming something of a peacock. The clothing he had selected were as fashionable as possible, given the choice. Erik had no doubt Luis was not simply speaking of high fashion in the abstract but was a man who had dressed for court functions before his temper and violent nature had brought him to low estate. He had said nothing of his past, but once had mentioned having been friends with the son of the Duke of Rodez.

They hurried to the smithy and Erik noticed with a sense of awe just how fast the forge and other equipment were being carried out of the building. Everywhere they looked, men were hurriedly tearing down all signs of occupation. Newcomers to the camp, workmen from somewhere—probably Krondor— were now starting to tear apart the three buildings that dominated the compound. Foster was waiting for them at the smithy and motioned for them to climb into a wagon. Two guards sat atop the buckboard and two more climbed in after the prisoners, who sat three to each side of the wagon as they had when arriving. Two more guardsmen, on horseback, moved in behind the wagon, and they set out.

Erik glanced around. Roo seemed half-excited, half-afraid of the significance of what was occurring. Luis watched carefully, as did Biggo. Billy seemed amused, and Sho Pi was looking off into the distance.

Some of the men whom Erik recognized as having been dressed in black were now dressed as were the prisoners, in a variety of clothing, ranging from almost ragged to nobles' finery. Some rode on horseback and others in wagons and more than a dozen were leaving the compound by foot. Two more riders approached, and Erik saw they were Robert de Loungville and Corporal Foster.

De Loungville pulled up next to the wagon and said, "All right, listen up. I was talking to Calis about hanging you all this morning, but we couldn't take the time. Nothing spoils my breakfast like a rushed hanging. Calis agrees with me that we can do it later when we can be more leisurely and do things properly. You men are going to live a few days longer. But don't think we've fallen in love with you; those two lads behind you with the crossbows have orders to shoot any one of you foolish enough to try to get down from this wagon. Understood?"

"Yes, Sergeant!" they all said.

"And another thing, until I tell you, no more of that shouting 'Yes, Sergeant.' It'll call attention to you. And attention's too much of what we have right now. So keep your mouths shut and do as you're told until we get where we're going." Without another word, he put heels to his horse and cantered off. Foster followed, only a length behind.

Erik looked around and noticed no one else seemed willing to risk a crossbow bolt by saying anything, so he settled down as best he could in the jouncing wagon and tried to relax.

★★

Along the road to Krondor they passed groups of men on foot, many dressed as common mercenaries, farmers, or laborers. Others rode in wagons and kept to themselves. A few passed by on horseback, each appearing oblivious to the others.

Other traffic appeared on the road, heading toward the capital of the Western Realm. Farm wagons heavy with late summer crops and the first of the early fall harvest rumbled toward Krondor. Traders with their goods piled high and the occasional noble's carriage joined the traffic.

There was no roadblock, and Erik and the others moved rapidly down the road leading to the southern gate to the city, the one closest to the palace in which they had all been condemned to die. In the midday light, the palace looked splendid, rising up as it did above the harbor. Towers were aflutter with banners, and the city spread majestically around the ancient hill upon which the first keep of the first Prince of Krondor had been constructed.

At the southern gate, guards waved them through, and the wagon started a convoluted course through the city. At last they entered the docks area near the poor quarter, and Foster suddenly appeared. Without raising his voice, he said, "You lot, get out of that wagon and get into that boat down there." He pointed to a longboat that bobbed on the tide at the bottom of a flight of stone stairs leading down from the quayside. Erik and the others hurried down the stone steps and entered the boat, each being told where to sit by a pair of sailors. As soon as Roo, last to enter, was seated, Foster joined them and the sailors pushed off. Expertly the two sailors rowed the longboat toward a ship in the harbor.

Erik knew nothing of ships. But this one dwarfed most of those nearby. It had three masts, rising high into the sky like bare trees, and it was painted a daunting black. Other ships near it were green or red, or blue, and there was even one that was a gaudy yellow, making the black ship all the more impressive for its somber appearance. The longboat reached the side of the ship and Foster said, "Up you go," pointing to a net hung over the side. Erik rose and gripped the netting like a ladder and started to climb. The weight of those below pulling on the net caused him to twist and dip a little, but he made it safely to the rail, where sailors half hauled him aboard.

A man in a strange uniform—blue coat cut high at the waist, white trousers, and a saber hanging from a baldric slung across his shoulder—motioned for Erik to stand away. When the others were aboard, Foster called up, "That lot is to be kept together, Mr. Collins!"

The man in the strange uniform leaned over the rail and said, "In with the others?"

"Yes," answered Foster as the longboat pulled away. "But in a corner, Mr. Collins!"

"Aye, aye, Corporal Foster."

The man named Collins turned and ordered, "Follow me."

He moved down a strange ladder, narrow and steep, into a square hatchway, forward of the main mast. Erik was the last into the hold, and his eyes took a moment to adjust to the gloom. They entered a cargo hold that had been reconfigured to act as a barracks. Erik saw that twenty triple bunks had been fastened to the bulkheads, ten to each side of the ship, lengthwise, creating a fairly wide aisle.

Between the head of one set of three bunks and the foot of the next set, large trunks had been affixed to the deck, in which men were busy stowing gear. Collins motioned for the six prisoners to follow him. He led them to the two sets of bunks farthest from the other men, set against the starboard bulkhead; those across the hold on the port side were empty. He motioned for them to occupy the bunks. "This is where you'll sleep. You'll eat on deck unless the weather's too rough, when you'll be eating here. You can store your gear in those two trunks." He pointed to the trunk closest to the bulkhead at the aft of the cargo hold and the one between the two sets of bunks they were assigned.

Roo said, "We've got no gear."

The man said, "You'll call me Mr. Collins, or sir, when you address me. I'm the Second Mate on *Trenchard's Revenge*. The First Mate is Mr. Roper, and the Captain is . . . You call him Captain. Is that clear?"

Roo said, "Yes, Mr. Collins. But they didn't give us any gear, sir."

"That's not my problem. Your officer will get you what you need, I'm sure. It's a long voyage, and you'll have ample time to get organized. Now stay here until you're sent for." He left.

Biggo took one of the lower bunks, with Sho Pi and Billy Goodwin above him, while Roo, Erik, and Luis took the other bunk, in descending order.

"What do we do now?" asked Roo.

Biggo grinned. "Nothing. I'm for a nap!" he added cheerfully.

Erik realized that he was also tired, but nervous, waiting to discover what fate held in store for them next. Still, the lulling of the ship as it moved gently on groundswells in the harbor quickly soothed his nerves, and soon he was asleep as well.

A CLATTER FROM above and a sense of motion, and Erik sat up, striking his head against the bottom of the bunk above. Wincing at the pain, he almost stepped on Roo as he got down from the middle bunk.

A grinding sound from above and a change in motion, coupled with the shouts of orders from above, and it was clear they were under way. The six prisoners stood unsure of what to do, while the thirty men at the other end of the hold seemed amused by their confusion.

One of them, a large man nearly Biggo's size, said, "Why don't you run up and tell Bobby de Loungville that he's been thoughtless in not telling you we was leaving this soon!"

This brought a burst of laughter.

Luis said, "Why don't you go ask him if he knows who your father might be. Your mother certainly didn't."

The man on the bunk was on his feet and two strides on his way toward Luis when Sho Pi intercepted him. "Now, a moment, my friend," said the Isalani.

"You're no friend of mine," countered the large man, now obviously ready to fight with anyone, as he put his hand on Sho Pi's chest to push him aside.

Suddenly the man was on his knees, pain etched on his face as Sho Pi held his hand in a torturous grip, pulling thumb back and palm reversed so the hand twisted back hard against its own wrist. A gasp of agony was the only sound he made.

"I was going to suggest," said Sho Pi, "that as this is going to be a very long and tedious voyage, it would be in all of our best interests to make peace and try to consider one another's feelings. I'm sure my friend here is more than willing to apologize for impugning your mother if you'll graciously grant him pardon."

Luis was now amused, and with a gesture of removing a nonexistent hat, he bowed like a courtier and said, "Sir, I was a boor and acted rashly and without thought. My behavior shames me. I crave your pardon, sir."

The gasping man, whose eyes were now watering so that tears streamed down his face, said, "Granted!" It was barely more than a croak of pain.

Sho Pi released his hand and the man almost fainted from relief. Billy helped him to his feet and escorted him back to his own companions, trying to keep from grinning as he did. The man kept rubbing his hand, as if expecting something to be broken, but nothing was. He shook it a few times as Billy returned to his own side of the hold.

The hatch above slid aside and two figures came down, de Loungville and Foster. Foster said, "Listen up!"

De Loungville stopped about halfway down the companionway so he could look around at all the men. "We're under way, which no doubt you know unless you're unconscious or even more stupid than I thought. We'll be between ninety and one hundred days at sea, weather permitting. There's plenty of work to do, and I'll not have you running to fat because you're not sailors. Besides, we may be coming home short-handed"—he got a faraway look for a second, as if that meant more than what it sounded like—"so knowing your way around a ship will prove useful. Mr. Collins will come down later with assignments and you'll do as told, no questions asked. He has as much rank as Knight-Captain in the King's Army, so don't go forgetting that because he looks like a common sailor."

He moved down the ladder, walked over to where the six prisoners were waiting, and motioned for them to gather around. "I'm only going to tell you this once. Ruthia must love you, because the Lady of Luck has seen fit to keep you alive a little longer. I was given two weeks to judge if you're fit to live, and as things were going, you were all heading back to the gallows." He glanced from face to face. "But I convinced Calis that I could hang you from the yard-arms as easily as I could from the gallows in Krondor, so you've only gained time.

"The next three months are going to be harsh. You'll work a full watch like every man on this ship, and another watch will be given over to some training you haven't had and those others have." He hiked a thumb over his shoulder to the men at the other end of the hold.

Biggo spoke, to everyone's surprise. "Are we to learn why?"

"Why what?" asked de Loungville.

"Why this great galloping charade, Robert de Loungville, Sergeant darling sir. You don't spend the Prince's gold and dragoon soldiers from all parts of the Kingdom, then go through all this to save murderers and thieves from fair justice. You want something from us and you're prepared to give us back our lives in exchange. Fair enough, and no questions asked, but men more stupid than me would know that it's better for us to know what's ahead and rest certain in that knowledge than to let imagination stir up horrors that might make us do something rash and foolish. If we get ourselves killed, we're not happy and you're not happy."

De Loungville studied Biggo's face for a moment; then his face split into a grin. "I liked you better when you were stupid, Biggo." He turned and as he left, he said, "Stay alive long enough, and I promise you you'll find out more than you want to know." As he reached the companionway, he turned again to add, "But for the time being, the trick is to stay alive."

He climbed the stairs, Foster, as ever, behind him, and as the hatchway closed, Biggo said, "Well, that's not really what I wanted to hear."

Luis said, "What do you think? Is he trying to scare us?"

Sho Pi said, "No, I think the problem is he's trying very hard not to scare us."

Erik returned to his bunk, and with a cold feeling inside, he knew that Sho Pi was right.

DAYS PASSED. THE first day they had been allowed up on deck, Erik saw another ship traveling a short distance away. A sailor had told him that it was the *Freeport Ranger,* another ship under Calis's command. Erik said he had thought all Kingdom ships were called *Royal* this or that, and the sailor merely nodded, then went back to work.

Erik didn't care much for the work, but it was outside and the weather was clement, despite its being early fall. Roo hated being a sailor, having some trouble with the heights, but he had the agility to get around in the yards that

Biggo and Erik lacked. Luis and Billy were steady hands, and Sho Pi took to the tasks put before him with the same easy grace he had shown in the camp.

After two weeks, Erik had gotten his sea legs and calluses on his feet; he had put his riding boots away, because they were dangerous on a ship and the salt water was bad for the leather. Only officers wore boots, for they never had to climb the rigging. Erik and the other men below went barefoot like the sailors and were learning the sailor's craft in a hurry.

A landlubber of the worst sort, he was no longer confused by such terms as "running out a sheet," or "securing a yard." As in the camp, the hard work was accompanied by good food, a fact remarked upon by more than one sailor. That they were eating better than was the norm was not lost on Erik, and he joked that they were being treated like prize horses being readied for a competition among nobles. He decided not to mention that such competitions frequently ended with an animal down with a broken leg, or a rider thrown to serious injury or death.

Even Roo, adverse to hard work his entire young life, was showing the effects of the hard regime and good food. There was wiry muscle on his scrawny frame, and he moved with a self-assurance Erik had never seen before. Roo had always laughed as a child, but there was a mean, dangerous edge to him, and his humor had often been cruel. Now he seemed more involved with the moment, as if it was slowly dawning on him what life was, as opposed to the mind-numbing fear that death was only a moment away. Erik sensed something had changed in Roo, but he couldn't rightly say what that change was.

Sho Pi observed that whatever awaited them, de Loungville wanted them fit and ready. Each day was an equal mix of hard work and battle training.

The second day out, Sho Pi had gone up on deck during his off watch, to practice a series of controlled movements that looked like nothing as much as a dance to Erik. Graceful and flowing, they still held a sense of menace, as if to quicken the action would turn graceful motions into killing blows. After he finished and returned belowdecks, Luis said, "What was that you were doing up there, Keshian?"

"Isalani," corrected Sho Pi, then as he swung into his bunk, he said, "It is called *kata,* and it is the heart of the arts I practice. It is a sense of movement and it taps the power around you, to give you balance and ease at the moment you need to draw upon that power."

Erik sat up in his own bunk. "Is that the trick you used to disarm the soldier?"

"It is, sad to admit, the same, but it is not a trick. It is an ancient art form, and it can be used to harmonize the self with the universe, as well as for self-defense."

Biggo said, "If you could show me how to kick de Loungville around the way you did, I'd be interested in learning."

"That would be an abuse of the art," said Sho Pi. "But should you wish to practice with me, you are welcome. Kata will relax you, calm you, and refresh you."

Billy said, "Sure. You looked so relaxed and calm when you kicked de Loungville."

Luis grinned. "Ah, but it was refreshing!"

They all laughed. Suddenly Erik was visited with an unexpected and extraordinary affection for these men. Murderers all, the dregs of Kingdom society—yet in each he sensed something that made him feel kinship. He had never experienced such a feeling before and it troubled him as much as it felt natural. Lying back on his bunk, he pondered this odd turmoil.

BY THE END of the next week, Erik and the others had joined Luis in taking lessons in kata from Sho Pi. For an hour after their watch, the six would stand in a relatively clear area of the deck, between the main hatch and the foremast, and follow his lead.

Erik found the admonitions to think of a spot of light, or a soft breeze, or some other relaxing image while he moved vigorously through a long series of classic Isalani movements silly at first. After a time, he sensed the calm that would come with accepting Sho Pi's advice. Despite the long, hard hours of work, the additional exercise didn't tire, it refreshed, and Erik had never slept better in his life.

A sailor, a LaMutian, whose father had been a Tsurani warrior, asked to join as well. He claimed that much of what Sho Pi taught was similar to what his father had shown him as a child, part of the heritage of the Tsurani "way of the warrior."

After the group had been practicing for a week, the large man whom Sho Pi had humbled came over to watch. After a few minutes he said, "Can you show me how to do that thing with the thumb?"

Sho Pi said, "It is but a part of this. You will learn many things."

The man nodded and stood next to Erik. Sho Pi nodded to Erik, who said, "Put your feet like so." He showed him. "Now balance your weight so it is neither too far forward nor too far back, but just in the middle, even on both feet."

The man nodded. "My name is Jerome Handy," he said.

"Erik von Darkmoor."

Sho Pi demonstrated the four moves they would practice, and slowly led the men through the series. Then, instructing them to try it again, he moved quickly among them, correcting position and balance.

From the quarterdeck, Foster and de Loungville stood watching. Foster said, "What do you make of that?"

De Loungville shrugged. "Hard to say, Charlie. It could be something just to kill the time. Or it could be something that saves some lives. That Keshian could just as easily have killed me as embarrassed me with those kicks. He pulled them, despite the fact he was mad at me." He was silent for a while, then said, "Let it be known that I won't mind if the others follow Handy's lead. It's about time our last six birds joined the rest of our flock."

Slowly, over the next few days, more and more of the other thirty men joined the group, until at the end of the third week all were practicing kata under Sho Pi's supervision.

"YOU'RE ALL PRISONERS?" asked Luis, incredulity on his face.

"Ya, man," said an ebony-skinned man from the Vale of Dreams named Jadow Shati. "Each man here took the fall in Bobby de Loungville's little drama. Each of us looked the Death Goddess in the eye, or at least thought we were going to." He grinned and Erik found himself smiling in return. The man's smile had that impact, as if all the sunlight and happiness reflected off teeth made brilliant white by the contrast with his dark skin, the blackest Erik had ever seen. In the short time he had known Jadow, Erik had discovered he had the ability to find some humor in almost any situation. He also had a way of putting things so that Erik almost always ended up laughing.

Roo threw up his hands. "Then why were you such a bloody bunch of bastards when we first came to camp?"

They were all sitting around in the hold barracks. Over the last few days, after practicing with Sho Pi, the men had begun speaking with one another and the barrier between the six men Erik had come to think of as "us" and the other thirty he thought of as "them" had started to weaken.

Jadow spoke with the patois common to the Vale, a no-man's-land claimed at various times by the Empire of Great Kesh and the Kingdom, where languages, blood, and loyalties tended to be mixed. It was a musical sound, softer than the harsher King's Tongue, but not as guttural as High Keshian. "Man, that was the drill, don't you know? Each time a new group came, we were to give them bloody hell! Bobby's orders. Not until he knew he wasn't going to have to hang us did he treat us better than dirt on the sole of his boot, don't you see? Then we got to take off the damn ropes, man. Then we began to think we might live a bit longer."

Jerome Handy sat across from Erik, the biggest man in the group after Biggo and broader across the shoulders. "Jadow and me were among the first six. Four of our mates died. Two tried to go over the walls, and those Pathfinders picked them off with their long bows like quails on the wing." He made a flying motion with his two hands, as if throwing shadow puppets on the wall, and made a funny flapping sound with his mouth. Then suddenly he turned his hands over and made a sign of a wounded bird falling. Erik had delighted in discovering that as rough and intimidating as Handy could be, he also could be very amusing given anything remotely like an audience. "One lost his temper and died in a sword drill. The other . . ." He glanced at Jadow.

"Ah, that was bad, man. Roger was his name," supplied the Valeman.

"Right. Roger. He was hung when he killed a guard, trying to escape."

"How long ago was that?" asked Erik.

"More than a year, man," said Jadow. He ran a hand over his bald pate, which he kept free of hair by dry-shaving with a blade every morning. While most of it was naturally hairless, the little fringe around the ears was persistent enough that Erik winced each time he saw the man give himself a trim.

"A year!" asked Billy Goodwin. "You've been at that camp a year?"

Jadow grinned. "Man, consider the alternative, don't you see?" He laughed, a deep-throated version of a child's delight. "The food was sumptuous, and the company"—he cast a mock-baleful look at Jerome—"diverting, if nothing else. And the longer we were there . . ."

"What?" asked Roo.

It was Biggo who answered. "The longer they weren't headed toward wherever it is de Loungville and the Eagle are taking us."

"Exactly."

"You've been playing soldier for a year, then?" asked Luis.

"More, and I don't call it playing when men die," said a man named Peter Bly.

Jerome nodded. "We thirty are what's left of seventy-eight who were put through the false hanging over the last year and a bit."

Sho Pi said, "Then this would explain why Corporal Foster and . . . what is Robert de Loungville's real rank—when first I saw him, I took him for a noble—does anyone know?"

Jerome shook his head. "Sergeant is all I've ever heard. But I've seen him give orders to a Knight-Captain of the King's own. He's the second in command, after the elf."

"Elf?" said Erik.

Luis said, "What some of the older guards call the Eagle. It's no joke. They call him that, but there's no disrespect in it. But they say he's not human."

"He does look a little odd," said Roo.

Jerome laughed, and Jadow said, "Look whose talking about looking odd!"

All the gathered men laughed and Roo flushed with embarrassment, waving off the remark. "I mean, he doesn't look like the rest of us."

"No one looks like the rest of us," said Sho Pi.

"We know what you mean," said another man whose name Erik didn't know.

Jadow said, "I've never been to the west, though my father fought there against the Tsurani in the Riftwar. Man, that was some fighting, to hear the old man talk. He saw some elves at the battle in the valley in the Grey Towers, when the elves and dwarves betrayed the treaty. He said the elves are tall and fair, though their hair and eyes are much like yours, from brown to yellow, don't you know? Yet he said there is something uncommon about them, and they carry themselves with a different grace—as if dancing while the rest of us walk, is what he said to me."

Sho Pi said, "The man called Eagle is that. He is one I'd not wish to face."

"You?" said Erik. "You've taken swords out of armed men's hands. I would have thought you were afraid of no one."

"I have taken the sword from an armed man's hands, Erik. But I never claimed I was fearless when I did so." His expression became reflective. "There is something very dangerous in the man called Calis."

"He's stronger than he looks," said Jerome with a frank look of embarrassment. "Early on, in the training, before he left everything to Bobby de Loungville, that's when I thought to bully him and he knocked me down so hard I thought he'd broken my skull."

"Too thick, man, much too thick," said Jadow, and the others laughed.

"No, I mean it. I pride myself on taking a blow with the best, but I've never felt anything like it, and I was certainly surprised." He looked at Sho Pi. "As surprised as I was when you twisted my thumb that time. Same thing. I moved, and suddenly I was on my back and my head was ringing like a temple gong."

Jadow said, "He never saw the blow, man. And neither did I, truth to tell. Calis is fast."

"He's not human," said another, and there was general agreement.

A warning creak on the companionway stairs had the men scrambling for their bunks before Corporal Foster was through the hatch. As he touched boot to deck, he shouted, "Lights out, ladies! Say good night to your sweethearts, and get your rest. You've a full day tomorrow."

Before Erik could get completely under the woolen blanket, the lantern was doused, and the hold plunged into gloom. He lay back and thought what it must have been like to live in that camp for a year, to see men you didn't know come in and see them die. Suddenly something Sho Pi had started to say registered.

Erik whispered. "Sho Pi?"

"What?"

"What were you about to say, about something explaining why Foster and de Loungville were doing something or whatever, when you asked about de Loungville's rank?"

"I was going to say that having so many men fail, even after the testing before and during their trials, even after having the woman read minds, explains why they are so worried about the six of us."

"What do you mean?"

"More than half the men saved from the gallows died before we got to the camp. By rights, three or four of us—you, me, Roo, Billy, Biggo, and Luis—we shouldn't be on this ship. We should be dead. De Loungville's taking a chance. Even after all of this, we still might fail."

Erik said, "Oh, I see."

He lay back, and sleep was a long time coming as he thought, *Fail at what?*

11

★★

PASSAGE

ERIK YAWNED.

While things were never dull on *Trenchard's Revenge,* there were moments of boredom, and this was one. He had finished his exercises with the other men, who formed what he now understood was Robert de Loungville's hand-picked band of "desperate men." Evening chow was over, and he felt like some fresh air. While the others were lounging in their bunks belowdecks, Erik waited by the fore rail, overlooking the bowsprit, listening to the sounds of the sea as the ship sped through the night.

The deck officer called out the hour's orders, and the lookout above answered that all was clear. Erik smiled at that. How the man knew all was clear was beyond him, unless he had some magic device allowing his mortal eyes to pierce the darkness. What he meant, thought Erik, was he couldn't see anything.

Yet that wasn't entirely true. There was a sea of stars above, with the little moon just rising in the east, and the middle and large moons not due to rise until just before morning. The familiar pattern of the stars above gave silver highlights to the water below. A half mile to starboard, the *Freeport Ranger* was holding a parallel course, her presence marked by lights upon her bow, stern, and masthead. Any other ship in the night should be running under lights as well, so if they were near, they'd stand out like a beacon.

"Fascinating, isn't it?"

Erik turned, startled that he hadn't heard anyone approach. Calis stood a few feet away, gazing at the sky. "I've been on ships any number of times, and when the moons are down and the stars are like this, it still makes me pause to watch and wonder."

Erik didn't know what to say. This man had spoken to them so rarely, most of the men below were in awe of him. And de Loungville seemed to take great pains to keep them in awe of him. Jadow and Jerome's narrative about him helped further that cause.

Erik said, "Ah, I was just—"

"Stay," said Calis, coming to the rail next to Erik. "Bobby and Charlie are playing cards, and I thought I'd get some air. I see I'm not the only one feeling the need."

Erik shrugged. "It gets close down below sometimes."

"And sometimes a man likes to be alone with his own thoughts, isn't that true, Erik?"

"Sometimes," said Erik. Not knowing why, he said, "But I don't dwell much on things. It's not my way. Roo, now, he worries enough for a whole family, but . . ."

"But what?"

"Maybe it was my mother," said Erik, suddenly missing her. "She was always worried about this or that, and, well, I never really had much on my mind most of the time."

"No ambitions?"

"Just to earn a forge of my own someday."

Calis nodded, the gesture half seen in the dim light of a nearby lantern. "A respectable goal."

"What of you?" Erik was suddenly embarrassed at his own presumption, but Calis smiled.

"My goals?" He turned and leaned upon the rail, both elbows resting on it as he gazed into the darkness. "It would be hard to explain."

Erik said, "I wasn't trying to pry . . . sir."

Calis said, "Start calling me Captain, Erik. Bobby's our sergeant and Charlie's the corporal, and you're part of the Crimson Eagles, the most feared mercenary band in our homeland."

"Sir?" said Erik. "I don't understand."

Calis said, "You will, soon enough." Looking at the horizon, he said, "We'll be there shortly."

"Where, sir . . . Captain?"

"Sorcerer's Isle. I need to speak to an old friend."

Erik stood silently, uncertain what to do or say next, until Calis relieved him of that burden. "Why don't you go below and join your companions," he suggested.

"Yes, Captain," said Erik and started to move, but stopped. "Ah, Captain, should I salute you or something?"

With a strange smile, what Owen Greylock called ironic, Erik thought,

Calis said, "We're mercenaries, not the bloody army, Erik."

Erik nodded and turned away. Shortly he was back in his bunk. While Jadow regaled the others with tales of women he had known and battles he had single-handedly won, Erik lay half listening, half wondering just what Calis had meant.

"CAPTAIN!"

Erik paused as he secured a line. The sound of the lookout's voice had carried a troubling note with it.

"What do you see?" came the Captain's reply.

"Something dead ahead, sir. Lights or lightning. I don't rightly know."

Erik quickly made the line fast and turned to look ahead. It was near dusk, but the sun off the port bow made it hard to see anything. He squinted against the sunset glare, then saw it: a faint flash of silver.

Roo came to stand next to his friend. "What is it?"

"Lightning, I think," said Erik.

"Great. A storm at sea," said Roo. It had been pleasant sailing for almost a month as they had fought a tacking course out of Krondor toward their destination. One of the sailors had said that had they been heading the other way, they could have made the trip in one third the time.

"You boys got nothing to do?" came a familiar voice from behind them, and Erik and Roo were back up the rigging before Corporal Foster could inform Mr. Collins that they needed to be assigned more work.

Reaching the top yard on the mainmast, they began securing lines that really didn't need securing. They wanted a look at the coming storm.

As the sun lowered beyond the horizon, there were no clouds ahead, but they could clearly see arcs of incredible brightness. "What is that?" asked Roo.

"Nothing good," said Erik, and he started making his way back down toward the deck.

"Where are you going?"

"To report to Mr. Collins I've secured the lines and to get orders. No sense staring at whatever's ahead, Roo. We'll get there soon enough."

Roo hung back, watching as the bright arcs reappeared against the darkening sky, silver bolts that arched into the heavens. He imagined they carried thunderous booms or sizzling discharges, but from this distance they were silent. He felt chilled, yet the evening air was warm. He glanced down and saw that half the crew was straining to see what was ahead.

He lingered a moment, then headed down after his friend.

THROUGHOUT THE NIGHT they drew closer to Sorcerer's Isle. Near dawn the first of the cracking sounds that accompanied the energy displays could be heard. By the time the day watch was to be roused, no man on the ship was asleep.

Word of their destination had circulated through the crew, though Erik had told no one what Calis had told him. Sorcerer's Isle, home to the legendary Black Sorcerer. Some called him Macros, while others said his name was a Tsurani one, and still others said he was the King of Dark Magic. No one knew the truth, Erik decided, but everyone who spoke knew of someone who knew someone who had talked to another who had barely survived a visit to the island.

Terrible stories of mayhem and horrors so vile that death was the least of them were passed around between sundown and dawn, so by the time Erik and his companions came up on deck, the mood of the ship was fearful.

Erik almost exclaimed at the sight that greeted him. An island lay off the starboard bow, large enough that it would take hours to sail around, and dominated by a high wall of cliffs. Atop the highest point of that cliff face, a black castle—a malignant-looking thing of four towers and stone walls—rose high against the sky. It sat atop a massive stone chimney, an upthrust finger of land, separated from the rest of the island by tidal action, which had cut a cleft as impassable as any moat. A drawbridge could be lowered to cross the cleft, but it was presently raised.

The castle was the source of the terrible arcs of energy, silver flashes that rose high into the sky, vanishing in the clouds, accompanied by a sizzling whine that hurt the ears.

Blue lights shone from a high tower window overlooking the ocean, and Erik thought he detected movement upon the walls. "Von Darkmoor!" Robert de Loungville's voice brought the young smith out of his revery.

"Sergeant?" said Erik.

"You, Biggo, Jadow, and Jerome will come with Calis and me. Get the longboat over the side."

Erik and the others named, aided by four experienced sailors, got the longboat off the davits and over the side in quick order. Calis came up on deck and without a word to anyone scampered down the ladder to the boat. De Loungville and two sailors came next, then Erik led the designated prisoners.

As Erik reached the rail, he was handed a sword and scabbard and a shield by Corporal Foster. He slung the baldric over his shoulder, secured the shield to his back, and went down the ladder. This was the first time he had been handed a weapon when it wasn't a training exercise, and it made him nervous.

The boat pushed away from the ship and headed toward a small beach that swept away from the rocky pinnacle upon which the castle rested. The sailors were experienced, and Erik and Biggo were strong, so the boat made quick time getting in to shore.

When they landed, Calis said, "Keep alert. You never know what to expect here."

Robert de Loungville nodded, a wry smile on his face. "That's the gods' awful truth."

Suddenly a figure reared up out of the bushes near the top of an overlooking ridge, beside a small path that led up from the beach. The creature was easily ten or eleven feet tall, clothed in black and waving long arms within huge sleeves. A spectral voice issued from within a giant cowl, hiding the creature's face. "Despair! All who trespass upon the Black One's island are *doomed!* Flee now, or be destroyed in agony!"

Erik felt the hairs rise on his neck and arms. Biggo made a sign warding off evil, while Jadow and Jerome both drew their swords and crouched low.

Calis stood motionless, while Robert de Loungville pointed a thumb at the creature with a backwards wave of his hand. "I think he means it," he said with a grin.

Facing the advancing creature, de Loungville said, "Why don't you come on down here, me darling, and I'll give you a big wet kiss."

Erik's eyebrows shot up, and Calis smiled at his friend. The creature tilted, as if the brashness of de Loungville's words caused it to lose its balance; then Erik was astonished to see it collapse.

He saw long wooden sticks fall within the hooded robe, and a small man emerged from inside the folds of black cloth. He was a bandy-legged fellow, obviously an Isalani from his appearance, and he wore a tattered robe of orange cloth, slashed at the knees and sleeves. "Bobby?" he said. Then his face split in a grin and he let out a yelp of pure joy. "Calis!" He raced down to the sand and almost leaped into de Loungville's arms. Erik thought the two men daft as they slapped each other on the back.

Calis embraced the little man. "That's quite a show you have going there, Nakor."

The little man's face split into a grin, and suddenly Erik realized that he was standing with his sword drawn, while his heart was still beating rapidly. He glanced around and saw the others were also holding their weapons ready.

The man called Nakor said, "Had some trouble with some Quegan pirates a few years back. That little blue light didn't scare them away, so I added those lightning bolts. Impressive, I think," he added with a self-congratulatory note. "It starts whenever someone gets close enough to see the island on the horizon. But when you kept sailing toward us, I thought I had better come down here and scare you away." He pointed to the fallen contraption of robe and sticks.

"The Black Sorcerer?" said Robert.

"For the time being," answered Nakor with a grin. He glanced at the four guards and said, "Tell your men I won't hurt them."

Calis turned and, with a wave of his hand, said, "Put your weapons away. He's an old friend."

"Where's Pug?" asked De Loungville.

"Gone," said Nakor with a shrug. "Left about three years ago. Said he'd be back one of these days."

"Do you know where he went?" asked Calis. "It's very important."

Nakor shrugged. "It's always important with Pug. That's why he left, I think. All the troubles down south—"

"You know?" said Calis.

Nakor grinned. "Some. You can tell me the rest. You want something hot to eat?"

Calis motioned yes, and Nakor waved for them to follow. Calis told the two sailors, "Take the boat back to the ship and tell the captain he's to do as I instructed. And have him send word to the *Ranger,* as well." To Erik and the other three guards he said, "Follow along, and don't be alarmed by anything you see. There are some very odd-looking creatures about, but none will offer you harm."

The little man named Nakor led Calis and de Loungville up the path. Erik and the others followed behind. They reached the crest of the ridge, but rather than follow the path toward the castle, they paused. Nakor closed his eyes and waved his hand in the air, and the lightning suddenly stopped. He put his hand to his forehead a moment, then said, "Oh, shutting that off gives me a headache." Then he turned and led them all down another path that led into what appeared to be a small valley overgrown by a thick forest.

Then suddenly the forest vanished, and Erik almost tripped, he was so startled. Instead of thick woodlands, he was now staring at a pasture that stretched away for nearly a mile. In the middle of it sat a large, sprawling estate, a low, white house with a red tile roof, and several outbuildings, all surrounded by a low stone wall.

In distant fields, Erik could make out horses and cattle, and what might be deer or elk. Around the estate, figures moved, but they didn't appear to be entirely human. But, keeping in mind Calis's instructions, he decided to trust his leader and follow orders.

They reached the small yard before the main house and Nakor opened the gate in the low stone wall. They entered, and from the door of the house a creature appeared. Erik glanced at Jadow, Jerome, and Biggo, and judging by their expressions, all were as astonished as he.

The creature was tall, man-size, and had blue-tinged skin, large ears, and a bony, heavy forehead. It smiled, revealing an impressive array of teeth; its eyes were black and yellow. Erik wasn't sure, but the creature resembled every description of a goblin Erik had ever heard.

But it was dressed in the height of court fashion: a tight-fitting blue jacket cut at the waist, over a loose, billowing-sleeved white shirt, tucked into a wide waistband of black silk. Tight grey hose and ankle-high boots finished the ensemble, and the creature looked like nothing so much as one of Prince Nicholas's court dandies.

"Refreshments are served," said the creature.

"Gathis," Calis greeted it.

"Master Calis," replied Gathis. "It's so nice to see you again. It has been too long between visits. And Master Robert. Good to see you as well."

Calis said, "Did Pug leave you in charge, Nakor?"

With a squint-eyed grin, the little man said, "No, Gathis runs everything. I'm still just a guest."

Calis shook his head. "Guest? For what, twenty years now?"

Nakor shrugged. "Lots of things to discuss. Lots of things to study. Let those fools in Stardock become constipated with their rules and vows of secrecy and orders and the rest of that foolishness." He made a chopping motion with his hand. "This is where the real learning is taking place."

Calis said, "No doubt."

Gathis said, "I'll see to your guards, sir."

Calis and Robert went inside, followed by Nakor. The creature turned to Erik and the others and said, "You men follow me."

He led them around the building, and Erik was surprised to discover that it was larger than he had first suspected as they had walked down the path from the ridge above. The building was, essentially, a large square, with entrances in all four walls. Through one they passed, Erik could see that the building was also hollow in the center, a large fountain at the heart of a garden glimpsed briefly as they walked past.

Behind the building, a pair of very odd-looking men, black as soot and with eyes of red, hurried by, and as the four guards turned to gawk, Gathis said, "Come along, please." He led them to the door of a large outbuilding and motioned for them to follow him inside. "You'll see many beings here you might count strange or fearsome, but none will offer you harm."

That was again reassuring to hear, because within the building they found what could only be called, in Erik's judgment, a demon. Jadow had his sword half out of his scabbard when the creature turned and struck him across the knuckles with a long wooden spoon. "Put that away," it said with a deep rumbling growl.

Jadow let out a yelp and released the sword hilt, letting the sword slide back into its scabbard. "That hurt!" he exclaimed while sucking on his bruised knuckles.

"Don't talk with your mouth full," admonished the creature, motioning for the four guards to sit at a table.

Erik paused and realized he was in a kitchen. The "demon" was a red creature, about as big as Jerome, looking as if its skin was two or three sizes too large. It seemed to droop around the creature's body in folds and creases, and to be thick, like hide. A large head without hair was dominated by two horns, which rose in front of fanlike ears, to arch back to points just behind the head.

It appeared to be nude, save for the large white apron it wore. Pulling a big bowl of fruit from a shelf, it placed it upon the table and said, "I'll have soup in a minute."

Gathis said, "Alika will care for your needs and send someone with you to show you where you'll sleep." As the cook crossed to the other side of the room, Gathis lowered his voice. "She's very sensitive, so say something nice about her cooking." Then he hurried off.

Biggo said, "She?" in low tones. Jadow grinned and shrugged, taking a large pear from the platter and biting deep into it. He closed his eyes as juice dripped down his chin, and made a satisfied sound.

Now Erik noticed the smells. Suddenly he was ravenous as hot spices filled the air, and he remembered what food not cooked aboard ship tasted like. He took an apple and bit into it, finding it crisp and sweet, and savoring the taste.

Then Alika was back with a large platter of bread and cheese. Placing them on the table, she turned away. Erik hesitated briefly before he said, "Thank you."

The creature paused and rumbled, "You're welcome."

Soon the four men were eating as well as they had back in camp, with far more leisure, as the cook produced a thick soup of creamed vegetables with spices, a full roast chicken for each man, and steaming greens piled high, buttered, and spiced. Ale, cold and foaming in pewter mugs, was placed at each man's elbow, and Erik hadn't recalled drinking anything quite so thirst-quenching.

Between mouthfuls, Biggo said, "I don't think I would have believed any man who told me of this place and these creatures."

Jadow said, "Man, it's far easier to imagine evil spirits and black sorcery than this.

" 'And you say the creature could cook?' " he mimicked someone questioning him.

" 'Ya, man, she cooked better than me own mother!' "

The others laughed. Jerome said, "I wonder why we came here?"

"Wondering's not good for the health," said Jadow.

Jerome said, "One thing we learned in camp. You follow orders, you stay alive. Don't volunteer, don't cause trouble. Each day after the gallows is a gift."

Erik nodded. He still had trouble not wincing when he remembered that fall with the rope around his neck. The sour taste of fear in his stomach was one he wished never to repeat.

The cook came back with more bread and Biggo said, "Alika?"

The cook paused. "Yes?"

"Ah, what are you?"

The creature fixed Biggo with a narrow gaze, as if weighing the nature of the question, then she replied, "A student. I work for my instruction."

"No, I mean, where are you from?"

"Targary."

"I've never heard of Targary," said Jadow.

"It is far away," she said, turning back to her work.

They ate in silence after that.

When they finished, a young girl, no more than ten or eleven by her appearance, but with grey hair and maroon eyes, escorted them to a room. In a voice tinged with alien nuances, she said, "Sleep here. Water there." She pointed at a basin and pitcher. "Relieve yourself outside," she said, making a general down-the-hall and out-the-door gesture. "You need. You call. I come."

She bowed and departed. Biggo said, "I swear that child's feet weren't touching the ground."

Erik removed his baldric and sat on the nearest bed, a thickly padded feather mattress with two pillows and a heavy comforter against the chill. "I am through with being amazed." He lay down with an exaggerated stretch. "This is the first bed I've been in . . ." He stopped and grinned at his friends. "This is the first bed I've been in!"

Biggo laughed. "You've never slept in a bed?"

"With my mother, when I was a baby, I guess, but I've been sleeping in the hayloft as long as I can recall, then prison, the camp, and the ship."

"Well, enjoy, Erik von Darkmoor," said Jerome as he lay down on his bunk. "I plan on sleeping until someone makes me get up to work." With that he closed his eyes and raised his arm to cover his face.

"Man, that is a fine notion," said Jadow.

Erik and Biggo followed suit, and soon the room was silent, save for the sounds of heavy breathing and snoring.

ERIK AWOKE TO the sound of voices. Sitting up, he was disoriented for a moment, then remembered where he was. The voices were coming through a window, one that looked out upon the garden.

The familiar voice of Robert de Loungville carried through the night as he and someone else approached. ". . . never seen him like this before."

"He has a great deal on his mind," said another; Erik recognized the speaker as being their host, Nakor.

"He took that last mission hard. We've had setbacks before, but nothing like that. If he hadn't carried me half the way, I'd have died on the banks of the Vedra River. Of the two thousand of us who went, only sixty returned."

"Ah, I had heard it was difficult."

"Whatever you heard, it was worse."

Erik felt awkward. He didn't think it was proper to eavesdrop, but this was the room he had been assigned and Nakor and Robert weren't taking pains not to be overheard.

"I hear this and I hear that," said Nakor, and Erik could tell they had stopped moving.

"It was the biggest battle so far. Calis put us in with Haji's Red Hawks and a half-dozen other companies that usually work out of the Eastlands. We joined up with the other defenders at Kisma-hal, a town between Hamsa and Kilbar. Ran into the Westland army skirmishes as we beat them back. Then their leading elements rolled through us and drove to the gates of the city. We fortified the garrison and beat back three assaults on the walls, and we sallied a few times, burning their baggage train and causing them a great deal of pain. Then the second wave of Westland infantry showed up and we were surrounded.

"Two hundred and sixty-five days of siege, Nakor. And those damn magicians. Nothing like those Tsurani during the Riftwar were supposed to have done, but enough to make a man hate all magic. The King of Hamsa's magicians barely kept us free of most of the worst, the lightning, fires, the freezing spells. But they couldn't protect us from the rest, and it was almost as bad: flies and mosquitoes in clouds appearing out of nowhere. Every barrel of wine in the city turned sour. After the first hundred and fifty days, we ate hard bread and drank foul water and we survived. After two hundred, we ate maggots in green meat, and we ate insects when we could find them and were thankful. We were close to eating our dead.

"Then, when the city surrendered, Calis took the head start rather than sell out the contract and join the invaders." Erik heard bitterness in Robert's tone. "Half our men were injured or sick. Half of those still living, I should say. We got our one day's grace; then they turned their cavalry after us. If we had headed south along the river, they'd have run us down for certain. We turned east and hid." Robert was silent for a time, then when he spoke again, Erik could hear the barely held-back emotions in his voice, as if he had never told the story to anyone before. "We killed our own wounded rather than leave them behind. As it was, the rest of us barely made it to the steppes. The Jeshandi covered our retreat from there, and the snakes were smart enough not to get into a running fight with them in their own territory. The Jeshandi fed us and nursed us, and we eventually got back to the City of the Serpent River."

Nakor said, "I remember the first visit, twenty-four years ago." There was a moment of silence. "Calis was very young then. He still is, by the measure of his race. Now he has much responsibility, and lacks Arutha or Nicholas at his side to instruct him.

"And now you plan this very dangerous thing."

"Desperate thing," said Robert de Loungville. "It was a long time in the planning, and getting the right men for the job was harder than we thought."

"These men, these 'desperate men,' they will be able to do this where so many experienced soldiers could not?"

There was another long silence. De Loungville finally said, "I don't know, Nakor. I don't know."

Erik heard the sounds of the two men walking away and after a moment he could hear them speaking again, though he couldn't understand what they were saying.

Erik lay awake a long time trying to puzzle out the significance of what he had overheard. He had never heard of those places, Hamsa or Kilbar, and didn't know who the Jeshandi were. But there was a note in de Loungville's voice he had never heard before. It was an overtone of worry, perhaps even fear. Erik found sleep came slowly, and when it at last found him, he didn't rest well.

NAKOR, CARRYING A travel bag slung over his shoulder, was waiting with Calis when Robert de Loungville called Erik and the others out of their room. The four guards said nothing but fell in behind Calis and the others.

Nakor kept up a nearly nonstop narrative of some of the things he had been involved in since the last time Calis and de Loungville had visited. From what Erik overheard, it sounded as if Nakor and Calis had known each other for a very long time. Erik remembered Nakor's having said something the night before about a visit somewhere with Calis twenty-four years earlier, which hardly seemed possible to Erik, as Calis didn't look much older than twenty-four. Then Erik remembered what Nakor said about "his race," meaning Calis's, and then the other remarks made in camp about Calis not being human.

Erik was so caught up in these reflections he hardly noticed when they climbed out of the vale and crested the ridge. He was surprised to see that the beach was covered with men, his own shipmates and the full company of soldiers who had been aboard the *Freeport Ranger*. They stood quietly waiting on the sand. Erik recognized a few faces from the *Ranger*'s company as guards who had served at the camp, but now they were dressed in all fashion of clothing, in the same manner as the *Revenge*'s company.

De Loungville motioned for Erik and the others to go over and stand next to their shipmates and he mounted an outcropping of rock next to the trail, so he could look down on the men. "Listen up!" he shouted.

Calis took his place on the rock and said, "Some of you know me well, and others here have never spoken with me. Most of you know by now who I am, or think you do." He glanced from face to face. "I am called Calis. I serve Prince Nicholas, as I did his father before. Some call me the Eagle of Krondor, or the Prince's Bird of Prey." He seemed amused by these titles.

"Twenty-four years ago a great raid was launched against the Far Coast.

Some here might remember the destruction of Crydee, Carse, and Tulan."

A few of the older soldiers from the *Ranger* nodded.

"Those events led us to travel halfway around the world, to the land called Novindus."

None of the men from the *Ranger* said anything, but Erik's company looked at one another amid a few muttered questions.

"Quiet, now!" commanded de Loungville.

"What we found down there was a plot to destroy the Kingdom."

Again there was some stirring among the men from *Trenchard's Revenge,* but no one spoke.

Calis continued. "Twice since, I have traveled to this far land, the last time with some of you."

The men from *Trenchard's Revenge,* almost to a man, turned to regard the guards from the compound, veterans from many different garrisons around the Kingdom. Those looked at Calis with a steady gaze, as if they understood exactly what was being said.

"So you who weren't with us know, I'll tell you a few things. Ten years ago word reached Prince Arutha that a great army was massing in that part of Novindus called the Westlands. That army swept down from an unknown place along the shore of an ocean they call the Green Sea. The first city to fall was Point Pünt. In this land there is nothing like our Kingdom Army. Cities may have militia, but most fighting is done by mercenary companies. There are rules of conduct and established protocols for how they are treated by those who are victorious in warfare. The conquerors gave the defenders of the city called Point Pünt the choice of serving or one day's grace to withdraw. That is normal, but what wasn't normal was that every man in the city was ordered to serve under arms or watch his wife and children, mother and father impaled before his eyes. After the first executions, the entire male population of the city joined that army.

"They then marched on the city of Irabek, and after bitter fighting it fell. Then Port Sulth, then all the towns along the Manstra River."

Erik had never heard of any of these places, but he listened, fascinated.

"From Point Pünt they launched an invasion along the river Dee, seeking to enter the area known as the Midlands, and they were unopposed until reaching the foothills of the Ratn'gary mountains. Dwarves—much like the race who live in the west of the Kingdom—turned them back for three years. At last this army of invaders threw up a stable frontier of fortifications and sought another way across Novindus.

"They came through the Forest of Irabek, darker and more fearful than our own Green Heart. They died in numbers getting through, but at last they did and then they struck the city of Hamsa. The King of Hamsa warred for five years with this army and hired mercenaries from as far away as the City of the

Serpent River at the other end of the continent. We have dealings with this city, which is how we came to hear of this invading army."

Calis paused. "Prince Arutha suspected who was behind this invasion and sent agents to discover if he was correct. Of thirty men, one returned, barely alive, and confirmed our worst fears.

"Six years ago I was given command of two thousand men and sent to bolster the defenses of the city of Hamsa."

Every man listening to Calis was motionless. Only the sound of waves breaking on the rocks below the castle and the cries of seabirds broke the silence.

"There is a race of creatures who live somewhere on Novindus. Some of you may have heard of them as creatures of legend. They are called the Pantathians."

Erik turned to look at his companions, and saw Jadow make a sign against evil. The Pantathians were called the Snakes Who Walk Like Men and were creatures of lore conjured up to frighten children into behaving. Unlike trolls and goblins, who were natural creatures living in the distant wilds of the frontier, the serpent men were legends, like dragons and centaurs, and no one believed them real.

As if reading Erik's mind, Calis said, "These are not legends. I have faced them, and so have these men over here." He motioned to the company from the *Freeport Ranger.* "You aboard *Trenchard's Revenge* will have the opportunity along the way to talk to these men, your former guards, and to get the benefit of their knowledge. They can tell you from bitter experience how all too real the Pantathians are.

"Two thousand men in ten ships went south to Novindus to battle the enemy as far from home as we might, and only sixty men came home. If you want the full story, there are others who will tell it. Of that sixty, the fifty-eight still living are here."

Looking directly at Erik for a moment, then at the other former prisoners around him, he went on. "Less than one in twenty who went before returned, and now, five years after returning home, we go to find these invaders again.

"Only this time they are more powerful, more entrenched, and more aware of our part. Each town they conquer joins with them or dies, and when Hamsa fell, of six thousand defenders, four thousand swore oaths to the invaders.

"Those mercenaries who would not were given a day's truce before they were hunted down.

"This army means to conquer all of Novindus. More, it means to sail here, to the Kingdom, and conquer us after.

"Some of you might think that such chaos would be your perfect chance to escape."

Erik glanced around and saw that more than one expression confirmed Calis's remark.

"If you attempt to leave without permission, at any point along our line of march, Robert de Loungville and I will personally hang you from the nearest tree.

"If you manage to escape, know that you are living on stolen time, for eventually that army will reach any part of Novindus you may hide in and you will serve or you will die.

"Why chance dying now rather than later?"

He was silent as the men thought on his question. "Because," answered Calis, "these creatures, these serpent men, will not end at conquest. They will eventually destroy everything, and you will die."

There was a bit of muttering at this, and to Calis's surprise it was Nakor who spoke next.

The bandy-legged little man said, "You foolish men! Listen to me! I have seen what these creatures do. They sought to send a plague to us nearly twenty-five years ago. They sought to kill everything in the Kingdom."

Jerome made bold to speak. "Why would any creature do such a thing?"

Nakor shrugged. "I could tell you, but I scarcely think you'd understand."

Jerome, whose temper was as bad as Luis's, narrowed his gaze at the Isalani. "I may have to take abuse from my officers, little man, but I'm not as stupid as you might think. If you speak slowly enough, I just might understand."

Nakor glanced at Calis, who nodded. Nakor said, "Very well. The Pantathians are not natural beings." When Jerome Handy gave him a puzzled look, Nakor said, "I'll speak slowly."

Some of the men laughed, but it was a nervous laugh. Calis said, "Continue."

"There was, ages ago on this world, a race called the Dragon Lords."

Some of the men made signs against evil and others scoffed openly. "Legends!" shouted one.

"Yes," said Calis. "Legends, but based upon history. Those being once ruled this world.

"And one of them, a powerful member of her race, created the Pantathians as her servants. They are an ancient race, raised up by this Dragon Lord from serpents in the swamps of Novindus. Artificial they may have been in their beginning, but they were bred to serve this one. She was called Alma-Lodaka.

"When the Dragon Lords vanished, this race of twisted creatures believed that they were to abide until her return. By means I will not reveal, they have found a way to call her back from the place she resides.

"The unfortunate consequence of such an act would be to destroy all life on this world."

"No," said several men. "That can't be possible," said another.

"Possible?" asked Nakor. "What is possible?" He reached into his sack and drew out an orange. He tossed it to Jerome. Then he took out another and threw it to Erik, and another to another man. After a few minutes, at least a score of oranges came out of the sack.

Calis said, "I thought it was apples?"

"I went back to oranges a few years ago," said Nakor as he kept pulling more and more oranges out of the little sack. He held up the sack and showed everyone that it was empty, even turning it inside out. Then he reached in and drew more oranges out and started throwing them to the other soldiers, until more than five dozen oranges had come out of that small sack. "Possible?" he asked.

He walked up to Jerome Handy, looked up at the big man, and said, "Do you think it possible that I could force you to your knees with one hand?"

Jerome's eyes narrowed and his complexion flushed, and he said, "No, I don't!" Erik cleared his throat, and when Jerome turned to look, Erik nodded once toward Sho Pi, who stood behind him. Jerome saw the other Isalani raise a questioning eyebrow; then he turned to Nakor and stared at him for a long moment. Lowering his voice, he said, "But maybe you could do it with two hands."

Nakor glanced over at Sho Pi and grinned. Turning away, he said, "Only need one."

To the assembled company he said, "Take it on faith, you desperate men. This the Pantathians can do: they can end life as we know it on this world. No bird will sing to greet the dawn, and no insect will buzz from flower to flower. No seed will take root. No child will cry for his mother's breast, and no thing that crawls, walks, or flies will survive."

A young man Erik didn't know well, David Gefflin, said, "Why would they do such a mad thing?"

"Because they think this Dragon Lord, this Alma-Lodaka, is a goddess. A powerful being she was, but no goddess. Yet to these sick creatures, whom she created from snakes, she was. Their Mother-Goddess they call her. And they believe that to return her to this lifeless world will bring them into a state of grace with her, that she will make them first among all the new creatures she creates. So they believe and so they act. And this is why they must be opposed."

"How can they do this?" asked Billy Goodwin.

"How we will not say," answered Calis. "We will only say that the King and a few others know this secret. No others need know. All we need know is that it is our job to stop them."

"How?" demanded Biggo. "You lost almost two thousand men, and from what you've said, their army is now twice the size of the one you faced."

Calis looked around. "Because we don't travel to Novindus to face this conquering army, Biggo. We travel to Novindus to join it."

12

★★

ARRIVAL

ERIK WINCED.

The roundhouse kick Nakor caught him with had been pulled, but it still stung.

"You still charge like a mad bull," scolded the Isalani. His face was like wrinkled leather, but his eyes showed a youthful merriment. Sho Pi watched closely as his older countryman spun again, unexpectedly. Erik moved just in time to keep from getting kicked in the chest again, and snapped off a kick of his own, coming quickly back to a defensive position.

"Why!" shouted Nakor, scolding. "Why did you draw back?"

Erik blew out hard, sucking in air as perspiration poured from his face and body. Puffing, he said, "Because . . . I would have been . . . off balance. That kick . . . was to get you to back off . . . not to hurt you. If I had followed up, you would have broken my neck."

Nakor grinned, and once more Erik was struck by how this strange man, aboard their ship for less than a month now, had come to be so liked by everyone. He told outrageous stories, almost certainly all lies, and his habit of winning consistently at cards caused Erik to think him probably a cheat as well. But if a liar and cheat could said to be trusted, Nakor was.

Sho Pi came to stand next to Nakor. "It is wise to know when to regroup, just as it is wise to know when to press." He bowed, and Erik returned the bow. At first, like the others, he had thought all the rituals strange, and had mocked them, but now, also like the others, he performed them without thought. In fact, he now admitted to himself that the rituals helped keep him focused.

"Master—" began Sho Pi.

"I tell you again, boy, don't call me master!"

The men laughed. Sho Pi had decided at some point during the week following Nakor's arrival that Nakor was the master he had been sent to find. This had brought a consistent stream of denial from Nakor that was now in its third week. At least once in every conversation, Sho Pi called Nakor master and Nakor demanded he stop.

Sho Pi ignored the instruction. "I think we should show the men shi-to-ku."

Nakor shook his head. "You show them. I'm tired. I'm going to go over there and eat an orange."

Erik flexed his left shoulder, stiff from the blow to his chest. Sho Pi noticed. "That is bothering you?"

Erik nodded. "Caught me here," he said, pointing to just below his right pectoral muscle, "but I can feel it all the way through to my neck and elbow. My shoulder is tightening."

"Then come here," said Sho Pi.

Nakor watched and nodded as Sho Pi indicated Erik should kneel. He made a gesture with his right hand, then laid his hands upon Erik's shoulder. Erik's eyes widened as he felt heat flowing from Sho Pi's hands. The throbbing in his shoulder quickly diminished. As he knelt there, Erik said, "What are you doing?"

Sho Pi said, "In my homeland it is known as *reiki*. There is healing energy in the body. It is what helps you recover from injuries and disease."

As the heat loosened the bruised muscle, Erik said, "Can you teach me to do this?"

"It takes a great deal of time—" began Sho Pi.

"Ha!" shouted Nakor. Moving from the rail, he tossed a half-eaten orange over the side and said, "More monastic mumbo-jumbo! Reiki is no mystic meditation; there is no prayer. It's a natural thing. Anyone can do it!"

Sho Pi smiled slightly as Nakor waved him aside. Standing over Erik, he said, "You want to do this?"

Erik said, "Yes."

Nakor said, "Give me your right hand."

Erik held it out, and Nakor turned it over, palm up. He closed his eyes and made some signs, then slapped Erik's hand, hard. Erik felt his eyes water from the unexpected blow. "What did you do that for?" he demanded.

"Wakes up the energies. Now, hold your hand here." Nakor moved Erik's hand to his shoulder. Erik felt the same heat flowing from his own hand he had felt from Sho Pi's. "Without prayer or meditation, it flows," instructed Nakor. "It's always on, so whatever you touch you will heal. Now I will show you what to touch." To Sho Pi he said, "I can teach these men to use the power in two days, boy. None of your mystic nonsense. The temples claim this is magic, but it isn't even a good trick. It's just that most people are too stupid to know they have the power or how to use it."

Sho Pi looked at Nakor and feigned a serious expression, but his eyes were amused. "Yes, Master."

"And don't call me master!" shouted Nakor.

He instructed the men to circle around and began talking about the body's natural healing energies. Erik was fascinated. He thought back to those horses he had treated, the ones who should have gotten better but didn't, and the ones that recovered from injuries against any reasonable expectation of success, and he wondered how much of it was their spirit.

"This energy is made of the stuff of life," said Nakor. "I think you are not stupid men, but you are also men who do not care much for those things I find so fascinating, so I will not try to explain to you what I think this stuff of life is. Leave it to say that this energy is everywhere, in all things living."

Calis came up on deck and caught Nakor's eyes. Something passed between them as Nakor said, "All living things are connected." Erik glanced back at where Roo sat, and noticed his friend had also caught the exchange.

Nakor went on to explain about how the body can heal itself, but that most people don't know how to accept their own power. He demonstrated a few things the men needed to know to take full advantage of the reiki—where best to place their hands to achieve the desired effect, how to identify different types of injury and illness—but the energy seemed always to be there whenever they touched themselves or one another after Nakor had "awakened the power" in their hands.

By midday all the men had been slapped on the hand and had spent hours practicing healing energies on one another. Nakor and Sho Pi had led them through a series of exercises designed to help them identify the sources of common problems and how to recognize the flow of energies in another's body. At the midday meal the men were joking about this laying hand on one another, but they were also obviously impressed at the ability of this simple act to relieve aches and reduce swelling and generally make them feel better.

After lunch, Erik and Roo were sent aloft, relieving sailors on the day watch so they could eat. Securing a sail that the Captain had ordered reefed as the wind freshened, Roo said, "What do you think of all that?"

Erik said, "What Nakor said: it's a useful tool. I don't care a fig for what Sho Pi says about its being a mystic thing. It works; I'll use it." With a near-wistful note in his voice, he added, "I wish I had known about it when I was tending Greylock's mare. It would have made her come back faster, I think."

Roo said, "I think anything we know that can keep us healthy is good."

Erik nodded. There was a grim reluctance among the men to consider the eventual end of their journey. After Calis had announced his intention to take them to join this invading host, he had briefly outlined their mission.

They would land a small party on a beach below a cliff where ships did not normally pass. The thirty-six prisoners and fifty-eight survivors of the last campaign, with Foster, de Loungville, Nakor, and Calis, would climb this cliff face. Once atop the plateau, they would travel overland to meet some allies of Calis's, then move to intercept the invaders at a city called Khaipur. Their mission was to discover what weakness, if any, existed in this host, and Calis and Nakor would be the ones likely to understand what that would be. But when it was discovered what that weakness might be, then it was every man's duty to return to the City of the Serpent River with the information, to get back to *Trenchard's Revenge,* and get the critical intelligence back to Prince Nicholas.

If they could contrive a way to balk the onslaught before the invaders could muster a host big enough to cross the waters and assault the Kingdom, all the better. But Calis drove home again and again the risk that hung over everyone. Erik remembered his last words on the subject: "No one will escape. This plague of invasion is but the first part of the destruction. Dark magic beyond your ability to comprehend will be unleashed in the end, and should you hide in the deepest cave in the farthest mountains of the Northlands, or in the remotest island on some distant sea, you will die. If we do not stop this host, we all will die." He had looked from man to man. "That is the only choice, win or die."

Now Erik understood why Robert de Loungville had needed "desperate men," because for all intents and purposes they were about to stick their neck back in the noose. Erik absently fingered the one he still wore.

"Mercy!" said Roo, bringing Erik out of his revery.

"What?"

"Speak of a demon and he appears! Isn't that Owen Greylock's silver scalp I see over there on the foredeck of the *Ranger?*"

Erik looked hard and saw the tiny figure on the nearby ship. "It could be. About the right size, and the hair has that silver streaking through it."

"I wonder why we didn't see him at the beach?"

Erik finished off tying a line. "Maybe he didn't come ashore. Maybe he already knows the tasks at hand."

Roo nodded. "In all of this there are still some things I don't understand. Who was this Miranda woman, anyway? Every man I mention her to has met her, sometimes under different names. And Greylock was your friend, maybe, but if he's on that ship, did he have something to do with our being captured?"

Erik shrugged. "If that is Greylock, we'll find out when we get where we're going. As for the rest, who cares? We're here, and we have a job to do. Thinking about why isn't going to change that."

Roo looked exasperated. "You have too accepting a nature, my friend. When this is all done, if we survive, I plan on getting rich. There's a merchant in

Krondor with a homely daughter who he wants to marry off. I may be just the lad for her."

Erik laughed. "You can be ambitious for both of us, Roo."

They continued to work, and when Erik glanced over at the *Ranger*, the figure who might have been Owen was gone.

Weeks passed. They sailed through the Straits of Darkness without mishap, though the weather was difficult. For the first time Erik felt what it was like to be at risk aboard ship, hanging from rigging as weather buffeted him. The old hands joked that this was a mild passage for the time of year in the Straits, and wove stories of impossible conditions, with mile-high funnel clouds and waves the size of castles.

It took three days, and when they had passed through, Erik had nearly collapsed on his bunk, as had his companions. The experienced sailors could sleep through the storm on their off watch, but the former prisoners weren't that blasé about it.

As life aboard the ship became more routine, the relationships between the men evolved. They would talk for days about the grim purpose behind their mission, then more days would go by without comment. Speculation would lead to dispute, followed by silent acknowledgment that each man, in his own way, was afraid.

Those former soldiers who came over from the *Ranger* to train with the prisoners were just as likely to give long narratives about the previous venture south as they were to remain silent. It depended upon the man and his mood.

Erik did discover one thing: Calis was nothing human, if the older soldiers were to be believed. Far more telling than Jadow's and Jerome's tales of his prodigious strength was one old soldier, a former corporal at Carse, who said that he had first met Calis twenty-four years previously, when the corporal had been a raw recruit, and Calis hadn't aged a day since.

Roo was learning to curb his temper, if not entirely master it. He had gotten into several arguments, but only one had come to blows, and that had quickly been ended by Jerome Handy's picking Roo up, carrying him up on deck, and threatening to drop him over the side. The crew laughed as Roo dangled over the water with Jerome gripping his ankles.

Roo had been more embarrassed than angered by the incident, and when Erik had spoken to him about it afterward, he shrugged it off. He said something that had stuck with Erik ever since. He looked his boyhood friend in the eye and said, "Whatever happens, I have been afraid, Erik. I cried like a baby and peed in my pants when they took us to the gallows. After that, what is there left to be afraid of?"

Erik enjoyed the sea, but he didn't think he could live the sailor's life. He longed for his forge and horses to tend. He knew that if he survived the coming battles, that would be his choice: a forge and maybe, someday, a wife and children.

He thought about Rosalyn and his mother, Milo and Ravensburg. He wondered how they were doing, and if they knew he was alive. Manfred might have mentioned it to a guard, who might have told someone in town. But there was certainly no one who cared enough about him or his family to ensure that his mother or Rosalyn knew. He had thoughts of Rosalyn, and found them strangely neutral. He loved her, but when he imagined a wife and children, Rosalyn wasn't there. No one was.

Roo had already made up his mind he would return to Krondor and marry Helmut Grindle's homely daughter. Every time he said that, Erik laughed.

As the days wore on, the men became more proficient in every aspect of their training. The stories of the surviving men from the last mission and their example, their own grim determination to excel, spurred on the former prisoners to match their achievements. As well as they could aboard ship, they practiced their weapons, and on calmer days Calis worked with them on archery. The weapon of choice was a small bow used by the horsemen of the Eastland steppes, the Jeshandi. Calis had his own longbow stored in his cabin, but used the shorter weapon with ease. About half the men turned out to be good to excellent with the weapon. Roo was better than Erik, but neither youngster was among the first thirty bowmen. Those would be issued bows, Calis had said, but he wanted every man at least familiar enough with the weapon to have some chance of hitting a target.

That seemed to be the underlying pattern to the training. De Loungville and Foster would drill men with every weapon they might be forced to use, from long poll arms to daggers. Each man was marked down in a journal as to his strengths and weaknesses, but none was spared the hours of drills, even with the weapons for which he showed no aptitude. What had begun at the camp outside of Krondor continued aboard ship. Each day Erik spent a half watch using a sword, spear, or bow, a knife, mauler, or his fists, but always he was expected to improve.

The hour with Sho Pi and Nakor became the high point of the day for Erik, and the other men seemed to enjoy the exercises as well. The meditation was strange at first, but now it refreshed him and made his sleep better.

By the third month, Erik was adept at open-handed fighting, as he thought of the strange Isalani dance Sho Pi taught them. No matter how strange at first, the movements wove themselves into an arsenal of moves and countermoves, and often without thought Erik found a sudden response, completely unexpected, coming from him during a combat drill. Once, when using knives, he almost cut Luis, who said something in Rodezian as he studied his onetime death cell companion. Then he had laughed. "Your 'dance of the crane' has turned into the 'claw of the tiger,' it seems." Both were moves taught him by Sho Pi, and neither had been conscious on his part.

Erik wondered what he was becoming.

"LAND HO!" CRIED the lookout.

For the last two days tension on the ship had mounted. Sailors had mentioned that they were close to the point where they should be making landfall, and now every man was conscious of how long he had been confined to the ship. These large three-masted warships were provisioned well enough for the long four-month voyage, but the food was now stale or old and tired. Only Nakor's ever-present oranges were fresh.

Erik went aloft and made ready to reef sail, as the Captain took the ship through a treacherous series of reefs. Moving past a clear patch of water, Erik looked down and saw what appeared to be part of a ship lying under ten feet of water.

An older sailor named Marstin standing next to him said, "That's the *Raptor*, lad. Old Captain Trenchard's ship, once the *Royal Eagle* out of Krondor. We sailors of the King became pirates for a time." He pointed toward the rocky shore. "A handful of us washed up there twenty-four years ago, and young Calis, with the Prince of Krondor—Nicholas, not his dad—and Duke Marcus of Crydee."

"You were among that party?" asked Roo on his other side.

"There's a handful of us still alive. I was on my first voyage, a seaman apprentice in the King's Navy, but I served on the best ship under the finest Captain in history."

Roo and Erik had heard several versions of the story about Calis's first voyage to the southern continent. "Where are you going once we're dropped off?"

Marstin replied, "City of the Serpent River. *Revenge* is going to wait for you men, while *Ranger* is going to refit and go home with the current news. That's what I hear, anyway."

Scuttlebutt they called it in the navy, but it was the same gossip they'd heard. Further conversation was cut off by the order to reef the sails, and Erik and Roo got to it.

When they were done scrambling around enough to take in their whereabouts, they saw they were lying off a long, empty beach beneath a huge wall of cliffs, easily one hundred feet high. The breakers and combers indicated the area was thick with rocks, and Erik was impressed with the Captain's ease at reaching this relatively safe anchorage.

"Muster on deck!" came the command, and Erik and Roo scrambled down to the deck with the others. De Loungville waited until the entire company was settled before he shouted, "We get off here, ladies. You have ten minutes to get below and gather up your kits and get back up here. The boats will be putting over the side at once. We don't dawdle. No one will be left behind, so don't get cute ideas about dodging into the rope lockers."

Erik was convinced the warning was unnecessary. The conversations he'd had with every other member of this company led him to judge that everyone understood there would be no quick escape from this mission. Some might not believe that everything was as Calis had said, but Nakor's words seemed to have reached all of them, and whatever the truth of it, this band of desperate men would meet the challenge face on.

HORSEMEN WAITED AT the top of the cliff. The climb had been relatively easy, as a rope-and-wood ladder had been installed on the face of the rocks. Anyone in poor health might have had difficulty with the long climb, but after four months of ship's duty, hard upon the heels of the training at the camp, Erik had no trouble climbing with his backpack and weapons.

At the top of the bluff, Erik saw a pleasant oasis hard against the edge of the cliff. A large pool of water was surrounded by date palms and other greenery. Then he caught sight of the desert. "Gods!" he exclaimed, and Roo came to his side.

"What?" asked the smaller youth. Biggo and the others came and looked where Erik pointed.

"I've seen the Jal-Pur," said Billy Goodwin, "and it's a mother's kindness compared to this."

In every direction, rock and sand greeted the eye. Save where the cliff showed ocean, there was only one color, a slate grey, dotted with darker rock. Even this late in the afternoon, the heat shimmer rising made the air ripple like bed sheets on a line, and suddenly Erik felt thirsty.

Biggo said, "I'd not wish this on a hound of hell."

The attention of Erik and his five companions was diverted by Foster suddenly shouting, "All right, ladies, enough time to take in the scenery later. Fall in!"

They were moved to where de Loungville waited. He pointed to a group of six men, the one that included Jerome and Jadow Shati. Erik knew them by name and had spoken to each from time to time on the long voyage. "This is the oldest team of six I have. They've been training for three years." Then he motioned toward Erik and his group. "This is the newest group. They'd been training for only a few weeks before we left." He addressed Erik's group. "Watch them. Do what they do. If you get into trouble, they will help you. If you make mistakes, they will help you. If you try to escape, they will kill you." Without another word, he moved away, calling Foster's name, he shouted instructions to get the men organized for a march.

The horsemen conferred with Calis, then turned and rode off. A short distance away, large bundles were tied down under canvas, staked to the ground by peg and rope. Foster ordered a dozen men to uncover them, and when they had finished, Erik saw a cache of arms and armor.

Calis held up his hand. "You are mercenaries, now, so some of you will dress like ragpickers, while others will look like princes. I want no squabbling over who takes what. The weapons are more important than the finery. Leave your Kingdom-made weapons here, and take what's under the canvas. . . ."

Roo whispered, "Wish they'd told us we wouldn't need all this armor before we lugged it up the cliff!"

Calis continued, "Remember, this is mummery, nothing more. Booty isn't our objective."

The men gathered closer, for Calis rarely addressed them and they were still not privy to much of what lay before them. "You know what you've been told," he continued. "Now you will know the rest. In ancient times a race was created, the serpent men of Pantathia." Instead of the usual muttering, the men were rapt and silent, for they knew their lives depended upon knowing as much about this mission as possible. "This race has lore as ancient as the Chaos Wars. They think their destiny is to rule this world, destroying all else who abide here." Looking around at the men, as if memorizing their faces, the young-looking elf-kin said, "They have the means, I think. Or at least it's our task to discover if they have the means.

"We came here twelve years ago, some of us." He nodded to a knot of soldiers from the last campaign. "We thought in simpler terms then: we would lend our weight to the struggle and turn back conquerors. We now know better." All the surviving soldiers of the first campaign against the Pantathians nodded in agreement. "Whatever these creatures plan, it is more than simple land-grabbing or raiding for booty. Twenty years ago they came against a small city on the far side of this continent, Irabek, and since then, any land they take falls behind a curtain of death and fire. We have no word from any place they have conquered. Those of us who faced them on the walls of Hamsa know what they are. Mercenary companies such as we pretend to be lead the wave, but behind them are fanatic soldiers. There are human officers and cadres of well-drilled fighting men, but more: there are also serpents who ride horses twenty-five hands high."

Erik blinked at this. The largest war-horse he had seen in Baron Otto's cavalry was nineteen hands. He'd heard of some being twenty hands, used by the Krondor Heavy Lancers, but twenty-five hands? That was nearly eight and a half feet at the withers. Not even the biggest Shire horse he'd seen came close to that.

"We've not seen these creatures," continued Calis, "but we have reliable reports. And behind these creatures come the priests themselves.

"Some men, we are told, are rewarded by being placed high within this company of well-drilled fightingmen. But all of them are willing servants of those who seek to dominate this land.

"Our mission is simple. We must get as close to the heart of this army of conquest and discover as much about it as we may. Then, when we have learned all we can, we must flee to the City of the Serpent River, and from there home, so that Prince Nicholas can prepare for the coming invasion."

There was a moment of silence; then Biggo said, "So that's all we need do, and then we can go home?"

Suddenly there was laughter. Erik found he couldn't hold it in. Roo looked at him, seemed to struggle to hold in his own guffaw, then abruptly was laughing as well.

Calis let the mirth go on for a moment before he held up his hands for silence. "Many will not return. But those of you who do will have earned your freedom and the praise of your King. And if we can defeat these murderous snakes, you may have the opportunity to live out that life as you choose. Now, get equipped. We have a long march across a difficult desert before we meet with friends."

The men fell upon the arms and clothing like children on gifts at the Midwinter Feast, and soon comments and friendly insults were flying.

Erik found a faded but serviceable blue tunic, over which he strapped on a breastplate of alien design, with a worn and faded lion's head embossed on it. A simple round shield, a long dagger in his belt, and a well-made longsword filled his needs. As men tried on various items and discarded them, a conical helm with a nasal bar rolled to his feet. He bent to pick it up, and a chain neck guard fell out. He tried it on. It fit comfortably, so he kept it.

As the men made ready, the mood turned somber. Calis saw they were finished and held up his hands. "You are now Calis's Crimson Eagles. If anyone recognizes that name, you're men from the Sunset Islands. Those of you who served before can tell the others what they need to know about the Eagles if they're asked. We are the fiercest fighters in the Kingdom, and we fear no man or demon. We got our backsides booted when last we came this way, but that was twelve years ago, and I doubt there's one man in a thousand alive who remembers. So, form companies—we're mercenaries, but we're not rabble—and check your rations. Each man's to carry three full waterskins. We're marching at night and sleeping during the day. Follow instructions and you'll live to see water again."

As the sun sank Foster and de Loungville got the men ranked into companies. Calis faced west, toward an angry sun, and led them into the heat.

ERIK HAD NEVER been so hot, tired, and thirsty in his life. The back of his neck itched, yet he couldn't spare the energy to reach up and scratch it. The first night had seemed relatively easy. The air had plunged from hot to brisk within hours, and as sunrise approached, it was cold. Yet even then it had been a very dry cold, and the thirst had begun. As instructed, they drank only when permitted by Foster and de Loungville, a mouthful every hour.

Near sunrise, they were ordered to make camp, and quickly had small tents erected, each large enough to shade six men. They quickly fell asleep.

Hours later, Erik awoke with a start, as the breath in his lungs seemed barely to hold enough air to keep him alive. He gasped and was rewarded with a dry lungful that was close to painful. Opening his eyes, he saw waves in the air as heat shimmer rose off the hardpan. Other men moved and tried to get comfortable in the heat. A couple had left the small tents, thinking the heat outside might somehow be less than the heat radiating through the canvas, and quickly they returned to the tiny shelter. As if reading minds, Foster's voice had cut through the air, warning any man caught drinking would be flogged.

The second night had been arduous, and the second day terrible. Now there was no rest in lying in the heat, only less energy expended than attempting to move. The night offered no relief, as the cold dry air sucked moisture from the men seemingly as quickly as the day's heat.

They marched on.

Foster and de Loungville were careful not to lose sight of each company, ensuring that no one at the rear stumbled and was left behind. Erik knew they were also ensuring that no one dropped any vital piece of equipment because they were fatigued.

Now it was the third day and Erik despaired of ever seeing water and shade again. Adding to the cruelty of the trek was the rising terrain before them. It had begun gently enough, but now it felt as if they were walking uphill.

Ahead, Calis stopped, but motioned for the others to come up to him. When they reached the crest of the rise, Erik could see that they had reached grasslands, and that from the crest downward, rolling hills of green led to a scattering of copses where broad branched trees offered shelter. In the distance, a line of trees meandered across the countryside, and it was there Calis pointed. "The Serpent River. You can drink your fill now."

Erik pulled up his last waterskin and drained it, finding it was almost empty. He was surprised; he had thought he had more water left, as he hadn't been allowed to drink enough to drain three skins.

Calis looked to de Loungville and said, "That was pretty easy."

Erik glanced at Roo, who shook his head. The order to march was passed along, and they moved toward the distant river.

HORSES MILLED IN large corrals and Calis spoke to a pair of horse traders. They had been at this place before, a prosperous-looking trading post called Shingazi's Landing. One of the older soldiers said it had been burned to the ground when Calis had first come to this land, twenty-four years ago, but had been rebuilt. Even though Shingazi had died in that fire years before, the new owners kept the name. So they were presently enjoying the hospitality of Brek's at Shingazi's Landing.

The food was simple but welcome after the rations of the last three days, as were the abundant wine and ale. The men waiting for them weren't the same riders that had met them on the bluffs. Those had been riders of the Jeshandi, Erik had been told, while these were city men, up from the City of the Serpent River.

A company of guardsmen were stationed with them, and their captain was known to Calis. They had gone inside the tavern to talk, while the mercenary company was left to itself outside. Every man had bathed in the river, drank his fill, and now they were resting before mounting up to ride.

Erik watched the horses with interest. Here was something he could understand. He saw that each mount was being given a snaffle bit, a cavalry saddle with a breastband, and saddlebags, with room for a sleeping roll or rolled-up tent behind the saddle's cantle.

Foster was walking nearby when Erik noticed something. "Corporal," he said.

Foster halted. "What?"

"That horse isn't sound."

"What?"

Erik moved between two rails of the corral fence and pushed past the milling horses near by. One of the horse trader's handlers shouted at Erik; he had tried to learn the language of this land on ship, and knew that man was ordering him to stay away from the horses, but he didn't have enough confidence in his ability to say he just wanted to look. He waved at the man as if returning a greeting.

Reaching the horse, he ran his hand down the left foreleg, picking it up. "Bad hoof."

Foster said, "Damn their greedy hearts."

The wrangler reached them, shouting at them to leave the animals alone. "You haven't paid yet! They are not yours!"

Foster unleashed his legendary rage. Gripping the man's shirt in one meaty hand, he raised him to his toes and screamed in his face. "I should have your liver for lunch! Get your master and tell him if he's not here before I lose my good mood, I'll kill him and every cheating whoreson of a city man within five miles!" He half pushed the man as he let go of his shirt, and the wrangler fell back against the horse, who snorted in protest and moved away. Turning, the man ran off to find his employer.

This exchange wasn't lost on the guards who came with the horse traders, and suddenly there were armed men in all directions moving to get ready for a fight. Erik said, "Corporal, was that wise?"

Foster only grinned.

A few moments later the horse trader was upon them demanding to know why they had assaulted his man. Foster said, "Assault? I should have your heads on pikes! Look at this animal!"

The man glanced at the horse and said, "What about him?"

Foster looked to Erik and said, "What about him?"

Erik suddenly found himself the center of attention of every man within view. He looked around and saw Calis and the leader of the city guardsmen coming out of the tavern. Someone had obviously alerted them to the possibility of danger.

Erik said, "He has a bad hoof. It's cracked and festering, and it's been painted over to look healthy."

The man began a stream of protests, but then Calis said, "Is this true?"

Erik nodded. "It's an old trick." He moved to the horse's head and looked into his eyes, then inspected his mouth. "He's been drugged. I don't know what, but there are several drugs that will deaden the pain enough to make him not limp. Whatever they gave him is wearing off. He's starting to show a hitch in his walk."

Calis came up to the horse trader. "You were given this commission by our friend Regin of the Lion Clan, were you not?"

The man nodded, attempting to bluff. "I was. My word is bond from the City of the Serpent River to the Westlands. I will find whichever one of my misguided retainers is responsible and have the man beaten. Obviously someone is attempting to curry my favor, but I will have no cheating of good friends!"

Calis shook his head. "Fine. We shall inspect every animal, and for each one we reject, you will be fined the price of a sound horse as well. This is one, that means we get one other sound mount for no charge."

When the man looked to the Captain of the company that had accompanied the horse man, he smiled. "Sounds fair to me, Mugaar."

Seeing no relief, the man touched his hand to his heart. "It is done."

As the defeated merchant stalked away, Calis said, "Hatonis, this is Erik von Darkmoor. He'll be inspecting each animal. If you would see he's not interfered with, I would be in your debt."

Erik extended his hand. The man shook it with a firm grip. He was a soldier of middle years, but only a little grey took away his youth. He was strong and looked like a seasoned fighter.

"My father would come back from the grave to haunt one such as that if he cast shame upon our clan," said the guard captain.

Turning to Erik, Calis said, "Can you vet more than a hundred horses by first light tomorrow?"

Erik glanced around and shrugged. "If I must."

"You must," said Calis, walking away.

Foster watched a moment, then turned to Erik. "Well, don't just stand there. Get to it!"

Erik sighed in resignation and, looking around, called for some of the men in his company to lend a hand. He couldn't get another expert to magically appear, but he needed men to walk and jog the animals and move the vetted ones to another location.

Taking a deep breath, he began with the closest horse.

13

★★

SEARCH

THE BARMAN LOOKED up.

The inn was crowded, and in the normal course of business, anyone entering should not have caused him to notice. But the figure who entered was not one of his ordinary customers, nor was the barman an ordinary barman.

The newcomer was a woman, tall and alert in her stance, wearing an all-concealing robe of sturdy weave, fine enough to mark her as more than a common street girl, but not so elegant as to mark her as nobility. For a moment the barman expected one or more men to follow her, escorts to protect her from the street's rougher denizens. When none appeared, he was certain there was nothing ordinary about this woman. She glanced around the room as if seeking someone; then she locked eyes with the barman.

She threw back the hood of the cloak, revealing a youthful appearance—though the barman knew well enough appearances were deceiving—with dark hair and green eyes. She was not pretty but striking, with a full mouth and good cheekbones. Her eyes were dangerous. Most men would have called her beautiful, but most men wouldn't have known how dangerous she was.

A young bravo stepped up to intercept her before she could reach the bar. He was at the peak of youth, feeling too much the rush of blood and ale. He was nearly majestic in appearance, half a foot taller than six feet, with shoulders broad with iron plates, and enough scars to ensure that few of his boasts were challenged as lies.

"Here, now!" he said with a drunken laugh, pushing back a crested helmet so he could see better. "What is so wonderful a wench doing without my company?"

This brought a laugh from two of his companions and a disapproving look from the whore who had counted on all three of these soldiers making her night profitable. The woman stopped as the young warrior stepped before her, and looked him slowly up and down. "Excuse me," she said softly.

The man-boy grinned and seemed about to say something. Then his smile slowly faded, until he looked down upon the woman with a puzzled expression. "I'm sorry," he said quietly as he stepped aside.

His friends looked on in amazement and one stood up to say something. The barman produced a light crossbow and put it on the bar, with the bolt pointed directly at the protester. "Why don't you sit back down and finish your drink!"

"Hold on, Tabert. We spend a lot of gold here! Don't be threatening us!"

"Roco, you get drunk on cheap wine down at the market, then stagger up here to grope and fondle one of my girls until closing, when half the time you don't have enough to pay for her company!"

The girl who had been sitting with the three men stood up and said, "And the half of the time they have money, they don't have any iron left in their swords from all that cheap wine, and even when they do, it's nothing much to brag on."

This brought a torrent of laughter and insults from the rest of the patrons of the commons. The third warrior, who had been holding the whore until she stood up, said, "Arlet! I thought you liked us!"

"Show me your gold, then I'll love you, darling," she said with a grin lacking any affection.

Tabert said, "Why don't you three boys head on down to Kinjiki's and annoy his girls for a while. He's Tsurani blood, so he'll bear up under the abuse with better grace than I."

The two companions looked ready to dispute this request, but the first, who had tried to stop the woman, nodded slowly and pulled his helm back down. Reaching under the table, he retrieved his weapon and shield. "Come on. We can find our fun somewhere else." His two friends were about to protest when he bellowed, "I said come on!" The abrupt rage startled the others and they hesitated, then agreed, following him out of the room.

The woman reached the bar. The barman knew her first question before she asked. He said, "I haven't seen him."

The woman raised one eyebrow in question.

"Whoever it is you're looking for, I haven't seen him."

"Who do you think I'm looking for?"

The barman, a stout fellow with muttonchop sideburns and a receding hairline, said, "There is only one kind of man who would bring a woman like you searching, and one like that hasn't come by recently."

"And what kind of woman are you taking me for?" she asked.

"One who sees things others miss."

"You're very observant for a barman," she countered.

"Most barmen are, though they learn not to show it. I, on the other hand, am not most barmen."

"Your name?"

"Tabert."

Lowering her voice, she spoke. "I have been to every shabby inn and dirty taproom in LaMut, seeking something I was told on good authority would be here. So far I get nothing but blank looks and confused stammering." Speaking even more softly, she said, "I need to find the Hall."

With a smile he said, "The back room."

He led her through a small back room, then down a flight of stairs. "This storage room connects with others, below the city," he said. He opened a door at the foot of the stairs and led her to the far end of a narrow hall. There was no door, only a small alcove doorway, hidden by a piece of cloth hung from a metal rod. As she reached the door, Tabert said, "You'll understand when I say if you're in this room, I can't help you. I can only show you the door."

Miranda nodded, though she wasn't entirely sure of the meaning of what he said. She stepped through into the small room. As she stepped across the threshold and passed under the rod, she felt the energy emanating from it. For a brief instant she saw a tiny storage room, stacked high with a few empty ale and wine casks and some crates, but instantly she understood the barman's words. She willed herself into phase with the energies coursing down from the metal rod, and an instant later she stood somewhere else.

THE HALL WAS endless. Or at least no creature able to communicate had ever discovered the end of it. Miranda saw that every so often a doorway, a rectangle of light, adjoined the Hall on the sides. Between the entrances a grey nothingness loomed. That she could see at all was something of a mystery, for there was no obvious source of light. Miranda shifted her perceptions and instantly regretted it. The darkness she experienced was so profound it produced an instant despair. She returned her sight to the magically tuned vision she had employed, and again she could see. She considered the barman's words. "You'll understand when I say if you're in this room, I can't help you. I can only show you the door." He knew of the magic portal into the Hall but could not empower anyone to enter. Only a talent like Miranda or a few others on Midkemia would have the means of entering the Hall and surviving once there.

She turned and looked at the door she had just stepped through, seeking to set it apart in her mind from the others, should she need to return this way. At first nothing out of the ordinary marked the doorway; at last she noticed faint runes hovering over the top of the door, difficult to see. She focused her attention on them and memorized the shape and formation, in her mind translating the glyphs to "Midkemia." Across from the door, only a featureless grey void beckoned. The doors were staggered on the left and right so that none faced another. She moved down and saw that the glyphs of the door on the other side of the one through which she had entered bore a different mark. She memorized that one as well. If she were to be turned around somehow and lose sight of where she was, a series of familiar landmarks would prove useful.

After memorizing a half dozen of the nearest door glyphs, she continued on—assuming that, without information, one direction was as apt as another—and began to walk.

THE FIGURE IN the distance appeared roughly human in shape, but it could have been a member of any number of races. Miranda stopped walking and watched. She was able to defend herself, but she thought it better to avoid rushing into trouble if she could avoid it. A door to her right provided the potential for escape, though she had no idea what was on the other side.

As if reading her thoughts, the figure yelled something, holding out its gloved hand to show it was holding no weapons. The gesture was less than reassuring, as the creature was otherwise bristling with more arms than Miranda thought anyone should be able to carry and still walk upright. Upon its head a full visor masked its features, while the body was covered in a material that looked as rigid as steel, yet gave the appearance of being more flexible. It was a dull, pale silver in color, almost white, and lacked the high reflective quality that most polished armor possessed. The creature carried a round shield on its back, giving it a turtle-like appearance. A longsword's hilt peeked over one shoulder, while what appeared to be the stock of a crossbow was visible over the other. At the right hip hung a short sword, and an assortment of knives and throwing implements hung around the figure's torso. A whip was rolled up and hung from the left side of the creature's belt. And over one shoulder a large sack was thrown.

Miranda called out in the Kingdom tongue. "I can see you are not carrying anything in your hand . . . at the moment."

The figure moved cautiously toward her and said something in a language different from the first it had used. Miranda answered in Keshian, and the slowly walking arsenal answered in yet another tongue.

At last Miranda spoke in a variant of the language of the Kingdom of Roldem, and the figure said, "Ah, you're a Midkemian! I thought I'd recognized Delkian a bit ago, but I'm rusty." He—for his voice sounded like that of a man—said, "I have been trying to tell you that if you jump through that door, you'd better be able to breath methane."

"I have means of protecting myself from lethal gas," answered Miranda.

The man reached up slowly and removed his helm, revealing a face that was almost boyish—a freckled visage set with green eyes and topped with a damp mat of red hair—a face split with a friendly smile. "Few who walk the Hall don't, but the stress is pretty awful. You'd weigh about two hundred times as much as you do normally on Thedissio—which is what the inhabitants call that world—and that can slow movement down a great deal."

"Thank you," Miranda said at last.

"First time in the Hall?" asked the man.

"Why do you ask?"

"Well, unless you're a great deal more powerful than you look—and I'll be the first to admit that appearances are almost always deceiving—it's usually first-timers whom we find wandering the Hall without company."

"We?"

"Those of us who live here."

"You live in the Hall?"

"You're a first-timer, no doubt." He set the bag down. "I am Boldar Blood."

"Interesting name," Miranda said, visibly amused.

"Well, it's not the one my parents gave me, certainly, but I'm a mercenary and one must attempt a certain level of intimidation in my line of work. Hardly credible, I know, but it does prove to be the case. Besides"—he pointed to his own countenance—"is this a face to inspire terror?"

Miranda shook her head and smiled in return. "No, I guess not. You can call me Miranda. Yes, it's my first time in the Hall."

"Can you get back to Midkemia?"

"If I turn around and walk about two hundred twenty doors, I suspect I'll find the right one."

Boldar shook his head. "That's the long way. There's a door a short way off that will put you in the city of Ytli, on the world of Il-Jabon. If you can get through the two blocks to another entrance without being accosted by the locals, you'll find a door that leads back into the hall next to the door that leads to . . . I forget which Midkemian door it is, but it's one of them." He leaned over, opened his bag, and took out a bottle. He fished around inside the sack and produced a pair of metal cups. "Care to join me in a cup of wine?"

"Thank you," said Miranda, "I am a little thirsty."

Boldar said, "When I first stumbled into the Hall—must have been a century and a half or so ago—I wandered around until I almost starved to death. A very agreeable thief saved my life in exchange for a seemingly inexhaustible series of reminders of that fact, usually in conjunction with a need for a favor from me. But he did save me a great deal of difficulty at the time. Knowledge of how to navigate the Hall is quite useful. And it's knowledge that I'm delighted to share with you."

"In exchange for . . ."

"You catch on quickly," said Blood with a grin. "Nothing is free in the Hall. Sometimes you might do something to build accounts and put others in your debt, but nothing ever goes without something in return.

"There are three types of people you'll meet in the Hall: those who will avoid you and spare you their society in passing, those who will try to bargain with you, and those who will try to take advantage of you. The second and third groups are not necessarily the same thing."

"I can take care of myself," Miranda said with a challenge in her voice.

"As I said earlier, you couldn't be here in the first place and not have some capacity. But remember this is also true of everyone else you meet in the Hall of Worlds. Oh, occasionally some poor soul without any powers, talents, or abilities blunders in unbidden. No one quite understands how. But quickly they walk out the wrong door or run into those who seek easy prey or step off into the void."

"What happens when you step off into the void?"

"If you know the right spot, you end up coming into a saloon of a great inn, known by many names, owned by a man named John. The inn is called simply 'The Inn,' and as John is known as, variously, 'John the Oathkeeper,' 'John Without Deceit,' 'John the Scrupulous,' 'John Who Has Ethics,' or any other of a half-dozen such honorifics, the saloon is usually called 'Honest John's.' There were, at last count, one thousand one hundred and seventeen known entrances to the saloon. If you don't know the right spot, well . . . no one knows, for no one has ever returned to tell anyone what exists in the void. It is simply *the void*."

Miranda relaxed. The mercenary's affable manner was such that she doubted he would attempt to take advantage of her. "Would you be willing to show me to one of these entrances?"

"Certainly, for a price."

"That being?" she asked, raising an eyebrow.

"In the Hall, there are many things of value. The usual: gold and other precious metal, gems and stones, deeds of ownership to estates, slaves and indentures, and, most of all, information. Then there is the unusual: items unique, services personal, manipulations of reality, souls of those who will never be born, things of those types."

Miranda nodded. "What would you?"

"What have you?"

They began haggling.

TWICE IN LESS than a day, Blood had proven his worth. Miranda was finding herself fortunate that he had been the first person she encountered, rather than a party of interdimensional slavers whom they encountered several hours later.

Miranda had a personal distaste for the institution of slavery, a bias now heightened by the attempt to reduce her and Boldar to inventory.

Boldar had disposed of the four guards and the slaver after attempting to allow them peaceful passage. Miranda thought she might have been able to cope with them alone, but she was impressed how Boldar had instantly recognized the moment the negotiations had soured and had disposed of two guards before she could begin to focus her mind on protecting herself. By the time she would have encased herself in a protective aura, the conflict was over.

The slaves had been freed—which had required a great deal of argument on Miranda's part, for now she had to make good on the portion of profit Boldar stood to make upon acquiring the slaves and selling them. Miranda pointed out that as he was currently in her employ, he was in fact acting as her agent, and she was free to do with the slaves what she chose. He found this proposition somewhat dubious, but after considering the difficulty of feeding and caring for the slaves, decided that accepting a bonus from Miranda would prove the better solution.

The second encounter had been with another band of mercenaries, who seemed inclined to give Blood and his employer a wide berth, but who, Miranda was certain, would have acted entirely differently had she been alone.

While they walked, she learned.

"So if you know the locations of the common doors, the journey through the Hall can be shortened?"

"Certainly," said Blood. "It depends on the world, how many doorways exist, and where they are relative to one another in the Hall. Thanderospace, for example"—he waved at a door they passed—"has but one door, which unfortunately opens into the hall of sacrifice in the most sacred temple of a cult of cannibalistic humanoids, who are less fussy about defining cannibalism than they are devoted to eating anyone who stumbles into their most holy of holies. This is a world seldom visited.

"Merleen, on the other hand"—he waved at another door a short distance ahead—"is a commerce world that is served by no less than six doors, which makes it a hub of trade, both among its resident nations and for other Hall worlds.

"The world from which you appear to hail, Midkemia, has at least three doors I'm aware of. Which did you use to enter?"

"Under a bar in LaMut."

"Ah, yes, Tabert's. Good food, decent ale, and bad women. My sort of place." He seemed somehow to be grinning behind the mask. How Miranda could tell she didn't know. Perhaps it was some subtlety in the mercenary's body language, or a note in his voice.

"How does one learn of these doors? Is there a map?"

"Well, there's one," said Boldar, "at Honest John's. It's on a wall in the public room. There you can see the known limits of the Hall. The last time I looked, there were something like thirty-six thousand–odd doors identified and catalogued.

"There are occasionally messages forwarded to the Inn from those who encounter new doors, either in the Hall or upon any world where a new passage is discovered. There's even one legendary lunatic whose name I forget who is exploring the far reaches and sending back messages, some which take decades to reach John's. He's getting so far from the Inn he's becoming a myth."

Miranda thought. "How long has this been going on?"

Boldar shrugged. "I suspect the Hall has existed since the dawn of time. Men and other creatures have lived here for ages. It requires a certain talent to survive for long within the Hall, so it has its appeal for those who seek a . . . higher-stakes sort of living."

"What of you?" asked Miranda. "You could live well on most worlds with the fee you charge me."

The mercenary shrugged. "I do this less for the bounty than for the excitement. I must confess that I do grow easily bored. There are worlds where I could rule as king, but that has little appeal for me. In truth, I find myself happiest in circumstances that would drive most sane men mad. War, murder, assassination, intrigue—these are my stock-in-trade, and there are few who match me in skill. I say this not to brag, for I have your commission already, but to tell you simply, once you grow used to living in the Hall, there is no other life."

Miranda nodded. The scope of the place was staggering; it was literally the sum of all known and quite a few unknown worlds.

Boldar said, "As much as I am enjoying your company, Miranda, and as much as I enjoy the wealth you promise, I grow tired; while time has no meaning here, fatigue and hunger are real in all dimensions—at least the ones I've visited. And you still haven't told me where you go."

Miranda said, "That's because I really don't know where I'm going. I'm looking for someone."

"May I enquire whom?"

"A worker of magic, by name Pug of Stardock."

Boldar shrugged. "Never heard of him. But if there is one place where both our present needs can likely be met, it is the Inn."

Miranda was uncertain, and wondered at her own reluctance to embrace the obvious. If there was a communal center to the Hall, then should Pug have come through the Hall, that was the most likely place to inquire. But she feared others might also be interested in his passing and thought it likely he would have avoided letting others know of his whereabouts. Still, it was better than wandering aimlessly.

"Are we far from the Inn?"

"No, actually," said Boldar. "We've passed two other entrances since we met, and there is another a short distance away."

He motioned for her to follow, and after progressing past another two doors, he pointed to the void. "This is very difficult the first time." He pointed to the door opposite the void. "Note that mark?"

She nodded.

"It's Halliali, a nice place if you enjoy mountains. One of the entrances to Honest John's lies across from it. Now, you simply step off and expect to meet a step a foot or so beyond the edge of the void." So saying, he stepped into the grey and vanished.

Miranda took a breath, then, as she started to duplicate his move, thought, *Step up or down?*

MIRANDA FELL FORWARD: the step was down and she had guessed up. Strong arms caught her, and she opened her eyes wide at the sight of white fur on them.

She tried remaining calm as she disengaged herself from her helper, a nine-foot-tall creature covered in that same white fur from head to foot. Black spots broke up the otherwise snowy surface, and two immense blue eyes and a mouth were the only visible features on a shaggy head. A plaintive grunt was followed by Boldar saying, "If you have any weapons, now is the time to surrender them."

She saw he was efficiently divesting himself of his arsenal, including several rather innocuous-looking items that had been secreted about his person. Miranda carried only two daggers, one in her waistband, and another strapped to the inside of her right calf, and she quickly surrendered them.

Boldar said, "The proprietor learned ages ago that his establishment thrives so long as it is neutral ground for everyone. Kwad ensures that no one who starts trouble remains inside the saloon any longer than necessary."

"Kwad?"

"Our large hirsute friend here," answered Boldar. As they left the doorway, he continued. "Kwad's a Coropaban; stronger by the pound than any creature known, almost completely resistant to any magic; and the most toxic poisons take a week or so to kill one. They make incredible bodyguards, if you can get one to leave their homeworld."

Miranda stopped and gaped. The saloon was immense, easily two hundred yards across, and twice that deep. Along the right wall, nearly the entire way, ran a single bar, with a dozen barmen rushing to meet their customers' demands. A pair of galleries, one above the other, overhung the other three sides of the hall, thick with tables and chairs, providing vantage points from which those drinking and dining could gaze down upon the main floor.

There every game of chance conceivable was being played, from several variations of dice to a knife duel in a small sandpit. Creatures of every imaginable conformation moved easily through the press, greeting one another as they chanced upon old acquaintances.

Creatures carried trays covered with a variety of pots, platters, cups, buckets, and bowls. Some were put before creatures that defied Miranda's sense of order. At least a dozen clearly reptilian creatures were dining in the hall, the mere fact of which caused her to be very uncomfortable. The majority of the clientele was humanoid, though an occasional insectlike being or something that looked like a walking dog could be seen.

"Welcome to Honest John's," said Boldar.

"Where's John?" she asked.

"He is over there." He pointed to the long bar. At the near end stood a man wearing a strange suit of shining cloth. It consisted of trousers that broke without cuffs at the top of shiny black boots with oddly pointed toes. The jacket was open in front, revealing a white shirt with ruffles, closed by pearl studs and sporting a pointed collar, set off with a cravat of bright yellow. Upon his head he wore a wide-brimmed white hat with a shimmering red silk hatband. He spoke closely with a creature that looked like a man with an extra set of eyes in his forehead.

Boldar waved as they approached and the man identified as John said something to the four-eyed man, who nodded once and departed.

With a wide smile, John said, "Boldar! It's been, what, a year?"

"Not quite, John. But close enough."

"How do you tell time in the Hall?" asked Miranda.

John glanced at Boldar, who said, "My current employer, Miranda."

With a theatrical gesture, John doffed his hat and swept it across his chest, bowing at the waist as he reached out with his other and took one of hers lightly in it. He then made a gesture of kissing it, though his lips never touched skin.

She withdrew it quickly, feeling somewhat awkward at the contact. John said, "Welcome to my humble establishment."

Suddenly Miranda's eyes widened. "What language are you—are we . . ."

John said, "Your first visit, I see. I thought it unlikely we should host as lovely a guest as yourself before without my notice." He waved them to a table located near the bar, and pulled out a chair. She blinked at it a moment before she realized he was waiting for her to sit. She was unused to this odd behavior, but considering the range of human custom, she chose not to offend and let him seat her.

"One of the few magic spells allowed. It is not only useful, it is necessary. It's not foolproof, I fear, for we do occasionally have the odd visitor whose personal frame of reference is so alien to the majority of sentient life that only the most basic communication is possible, if any, and we also do get the occasional fool."

Boldar chuckled and said, "That we do."

John waved his hand. "Now, as to your first question, measuring time is simple. Outside the Hall, time passes as it does everywhere else in the universe, as far as I know. But to answer what you meant to ask, we measure it as we did on my homeworld. It's a vanity, but as I am the owner of the establishment, it's my right to make the rules. What world do you hail from, if I might know?"

"Midkemia."

"Ah, then, it's very close to what you're used to. Mere hours different per year; enough to trouble scribes and philosophers, but in the course of a normal lifetime, you'd only be off by a few days on your birthday between the two calendars."

Miranda said, "When I first learned of the Hall, I thought it a magic gate through which I might seek other worlds. I had no idea . . ."

John nodded. "Few do. But humans, for that is what I judge you to be, are like most other intelligent creatures—they adapt. And they find things that are useful and continue to do them. Likewise, those of us who are privileged to walk the Hall, well, we adapt, too. There are too many reasons to stay within the Hall, too many benefits, once one finds one's way into it, to ignore, so most of us become citizens of the Hall, abandoning our former ties or at least neglecting them shamefully."

"Benefits?"

John and Boldar exchanged looks. "So I don't bore you, my dear, why don't you tell me what you know about the Hall?" suggested John.

Miranda said, "In my travels I have heard of the Hall of Worlds several times. I had to look for quite some time to find the entrance. I know it is a means of traveling through space, to reach distant worlds."

"And through time, as well," said Boldar.

Miranda said, "Time?"

"To reach a distant world by conventional means takes lifetimes; the Hall reduces transit to days, in some cases hours."

John said, "Then to the heart of the matter: the Hall exists independent of objective reality as we like to define it when standing on the surface of our homeworlds. It links worlds that may be in different universes, different space-times, for lack of a better term. We have no way of knowing. For that matter, it may link worlds at different times. My homeworld, a not very distinguished sphere orbiting an unremarkable sun, may very well have died of old age before your world was born, Miranda. How would we know? If we move through objective space, then why not through objective time?

"And because of that, we have here, within the Hall, everything. Or if not that, then as close as a mortal can wish. We trade in wonders, in the Hall, and in the prosaic, every chattel and species, every service and debt. If you can imagine it, if it can be found anywhere, it can be found here, or at least here you can find someone to take you to it."

"What other benefits?"

"Well, for one, you don't age in the Hall."

"Immortality?"

"Or something close enough to it to make little difference," said John. "It may be that those of us able to find the Hall possess this gift already, or it may be that by living within the Hall we avoid Death's icy hand, but the gains in time are not trivial, and few give them up willingly." He waved his hand to the gallery above. "Those who inhabit my guest quarters number several hundred who fear to ever again leave the Hall, conducting their businesses in their entirety in rooms I lease them. Others come here as the only possible refuge from all danger, while yet others spend part of their days on other worlds and part of them here. But no denizen of the Hall will give up its lure after becoming aware of the benefits."

"What of Macros the Black?"

At the mention of that name, both John and Boldar looked uncomfortable. "He's a special case," answered John after a while. "He may be an agent of some higher power, or even a higher power himself; at the very least, he's something beyond what we would count mortal here in the Hall. How much of what has been placed at his feet is true and how much legend, only a few can tell. What do you know of him?"

"Only what was told me in Midkemia."

"Not the world of his birth," said John. "Of that I am almost certain. But what brings his name into this conversation?"

"Only that he's a special case, as you have said. So there might be others."

"Perhaps."

"Such as Pug of Stardock?"

Again John looked discomforted, though Boldar hadn't so much as blinked at mention of Pug's name. "If you seek Pug, I may not be able to offer you much by way of encouragement."

"Why is that?"

"He passed through here quite a few months ago, ostensibly on his way to some odd world I can't remember, to do research, but I fear that is a ruse."

"Why do you say that?"

"Because he hired several of Boldar's friends to prevent anyone who asked for him from following after."

"Who?" said Boldar, looking around the room.

"William the Gripper, Jeremiah the Red, and Eland Scarlet, the Grey Assassin."

Boldar shook his head. "Those are three likely to cause some trouble." He leaned forward to Miranda. "I could most likely best Jeremiah; his reputation is built mostly on rumor. But William and Eland both possess the death touch, and that makes it dicey if they're working together."

Miranda said, "Do I look like a Pantathian?"

John said, "My dear, after as many lifetimes as I have spent in the Hall, looks are the last thing I would depend upon. You, for all your evident charms, could turn out to be my own grandfather and it would barely surprise me—though I fervently hope the old boy is dead, as we buried him when I was fourteen years old." Rising, he said, "Pug of Stardock is another, like Macros, who is not of the Hall, but utilizes it occasionally. But his word is good and so is his gold. He paid for protection, and such he will get. My advice is not to let anyone else in this room know you seek him and to find some other means to trace his whereabouts, or be prepared to meet two of the Hall's most reputable mercenaries and one of the most feared assassins, no less than one minute after you leave this place."

He bowed. "Please have refreshments as my guest." He signaled a small man and said something to him, indicating that a round of drinks should be produced. "Should you need quarters for a time, you'll find us reasonable. If not, I trust you'll enjoy yourself as long as you're here, and return to us soon." He bowed, tipping his white hat, and left to return to the bar and his conversation with the four-eyed man, who had just returned from whatever errand he had been on.

Blood let out his breath in a dramatic fashion. "What do you choose to do?" he asked.

"I intend to keep looking. I mean Pug no harm."

"Would he think that?"

"We've never met. I know him by name only. But he would not think me dangerous, I know."

"I've never met him, either, but John recognized his name instantly. That means his reputation is spreading, and for that to occur in the Hall, one must possess a significant level of gifts. For him to worry about being followed . . ." He shrugged.

Miranda was inclined to take Boldar at face value, and nothing he had said was inclining her to suspect him; still, the stakes were too high for her to take chances. She said, "If he doesn't want to be followed, enough to take such precautions, how would one follow his trail?"

Boldar blew out his cheeks. "There are several oracles. . . ."

"I've consulted with the Oracle of Aal."

"If she doesn't know, then none of them do," he observed. "There's the Toymaker."

"Who is he?"

"A creator of devices, several of which may be used to spy out people who don't wish to be seen. But he's somewhat mad and therefore undependable."

"Who else?"

The waiter appeared with a round of drinks, placing a frosty mug of something that looked like ale before Boldar and a large crystal goblet before Miranda. He made a show of unfolding napkins and placing one in Miranda's lap and the other in Boldar's. He said, "Compliments of my master," and withdrew.

The wine was delicious and Miranda drank deeply, discovering she was quite thirsty—and hungry.

"There's Querl Dagat," said Boldar. "He deals in information; the more improbable, the better he likes it . . . as long as it's true. For that reason, he's a full cut above the average rumormonger hereabouts."

Miranda picked up her napkin to blot her lips, and a folded piece of paper fell to the floor. She looked down, then at Boldar, who bent over and picked it up. He handed it to her unopened.

She took it and unfolded it to find a single word. "Who's Mustafa?" she asked.

Boldar slammed his hand down upon the table. "The very fellow we must see."

He glanced around and said, "Up there," pointing to the gallery.

He rose and Miranda followed; they wended their way through the press of tables and alien bodies. Reaching a stairway, they climbed to the first of the two overhanging galleries. Miranda was surprised to discover that the gallery was but one side of a wide promenade, which had large corridors stretching away. "Is all this part of the Inn?"

Boldar said, "Certainly."

"How big is it?"

"Only Honest John knows for certain." He led her past booths offering all manner of goods and services, several lewd, a score or more clearly illegal anywhere Miranda had ever been, and many incomprehensible. "Rumor has it that John was a barkeep on his homeworld who was run out of his birth city over some dispute. A roving band of some sort of aboriginal people chased him, and he blundered into the entrance to the Hall. As fate would have it, he appeared in the Hall in the midst of a battle. It has been said that, not knowing any better, he jumped into the void opposite the door he had entered, discovering the first entrance into the stable place in which the Inn is now housed."

Boldar moved down a side corridor. "He blundered around in a strange darkness, then somehow found his way back to the Hall, moving back to his homeworld once he was certain the aborigines were gone and returning to his birth city. Over the years he came back to the Hall, exploring and trading. When he finally had some sense of the society within the Hall, he decided the Inn was what would make him rich. He made some deals, hired some workers, and returned here to establish his small inn. He's added onto it over the years, until now it's a small township. Whenever he adds onto the building, he encounters no limit to the size he can increase his holdings, or at least not so far."

"Has it?"

"What?"

"Made John rich?"

Boldar laughed, and again Miranda was struck by how boyish the mercenary looked. "I suspect that by any reasonable measure, John is the richest man in creation. He could buy and sell worlds should he choose. But like most of us, he's found that after a while riches are only a means to keep oneself amused or to keep tally on how well one does in the various games and transactions in the Hall."

Reaching a doorway hung with a curtain, Boldar called, "Mustafa, are you in?"

"Who wants to know?"

That got a laugh from Boldar, who swept aside the curtain, indicating Miranda should enter. She did and found herself inside a small room with but a single table, upon which a solitary candle burned. Otherwise, the room was without distinction—no wall hangings or other furniture, just another door in the wall facing the one through which they'd entered.

A man stood behind the table, his face nearly black, like aged and oiled leather. A white beard adorned his cheeks and chin, though his upper lip was shaven, and his head was covered with a green turban. He bowed. "Peace be upon you," he said in the language of the Jal-Pur.

"Upon you be peace," answered Miranda.

"You seek Pug of Stardock?" he asked.

Miranda nodded. Glancing at Boldar, she raised an eyebrow in question.

Boldar said, "Mustafa's a fortune-teller."

Mustafa said, "You must first cross my palm with gold." He held out his hand. Miranda reached into her belt and withdrew a coin, placing it upon his hand. He put it in his own belt pouch without looking at it. "What do you seek?"

"I just told you!"

Mustafa said, "You need to say it aloud!"

Fighting off irritation at what she thought was needless show to convince gullible travelers, Miranda said, "I need to find Pug of Stardock."

"Why?"

Miranda said, "That is my business, but the need is great."

"Many look for this man. He has taken precautions against being followed by those he would rather not encounter. How may I know you are not such a one?"

Miranda said, "One may vouch for me, but he is back upon the world of Midkemia: Tomas, friend of Pug."

"The Dragon Rider." Mustafa nodded. "That is a name few would know who meant to harm Pug."

"Where might I find him?"

"He seeks alliances and goes to speak with the gods. Seek him in the Celestial City, in the Hall of the Gods Awaiting."

Miranda said, "How do I get there?"

"Return to Midkemia," answered Mustafa, "and get you to the land of Novindus. In the great mountains, the Pillars of the Stars, find the Necropolis, the home of the Dead Gods. There, atop the peaks of the mountains, there is a hall in which those gods waiting to be reborn abide. Go there."

Miranda didn't wait, but rose and left, leaving Boldar standing alone with Mustafa. After a second, Boldar said, "Is this true? Or are you doing one of your carnival acts?"

Mustafa shrugged. "I don't know if it's true. That's just what I was paid to say."

"Who paid you?"

"Pug of Stardock." The old man took off his turban, revealing a nearly bald pate. Scratching his head, he said, "I suspect it's probably another false lead. I have the distinct impression this Pug is a man who doesn't wish to be found."

Boldar said, "This gets interesting. I think I'll catch up with her and see if she needs help."

Mustafa shook his head and said, "Find him or not, I have a feeling she's going to need a great deal of help before this is over. Some idiot left open a critical gate to the demon realm, and a couple of realities could be in jeopardy as a result." He yawned.

Boldar was about to ask what that meant, but considered Miranda getting too far ahead, so he said nothing and left.

A moment after Boldar left, the other door opened and a man stepped through. Small but striking, he had dark hair and eyes and a closely trimmed beard, and wore a simple robe of black. He reached into a pouch at his belt and pulled out some gold coins. Handing them to Mustafa, he said, "Thank you. You did well."

"Anytime. What are you going to do now?"

"I think I'll go set up a small test."

Mustafa said, "Well, enjoy yourself. And let me know how the situation with the demon realm turns out; things could get busy around here if they get loose."

"I will. Good-bye, Mustafa," said the man as he began to move his hands.

"Good-bye, Pug," responded Mustafa, but by the time he had spoken, Pug of Stardock had vanished from sight.

14

★★

JOURNEY

ERIK DISMOUNTED.

Roo grabbed the reins of Erik's and Billy's horses and led them away. Erik and Billy ran forward, weapons at the ready, while the maneuver was repeated up and down the line.

Since leaving Brek's at Shingazi's Landing two weeks before, Calis had been drilling the men continually. They were now being trained as mounted infantry. At the first sign of attack, one man in three would lead the horses to be staked behind the line while the other two made a defensive position where instructed. The men had complained about this, saying it made no sense to leave a perfectly good horse and get down to fight, but the complaints had fallen on deaf ears.

Nakor had laughed it off, saying only, "Man and horse gives a much bigger target than man on foot hiding behind a rock."

The drills were becoming second nature to Erik and the others, who now waited to see what would happen next. Sometimes, nothing; other times, Hatonis's company of clansmen from the City of the Serpent River would "attack," and the results could be painful. The drills were conducted using heavy wooden swords, weighted with lead rods, that were twice the heft of a normal shortsword. Erik swore his own sword was feather-light in his hand after weeks of drilling with the false swords, which he supposed was the point of it all, but the wooden swords could leave heavy welts and even break bones, and the clansmen from the City of the Serpent River seemed to take delight in embarrassing Calis's company.

220 RAYMOND E. FEIST

Erik didn't understand the politics of this strange land; he knew that Calis and Hatonis were old friends, or at least friendly acquaintances, but the other men from that distant city seemed either suspicious or contemptuous of Calis's men. He asked and was told by one of the soldiers from Calis's last voyage that clan warriors simply didn't have much use for mercenaries. Erik took this to mean that only a few leaders, such as Hatonis, knew of their real purpose in coming to this distant land.

Erik heard a rattle behind him and knew that Roo had returned and was laying down the odd short spears they had picked up at Brek's. Soft iron, they were designed to be thrown at charging opponents, either injuring them or fouling their shields. Once they struck something, they were useless, as they bent easily, so the enemy couldn't throw them back. A shout went up from a crest nearby and suddenly it was raining arrows. Erik raised his shield, crouching low behind it, and felt two shafts strike and shatter on the heavy metal and wood. A curse nearby told Erik that Luis hadn't been as fortunate, and had been struck by the dull point of a practice shaft. Not lethal, these shafts nevertheless stung when they struck, and occasionally they could cause real injury.

Then another shout signaled the charge, and Erik rose, gripping one of the heavy iron spears. "Ready!" shouted de Loungville. As the charging clansmen came near, Erik tensed, and as if reading his mind, de Loungville shouted, "Wait for it!"

As the clansmen bore down upon them, the men of Calis's company waited until de Loungville shouted, "Throw!" and Erik and the others motioned throwing the pilum, as the short soft spear was known in the Quegan tongue. Having no practice pilum to use, they couldn't throw the weapon, so after pantomiming a cast, each man dropped his spear next to where they waited and, with a few audible groans, readied the ponderous practice swords.

Erik recognized the man bearing down on him, a large somber fellow named Pataki. Erik braced himself and let the man throw the first blow, which he easily caught on his shield. He stepped slightly to his left and threw a roundhouse blow with his sword that got over the top of Pataki's shield and caught him behind the head. Erik winced, for he knew the blow must hurt, despite the helm the other man wore.

Glancing around, he saw that his companions were easily repulsing the attackers, and within a minute the clansmen threw down their swords and removed their helms in the mercenary's sign of surrender. A few of Calis's company cheered the victory, but the majority were content to stand motionless for a few minutes. Riding most of the day, then suddenly fighting a battle—even if only a mock skirmish—took its toll; most of the men learned to steal rest whenever it was possible, even if only for a minute.

"All right," shouted Foster. "Pick 'em up!"

Erik got his practice sword under one arm and was starting to retrieve his pilum when he heard Billy say, "This one's not moving!"

Erik saw that Pataki was still lying facedown in the dust. Roo was the first to reach him and rolled the bulky man over. He then leaned over and after a moment said, "He's still breathing, but he's out cold."

De Loungville hurried over. "What's this?"

Erik picked up his pilum. "I caught him on the back of the head. I hit him harder than I intended, I guess."

"You guess," said de Loungville, his eyes narrowing as if he was about to launch into another reprimand. Suddenly he grinned and said, "That's my lad!" He told Roo, "Toss some water on him and get your kit together."

Roo rolled his eyes heavenward and hurried to where the horses were picketed. He fetched a waterskin and doused the motionless man. Pataki came awake, spitting out the water, and once he had regained his feet, returned to his own company.

Erik carried his set of pilum, practice sword, and shield to where the horses were waiting. He loaded up his equipment, then waited for Roo to catch up. When the shorter man returned, he said, "You really caught him with that head shot."

"You saw?"

"I was unoccupied at the moment. The fellow who came at me was blindsided by Billy, so I had nothing to do."

"You could have lent me a hand," Erik said.

"As if you needed one," said Roo. "You're turning into something of a terror with that practice sword. Maybe you ought to keep with it when the real fighting starts. You can bludgeon with it better than most men can cut."

Erik half smiled and shook his head. "Maybe I'll find one of those big dwarven war hammers and smash rocks, too."

"Mount!" came the order from Foster, and with accompanying groans the men complied.

Moving into position, Erik and Roo fell in with Sho Pi, Biggo, Luis, and Billy. The company waited. Then came the order to ride. There was at least another hour of daylight before they'd be ordered to make camp, and that would entail another two hours of work. Erik glanced at the sun, an angry red globe lowering in the west, and said, "It's too damn hot for this time of year."

From behind him, Calis said, "The seasons are reversed here, Erik. It's winter in the Kingdom, but it's early summer here. The days are getting longer and hotter."

"Wonderful," said Erik, too tired to wonder how the Captain had come to be riding next to him.

"When we spar with the clansmen," said Calis, with a faint smile, "try to be a little more subdued with them. Pataki's a nephew of Regin, the Lion Clan chieftain. If you'd broken his head, it would have strained things a bit."

"I'll try to remember, Captain," said Erik without humor.

Calis set heels to his horse and moved toward the head of the line. Roo said, "Was he joking?"

"Who cares?" said Billy Goodwin. "It's too hot, and I'm too tired to worry about it."

Biggo, who rode next to Billy, said, "That's strange."

"What?" asked Roo.

"The sun's so red, but it's another hour or more to sunset."

Looking toward the west, they nodded. "What could be causing it?" asked Luis, from his place behind Biggo.

"Smoke," answered a clansman who was riding past. "Word came last night that Khaipur was falling. That must be it burning."

Roo said, "But that's hundreds of miles from here! At least, that's what the Captain said!"

Sho Pi spoke softly. "Very big fire" was all he said.

THE TRAINING WORE on, and Erik and the others no longer had to think about what to do; they just did it. Even the routine of building fortifications every night became commonplace; Erik ceased being astonished at how much work the seventy-five men could accomplish.

Once the routine was established, Calis and de Loungville would disrupt it, seeking to keep the men constantly alert. As the days wore on, Erik thought it unnecessary.

Riders came and went as messages were carried from various agents Calis had established over the years. Rather than take years to establish its control over the surrounding countryside, the host of the Emerald Queen was driving on the city of Lanada.

Riding in the second company, Erik heard Calis speaking to Hatonis and one of the riders who had just brought that news. "It was seven years between the fall of Sulth and the assault on Hamsa."

Hatonis said, "But the invaders had to fight through the Forest of Irabek."

"Three years between Hamsa and Kilbar, then a year between Kilbar and Khaipur."

Calis nodded. "As they control more of the continent, they seem more intent on accelerating their advance."

De Loungville speculated, "Maybe the army's getting too big to control and its generals have to keep it busy with conquest."

Calis shrugged. "We need to change our line of march." To the rider he said, "Rest with us tonight and tomorrow return north. Carry word to the Jeshandi we will not be coming their way. We are going to leave the Serpent River and turn straight west. Pass the word to those who seek us that we are going to attempt to intercept the invaders between Khaipur and Lanada. Look for us at the Mercenaries' Rendezvous."

Erik and the others turned to look across the Serpent River, where in the distance they saw a vast valley of forests and meadows, and beyond that a small range of mountains. They would have to cross the river, ride through that and, once across the mountains, down into the river lands of the Vedra.

De Loungville said, "Do we turn around for the crossing point at Brek's?"

Calis said, "No, it would lose us too much time. Send scouts ahead and find us a place to cross."

De Loungville ordered riders forward, and two days later they reported a broadening of the river where the current was slow enough that rafting might be possible. Calis reached that point and agreed it was worth the try. He ordered the men to cut what little growth there was along the river to make a set of small rafts. A dozen men, including Erik and Biggo, made the treacherous crossing, poling their way from one side to the other, carrying lines that would be used to get the others across. On the far bank, the dozen men cut enough trees of a size to lash together logs into four rafts, each large enough to hold four horses. The horses for the most part cooperated, though one raft was lost on the second-to-the-last trip as a line parted and the logs broke apart. The horses and men jumped into the water as the raft disintegrated, and all the men were pulled out downstream, but only one horse made it to the shore.

There were sufficient remounts so that the losing of three horses was not a serious deprivation, but the thought of the animals drowning bothered Erik. He found that disturbing, for the specter of battle and men dying held no pain for him, but the idea of a horse, terrified as it was being swept downriver, made him very sad.

The valley swept from the fork in the river to the west, ending in a series of rising meadows, until at last they would have to crest the ridge of mountains. On the tenth day of the march, a scout returned to tell Calis of a party of hunters he had encountered ahead.

Erik, Roo, and four other men were sent ahead with Foster to negotiate with the hunters. Erik was grateful for anything that broke the monotony of the march. Every day had been toil without respite. As much as he enjoyed horses and working with them, Erik had never been a great rider. He found twelve hours in the saddle, interrupted only by walking beside the horses to rest them, making and breaking camp, mock combats, and a steady diet of dried rations more drudgery than even his worst days at the forge.

The countryside was sloping hills, all moving quickly up into peaks and crests. The mountains of this region topped out at a lower elevation than the biggest Erik was used to at home, but there were far more of them here. The three major peaks of Darkmoor were surrounded by many hills, but otherwise few true mountains. Mostly they were high plateaus and sloping hillsides. But here, while modest in altitude, the mountains were plentiful and steep, with quickly rising buttes and prominences, dead-end valleys and box canyons, hard granite cut by streams and rivers. Trees grew in abundance and none of the surrounding peaks rose high enough above the timberline to give them a clear point of reference as they traveled through the dense woods. Erik suspected this range of mountains might prove a hazard as well as an inconvenience.

The hunters were waiting at the agreed-upon location. Erik reined in as Foster dismounted, removed his sword belt, and approached with his hands open. Erik studied the hunters.

They were hill people, dressed in fur-covered vests and long woolen trousers. Erik suspected there were herds of sheep or goats secreted away in the local meadows. Each man carried an efficient-looking bow, not quite as impressive as the Kingdom longbow, but clearly powerful enough to kill a man or bear as well as a deer.

The leader was a grey-bearded man who stepped forward to speak with Foster, while the other three stood motionless. Erik glanced around and saw no sign of any horses; these men hunted on foot. Given the terrain, Erik judged that more sensible than trying to convince a horse to act like a donkey or goat. If the hunters' village was any higher up the slopes, horses would be less than an inconvenience; they'd be a danger.

Two of the other men bore a strong resemblance to the leader, while the third appeared like him in manner only. Erik guessed they were a family, with the odd man perhaps being married to a daughter.

Foster nodded, reached into his tunic, and pulled out a heavy purse. He counted out some gold pieces and returned to where Roo held his mount. "You men wait here." With a motion of his head he made it clear that they were to keep the hunters from running off with the gold he just gave them. "I'll bring up the rest of the company. These fellows have a way over the mountains that's safe for the horses."

Erik glanced at the steep rise of the landscape before him and nodded. "I hope so."

While they waited, the hunters talked among themselves. The one who didn't resemble the other three listened as the leader spoke, then without comment he turned and began to trot toward the tree line.

One of the soldiers, a man named Greely, shouted, "Where does he think he's going?" The hunter stopped. Greely's command of the local language, learned on ship and while traveling, was better than Erik's, but his accent obviously struck the hillmen as odd enough that they looked puzzled by the question.

The leader looked at him. "Do you think treachery?"

Seeing that all four hunters were ready to unsling bows and start firing if the wrong answer was forthcoming, Erik glanced at Roo; suddenly Roo said, "He's sending his son-in-law home to tell his wife and daughter that he and his sons won't be home for supper tonight. Am I right?"

The lead hunter nodded, once, and waited. Greely said, "Well . . . I guess that's all right."

The leader made a curt gesture and the fourth hunter began trotting off again. Then the leader of the hunters said, "And tomorrow, too. It's a harsh two days over the ridge, with no easy time going down the day after, but once on the trail you'll have that well enough without my help." He leaned upon his bow once more.

About fifteen minutes of silence followed, then the sound of horses approaching from the rear heralded Calis and his company's approach. Calis rode at the head of the company and when he pulled up he spoke rapidly to the hunter. The exchange was so quick and heavily accented that Erik couldn't follow most of it.

But in the end Calis seemed satisfied and turned to the others, who were still riding up behind. "This is Kirzon and his sons. They know a trail over the ridge and down into the Vedra River valley. It's narrow and difficult."

For two hours they followed the hunters along a narrow trail, winding up into the hills. The way was dangerous enough that they took it at a slow pace, since any mistake could cause an injury to horse and rider. After reaching a small meadow, the hunter turned to confer with Calis. Calis nodded, then said, "We'll camp now and leave at first light."

Suddenly de Loungville and Foster were shouting orders and Erik and Roo were snapping to without thought. Getting the horses in picket, unsaddled and placed so they could crop the long grass, proved more time-consuming than if they had simply been staked out in a line and had fodder carried to them.

By the time Erik and the others in charge of the horses were finished, the rest of the company had already dug most of the moat, throwing up dirt on four sides in a breastwork. Erik grabbed a shovel and jumped down next to the others. Quickly the defense was made ready. The drop gate was assembled, interlocking planks of wood carried on a baggage animal that, when run out, served as a broad bridge over the trench. Then Erik climbed out as others were doing, on the short side of the trench, walked to the gate and crossed over, and began tamping the earth of the breastwork. Roo came over with a set of iron-tipped wooden stakes, which he inserted at a set distance along the top of the breastwork. Then they hurried to join with the rest of the men and erect their six-man tent, fashioned with interwoven pieces of fabric, one section carried by each man. They placed their bedrolls inside and returned to the commissary area, where soup was being boiled.

On the march they ate dried bread and fruits, with vegetable soups whenever possible. At first Erik and some others grumbled over the lack of meat in the diet, but he now found he agreed with the older soldiers that heavy food weighed them down in the field. He knew that while the thought of a steaming roast or a joint of mutton, or his mother's meat pies, could make his mouth water, he hadn't felt stronger in his life.

Wooden bowls were handed out, and each man came away with a steaming helping of stewed vegetables, with just enough beef suet and flour to give it some texture. Sitting near the campfire, Roo said, "I'd love some hot bread to soak this up with."

Foster, who was walking by, said, "People in the lower hells would love a cool drink of water, me lad. Enjoy what you have. Tomorrow we're on trail rations."

The men groaned. The dried fruit and hardtack was nourishing but almost tasteless, and a man could seemingly chew for hours without making the mess any easier to swallow. What Erik found himself missing most was wine. Growing up in Darkmoor, he had taken wine for granted. The quality of the wine made in the region was near-legendary, and this made even the cheapest "plonk" drunk at meals by the commoners a cut above the usual. Until he reached Krondor, he had no idea that wine that was too inexpensive to justify transport would have earned a fair return in the taverns and kitchens of the Prince's City.

He remarked on this to Roo, who said, "That might be just the ticket for an enterprising lad such as myself." He grinned and Erik laughed.

Biggo, who was sitting on the other side of the fire, said, "What? You going to truck bottles of the stuff into Krondor and lose money?"

Roo narrowed his gaze. "After my father-in-law, Helmut Grindle, advances me enough gold to work with, I have a plan that will put good wine on every table in the Western Realm."

Erik laughed. "You haven't even met the girl! She may be married with a brace of children by the time you return!"

Jerome Handy snorted. "If you return."

They fell silent.

HORSES ARE CONTRARY creatures, thought Erik as he blinked dust out of his eyes. He had been given the responsibility of herding the remounts over the mountains and had picked a half-dozen of the better riders to ride herd. One surprise had been Nakor volunteering. Most men would find riding behind the herd—"drag," as the position was called—choking on their dust, poor duty, but the chronically curious Isalani found the entire process fascinating. And it turned out, to Erik's relief, that the man was a competent enough horseman.

Twice, horses had been content to walk down a bluff that would have taken them to a place where they would either have to back up—one of the least-favored choices of most horses—or learn to fly, which Erik judged even less likely. "Whoa!" he shouted at one particularly troublesome horse who was determined to walk off the mountain. He shied a rock at her, which bounced off her right shoulder, turning her in the direction he wanted. "Stupid bitch!" he shouted. "Trying to turn yourself into crow bait?"

Nakor rode closer to the edge than any sane man was like to do and seemed ready to somehow will his horse into flight so he could interpose himself between a horse bolting the wrong way and thin air. Whenever Erik mentioned he might come in a bit, the little man just grinned and told him everything was fine. "She's in season. Mares get very stupid when in heat," he observed.

"She's not overly bright even when she's not ready to breed. At least we have no stallions along. That would make life interesting."

"I had a stallion once," said Nakor. "A great black horse given me by the Empress of Great Kesh."

Erik regarded the man. "That's . . . interesting." Like the others who had gotten to know Nakor, he was reluctant to call him a liar. So much of what he said was highly improbable, but he never said he could do anything he couldn't back up, so the men had come to take most of what he claimed at face value.

"The horse died," Nakor said. "Good horse. Sorry to see him go. Ate some bad grass; got colic."

A shout from ahead warned Erik the herd was bunching up, and he sent Billy Goodwin forward to help keep the horses moving through a narrow defile that cut across the ridge of the mountains. Once through that, they would be heading downward into the valley of the Vedra River.

Erik shouted for Billy to come back to the rear and ride drag while he urged his own horse on, to the head of the thirty horses that served as the company's remounts. A balky gelding was trying to turn around, and Erik used his own horse to push the recalcitrant animal into the gap, and then the horses were moving in orderly fashion. Erik pulled up and waited for the rest of the animals to pass, then joined again with Billy and Nakor in back.

"Downhill from here," said Billy.

Suddenly Nakor's mare took a bite at Billy's horse, and his animal reared. Nakor shouted, "Look out!"

Billy lost his grip on his reins and fell backwards, and landed hard on the ground. Erik jumped down from his animal and ran over while Billy's horse ran after the herd.

Leaning over, he saw Billy staring up into the sky. His head rested upon a large rock while a crimson pool spread behind him.

Nakor shouted, "How is he?"

Erik said, "He's dead."

There was a moment of silence, then Nakor said, "I'll follow the horses. You bring him along to where we can bury him."

Erik stood up, started to reach down to grab Billy, and suddenly remembered having to pick up Tyndal's body. "Oh, damn," he said as tears came unbidden to his eyes.

He found himself trembling as he realized that of those who had been sentenced to hang that day, Billy was the first to die. "Oh, damn," he repeated, as he stood clenching and unclenching his fists. "Why?" he asked the fates.

One moment Billy had been sitting astride his horse; the next he was dead. And nothing more important than a stupid, poorly trained gelding shying from a bite by a mare in heat had caused it.

Erik didn't know why he suddenly felt so sad at Billy's death. He felt his body tremble, and realized he was afraid. Sucking down a lungful of air, he closed his eyes and bent and picked up Billy. The body was surprisingly light. He turned and moved to his own horse, who started to shy as he approached. "Whoa!" he commanded, almost yelling, and the horse obeyed.

He lifted Billy across the horse's neck and the front of the saddle, then swung up behind. Sliding into the saddle, he lifted Billy enough so that he could rest him as much as possible across his upper thighs, so the horse could manage the weight. Slowly he moved after the distant herd.

"Damn," he whispered again as he willed his fear and anger back deep inside himself.

A MAN NAMED Notombi, with a heavy Keshian accent, was moved into their tent, taking Billy's place. The five remaining members of Erik's company were cordial, but distant. While he was an outsider, his training made him mesh quickly, knowing exactly which duties to perform without being told.

Two days after crossing the ridge of the mountains, Kirzon and his sons pointed the way down and returned to their hunting. Calis paid them off in gold and bade them farewell.

Erik returned to the routine of travel, though the difficult descent into the hills west of the mountains gave little time for reflection. He buried all his memories of his feelings at Billy's death and continued as before.

Five days after crossing the mountains, they encountered a difficult rise. Erik went ahead with Calis to scout out a clear trail before allowing the full company to proceed. Turning around nearly seventy-five riders and another thirty remounts was tricky business under the best of conditions. In tight quarters, it was nearly impossible.

Reaching a crest, they reined in and Erik exclaimed, "The gods weep!"

In the distance, to the north, the great tower of smoke that had been turning the sun red could now be seen. "How far is that?" asked Erik.

"Still more than a hundred miles distant," answered Calis. "They must be burning every village and farm within a week's ride of Khaipur. The wind's blowing it east, else we'd be tasting that soot as well as seeing it."

Erik's eyes stung slightly. "I'm feeling it now."

Calis smiled his strange half-smile. "It would be worse if you were closer."

Riding back, they found an easier trail than the first, and as they moved toward the company, Erik said, "Captain, what are our chances of getting home?"

Calis laughed, and Erik turned to regard him. "You're the first with the grit to come out and ask; I was wondering who it would be."

Erik said nothing.

Calis said, "I think our chances of getting home are as good as we can make them. Only the gods know just how mad this plan is."

"Why couldn't you sneak one man in, have him look around, then sneak him out?"

"Good question," said Calis. "We tried. Several times." He glanced around as he rode, as if scouting was a habit. "This land is a land of few standing armies, as we know them in the Kingdom and Kesh. Here you're either a swordsman for your family or clan, or you're in the palace guard of some city ruler, or you're a hired sword. Mercenary armies are the rule."

"I would think that with hired swords on both sides, it would be easy enough to slip a man across the lines."

Calis's expression showed it was a fair observation. "One would think that. But a single man attracts notice, especially one who is ignorant of basic customs and attitudes. But a company of freebooters from a distant land? That's not unusual in these parts. And reputation counts for much. So, I am Calis, and we're the Crimson Eagles, and no one looks twice at an elf living among humans here. A 'long-lived' leading such a company is rare but not unheard of. You would be found out by magic or treachery were you to come here alone, Erik. But as a member of my company, no one will pay you the least heed." He said nothing for a while, looking down on the rolling hills that led down to the river. After a while he said, "This is a beautiful land, isn't it?"

Erik said, "Yes, it seems so."

Calis was silent for a moment, then said, "Twenty-four years ago I came to this country for the first time, Erik. I've been back twice since then, once with my own army. I've left graves behind me in numbers you can't imagine."

"I overheard de Loungville and Nakor, back on Sorcerer's Isle," admitted Erik as he reined his horse around for better footing on the trail. "It sounded terrible."

"It was. Many of the Kingdom's best soldiers died on that march. Hand-picked men. Foster, de Loungville, and a few others were able to escape with me, and only because we took a chance and went where the enemy didn't expect us to go." Calis was again silent a moment. "That's why I agreed with Bobby's plan, and convinced Arutha that only men desperate to stay alive would serve. Soldiers are all too willing to die for the colors, and we need men who would do everything in their power to stay alive, short of betraying us."

Erik nodded. "And soldiers don't make convincing mercenaries."

"That, too. You're going to meet some men who will change your thinking about what humanity is capable of, and you won't be better for knowing them." He looked at Erik as if studying him. "You're part of an odd lot. We searched for those things in each man that would give us all the chance of blending in—an ability to be violent, no pretension of ideals, just men who are as rough as those we must go among—but we also needed men who were more than the common scum the tides of battle usually wash ashore. We needed men who, when it came time, would answer the call rather than run." He smiled and it was a smile of genuine amusement. "Or at least they would run in the proper direction, and keep their wits about them." As if a thought struck him for the first time, he said, "I think I had better keep you and your company close by. Most of the men we've selected are cutthroats who would happily kill their grannies to earn a gold piece, but your little band numbers some of our oddest characters. If your friend Biggo starts talking about the Death Goddess—who is a figure of terror in this land, named Khali-shi, and who is only worshiped in secret—or if Sho Pi starts discussing philosophy with some of the blood drink-ers we're going to hook up with, we'll have hell to pay. I'll tell de Loungville when we camp tonight that your six is to be billeted closest to my tent."

Erik fell silent. He was surprised that Calis knew enough about them as individuals to know about Biggo's theories on the Death Goddess or Sho Pi's odd views of things. And he didn't know if being close to the Captain, de Loungville, and Foster was a comfort or nuisance.

Days of cautious travel at last brought them to rolling lowlands. Then on the fifth day after leaving the mountains, they approached a village, one that sat athwart the major north–south road between Lanada and Khaipur. They found the houses abandoned, for the presence of a company of armed men usually meant a raid in this land. Calis waited an hour in the small town square, his men tending their horses with water from the well, but otherwise leaving everything untouched.

A young man in his early twenties appeared from hiding in a stand of trees close by. "What company?" he called out, ready to duck back into the shelter-ing copse at the first sign of trouble.

"Calis's Crimson Eagles. What village is this?"

"Weanat."

"Whom do you serve?"

The man, eyeing Calis suspiciously, said, "Are you pledged?"

"We are a free company."

That answer didn't seem to sit well with the villager. He spoke softly, conferring with someone hidden behind him, then at last he said, "We tithe the Priest-King of Lanada."

"Where lies Lanada from here?"

"A day's ride south along that road," came the answer.

Calis turned to de Loungville. "We're farther south than I wanted to be, but the army will catch up with us, sooner or later."

"Or grind over us," answered de Loungville.

"Make camp tonight in that meadow over to the east," instructed Calis. Turning to the still-half-hidden villager, he said, "We'll need a market. I need feed, grain for bread, chickens if you have any, fruit, vegetables, and wine."

"We are poor. We have little to share," said the man, backing deeper into the shadow of the trees.

Erik's squad was stationed right behind Calis, and Biggo, who had listened to the exchange, whispered to Erik, "And I'm a monk of Dala. This is rich land, and those beggars have whatever they own stashed away somewhere in those woods."

Luis leaned down from where he still sat his horse, and said, "And we are probably being watched over a half-dozen arrows."

Calis called out, "We'll pay in gold." He reached into his tunic, pulled out a small purse, and turned it over, emptying a dozen pieces of gold onto the ground.

As if signaled, a score of men appeared, all holding weapons. Erik studied them, making a comparison to the townspeople he had grown up with. These were farmers, but they also held their weapons in a sure-handed fashion. These men had to fight to keep what was theirs, and Erik was glad that Calis was the sort of leader who paid for what he needed rather than taking it.

The leader, an older man with a limp who carried a large sword strapped across his back, knelt and picked up the gold pieces. "You'll bond peace?" he asked Calis.

"Done!" said Calis, throwing the reins of his horse to Foster. He held out his arm and the village leader gripped his wrist, as Calis gripped in return. They shook twice and let go.

Abruptly the trees emptied of men, followed a short time after by women and children. Before Erik's eyes he saw a market take form in the small square of the village.

Roo said, "I don't know where they kept all this," as he motioned to pots of honey, jars of wine, and baskets of fruit that seemed to have materialized out of nowhere.

"Get raided often enough and I expect you learn how to hide things in a hurry, fella-me-lad," observed Biggo. "Plenty of basements with hidden traps, and false walls in those buildings, I'm thinking."

Sho Pi, who motioned for the others to follow to where camp was being set up, said, "They have the look of fighting men, those farmers."

Erik agreed. "I think we're in a beautiful but very harsh land."

They picketed their horses where instructed by Corporal Foster, then began the routine of making camp.

THEY RESTED WHILE Calis waited. What he was waiting for wasn't clear to Erik and the others, and Calis wasn't taking them into his confidence. The villagers were guarded in dealing with the mercenaries; approachable, but not warm. There was no inn, but one of the local merchants had erected a pavilion and served average-quality wine and ale. Foster warned against any public drunkenness, promising a flogging to any man who couldn't pull his weight the next morning because of a thick head.

Each day brought more drills and new practices. For three days they worked on holding their shields above their heads while moving heavy objects about. Foster and de Loungville stood on top of a hillock nearby throwing rocks into the air so they would fall straight down on the drilling men, reminding them to keep their shields up.

After a week had passed, one of the guards set at the north end of the town cried out, "Riders!"

Foster barked out orders for the men to get ready, and practice swords were discarded, replaced by steel. Those men selected as bowmen hurried to a position overlooking the town, under Foster's command, while de Loungville and Calis moved the rest of the company to defensive positions at the north end of the village.

Calis moved to where Erik and his companions waited, and said, "They're coming fast."

Erik squinted and saw a half-dozen men racing down the road that led into the village. As they drew near, they reined in, probably having seen a glint of metal or the movement of men.

Biggo said, "They're not so quick to come rushing in now that they know we're here."

Erik nodded. Roo said, "Look over there."

Erik turned to where Roo pointed, back into the village, and was astonished to see it was once again deserted. "They do know how to make themselves scarce, don't they?"

The riders began to trot toward the village, and when they were close enough to be seen clearly, Calis shouted, "Praji!"

The leader waved and spurred his horse into a canter, while his companions followed. As they neared, Erik saw that the six men were mercenaries, or at least dressed as such, and that the man in the van was easily the ugliest person he had ever seen. A face like seamed leather was dominated by an improbably large nose and a huge brow. His long hair, mostly grey, was tied back. He rode poorly; his hands were far too busy, and it was irritating his horse.

Getting down, the man walked toward the defensive position. "Calis?"

Calis walked forward and the two men embraced, with heavy back-slapping on both sides. The man pushed Calis away and said, "You don't look a damn day older; curse you long-lived bastards—steal all the pretty women, then come back and steal their daughters."

Calis said, "I expected to see you at the rendezvous."

"There isn't going to be one," the man called Praji said; "at least not where you'd expect it to be. Khaipur has fallen."

"So I heard."

"That's why you're here and not marching up the banks of the Serpent River," said Praji.

Foster motioned for Erik and five other men to take the horses. As they gathered the animals, they studied the other five riders. Hard men all, they had a beaten, tired look. Praji said, "We got our tails singed, for sure. I barely got out with a score of our men; we got as close to the siege as we could, but the greenskins had outriders and they came down on us hard. I didn't even have time to claim we were looking for work. No truces. You're either with them or you're attacked." He hiked a thumb at his companions. "After we got loose, we split up. Half the lads went with Vaja to the Jeshandi. Figured you'd be coming up that way, but in case you put in at Maharta I was heading that way. Figured you'd send word through our agents where you were if I was wrong. Give me something to drink; my throat's coated with half the dirt between here and Khaipur."

Calis said, "Let's get a drink and you can tell me more."

He took the man over to the pavilion, and as they moved, villagers began to appear as if from the air. Erik and the other men detailed to the horses took the riders over to the remounts, and Erik inspected them all. They had been ridden hard; they were heavily lathered and breathing deep. He unsaddled the horse he led, and told the other men to start walking the animals. They needed an hour's cooling at least, he judged, before they could be allowed to eat or drink, lest they become colicky.

After the horses were cooled, Erik staked them out and rubbed them down, checking to make sure none was injured or coming up lame. When he was satisfied the horses were all right, he returned to his own tent.

With the arrival of the riders, order in camp was lax, and he found his five bunkmates lying on their bedrolls. He knew that it could be seconds before the order to fall to was issued, so he luxuriated in the first moment he felt the bedroll under him.

Natombi said, "Legionaries always grab whatever rest they can, minute to minute."

"Who?" asked Luis.

"You call them Dog Soldiers," said the Keshian. "In ancient times they were kept away from the cities, penned up like dogs, to be unleashed upon the Empire's enemies." Like Jadow, Natombi shaved his head, and his dark skin made the whites of his eyes and his teeth appear in stark contrast when he spoke. The nearly black irises made Erik think of deep secrets.

"You're a dog, then, you're saying?" asked Biggo with mock innocence.

The others laughed. Natombi snorted. "No, stupid-head, I was a Legionary." He sat up on his bedroll, his head almost touching the canvas above. He placed his fist on his chest. "I served with the Ninth Legion, on the Overn Deep."

"I've heard of those," said Luis, making a display of not being impressed by shaking his open hand back and forth.

Sho Pi rolled over and raised up on his elbows. "In my country, Kesh is the heartland of the Empire. Isalani is my nation, but we are ruled by Kesh. Those he speaks of are the heart of the army. How did one from the Legion come so far?"

Natombi shrugged. "Bad company."

Biggo laughed. "This isn't an improvement, I'll wager."

"I was serving with a patrol that was to escort a man, a very important man of the Trueblood. We traveled to Durbin, and there I fell into disgrace."

"Women, gambling, or what?" asked Biggo, now genuinely interested. Natombi was something of a mystery to the others, even though they had shared the same tent with him for more than a week since Billy's death.

"I let the man die at the hands of an assassin. I was disgraced and fled."

"You let him die?" asked Roo. "Were you in charge?"

"I was a captain of the Legion."

"And I was Queen of the Midsummer Festival," said Biggo with a laugh.

"It's true. But now I am as you, a criminal living on time given to me by another. My life is over, and now I live another man's life."

"That doesn't make us particularly unique," observed Biggo.

Roo said, "What was it like in the Legion?"

Natombi laughed. "You know. You live like a Legionary."

"What do you mean?" Roo looked confused.

"This is a Legion camp," said Natombi.

"It's true," agreed Sho Pi. "The formations, the way we march, the practices, this is all of the Legion."

Natombi said, "This man Calis, our Captain, he is a very smart man, I am thinking." He tapped his head to make the point. "This Captain, he trains us to survive, for, man to man, there is no army on this world that can face the Legion of the Overn and survive. No army here has faced the Legions of Kesh, and when you fight someone, it's good to fight them with tactics they've never encountered before. Makes even better the chance to survive."

Luis was cleaning his fingernails with his dagger. Flipping it up, he balanced it on the tip, resting lightly upon one finger point, then he let it slip, caught it by the handle, and slammed it point first into the dirt. Watching it vibrate from the impact, he said, "And that's what it's all about, isn't it, my friends? Survival."

★★

15

VILLAGE

THE LOOKOUT SHOUTED.

"Riders!"

Erik and the others moved away from their various tasks and put on their weapons. Since arriving the week before, Praji had warned Calis's men that companies fleeing the fall of Khaipur would be heading south. Twice already bands of fighters had passed, avoiding the village after having seen the fortifications Calis had ordered constructed after conferring with the villagers.

Erik was uncertain if the Captain intended to truly defend this village or simply wanted to drill the men in another aspect of warcraft. Where just another village had stood, now a respectable fortification sat athwart the road. A full-scale moat had been dug around the village, with the earth from it serving as the foundation of the palisades. Two gates bound with iron had been hung, one at the north end and one at the south of the village, each securely attached to gateposts carved from the trunks of oaks from across the river. Erik had overseen the forging of the hinges, pins, and bands.

The village smithy had been abandoned years before when the last smith died, but the old forge still stood. Lacking a full set of smith's tools, Erik had made do with those carried in the baggage train so he could shoe the horses. Given enough time, he could use those tools to make other tools, and eventually restore the smithy completely. Each time Erik looked at the gates he felt a sense of pride. It would take a serious siege engine to knock them down. Glancing around, he thought he'd rather attempt to breech the log wall, perhaps burning it, than to send a company against either gate, while being fired upon by the men on the wall.

He looked over his shoulder as he put on his armor, and saw Foster and de Loungville, following hard on the heels of Calis, as they came down from the tower that was being erected in the center of the village. This tower, built atop a huge mound of earth, when finished would give them an unobstructed view for miles, and prevent any company of significant size from approaching unnoticed.

Erik and Roo hurried to their appointed places, each silently checking to see that all weapons and supplies were where they needed to be. Roo carried a half dozen of the heavy iron spears, and Erik found himself amazed at the wiry strength his friend had developed since they had run from Ravensburg.

He felt a stab of unexpected pain at a fleeting memory of his mother and Rosalyn, then let the thought go as the riders came clearly into view.

It was a company of at least thirty men, all seasoned warriors by their look. At the head of the company rode a heavyset man of middle years, his grey beard hanging down to his stomach. He signaled for a pair of his men to circle out and around the fortress, and slowed as he approached. As soon as he came within hailing distance, he shouted, "Hello, the fort!"

From the wall, Calis shouted back, "Who rides?"

"Bilbari's Regulars, fresh from the fall of Khaipur," and, glancing around, he added, "or what's left of us."

The outriders returned and Erik assumed they were informing their leader that it was a closed fortress, not a simple barricade. Calis called back, "Who commands? I know Bilbari, and you're not he."

The leader again looked around. "I guess I do. Bilbari died at the wall"—he spit and made a sign—"and we took the day's grace after the fall. My name is Zila."

Praji came to stand next to Calis, and Erik could hear him say, "I know them. A good enough band for butchery, though I'd not want any of them sharing my bunk. They'll honor the peace of the camp, more or less."

"I can give you the peace of the camp," said Calis.

"How long?"

"Two days," answered Calis.

"Fair enough." Then Zila laughed. "More than fair. Who commands here?"

"I do. Calis."

"Calis's Crimson Eagles?" asked Zila as he dismounted.

"The same."

"I heard you died at Hamsa," he said as Calis motioned for the gates to be opened.

As Erik and the others waited, Foster came by and said, "Stand down, but be alert. These wouldn't be the first to promise the peace of the camp but change their minds once inside."

All thought of such betrayal vanished when the company entered the village. They were beaten men. Erik noticed that several horses were injured and all were footsore. Even two days of rest would not be enough to bring some of those mounts to soundness.

Erik heard Zila snort, clear his throat, and spit. "Damn dust," he said. "The smoke was worse. Fires from one horizon to the other." He glanced at the men of Calis's company. "You did well to avoid that one." Motioning to his horse, he asked, "Got a smith in your company?"

Calis motioned for Erik, who handed his sword and shield to Roo. "Put these away for me, would you?"

Roo's answer was rude, but he took the armor and headed off toward their tent. Erik came up to Zila, who said, "Threw a shoe somewhere along the way. She's not lame, but she's going to be."

Erik only needed a glance to tell Zila was right. He picked up the horse's leg and saw that the frog of the hoof was bloody. "I'll clean this and dress it. With a new shoe, packed and padded, she should be all right if you don't push her too hard."

"Ha!" said Zila. To Calis he said, "There's an army of thirty thousand or more coming this way. They just kicked hell out of us. Unless someone organizes a rendezvous north of here soon, we're but the first of maybe a hundred or more companies that are going to come riding this way, and most of those lads are damn out-of-sorts over having been butchered by the lizards—"

Calis said, "Lizards?"

Zila nodded. "For a drink, I'll tell you about it."

Calis instructed Erik to care for the newcomers' horses, and Erik signaled the nearest men to take charge of the others as he took Zila's mount in tow. The animal was limping, and by the time they reached the pen for remounts, Erik was certain she would have been useless in another day, two at the most.

The newcomers were split equally between those who were content to let Calis's men treat their animals and those who insisted on following along to ensure their animals were well cared for; Erik was completely unsurprised to see that those who came along had the best mounts. Despite the hardships, those horses were the fittest and should recover after resting up. The others were a poor lot at best, and Erik suspected that others besides Zila's would soon be unable to carry their riders.

Erik had each horse inspected and made a mental list of which animals would be worth caring for and which would be best killed today. After conferring with a couple of the more experienced horsemen in Calis's forces, he found no argument.

As he moved away, one of the newcomers approached. "You. What's your name?"

"Erik." He paused and waited to see what the newcomer had to say.

Lowering his voice, the man said, "Mine is Rian. You know your way around horses." He was a large man with a flat face, reddish from the sun and covered in road dust. His eyes were dark, but his hair was reddish brown, his beard grey-shot. He carried himself easily, one hand absently resting on a long-sword.

Erik nodded, but said nothing.

"I could use another horse. Mine will come sound if I don't ride her for another week. Do you think your Captain would sell me one?"

"I'll ask him," Erik said, and started to move off.

Rian restrained him with a gentle touch to the arm. "Zila's a good enough fighter in a brawl," he whispered, "but he's no proper Captain. We were heading down to Maharta to seek service with the Raj. It should take the better part of the next year for that lot up north to get past Lanada."

He glanced around to see if anyone else was listening. "Your Captain seems to know his way around a fortification, and you seem more like garrison soldiers than hired swords."

Every man in Calis's company had been warned against spies, so Erik responded without having to think. "I just follow orders. Captain Calis has kept every man here alive at least once, so I don't question him."

"You think he's got room for another sword?"

"I'll ask. But I thought you were heading for Maharta?"

"After the beating we took at Khaipur, you'd think a year or two of resting up and waiting might be nice, but truth to tell, there's no booty and I get bored easily."

"I'll tell him that, too," Erik said, leaving the man with the horses.

He moved through the village, and several of the villagers nodded greeting. Calis's men weren't treated with open fear anymore, but the villagers were equally split between those happy to have their swords around for protection as well as their gold and those who feared that the fortification would attract unwanted attention. The village was routinely raided over the years, and the villagers had a time-tested method of fleeing into the nearby hills. Few died if there was any advance warning. But this fortress on the road: that was both a protection and a trap.

Someone called Erik's name, and he glanced over to see Embrisa, a girl of fourteen who had taken a liking to him. She was pretty in a large-boned way, with pale blue eyes her most striking feature, but Erik knew that she would be old before she was thirty, probably with three or four children and a husband who worked her from dawn to dusk. A town-bred boy, Erik had little sense of what real poverty and hard work were until he had come to this village.

He spoke a quick greeting, then excused himself as he went to the pavilion that served as an inn. Rough wooden benches and tables had been fashioned by an enterprising farmer named Shabo who had used the profits from serving

Calis's men poor wine and ale to build a wooden trellis alongside his rude hut. Erik considered that if they stayed long enough, Shabo would be a proper inn-keeper, as he kept using his profits to improve his little enterprise. His latest innovation had been to knock out a second door to the hut so he could serve across a newly built bar that ran the length of the building. Erik considered the hut might get very cold during winter, though he had no idea how cold it got in these parts.

Calis and Zila and some others sat at one table, while other men in Zila's company drank heavily and did indeed look like beaten men. Praji had joined Calis and was nodding as Zila said, "I've seen thirty years of fighting, man and boy, but nothing like this." He drained his tankard and wiped his mouth with the back of his hand.

Calis raised an eyebrow at Erik, who said, "Half the mounts either need a month of grazing and no work or need to be put down. The rest could be ready to be ridden if they lay up a week."

Calis nodded. Zila said, "We don't have much—being on the losing side pays little—but we'll buy some mounts from you if you'll sell them."

"What are you planning to do?" asked Calis.

"We're heading for Maharta. The Raj is sending his Royal Immortals to help the Priest-King of Lanada defend against the greenskins and their army. That means his war elephants and those drug-crazed maniacs of the Priest-King are on the same side for a change."

Praji said, "Things must be grim to make those two old enemies take the same cause."

Zila waved for another tankard, and Shabo hurried over to replace the empty one. "Yes, but it also means the Raj will need more fighters to keep peace around his city, so there will be work for us. I could use a couple of years of keeping farmers in line after what we just went through." He looked at Praji and Calis. "You say you were at Hamsa?"

"Yes," they both answered.

"It was ten times as bad at Khaipur. Before this war began, we were like you, a company of mercenaries who plied our trade between Khaipur and the Meet-ing Place"—Erik knew he spoke of the annual meeting of the Jeshandi horse-men and other tribes who came to the boundary of the steppes to trade with the nomads of the eastern grasslands—"or we worked along the central Vedra. Once we even took a caravan across the Plain of Djams to Palamds on the Satpura River." He shook his head. "But this war, this was like nothing I've seen. We signed on after the fall of Kilbar. I've heard enough from those who survived to know it was bad, but nothing prepared us for what happened at Khaipur." He stopped as if collecting his thoughts. "Bilbari signed us on to ride picket and run messages. The Raj of Khaipur had one of those pretty little armies that look so nice on parade, but he knew he needed veterans to slow down the invaders while he hired some mother-killers to train his army and make real fighters out of them. My comrades and I aren't Jeshandi, but we ride and fight well enough for the job.

"A month after we signed on, we got our first glimpse of the invaders. A company much like yours, about sixty seasoned fighters, rode skirmish against our forward position, then retreated without doing or taking much harm. We reported the contact and settled into wait for the next assault.

"We woke up one day and the sky was brown with dust to the northwest. A week later, ten thousand men and horses rode into view."

Zila laughed a bitter laugh. "Old Bilbari messed his pants but good, and I'll tell you he wasn't the only one with brown breeches that day. There were maybe two hundred of us in a fortification not as stout as this one, and it took us all of a minute to decide to get the hell out.

"By the time we reached the city walls, every company to the north and west of the city was also heading in. There was no fighting except at the city wall. Then from that day forward, they just came at us."

He glanced at the faces in the pavilion, as now every eye was upon him and every man listened closely. "Some of the boys gave as good as they got, and by the third month of siege, those pretty home-guard soldiers of the Raj had turned into as tough a bunch as I've seen. And they fought for their homes, so they were more motivated than we were."

He fell silent. Calis said nothing for a long while, until finally he asked, "When did they call for surrender?"

Zila looked uncomfortable. "That was what caused everything to fall apart."

Erik knew from what he had heard around camp that the behavior of mercenaries was strictly governed by convention and tradition. Zila's manner suggested something out of the ordinary had occurred.

At last Calis asked, "What?"

"They didn't call for surrender. They just came to the limit of our arrows and started digging, setting up their siege trenches and readying their engines. For a week there was no real fighting, just a few shots from the walls to keep them alert. The Raj was a brave enough man for someone who had never held more than a ceremonial sword in his life, and he stood at the head of his army. . . ." Zila closed his eyes. He covered them with his hand, and for a moment Erik thought he might be weeping. When he removed his hand, Erik didn't see tears, but he did see bottled-up rage.

"The silly bastard stood there, wearing a gods-thrice-damned golden crown, holding a peacock fan of office, while those lizards rode around below his walls. He *commanded* them to leave."

Calis said, "What else?"

"He couldn't understand that this was no war out on the plain over control of trading routes or to settle some matter of honor with the Raj of Maharta or the Priest-King of Lanada. He didn't understand even when they swarmed into his palace and started cutting up his wives and children in front of his eyes. . . ." Zila closed his eyes, and then whispered, "I don't think he understood when they hoisted him up and impaled him before his own palace."

"Impaled him?" blurted Erik.

Calis looked at him for a moment, then said, "What aren't you telling?"

"Ah, it's a nasty business," said Zila. "And I speak ill of the dead to repeat it. And of myself, truth to tell."

"You're protected by the peace of the camp," reminded Praji, his ugly face turned even less appealing by dark suspicion. "Did you turn coat?"

Zila nodded. "My captain, and the others . . ." He seemed lost in the tale and said, "You know there are ways in and out of a city under siege, for a crafty man with enough money. The lizards didn't ask for our surrender. They just came at us again and again. The men fighting with them were worse than any I've met, and I've met some black-hearted murderers in my time. But the lizards . . ." He took a long drink. "They stand nine, ten feet tall, and they're as broad as two men across the shoulders. One blow with their sword can numb a strong man's arm to the shoulder or split a shield. And they have no fear. They didn't attack until the wall was breached." He shook his head. "Until we quit the wall and gave it to them.

"They sent an agent who found my captain and some others and told us there would be no formal offer of truce and that after the battle, those in the city would be put to the sword. They said those of us who abandoned the walls and stood aside would be free to join in the looting."

Praji looked ready to attack the man, as he slowly rose. He stared at Zila for a long, dark moment, then spit on the ground and left. Calis seemed more interested in facts than in condemning the man. "What else?"

"The captains brought the offer to us. We knew we were beaten. Every day more men and supplies would come downriver to bolster them, while we grew weaker. Someone had set fire to a grain warehouse"—Erik winced in anticipation; he knew that grain dust in the air could explode if touched by spark or match; that was why no fire was permitted near the mill or the grain silos near Ravensburg—"and the explosion took out half the supplies of grain as well as a block of dwellings. Someone else poisoned a good amount of the wine being harbored near the palace, and at least a score of men died screaming as they held their bellies." He closed his eyes, and this time a tear did fall, one of rage and frustration as well as regret. "And their damn spellcasters. The Raj had hired his own, and some were good. A few priests were there, too, healing the wounded and sick. But the lizard magicians were stronger. Strange noises would come during battle, and a man would feel terror no matter how well the fight went. Rats came boiling out of the sewers in broad daylight to bite your ankles and climb up your legs. There were clouds of gnats and flies so thick you inhaled them, or swallowed them if you opened your mouth.

"Fresh bread turned moldy moments after being taken from the oven, and milk soured in the bucket below the cow. And every day the lizards dug their trenches and turned their siege engines and kept hammering at us."

Zila looked around at the faces. "I don't know if you'd have done different in my place, but I doubt it." His tone was defiant. "My Captain came to us and told us what was going to happen, and we knew he wouldn't lie to us. We knew he was no coward." He said to Calis, accusingly, "You said you knew him?"

Calis nodded. "He was no coward."

"It was the lizards that broke the compact. They changed the rules of war. They gave us no choice."

"How did you escape?" asked a voice from behind, and Erik turned to see de Loungville, who had come up sometime during the narrative.

"Something the lizard's agent said bothered my Captain. I don't know exactly what, but I do know that when they impaled the Raj in front of his own people, they told everyone still alive that they could either sit a stake next to their former ruler or serve."

"You weren't given the day's grace to quit the field?" said Foster, from behind de Loungville, and Erik stepped aside so they could see Zila better.

"We weren't given enough time to pick up our own kits! But Bilbari knew they were up to something and had us gather by the smallest gate to the south. We fought our way out, and they were too busy to send anyone after us. That's where our Captain died, leading us out of the city we had betrayed."

Calis said, "It was your Captain's choice."

Zila said, "I'd be a liar if I told you. We're regulars, and until then every man had a contract with Bilbari. We voted on it, like regulars do."

"How did you vote?" demanded de Loungville.

"Does it matter?"

"You're damn right it matters," he answered, his face set in an angry mask. "Turning coat is the lowest thing a man can do."

Zila said, "Every man voted to leave."

Calis said, "You have the peace of the camp until sunrise the day after tomorrow. See that you're gone by then."

He rose, and as he left the pavilion, Erik hurried after him. "Captain!"

Calis halted, and Erik was shocked at the anger he read in the half-elf's face. "What?"

"Some of their horses need to lie up. If they don't, give them another couple of days and they're useless."

"That's Zila and his companions' problem."

"Captain, I don't give a nail's head for Zila and his men. I'm thinking of the horses."

Calis looked at Erik, then said, "Tend the horses as best you can, but do nothing special for them. Hay and water, that's all we'll give them. What they buy from the villagers is their own business."

"There's a man named Rian who wants to know if we'll take him. Says he doesn't want to lie around Maharta."

Calis was silent for a moment. Finally he said, "If one of those turncoats is in sight when the sun reaches the sky the day after tomorrow, he will be killed."

Erik nodded and returned to the remounts. There he found Rian and said, "My Captain says we have no room."

The man's expression shifted, and for an instant Erik thought he'd appeal, but at last he said, "Very well. Will you sell horses?"

Erik said, "I don't think it would earn me my Captain's thanks to keep you here." Lowering his voice, he said, "Keep what little gold you have. Take that buckskin gelding over there." He motioned toward the horse. "He's just come sound from a stocked-up leg—he got it kicking out for no damn reason at all—and he's got rocks for brains. But he's fit enough to get you out of here in two days."

The man named Rian said, "I don't think I'll wait that long. My Captain's dead, and so are Bilbari's Regulars with him. I'm heading south to find a billet before word gets down there. Once a man's labeled turncoat, no one will ever trust him."

Erik nodded. "Zila said you had no choice."

Rian spat. "A man always has a choice. Sometimes it's to die with honor or live without, but there's always a choice. That pretty Raj was a man. He might never have fought a day in his life, but when it came time to surrender he spit over the wall. He cried like a baby when they hoisted him up onto the stake, and he howled like a broken-backed dog when he felt it coming up his gut. But even while he hung there with his own shit and blood running down the pole, he never asked for mercy, and if Khali-shi"—he used the local name for the Goddess of Death, who judges the lives of men—"has any goodness in her, she'll give him another chance on the Wheel."

Erik said, "Zila said you were never offered the chance of surrender."

"Zila's a lying sack of pig guts. He was our corporal, and with the Captain and sergeant dead he thinks he's our Captain. No one's killed him yet because we're all too damn tired."

"Come with me," said Erik.

He led Rian to the hut Calis used as his office and quarters and asked to see the Captain. When Calis appeared, he looked at Rian, then at Erik. "What?"

"I think you should hear this man out," said Erik. Turning to Rian, he said, "What about the offer to surrender?"

Rian shrugged. "The Raj told the lizards he would burn in hell before he'd open the gates of his city to them. But he offered any captain who wanted to quit the city the chance to leave—without pay, of course." Rian sighed. "If you knew Bilbari, you'd know he was one greedy son of a mule. He took a bonus for staying, then made a deal with the lizards to betray the city and join in the looting." He shook his head. "But that was the joke. It was the worst betrayal of all: as soon as the fires started and the looting began, they hunted down the mercenary companies one at a time. Those that stood died, and those that surrendered were given the choice of swearing service or taking the stake. No day's grace, no laying down of weapons and walking away, nothing. Serve or die. A few of us managed to get free."

Calis shook his head. "How could you betray your vow?"

"I never did," said Rian, with what was the closest to a show of emotion Erik had seen so far. He stared Calis in the eyes and repeated, "I never did. We were a regular company, soldiers for life, sworn in oath as brothers. We voted, and those who voted to stay and fight were on the losing side. But we swore an oath to each other long before we took the Raj's gold, and damn me if I'd leave a brother for being wrong-headed."

"Then why did you seek service with us?"

"Because Bilbari's dead and our brotherhood is broken." He looked genuinely sad. "If you knew Bilbari, you also knew he had his own way of taking care of his men. Some of us were with him ten, fifteen years, Captain. He was nobody's father, but he was everyone's eldest brother. And he'd kill the first man who harmed one of his own. I've been selling my sword since I was fifteen years old, and it's the only family I've known. But it's a dead family now. After Khaipur, no man will have us to service, and that means being a bandit or starving."

"What will you do?" said Calis.

"I'd like to head out tonight and get a march on this news heading south. Maybe catch a boat out of Maharta if I can't find a billet there, head up coast to the City of the Serpent River or down to Chatisthan, someplace nobody knows me. I'll find another company who'll hire me, or a merchant needing a bodyguard." He looked to the north for a moment with a thoughtful expression. "But with what's up there, I don't know that any of us can find a peaceful life anywhere. I've never seen war like this before. You saw the smoke, Captain?"

Calis nodded.

"They fired the city when they were through. I don't mean a fire here or there, but the entire city. We saw from a ridge to the south before we ran for our lives, but we saw." His voice lowered as if he was afraid someone might overhear. "From one end to the other the fire burned, and the smoke rose so high it flattened and spread through the clouds like a big tent. Soot rained from the sky for days. Twenty, thirty thousand soldiers standing shoulder to shoulder before the gates, shouting and laughing, chanting and singing as they killed those who wouldn't serve their cause. And I saw her."

"Who?" said Calis with sudden interest.

"The Emerald Queen, some call her. In the distance. Couldn't see her face, but I saw a company of lizards on those damn big horses of theirs, and a big wagon, bigger'n anything I've ever seen before, and on the wagon was this big golden throne, and this woman sat there, in a long robe. You could see the green flicker of the emeralds at her throat and wrists, and she had a crown with emeralds. And the lizards all went wild, hissing and chanting, and even some of the men, those who'd been with them long enough, they all bowed when she came by."

"You've been helpful," said Calis. "Take a fresh horse and whatever food you need and slip out at the guard change at sundown." Rian saluted and left.

Erik turned to leave and Calis said, "Keep what you heard to yourself."

Erik nodded. Then he said, "Captain, the horses?"

Calis shook his head. "Very well. Do what you can, but nothing that diminishes our ability to care for our own animals. No medicines you can't replace . . . easily replace."

Erik was about to say thank you, but Calis turned and reentered the hut, leaving him alone. After a moment he headed back to the horses; there was a great deal of work to do, and some of Zila's companions would be leaving on foot in two days if he didn't work miracles.

"ERIK!"

Erik looked up to see Embrisa standing nearby, just outside the corral where he was examining a horse's leg, and he said, "Hello."

Shyly she said, "Can you have supper tonight?"

Erik smiled. The girl had asked him twice before, so he could meet her father and mother—though he already had in the market and knew them by sight, she wanted a formal meeting. It was becoming clear she had decided that Erik should court her, and he was both flattered and disturbed by the attention.

She would be of marrying age in another two years in Ravensburg, but that was Ravensburg. The people here were much poorer, and children meant hands that could work at three years of age, out in the field gleaning grain that fell from the stalks as the crops were harvested, helping with the heavy work by six or seven years. A boy was a man at twelve, and a father at fifteen.

He crossed to the rails, and climbed over, stepping down next to her. "Come here," he said quietly. She stepped closer and he looked down and put his hand on her shoulder. He kept his voice low as he said, "I like you very much. You're as nice a girl as I've met, but I'm going to be leaving soon."

"You could stay," she said in a rush. "You're only a mercenary, and you can leave the company. A smith would be a man of importance here, and you'd quickly become a leader."

Erik was suddenly aware that besides being pretty, she was also a cunning girl who had sized up the most likely man in the company to become rich—at least by village standards—should he remain and ply a trade.

"Isn't there a boy here—" he began.

"No," she said, half in anger, half in embarrassment. "Most of them are already married or too young. The girls outnumber them because of the wars."

Erik nodded. His own company, though composed of condemned men, numbered more than one former farmer's son who had left home to seek his fortune as a soldier or bandit.

Suddenly Roo was standing beside them, and Erik knew he had overheard the entire conversation, though he pretended not to, by saying, "Embrisa! I didn't see you there. How are you?"

"Fine," she said, lowering her eyes; her sullen tone showed she wasn't.

As if nothing was amiss, Roo said, "Did you talk to Henrik today?"

Erik knew who Roo spoke of, a young man from a village not too far from Ravensburg who served with another squad, but one whom he had barely exchanged a dozen words with over the course of his travels. Henrik was a dull man with little to say.

"No, not today," answered Erik, wondering what Roo was leading up to.

Lowering his voice, Roo said, "He says he might come back here after we're done. Says he likes it and might just settle down"—he looked at Embrisa—"find a wife, and set up a mill."

Embrisa's eyes widened. "He's a miller?"

"His father was one, or so he says."

Embrisa said, "Well, I must go. Sorry you can't come to supper, Erik."

After the girl was gone, Erik said, "Thanks."

"I was over there and heard what was going on," said Roo with a grin. "I figure a miller is the only one likely to make more money here than a smith, so I thought I'd give your young friend another target."

Erik said, "Is Henrik really thinking of staying, or are you just making trouble?"

"Well, I don't know how much trouble, given she's a saucy lass with an ample bosom and a firm young bottom. If she nets our friend the miller's son, who knows? It could be true love, and he could indeed be thinking of staying by tomorrow."

Erik shook his head. "Or hiding from her father."

"Maybe, but as her father's downriver with his wife and their sons, leaving Embrisa here alone, I suspect she was laying a snare for you." He glanced at where the girl had gone. "Though I think it might have been a pleasant one for a night."

"The girl's not yet fifteen years old, Roo," said Erik.

"Around here, that's old enough for motherhood," answered Roo. "Anyway, it won't do the lass much good getting either of you in her bed, 'cause the Captain's not likely to let any of us wander off."

"True," agreed Erik.

"And besides, we're leaving in two days."

"What?"

"Riders from the south came in about ten minutes ago with messages. Some more soldiers are joining us in two days' time, and we all ride north."

"Well, I'd better get to work," said Erik. "I've got to sort out this horse business with Zila's men. I think we'll have to leave about a dozen horses here."

"The villagers will love that," said Roo with a grin. "The ones they can't use for plowing they'll eat."

Erik nodded, knowing he wasn't really joking. "Come on, give me a hand."

Roo grumbled, but he followed Erik back into the corral to cut out the lame horses.

ERIK LOOKED TOWARD the southern gate expectantly. Zila and his renegades had left the night before, as agreed, and now the new company from the south that was to join them was coming in ahead of schedule. De Loungville had already passed word: if the southern riders showed up before noon, they were off as soon as the company was mustered, all save a dozen men who would hold this fortress against the need of a southern retreat. Now the work made sense to Erik. A dozen well-armed soldiers could hold this village against up to three times that number of bandits, and if the villagers joined in the fight, it would require a small army to take it.

Already, without the order being given, men were hurrying to get ready to move out. Then Erik caught sight of a familiar figure among those riding in the gate. "Greylock!" Erik exclaimed.

Owen Greylock turned. Gripping Erik's arm in a gesture of greeting, he then pulled him to his chest with a slap on the back. Releasing the young man, he said, "You look well."

"We thought we spied that grey banner of yours on the deck of the *Ranger* one day in passage, but we didn't see you come ashore."

Pulling loose a scarf that had been around his face to cut the road dust, the former Swordmaster of Darkmoor said, "That's because I didn't. I sailed on with a couple of others to the City of the Serpent River to make some arrangements, then on to Maharta to take care of some other matters. After the *Ranger* left for Krondor, it was ride like hell for a week getting up to Lanada, then another back-breaker getting here."

Soldiers in various dress were riding in the south gate. "Who are they?" asked Erik dubiously.

"Don't let the ragged cut of their outfits fool you. Those are some of the best soldiers from around these parts, hand-picked by our friend Praji over the last few years." Lowering his voice, he said, "We need to blend in."

"What are you doing here?" asked Erik. "Last I saw of you was before I was arrested."

"Long story. Let me report to Calis, and after we've watered our mounts, share a cup of wine with me and I'll tell you all."

"It's going to have to be at camp tonight," answered Erik. "We leave in an hour. You've only got time to pick some fresh mounts and grab a bite before we're on our way."

Greylock groaned. "That bastard isn't giving a man's spine a hope of recovery, is he?"

"I fear not. Come on, I've got some fine horses and I'll pick out one for you with a soft back."

Greylock laughed and said, "Lead on."

16

★★

RENDEZVOUS

CALIS SIGNALED A halt.

Erik and his companions, first company in line behind Calis and de Loungville, reined in and passed word back for the halt. Owen Greylock was riding with Calis, and Erik hadn't found the opportunity to talk to him.

Two scouts who had ridden ahead at first light were galloping down the road. One of them, a clansman whose name was unknown to Erik, said, "A merchant caravan's been taken an hour ahead. They tried to stand and fight, but there were no more than six guards for six wagons."

De Loungville said, "The merchant was traveling light."

The other scout, a man named Durany, said, "They didn't even have time to stop the wagons. Looks like the raiders swooped down out of the trees and shot them full of arrows before they knew what was happening. The murderers stripped everyone down to the skin, and took their armor and weapons and everything else they could carry."

Calis asked. "How many?"

The clansman said, "Twenty or twenty-five, maybe more."

Erik said, "Where are the bandits?"

Ignoring the source of the question, Calis nodded, and Durany said, "They headed back into the trees. We followed their tracks about a hour's ride into the woods, where they turned south. They've been shadowing the road since." He looked around. "We never overtook them. They may be looping behind us already."

"What about the village?" asked de Loungville.

Calis said, "Our twelve can hold the village if they get advance warning. But these raiders are acting more like a mercenary company on a rampage than bandits. If they come up on the village undetected . . ." Turning to de Loungville, he said, "Bobby, take six men and head back to the village to warn them. That's the most we can do. Then catch up as soon as you can."

De Loungville nodded. "You come along with me," he said to Erik and as they rode past, he motioned for Erik's five companions to fall in. They pulled out of line, and soon the seven of them were riding back to the village of Weanat.

SMOKE TOLD THEM they were too late even before they could see the fort. As they crested a rise in the road, they saw the charred ruins of the outer wall and the still-unfinished tower now blazing like a banner.

Without waiting for orders, Erik spurred his horse forward to a canter and got as close to the fire as he could. He called out a few names of villagers he had come to know, and after a moment a man emerged from the woods.

"Tarmil!" shouted Erik. "What happened?"

The villager was covered in soot and looked tired but otherwise unhurt. "Those men who were supposed to leave yesterday morning came back last night with another band of men, asking to buy provisions. Your soldiers said no, and they got into an argument over giving their word and leaving and things I didn't follow." He waved up the road. "While they were shouting at each other at the south gate, this other group climbed over the north wall and opened the north gate.

"Your men tried to fight, but they were cut down from two sides. Most of us who could slipped out the south gate, or climbed the walls; then someone set a fire. The bandits didn't trouble most of us after that; they were too busy trying to steal whatever they could before everything burned up."

"Did everyone get out?"

Tarmil shook his head. "No. I don't think so. Some of the men, I don't know from which band, took out to the hills there, with two of our women. Drak's wife, Finia, and Embrisa, maybe some others."

De Loungville came up and said, "Don't you ever go riding off like that without leave."

"They've taken some of the women up into the hills."

De Loungville swore. "I told Calis—" He cut himself off before he said anything more. He looked at Tarmil. "How long ago and how many men?"

"Less than an hour and about five or six."

"Spread out," ordered de Loungville. "See if you can spot any tracks."

Natombi found tracks indicating that a large band of riders went south, while Sho Pi found signs of another, smaller, group heading into the hills. De Loungville motioned for the former monk and Keshian Legionary to take the point and begin to follow.

They had only a short way to go before the screams of women revealed the bandits' whereabouts. De Loungville motioned for the six riders to dismount and spread out, and moved quietly toward the sounds.

Erik had his shield on his arm and his sword out a moment after tying his horse, and glanced over to see Roo on his right and Luis on his left. They crept forward through the trees, and came upon a sight that set Erik's teeth on edge.

Two men were lying on top of two women, one who was struggling. The other lay motionless. Three other men sat close by, drinking from an earthen jug as they watched the rape. A sad cry was followed by a convulsion as one of the men finished and stood up, and started pulling up his trousers. One of the men who had been drinking tossed aside the jug and started unfastening his trousers as he came to take the first man's place.

He halted and looked at the still form on the ground, then said, "Gods and demons, Culli, you killed her, you fool!"

"She was biting, so I covered her mouth."

"You smothered her, you idiot!"

"She's not more than a minute or two dead, Sajer. Go ahead; she's still warm."

Erik saw the body and felt his heart lurch. The corpse was Embrisa. Something strangely familiar struck him, and for an instant he saw Rosalyn in a similar position, her clothing torn away. Without thought he rose up and moved toward the nearest men. One was watching the argument between his companions, but the other started to rise. He was halfway off the log where he had sat when he died: with a single sweeping motion Erik cleaved his head completely from his shoulders.

Erik's companions charged and shouted, and the four remaining men scrambled to defend themselves. Erik crossed to where the man named Sajer stood, while the one called Culli dashed to where his sword and shield lay. Sajer pulled his only weapon, a dagger at his belt, and Erik advanced upon him like death come into human form.

Fear crossed the man's face as Erik bore down on him, and he made ready to defend himself as best he could. He lunged in feint with his dagger, but Erik only stepped forward, bashing with his shield, knocking him to the ground. He raised his sword above his head, then brought it down with a thundering blow, cutting completely through Sajer's upraised forearm, slicing him from shoulder to belly.

Erik had to put his foot on the man's chest to pull free his sword, and when he did he turned to see that the remaining three men had taken off their helms and thrown weapons to the ground, the sign among mercenaries of surrender.

Erik's eyes were wild and wide as he looked at the man named Culli. He walked purposefully toward him.

De Loungville stepped before Erik and, using all his strength, pushed him backwards. It was like trying to move a tree, but he did slow Erik's forward advance. "Get a hold of yourself, von Darkmoor!" he commanded.

Erik paused at the sound of his name. He looked to where the two women lay. Finia had all her clothing torn from her, and lay motionless in the grass, the only sign she was still alive being the slow rise and fall of her small breasts. Embrisa lay a short distance away, also nude, but bloody from belly to knee. Erik turned to stare at the man named Culli. "He dies. Now. Slowly."

De Loungville said, "Did you know her?"

"Yes," answered Erik, part of his mind being surprised de Loungville didn't. "She was fourteen."

One of the captives said, "They was villagers! We didn't know they belonged to anyone."

Erik advanced, and this time de Loungville threw his shoulder into him, knocking him back a step. "You stand fast when I tell you!" he shouted at Erik.

Turning to face the three men, he said, "What company?"

The man named Culli said, "Well, Captain, we've been sort of looking out for ourselves lately."

"Did you hit that caravan a half day's ride north of here?"

A grin of broken and blackened teeth greeted the question. "Well now, it wouldn't be the truth if we took credit for it all by ourselves. There were another six or seven boys in on that one. But they joined up with some men who wanted to raid that fort at the village. Fat man, rode a big roan horse, he took them all together."

"Zila," said de Loungville. "I'll settle up with him someday."

Culli continued, "We was watching from the woods and got in to grab what we would when they started to leave. We saw these two women getting out of a burning house, so we decided to have some fun." He nodded at the still-living but stunned Finia and the dead Embrisa. "We didn't mean to be so rough, but these was the only two we could find, and there's five of us. We'll pay you gold if they was yours, Captain, to make up for it, you see. We won't even say nothing about the two boys you already killed. We only killed the one. Two for one seems more than fair. Give the other a couple of hours to rest and, why, she could service all six of you and a couple of us in the bargain."

"On your knees," commanded De Loungville. Biggo, Natombi, and Luis forced the three men to their knees, holding them fast.

"I want that one," said Erik, pointing at Culli. "I'm going to stake him out facedown over an anthill and watch him die screaming."

De Loungville turned and struck Erik as hard across the face as he could.

Erik staggered, fell to his knees, and could barely retain consciousness from the unexpected blow.

When his vision cleared, he saw de Loungville come up behind the first man. With an economy of motion he pulled his dagger, grabbed the man's hair, and pulled back his head, cutting his throat with a single slice.

The other two tried to rise, but Biggo and Luis kept them under control. Before Erik could regain his feet, the other two men had been executed. Erik took one staggering step, then shook his head to clear it. He came to stand over the body of Culli and looked at de Loungville, who said, "See to the woman." When Erik hesitated, he shouted, "Now!"

Erik and Roo moved to where Finia lay, eyes staring vacantly at the sky. When they knelt over her, her eyes seemed to focus for the first time. Recognizing Erik and Roo, she said in a whisper, "Is it over?"

Erik nodded, and Roo took off his cloak and used it to cover her. Erik helped the woman get to her feet, and she wobbled as she rose. Roo put his arm around her, to steady her, and she looked over at Embrisa. "I told her to do as they said. She scratched and bit them. She was screaming and crying, and her nose stuffed up; when they covered her mouth, she couldn't breathe."

Erik inclined his head to Roo to take her to where the horses were. He took off his own cloak and wrapped Embrisa in it. Lifting her, he carried her as if she were asleep. Softly he said, "Now you'll never find that rich husband."

Erik was the last to reach the horses, and found de Loungville holding his reins. He handed the girl's body to the sergeant, mounted, then took the corpse as de Loungville handed her up to him. After the sergeant had mounted his own horse, Erik said, "You let them off easy."

De Loungville said, "I know."

"They should have died over a slow fire."

"They deserved to suffer, but I'll not visit that on any man."

"Why? Why do you care what happens to scum like them?"

De Loungville moved his horse alongside Erik's, so he was almost nose-to-nose with Erik when he answered. "I don't care what happens to scum like them. You could cut off a piece at a time over a week and I wouldn't give a whore's promise for what it would do to them. But I do care what it would do to you, Erik."

Without waiting for an answer, de Loungville moved away and shouted, "Let's get back to the village. We've got a hell of a ride before we catch up with the Captain."

Erik rode after him, not sure what de Loungville had meant, but feeling troubled by what he had said.

★★

THEY REACHED CALIS's camp an hour after dark. As before, he had ordered a complete fortification dug, and as de Loungville and the others approached, a guard challenged them.

"Well done," said a weary de Loungville. "Now, lower the gate or I'll rip your ears from your head."

No one in Calis's company could fail to recognize that voice, so without a further remark the drop bridge was run out across the trench surrounding the camp. The horse's hooves clattered on the wood and iron as the riders crossed, and when they reached the center of the camp, Calis stood waiting.

"Zila and the bandits joined up and fired the village. Most got away." He glanced at Erik. "They killed a girl and we killed the five of them that did it."

Calis nodded, motioning for de Loungville to join him in his command tent. Erik took the reins of de Loungville's horse and led him with his own to where the remounts were waiting. It took him better than an hour to cool down the horses, clean hooves and saddle marks, and bedded them down with fresh fodder. By the time he was finished, he was aching to his bones, and he knew it was more than just the fatigue of the ride and fighting. The killing of the men had been so effortless.

As he walked back to where his companions were erecting their tent, he recalled what he had done. The first man he had struck had been an obstacle, nothing more. He hadn't been trying to decapitate him, only to brush him aside. Luis had said something later about its being a terrible blow, as was the cleaving of the second man Erik had faced, but Erik thought it a distant act, as if someone else had been doing the fighting. He could remember the smells: the smoke of the burning village and the campfire in the clearing, the stench of sweat and feces mixed in with the iron bite of blood and the stink of fear. He felt the shock of the blows he delivered running up his arm, and the pounding of his own blood in his forehead, but it was all distant, muted, and he couldn't find it within himself to grapple with and understand what had occurred.

He knew he had wanted Embrisa's killer to suffer. He knew he wanted the man to feel her pain a thousand times over, yet now he was dead, feeling nothing. If Biggo was to be believed, the man was being judged by the Death Goddess, but whatever the truth, he was feeling none of this life's pain.

Maybe de Loungville was right. Erik thought he was the one who was now suffering, and it made him both sad and angry. He reached the tent and found that Roo had taken Erik's section of tent and erected it, so that the six-man dwelling was up and waiting for him.

Erik looked at his boyhood friend and said, "Thank you."

Roo said, "Well, you spend enough time looking out for my horse."

"And mine," said Biggo.

"And everyone else's," said Luis. "Do you think we should pay this boy for being so good to us?"

Erik looked over at Luis, whose sense of humor was rarely in evidence, and saw that the often short-tempered Rodezian was looking at him with a rare warmth in his expression.

Biggo said, "Well, maybe. Or we could do his bit with setting up and tearing down the tent, like we did tonight."

"I can manage my own weight," said Erik. "No one needs to do for me." He heard an irritation in his voice that was unexpected. Suddenly he discovered he was feeling very angry.

Biggo reached from his bedroll across the narrow aisle separating the three bunks on each side and said, "We know, lad. You do more than your share, that's all. No one's said anything, but you've become the Horsemaster for our little company of cutthroats."

At the mention of the word "cutthroat" Erik was struck by the image of the three men being butchered by de Loungville. Suddenly he felt sick and his body felt flushed, as if fever was coming over him. Closing his eyes a second, he said, "Thank you. I know you mean well. . . ." He paused for a moment, then stood as upright as he could in the low tent and walked away. "I'll be back. I need some air."

"Guard duty in two hours," Roo called after him.

Walking through the camp, Erik tried to calm himself. He found his stomach clenched and he felt as if he might be sick. Running for the privy trench, he barely got there in time to keep from fouling his pants.

After agonizing minutes of squatting and feeling as if he was passing fire, he felt his stomach twist, and suddenly he was vomiting into the trench. When he at last finished, he felt as if he had no strength left. He went to the edge of the nearby stream and cleaned himself up, then he returned to the cookfire, where he found Owen Greylock helping himself to a bowl of stew and a hunk of bread.

Despite having lost everything in his gut only moments before, Erik was suddenly ravenous as he smelled the stew. He grabbed a wooden bowl as Owen greeted him and watched while Erik scooped out a large bowl of stew, ignoring the hot liquid as it covered his hand to the wrist.

"Look out!" said Owen. "Gods, you're going to boil yourself."

Erik lifted the bowl to his lips and took a long sip, then said, "Heat doesn't bother me. I think it's the years at the forge. Now, cold, that makes me hurt."

Owen laughed. "Hungry?"

Erik tore a large piece of bread off one of the loaves on the serving table and said, "Can we talk for a minute?"

Owen motioned for Erik to sit on a log that had been felled to provide a rude bench for men eating. No one else was nearby save the two men who would clean up the cook area and ready it for the morning meal before turning in.

Owen said, "Where do you want to begin?"

Erik said, "I want to know how you got here, but first, can I ask you something?"

"Certainly."

"When you kill a man, how does that make you feel?"

Owen was silent and then blew out his cheeks and let a long breath slowly escape. "That's a difficult one, isn't it?" He fell silent a minute, then said, "I've killed men two ways, Erik. As my lord's Swordmaster I was dispenser of the high justice and I've hung more than one man. It's different each time, and never easy. And it depends on why I'm hanging them. Murderers, rapists, thugs, they . . . I don't feel much of anything, except relief when it's over. When it's something dicey, like your execution was set to be, then it's a nasty business. I feel like taking a long, long hot bath afterward, though I rarely get the chance.

"When it comes to battle, things just happen too quickly and you're usually too busy staying alive to think about it. Does that answer you?"

Erik nodded as he munched on soggy vegetables. "In a way. Did you ever want to see someone suffer?"

Owen scratched his head at this. "Can't say as I have. I've wanted to see a few men dead, but suffer? Not really."

"I wanted to see a man feel pain today." Erik explained about Embrisa and how he had wanted to make her killer experience a long, slow, terrible death. When he finished, he added, "Then I found I could barely keep my arse closed. Flux and then throwing up. Then suddenly I'm here eating like nothing happened."

"Rage does strange things to you," Owen said. "You're not going to like hearing this, I think, but the only two other men I've known who felt as you say you did were your father and . . . Stefan."

Erik shook his head and laughed ruefully. "You're right. I didn't like hearing that."

"Your father only got that way with rage. If he was angry, he'd rather have seen his enemy injured and in pain than dead. But that was the only time." His voice lowered. "Stefan was worse. He really enjoyed watching people suffer. He got . . . excited by it. Your father had to bribe more than one father off because his daughter was . . . damaged."

"What about Manfred?"

Owen shrugged. "Given who his parents are, he's a decent enough person. You'd like him, given a chance to know each other, but that's neither here nor there." Owen studied Erik, then said, "I've known you a long time, since you were a baby, Erik, and while you have some of your father in you, you don't have *only* your father's blood in you. Your mother can be a hard woman, but she was never a mean one. She's never hurt anyone for pleasure. And you can bet that Stefan was the worst mix of his father and mother.

"I think I can understand why you'd be so ferocious with the man who killed the girl. You were fond of her, I take it?"

"In a way." Erik smiled. "She tried to cozen me into her bed so she could be the village smith's wife." He shook his head in regret. "She was so obvious and there was no art to it, but in a way . . ."

"It made you feel good?"

"Yes."

Owen nodded. "We all have our vanity, and a pretty girl's attentions are rarely unwelcomed by any man."

"But it doesn't explain why I wanted to see that man hurt so much. I can still feel it, Owen. If I could raise him from the dead and cause him to scream in agony, I think I'd do it."

"Justice, maybe. The girl died in agony, and he got a simple death in return."

A voice from the dark said, "Sometimes revenge goes disguised as justice."

Both Owen and Erik turned to see Nakor entering from the darkness. "I was out walking and heard you talk. Sounds like an interesting discussion." Without asking their leave, he sat down.

Erik said, "I was telling Owen here what happened today. Have you heard?"

Nakor nodded. "Sho Pi told me. You were in a rage. You wanted to cause this man pain. Bobby kept you from indulging in his suffering."

Erik nodded.

Nakor said, "Some men take to the pain in others the way other men take to strong drink or potent drugs. If you recognize that appetite in yourself early and learn to master it within yourself, you'll be the better man for knowing, Erik."

"I don't know what I wanted," Erik admitted. "I don't know if it was that he didn't suffer enough or if I really wanted to see something in his eyes as he died."

Owen said, "Most soldiers are struck by others' death after the fact. That you got sick—"

Nakor said, "You got sick?"

"Like I had eaten green apples," admitted Erik.

Nakor grinned. "Then you're not a man to eat poison and like it. If you hadn't gotten sick, it would be because that poison of hate found a home in your gut." He reached over and poked a finger into Erik's side. "You ate the hatred, but your body threw it up as if it were those green apples." He smiled, apparently satisfied with the explanation. "Do your reiki each night and let your mind seek calmness and you will survive the terrors you've just met."

Owen and Erik exchanged looks that said neither man knew what Nakor was talking about. Erik said, "Now tell me how you came here?"

Owen said, "That was due to you."

"Me?"

Owen said, "When you were caught, my lady Mathilda and your half brother raced to Krondor, to ensure the Prince knew you were to be hung without question.

"When we got there, I asked a friend in the Prince's court to grant me an audience with Nicholas, and I tried to give him some idea of how you'd been dealt with as a child." He shrugged. "It obviously didn't do any good, as you were to be hung, and the Dowager Baroness discovered I had tried to intercede upon your behalf." He looked at Erik and smiled. "I was asked to retire from my office. Manfred said he regretted to ask, but she is his mother, after all."

"I've never met her, but she seems a most persuasive woman, by all reports," offered Nakor.

"That's one way of putting it," said Owen. "Well, there isn't a great demand for discharged Swordmasters, so I applied to the Prince's Guard for a billet. I was prepared to stand down to man-at-arms if needs be, or to attempt to gain a commission on the frontier. Failing that, I was going to try my hand at the mercenary trade, providing escort for merchant trains down into the Vale of Dreams and Great Kesh.

"But that black heart Bobby de Loungville found me at a tavern and got me very drunk, and I woke up the next day and discovered I was going to be running like a madman from Questor's View to Land's End on one errand or another for Prince Nicholas and Calis."

Owen continued, "That's a strange customer, our Captain. Did you know he ranks in the court as a Duke?"

Erik said, "I only know him as—"

"The Eagle of Krondor," finished Owen. "I know. He's important, that's all I know. But when the dust settled, I was on the *Freeport Ranger*, with a list of missions to last three months, and one month to finish them when we made port in Maharta."

Erik finished his food and said, "Sorry to have put you to this, Owen."

Owen laughed. "It was in the cards, as the gamblers say. And truth to tell, I was growing bored at Darkmoor. The wine's the best in the world, and the women as fair as anywhere, but there's little else to stir a man there. I've grown tired of hanging bandits and running escort from one safe city to another. I think it's time for something grand."

Nakor shook his head. "There's little grand ahead of us." He stood up, yawning. "I'm going to sleep. We have three long days ahead."

"Why?" asked Erik.

"While you were killing those men, we got word of a rendezvous."

"What is that?" asked Erik. "I've heard that term before."

"Meeting," said Owen.

"A great camp," offered Nakor. With a grin he said, "It is where the two sides in this war will come to make offers for the service of companies like ours.

It's where we will find the army of this Emerald Queen, and then friend Grey-lock's adventure will begin." He wandered off into the gloom.

Owen said, "He may be the strangest man I've met. I've only talked to him a couple of times since yesterday, but he has some of the oddest notions I've ever encountered. But he's right about one thing: it's a long day tomorrow and we both need to sleep."

Erik nodded and took Owen's bowl. "I'll wash that up. I'm doing mine anyway."

"Thank you."

"And thank you," replied Erik.

"For what?"

"For talking."

Owen put his hand upon Erik's shoulder. "Anytime, Erik. Good night." He walked after Nakor.

Erik went to the bucket used to clean the wooden bowls and rinsed them with water, scoured them with cleaning sand, then rinsed with fresh water again. He put the bowls where the men who would make the morning mess would expect to find them, and returned to his own tent.

The others were sleeping, except Roo, who said, "Are you all right?"

Erik sighed and said, "I don't know. But I am better."

Roo seemed about to make a remark, then thought better of it and turned over to go to sleep. Erik lay in the darkness, and while he intended to practice the self-healing Nakor had taught him, sleep was on him less than a minute after Roo.

THE CAMP WAS immense. At least ten thousand armed men were scattered across a low valley that ran from the hills on the east to the river on the west. Cutting through the middle was a smaller tributary to the Vedra, and along this smaller river camps had been made.

The brokers who were conducting the contracts were arrayed under a large canopy, ocher in color, at the heart of the valley. Erik rode with his companions in their usual position near the head of the column, near enough to Calis to overhear his conversations with the men around him.

Praji pointed. "Some of those banners are damn strange; I thought I knew every company worth talking about in this gods-forsaken continent." He glanced around. "Some of these others are a long way from home."

"How is it shaping up?" asked de Loungville.

"It's early yet. Khaipur fell less than a month ago. If the Emerald Queen's representatives get here in the next week I'll be surprised. But I'll bet you a whore's hoard that the Priest-King of Lanada is spending money like a sailor in port." Looking around, he said, "We'd better head up the valley and see if there's anywhere good near the river." He sniffed the air. "With the number of these fools pissing in the water after they get drunk, downstream's the last place I want to be."

De Loungville laughed. "Looks like the best places are taken."

"Only if you like the taste of another man's piss in your water," said Praji. "This is just the start. The word's been about for five years now. There's a big war to end all wars coming, and any man with a sword who doesn't get in now will be out of the looting." He shook his head. "Doesn't make much sense, does it? You'd think any man with eyes in his head could see—"

Calis cut him off with an upraised hand. "Not here. Too many ears."

Praji nodded. "Look for a red eagle banner, twin to your own. That'll be Vaja if he's found his way here."

Calis nodded.

They rode into the camp area, and Erik felt his pulse race. Never had so many pairs of eyes regarded him with suspicion. The rendezvous was neutral ground, where both sides in the coming conflict could recruit mercenary companies to their cause, openly bidding against one another, and tradition bound every man who entered sight of the tent to keep his sword sheathed. But tradition and enforceable law were two different things, and more than once a battle had erupted at such a meeting. Men in this camp knew only that those in their own company were allies. Anyone else might be someone they would see across the field of battle mere days or weeks after leaving the rendezvous.

They passed by the large yellowish tent, though on the other side of the water, as they picked their way upriver, and away from the main body of men camping. Calis found a small rise with a flat top that gave a commanding view of the valley below and motioned to de Loungville that they would camp there. "No fortifications; it's against the compact, but I want double guard. When the whores come by, let the men indulge, but no strong drink and no drugs—chase the peddlers away. I'll not have some fool start a war because he sees the ghost of some enemy in the smoke and pulls his sword."

De Loungville nodded and gave the order. Without the need to dig a trench and rampart, making camp took little time. When Erik's squad had finished erecting their tent, Foster came by and gave the rotation for guard duty. Erik groaned when he was told the second watch, which was from midnight to two hours before dawn. Sleep interrupted was as good as not sleeping from his point of view.

Still, after three days in the saddle, a little time to lie around would be welcome. And if he had the midnight watch tonight, that meant the dawn watch tomorrow, and the day after, no watch at all. He found that a little gratifying, and was glad to have found any reason to feel good whatsoever.

★★

TRUMPETS BLEW AND Erik came awake with a start. They had been in camp for five days now and he was back to a split night of guard duty. He rolled out of his tent and saw that everyone was looking down into the valley below.

Roo came to his side and laughed. "Looks like an anthill with a stick in it."

Erik laughed, for Roo was right. There was motion everywhere. Then Foster was hurrying through camp shouting, "Every man to horse! We muster for inspection!"

Erik and Roo turned and went back into their low tent, grabbing their swords and shields. They hurried to where other men were already saddling their horses and got theirs ready. When the order to fall in came, they swung up into saddle and moved the horses to their position in the column. Foster rode by and said, "Rest awhile, lads. The shopping is beginning and you'll be doing little for a day. When the brokers come by, do your best to look fierce."

This got a laugh, and Jadow Shati's bass voice carried from somewhere back in line. "Just put Jerome in front, man. That will scare them, don't you know!"

This brought another laugh, and then de Loungville's voice cut through the air. "Next man who says anything better make me laugh, or he'll wish his mother had taken holy vows of celibacy before he was born!"

The company fell silent.

A hour later the sound of riders came from up the valley and Erik turned to see a small company of a dozen men heading their way. At their head was a large man, grey of hair, but otherwise young-looking. He wore foppish regalia, and obviously had put much thought into his appearance, despite being covered with road dust. At his side rode another carrying a crimson eagle banner.

"Vaja!" cried Praji as they pulled up. "You sorry old peacock! I thought someone had killed you out of mercy. What took you so long?"

The other man, handsome despite his years, laughed, and said, "You found them. If I hadn't heard of the rendezvous I would still be on my way down to the City of the Serpent River looking for our good Captain and this company of sorry fools."

Calis came riding over as Vaja and his men dismounted. "You've come just in time. The muster begins today."

Vaja looked around. "There's plenty of time yet. We'll have three or four days of this at least. Are both sides here?"

"No word of the Emerald Queen's agents. Just the Priest-King," answered Calis.

Vaja said, "Good. That gives me ample time to bathe and eat. You won't be taking any offer for days."

Calis said, "You know that and I know that, but if we're to be convincing, they"—he hiked his thumb over his shoulder in the general direction of the brokers' tent—"can't know that. We have to look as if we're weighing all offers equally."

"Understood," said Vaja. "But I still have time for a bath. I'll be back in an hour." He turned and led his companions away.

Praji said, "Twenty-nine years I've fought at his side, and I swear to this day no man more vain exists on this world. He'd primp for his own execution."

Calis smiled, and Erik realized it was one of the few times he had ever seen the Captain smile.

FOR DAYS THEY would muster on command, and brokers would come by to look over the company. With Vaja's men and the men under Hatonis, they numbered better than one hundred swords: a significant enough troop to be taken seriously, but not so large as to bear special scrutiny.

After the third such day, offers began to come in and Calis listened to them politely. He remained noncommittal.

A week after the mustering had started, Erik noticed a few companies departing. He asked Praji about this over supper, and the old mercenary said, "They've signed on with the Priest-King. Probably poor captains running low on gold to pay their men. They have to find employment quickly or lose their fighters to richer companies. Most are waiting around to hear what the other side has to offer."

Still more days passed and the other side didn't appear.

TWO WEEKS AFTER arriving, Erik had requested permission to move the horses upriver, as they had grazed the area clean, and the hay and grain brokers were charging outrageous prices. Calis gave permission, but instructed Erik to make sure a full guard company surrounded the animals at all times.

Another week went by.

ALMOST A MONTH after arriving, Erik was walking back from having checked the horses, a three-times-daily ritual now, to hear a series of loud trumpet calls from the heart of the camp. The weather was hot, the hottest part of the summer, he had been told by one of the clansmen, and soon summer would be waning. It felt odd to lose a winter, to leave in fall and return to spring. Erik was sure Nakor could explain this backwards season to him, but he wasn't sure he was up for hearing the little man's explanation.

Trumpets continued, insistent, and Erik started to hurry to see what the matter was. As he neared his own tent area, Foster came running toward him and shouted, "Get those horses down here! That's a call to quarter! We're being put on notice a fight's going to break out!"

Erik dashed back up the hill and down into the next small valley, and waved his hand as he shouted to the men standing guard. "Bring as many as you can lead!" He hurried past to the most distant picket line, and managed to lead four horses away. Others came hurrying past, and before he had reached the main camp, every horse was being led after him.

The men broke camp faster than Erik had ever seen. Calis gave orders for a defensive perimeter to be established, and a company began digging a breast-work. Archers scanned the hill below for signs of anyone heading their way.

Despite the sound to quarter, no sounds of battle erupted from below. Instead, a strange buzzing sound carried up the hill, and it took Erik a long minute to realize he was listening to men's voices. Arguments and curses carried up the hillside, and the sound carried a frantic quality, but there were still no sounds of fighting.

At last Calis said, "Bobby, take some men down there and find out what's going on."

De Loungville said, "Biggo, von Darkmoor, Jadow, and Jerome, with me."

Roo laughed. "He's got the four biggest men in the company to hide behind."

De Loungville turned in a single motion, looked at Roo, and said, "And you, my little man." With evil delight in his eyes, he grinned as he said, "You can stand on my shield side. If trouble erupts, I'm going to pick you up and throw you at the first man heading my way!"

Roo rolled his eyes heavenward and fell in beside Erik. "That will teach me to keep my mouth shut."

Erik said, "I doubt it."

They made their way down into the camp below on foot, trying not to call attention to themselves as they approached another campsite. Men were arguing with one another as they came within earshot.

"I don't care, it's an insult. I say let's ride south and take whatever the Priest-King offers."

Another voice said, "You want to fight your way out, so you can turn around and fight again?"

Erik tried to make sense of the remarks, but de Loungville said, "Follow me."

He made his way through several such camps, more than one marked by a busy attempt to get ready to ride. One man said, "If you break to the east, up this river, then cut through the hills to the south, you will probably get free."

The man next to him answered, "What? You're an oracle now?"

De Loungville led them to the area surrounding the brokers' tent, where he found a knot of terrified brokers standing outside their own tent. He pushed past and entered.

A low wooden desk was used by the brokers, and behind it sat a large man in fine armor, well cared for but obviously used often. His feet rested on the polished wood, mud scattering all over the documents still upon them. He looked little different from the other soldiers in camp except that he was older, perhaps older than Praji and Vaja, the oldest men in Calis's company. But rather than of age, his aura was that of a man of profound experience. He calmly looked at de Loungville and his companions as they entered, and nodded to another soldier who stood behind him. Both wore an emerald green armband on their left arm, but otherwise they wore no distinctive markings or uniform.

De Loungville stopped and said, "Well then, what fool blows a call to quarters?"

"I have no idea," said the old soldier. "I certainly didn't want to cause this much commotion."

"Are you the Emerald Queen's agent?"

The man said, "I am General Gapi. I'm no one's 'agent.' I'm here to inform you of your choices."

Erik sensed something in this man he had seen in a few others—the Prince of Krondor, Duke James, and Calis upon occasion. It was a sureness of command, an expectation that orders would be followed without debate, and Erik decided that this man's title was no mercenary vanity. This man commanded an army.

De Loungville put his hands on his hips and said, "Oh, and what choices are those?"

"You can serve the Emerald Queen or you can die."

With a slight gesture of his head, de Loungville instructed the men around him to spread out. Erik stepped to his right, until he stood opposite the single soldier in the tent behind Gapi. De Loungville said, "Usually I get paid to fight. But your tone makes me think I might be willing to forgo payment this one time."

Gapi sighed. "Break the peace of the camp at risk, Captain."

"I'm no Captain," said de Loungville. "I am a sergeant. My Captain sent me down to see what the fuss was."

"The fuss, as you call it," answered Gapi, "is the consternation of men too stupid to realize they have no choice. So you don't hear a garbled version of what was said here an hour ago, I'll repeat this so you can tell your Captain.

"All companies of mercenaries mustering in this valley must swear fealty to the Emerald Queen. We begin our campaign downriver against Lanada in a month's time.

"If you attempt to leave to take service with Our Lady's enemies, you will be hunted down and killed."

"And who's doing this hunting and killing?" asked de Loungville.

With an easy smile, Gapi said, "The thirty thousand soldiers who are now surrounding this pleasant little valley."

De Loungville turned and glanced outside the tent. He searched the ridges above the valley and saw movement, a glint of light upon metal or a flicker of shadow, but enough to tell him that a sizable force was ringing the valley. Letting out an exasperated sound, he said, "We wondered what was taking you so long to reach here. We didn't think you'd be coming in force."

"Carry word to your Captain. You have no choice."

Looking at the General, de Loungville seemed about to say something. Then he just nodded and motioned for the others to follow him.

They were silent until they were away from the main camp, when Erik said, "You look bothered, Sergeant. I thought the purpose was to join this army."

"I don't like it when the other side changes the rules," said de Loungville. "Around here you pay a man to fight. I think we may be getting sucked deeper into the sand than we thought.

"Besides," he added, "when I'm going to get buggered, I like to be asked nicely first. It annoys me when I'm not."

17

★★

DISCOVERY

ROO POINTED.

In the distance, fire marked a skirmish. True to his word, General Gapi attacked any band seeking to leave to the south. A few captains were stiff-backed enough to try to smash their way through the encircling army, and they were met with the full weight of those soldiers already in better positions and dug in.

The valley might have made a pleasant enough place for the rendezvous, but as a place from which to launch an attack it had little to recommend it. Since it was narrow and steep to the north and south, the only possible means of escape was through the eastern end, the way Vaja and his companions had come, which he reported as being treacherous hills with unforgiving trails for those taking a wrong turn. Still, some smaller bands attempted to leave this way.

Others moved out as did Calis's Crimson Eagles, either to serve and take whatever recompense might be forthcoming through looting or other rewards, or to steal away at some future opportunity. Everywhere Erik looked he saw unhappy men. De Loungville wasn't the only one feeling buggered without leave.

Those who obeyed General Gapi's orders mustered in columns at the lowest end of the river, just before it joined with the larger Vedra. A bridge, long burned out in some forgotten war, marked the place, and a series of ferries had been established to provide transport from north to south on the east side of the Vedra or from east to west below the nameless tributary.

Calis's company was among the last to reach the ferry, having quartered higher up in the valley than most, and as a result they were afforded a longer opportunity to sit and watch than those who came before. Men, and a few women, from every corner of Novindus were moving across the river, crossing to join those, like Calis's, already on the south bank.

A man wearing a green armband rode up and said, "What company?"

De Loungville pointed at Calis, who sat next to him on the left, and said, "Calis's Crimson Eagles, from the City of the Serpent River."

The man frowned, looking at Calis. "From the siege at Hamsa?"

Calis nodded.

The man grinned and there was nothing friendly in the expression. "I almost had you, you slippery bastard. But you went east to the Jeshandi, and by the time my company doubled back, you were into the steppes." He looked hard at Calis. "Had I known you were of the long-lived I would have headed east straight away. A lot of your kind with the Jeshandi."

He took out a parchment and a charcoal stick, made some marks, and said, "But Our Lady accepts all who come to her, so we're on the same side now." He waved toward the south. "Make your way downriver about a mile. Find the Master of the Camp there and report in. In a few days you'll get orders. Until then the rules of the camp are simple: any fighting, and you're killed. We're all brothers now, under the banner of the Emerald Queen, so any man who starts trouble goes to the stake. I don't recommend it; I've seen some men twitch for an hour or longer."

He didn't ask if the order was understood, simply putting heels to his horse and riding off toward the next company.

"That was simple," said Praji, who sat on Calis's left.

Calis said, "Let's find this Master of the Camp and report in. We might as well get situated as quickly as possible." He nodded at Praji and Vaja, who peeled off from the company without comment.

"What's that?" asked Erik quietly.

Foster, who was riding next to Erik, said, "Keep your mouth shut."

But Nakor laughed. "With all the confusion, it's easy to get separated from one's own company. It may take Praji and Vaja days to find out where we're camped. They'll have lots of time to hear many things."

Calis shook his head and looked over his shoulder, as if warning the Isalani to keep this to himself, but the little man giggled in delight at the notion. He said, "I think I'll get lost for a while, too." He tossed his reins to Luis, saying, "I do better on foot," and slid off his horse.

Before Calis could object, he was scampering down to where a huge company of horsemen was disembarking from barges while another large company rode in from the west. Within minutes the two companies were locked in milling confusion and Nakor had vanished into the press, ducking between horsemen who shouted curses as their horses shied at Nakor's sudden movements.

Calis said, "He's done this before."

Foster looked after Nakor with black murder in his eyes, but Calis and de Loungville only shook their heads.

THEY FOUND THE Master of the Camp hours later. A narrow face with dark, darting eyes regarded them as Calis reported in. He made a mark on a document, then waved toward the riverbank. "Find a spot between here and two miles downriver. There are other companies scattered along both sides of the road. Find a campsite between the river and the road. There should be a company calling itself Gegari's Command, just to the north of you. Across the road will be a company under a captain named Dalbrine. If you move south of that position, you will be assumed to be deserting and you will be hunted down. Those not killed will be brought back for public execution. And do not try to cross the river." He made a vague motion across the river, where in the distance they could see a company of horse riding along at an easy lope.

Something bothered Erik, and then he realized that the riders and horses were far too large for the distance and the speed they were moving. He blinked as he tried to make sense of the image, then he realized what he was seeing. "Lizard men!" he said aloud without thinking.

The Master of the Camp said, "Our Lady's allies are called the Saaur. Do not call them 'lizards' or 'snakes,' lest you incur her wrath." He motioned for Calis to lead his company away as another company approached from behind.

Squinting against the afternoon sun, Erik tried to make sense of the distant riders.

"Those horses must be twenty hands," said Sho Pi.

"Closer to twenty-two or -four," said Erik. "They're bigger than draft animals, but they move like cavalry mounts." As the riders moved away, he admired the fluid motion of the horses. The Saaur rode with an easy rocking seat, though their bodies looked oddly top-heavy, as their armor was cut in an almost triangular configuration due to flaring shoulder guards and a cinched waist. "I'd like to get a closer look at one of those horses," said Erik.

"No you wouldn't," snapped de Loungville. "At least, not one with a rider on his back."

Erik shook his head in wonder as the riders were lost in the distant afternoon haze.

THEY LOCATED THE campsite, and Calis made a guarded introduction to his neighboring captains. It was clear that no one was feeling talkative, as none of the companies knew if those next to them were actively supporting the cause of the Emerald Queen or were those coerced into serving.

Erik was no military expert, but he got the feeling that in this strange country, with its custom of hiring men to fight as opposed to supporting standing armies, having men without loyalty under arms was not a very smart thing to do. Still, no general uprising seemed to be taking place, so Erik assumed those in command of this host knew something he didn't, and left it at that.

Calis ordered the men to bed down without erecting tents. There was no order given to dig a perimeter defense or erect a breastwork. It was clear without being said that he wanted the men to be up off the ground and on horseback in the shortest possible time if the need arose.

After the second day, the surrounding camps became small communities, to be visited if the men weren't on duty. Bartering, gambling, swapping stories, or just alleviating the boredom of a camp between battles, the men wandered as far as they could without causing trouble. The level of trust was rising, albeit slowly, as those forced to serve grew more accepting of fate. They might resent having no choice as to who their new master was, but for most captains, one side was as good as the other, and booty was booty.

Some companies had an open attitude, welcoming a new face who might bring some news, gold to gamble, or just a break from the routine. But others were still wary, and twice Roo and Erik had been told to keep moving when they approached one of those camps.

The second night, Foster walked through the camp, stopping at every group of men to speak with them. He came upon Erik, Roo, Sho Pi, and Luis, who were sitting around a fire, watching as Biggo and Natombi took their turn cooking for the squad. "Here!" he said, motioning for the men to stand.

When they did, he opened a purse and counted out two golden coins and five silver for each man. In a low voice he said, "Mercenaries get paid, and if you can't buy something from a vendor or whore now and again, you'll get people asking questions about us. And the first man who gets drunk and says the wrong thing into the wrong ear, I'll personally have his liver on a stick!"

Erik hefted the coins, feeling them cold in his hand. He hadn't held coins since leaving Darkmoor, he realized, and it made him feel good to be able to buy something. He put them into a pouch sewn into a seam in his tunic, where they would be safe.

Whores appeared later that night, plying their trade. Without tents, there was little privacy, but that seemed to bother few of the men. Many simply pulled the woman of their choice under a blanket and ignored whoever might be sitting a few feet away.

A pair of them came by where Erik and Roo sat, and one said, "Looking for some company, boys?"

Roo grinned and suddenly Erik found himself flushing with embarrassment.

The last time whores had visited their camp, at the other site up on the tributary of the Vedra, he had been looking after the horses and they had moved on by the time he returned. He was certain he was the only man in camp who had never lain with a woman. Erik thought, *I might never get the chance again.* He looked at his friend, whose smile spread ear to ear, then found himself grinning back. "Why not?" he asked.

One of the women said, "We get paid first?"

Roo laughed. "And pigs fly." He waved at the camp. "We're not going anywhere, but we can't say the same for you, now, can we?"

The whore who had spoken gave him a sour look, but she nodded. "You're not as young as you look, I wager."

Roo stood up. "I'm older than I've ever been before in my life."

The whore looked confused by the statement, but followed Roo as he motioned for her to follow.

Erik stood, finding himself alone with the other woman. She could have been young, but it was difficult to tell. A hard expression and the dim campfire light made it impossible to tell if she was closer to fifteen years or forty. Some grey in her dark hair convinced him she was older than he, but he didn't know if that made him feel more comfortable or less.

"Here?" she asked.

"What?"

"Do you want to do it here, or somewhere else?"

Suddenly feeling profoundly embarrassed, Erik said, "Let's go down by the river."

He stuck out his hand awkwardly and she took it, her grip firm and her hand dry. He suddenly felt regret for the gesture, as his palm was damp and his grip uncertain.

She laughed softly and he said, "What?"

"First time, is it?"

He said, "Why . . . of course not, it's just . . . been a long time, with travel and . . ."

"Of course," she said. Erik couldn't tell if there was warmth in her amusement or contempt. He led her down to the bank of the river, and nearly stepped on a couple who were in a frantic embrace. He moved to where it was relatively dark, and stood there uncertain.

The woman quickly was out of her clothing, and Erik felt his own body respond to the sight of her. Her body was nothing extraordinary, a little plump around the hips and thighs, and her breasts sagged, but he suddenly thought of what he was about to do and he couldn't get out of his clothing fast enough. He had his tunic off and was working on his boots when she said, "You're a big lad, aren't you?"

Erik looked down at his own body as if noticing it for the first time. The passage of time and the rigors of his life since being taken prisoner had hardened him to a fitness beyond what he had known at Ravensburg. Always strong, he had lost a softer outer layer of fat and now his powerful smith's chest and shoulders were rippling muscle, as if he had been carved by a sculptor of the heroic. He said, "I've always been big for my age."

He sat and pulled off his boots, and she came over, and took the top of his pants in a firm grip. Her voice was husky as she said, "Let's see how big." She pulled off his pants, and looking at his obvious readiness, she laughed and said, "Big enough!"

Considering her profession, she was tender. She took her time and didn't laugh at Erik's awkward fumbling. She calmed him when he needed it, and while their coupling was frantic and quick, there was some sense of caring in it. After it was over, she quickly dressed, but stayed a moment after he paid her. "What's your name?"

"Erik," he said, not sure if he was comfortable telling her.

"You're a wild boy, Erik, in a man's body. The right woman's going to come to love your touch if you always remember how strong you are and how tender her flesh is."

Suddenly he felt self-conscious. "Did I hurt you?"

She laughed. "Not really. You were . . . enthusiastic. I'll have a bruise or two on my backside from hitting the damn ground so hard at the end there. But nothing like when those lads who like to slap a whore around get done with me."

Pulling on his clothing, Erik said, "Why do you do it?"

The woman shrugged in the gloom, the gesture almost lost, as she dressed. "What else can I do? My man was a soldier, like you. He died five years ago. I have no family or rank. I can steal or whore." She repeated, without apology or regret, "What else can I do?"

Before he could say anything more she was gone to seek another customer. Erik felt both relieved and empty. There had been something missing in their coupling, and Erik couldn't tell what it was, but he also knew he was already anxious to try this wonderful thing again.

SIX DAYS AFTER making camp, Erik saw Praji and Vaja riding up. Calis motioned for them to come over to where he sat, a short distance from Erik and his squad, who had just finished their midday meal. Men nodded greetings to the two old mercenaries, who walked to where Calis waited and knelt down next to him.

"What did you discover?" asked Calis.

Praji said, "Nothing terribly surprising." With a wave of his hand to indicate those companies mustered on all sides, "We're all boxed in between a range of hills to the east, the river over there, about twenty, twenty-five thousand swords to the north of us, and the armies of Lanada and Maharta mustering about fifty miles south of here."

"The Raj of Maharta sent his army that far north?"

"That's the rumor," said Vaja, keeping his voice low so only those near Calis's campfire could hear him.

Praji said, "This campaign's been going on for a dozen years, since the fall of Irabek. Sooner or later you'd think the Raj would figure it out. One by one, the cities of the river have fallen, each hoping its neighbor to the north would be the last the Emerald Queen took."

Calis said, "What else?"

"We're moving out in a few days, a week at the most, I think."

"What did you hear?" asked Calis as Robert de Loungville and Charlie Foster approached to stand behind Calis.

Praji said, "Nothing that said, 'We march in three days.' Just watching and listening."

Vaja waved to the north. "They're building a large bridge across the river where the ferry is. Got at least six companies of engineers and a couple of hundred slaves working on it all day and all night."

"No one from this side can go north without a pass," said Praji.

"And no one can leave this area unless they have signed orders," added Vaja.

"On the north side of the river," continued Praji, "there's where all the old vets are gathered, the ones who've been at the heart of this campaign from the start, them and the Saaur lizard men."

Calis was silent for a moment. "So we're wall fodder?"

"Looks like," said Praji.

Erik turned to the other men in his squad and whispered, "Wall fodder?"

Biggo kept his voice low so the officers wouldn't hear him when he answered. "First to march to the wall, old son. You get 'fed' to the wall, as it were."

Luis made a motion of drawing a blade across his own throat. "First companies to hit the wall lose the most men," he added softly.

Calis said, "We need to be alert. We've got to get closer to this Emerald Queen and her generals to find out what we really need to know. If that means we're the first through the gate or over the wall to prove our worth, that's what we'll do. Once we know what we need to know, then we'll worry about how we get the hell out of here."

Erik lay back on his pallet, arm behind his head. He watched as clouds scurried by overhead in the late afternoon breeze. He would have night watch, so he thought he'd try to get some rest.

But the thought of being the first to attack the wall of a city, that image returned again and again. He'd killed four men so far, on three different occasions, but he'd never been in battle. He worried he would somehow do something wrong.

He was still contemplating the coming campaign when Foster came along and kicked his boots, telling him it was time to get to his post. Erik found himself surprised that it was now night. He had lost himself in contemplations of the coming struggle, and the sun had set without his noticing. He rose and got his sword and shield and moved down toward the river, to spend the next few hours watching for trouble.

He thought it ironic that he was on guard in the midst of an army that would turn on Calis's Crimson Eagles in an instant if they understood their real purpose, and from what he had no idea, as no enemy was closer than fifty miles. Still, he was told to go stand guard, and that he did.

NAKOR STOOD AT the edge of the crowd, watching the priest lift up the dead sheep. The Saaur warriors closest to the fire let out a yell of approval, a deep-throated hissing, that echoed through the night like a chorus of enraged dragons. Those humans behind the circle of lizard men watched in fascination, for these rites were unknown to any but the Saaur. Many humans made signs of protection to their own gods and goddesses.

A great celebration was under way and Nakor was wandering freely through the various companies of men. He had seen many things and was both gratified and horrified: gratified that he had uncovered several key elements of the mystery that would help Calis best decide what to do next, and horrified because in his long life he had never met a gathering of evil men so concentrated in both numbers and malignancy.

The heart of this army was the Saaur, and a large company of men who called themselves the Chosen Guard. They wore both the common emerald armband and green scarves tied around their heads. Their malignancy was clearly demonstrated by one of their number who stood a short distance from Nakor, wearing a necklace of human ears. Rumor in the camp had it these were the most violent, dangerous, and depraved men in an army of dark souls. To join their ranks, one must have endured several campaigns and distinguished oneself by deeds black and numerous. It was rumored that the final act of acceptance was ritual cannibalism.

Nakor didn't doubt it. But having visited cannibals in the Skashakan Islands in prior years, he also knew these men indulged in practices that would have revolted most cannibals.

Nakor nodded and grinned at a man covered in tattoos who held a young boy tightly to him. The boy had an iron collar around his neck and his eyes had a drug-induced vacancy in them. The man snarled at Nakor, who merely grinned even more as he moved away.

Nakor was trying to move around the largest clump of celebrators so he could gain a vantage point from which to see the Emerald Queen's pavilion. Strange energies floated on the night wind, and old, familiar echoes of distant magic sounded between the notes of song; and Nakor was coming to a conclusion about who and what he would find there.

But he wasn't certain, and without certainty he couldn't return to find Calis on the other side of the tributary to tell him what he must do next. The only thing of which he was certain was the need to return to Krondor, to warn Nicholas that whatever he had feared was occurring in this distant land, far worse forces were being unleashed. Subtle, behind the ancient magic of the Pantathians, a lingering scent of alien origin hung in the air.

Glancing skyward, Nakor smelled demon essences in the clouds, as if ready to fall like rain. He shook his head. "I'm getting tired," he muttered to himself as he picked his way among giant Saaur warriors.

One of Nakor's better tricks, as he called his abilities, was the knack of moving in crowds without attracting undue notice, but it didn't always work, and this moment was one such time.

A Saaur warrior looked down and snarled, "Where do you go, human?" Its voice was deep and its accent sounded harsh to Nakor.

Nakor regarded the hooded eyes, deep red irises surrounded by white. "I am insignificant, O mighty one. I cannot see. I move to a place from which I may better observe this wondrous rite."

Nakor had been curious about the Saaur when he had first reached the heart of the camp, but now he was anxious to remove himself from them. They were still a mystery to him. They bore as much resemblance to the Pantathians as humans did to elves, which was to say that superficially they looked very similar, but upon close examination they were totally unrelated. Nakor was almost certain they came from another world entirely, and that they were warm-blooded creatures, like men, elves, and dwarves, while he knew the Pantathians were not.

He would have liked to be able to discuss such theories with an educated Saaur, but all he had encountered were young male warriors with an attitude toward humans that could only be called contemptuous. He had no doubt that should the men in this camp not be servants of this Emerald Queen, the Saaur would have been delighted to murder every human in the camp. They could barely keep their antipathy for humans in check.

The average Saaur stood between nine and ten feet in height. The Saaurs were massive in chest and shoulder, but strangely delicate of neck, and while their legs were strong enough to control their massive horses, they didn't seem to be a race of runners or jumpers. On foot, any good company of humans should prove their match, thought Nakor.

The lizard man grunted, and Nakor didn't know if that was approval or not, but he took it as permission to move on and he did so, judging he would deal with the consequences of being wrong if he turned out to be.

He was not. The warrior returned his attention to the welcoming ritual.

The pavilion of the Emerald Queen was raised up on a giant dais, constructed either of wood or of earth—Nakor couldn't tell which—but six feet higher than the other tents in this part of the camp. The structure was surrounded by a host of Saaur, and for the first time Nakor saw Pantathian priests beyond. Even more, he saw Pantathian warriors as well. Nakor grinned, for this was a new thing to his experience, and he always enjoyed discovering the unfamiliar.

The priest now turned and threw the slaughtered sheep onto a pyre and then cast scented oils after it. The smoke that rose was fragrant and thick, dark and coiling. The priest and the rest of the Saaur watched intently. Then the priest pointed and spoke in an alien language, but the tone was positive, and Nakor guessed he was saying the spirits were pleased with the offering or the portents were good, or some other priestly mumbo-jumbo.

Nakor squinted as a figure emerged from within the depths of the pavilion: a man in green armor, followed by another, who made way for a third, whose green armor was trimmed in gold. This powerful-looking man was General Fadawah, First Commander of the host. Nakor sensed evil hung around the man like smoke around a fire. For a soldier, he fairly reeked of magic.

Then came a woman with emeralds at her neck and wrists, dressed in a green gown cut low in front so that the fall of emeralds at her throat could be better shown. Upon her raven hair she wore a crown of emeralds.

Nakor muttered, "That is a lot of emeralds, even for you."

The woman moved in a way Nakor found disturbing, and when she came forward to answer the cheers of her army, he became deeply troubled. Something was profoundly wrong!

He studied her and listened as she spoke. "My faithful! I who am Your Lady, who am but a vessel for one much greater, I thank you for your gifts.

"The Sky Horde of the Saaur and the Emerald Queen promise you victory in this life and immortal reward in the next. Our spies return to tell us the unbelievers lie in wait just three days' march to the south. Soon we shall move to crush them, then fall upon the heathen cities and reduce them to cinders. Each victory comes more swiftly than the last, and our numbers grow."

The woman called the Emerald Queen stepped forward to the very edge of the dais and looked down on the faces of those nearest to her, both Saaur and human. Pointing to one man, she said, "You shall be my messenger to the gods this night!"

The man raised his fist in triumph and ran up the first four steps to the dais. He threw himself across the final two, so his head was on the floor before his mistress. She raised her foot and placed it on the man's head for a moment in ritual, then removed it, turning to move back into the tent. The man rose with a grin, winked back at his comrades who cheered him, and followed the Queen into her pavilion.

"Oh, this is very bad," whispered Nakor. He glanced around and saw the celebration was building in intensity. Soon men would be drunk and fighting, as much as was allowed, and given the lax discipline Nakor had seen in this part of the army, he suspected much brawling and even bloodshed were tolerated.

Now he would have to work his way through a company of very drunk, drug-crazed killers, and seek a way across the river to Calis—assuming he could locate Calis's camp.

Nakor was never one to worry, and this certainly wasn't a time to begin. Still, he was anxious that he not delay too long, for now he knew what was behind all the conflict that had been under way for the last twelve years, and what was more, he realized he might be the only man on the world who would fully understand all the different aspects of what he had just seen.

Shaking his head in consternation at the complexities of life, the little man started negotiating his way back away from the edge of the Emerald Queen's pavilion.

A COURIER RODE up and asked, "Are you Captain Calis?"

Calis said, "I am."

"Orders. You're to take your company and ford the river"—he motioned to some place to the north of him, so Erik, who sat nearby, assumed a ford must be close at hand—"and conduct a sweep along the far bank, for ten miles downstream. Gilani tribesmen were seen by one of our scouts. The generals want to keep the opposite bank free of such pests."

He turned and rode away as Praji said, "Pests?" Looking after the retreating courier, he shook his head in disbelief. "Obviously that lad has never encountered any of the Gilani."

"Neither have I," said Calis. "Who are they?"

Praji spoke while he casually picked up his kit and made ready to ride out. "Barbarians." He paused and said, "No, savages, really. Tribespeople. No one knows who they are or where they come from. They speak a tongue only a few can master, and they rarely give anyone from outside a chance to learn it. They're tough, and they fight like maniacs. They wander the Plain of Djams or up in the foothills of the Ratn'gary, hunting the big bison herds or chasing elk and deer."

Picking up his own bedroll, Vaja said, "Most of the trouble folks on this side of the river have with them is over horses. They're the best damn horse thieves in the world. A man's rank is earned by how many enemies he's killed and how many horses he's stolen. They don't ride them; they eat them. So I heard."

"Will they give us much trouble?" said Calis.

"Hell, we probably won't even see one," answered Praji. He tossed his bed-roll to Erik and said, "Hang on to that for me for a minute." He bent to get a bag that contained the rest of his personal belongings. "They're tough little guys, about half again the size of dwarves," and with an evil grin he pointed at Roo: "just like him!"

The men laughed as Praji reclaimed his bedroll from Erik and they started moving toward the picket line of horses. De Loungville and Foster began call-ing orders to the company to ride. Praji said, "They can vanish into that tall grass across the river like they were spirits. They live in these low huts they put together out of woven grass, and you can be standing ten feet from one and never see it. Difficult folks to figure."

"But they can fight," said Vaja.

As they started readying their horses, Praji said, "That, indeed, they can do. There, Captain, now you know as much about the Gilani as just about any man born in these parts."

Calis said, "Well, if they want to avoid trouble, we should be able to make a swing ten miles to the south and back before sundown." As if concerned over something, he looked back at the main body of the camp, then said to De Loungville, "Leave a squad to look after things." Lowering his voice, he said, "And tell them to keep an eye out for Nakor."

Foster motioned to another squad that was moving to saddle their horses and gave them instructions. Erik glanced back as he lifted his saddle to place it on the back of his own mount. Where *was* Nakor? he wondered.

NAKOR GRUNTED AS he picked up the plank, silently cursing the fool at the other end who didn't seem to realize something existed called "coordinated effort." The man, whose name was unknown to Nakor but whom he thought of as "that idiot," insisted on lifting, moving, and dropping without bothering to mention it to Nakor. As a result, over the last two days, Nakor had ac-cumulated an astonishing collection of splinters, scrapes, and bruises.

Nakor had encountered difficulties returning to Calis's company. The mus-ter had finally halted with the core army to the north of this tributary to the river Vedra, while Calis and other other new mercenary companies were to the south. Passing across the smaller river was now accomplished only by riders with official-looking passes, issued by the generals. Nakor had three such passes in his bag, having stolen them two nights before, but he didn't want to try to use one until he could study it, and there hadn't been any place to study the documents without attracting attention. Besides the risk of losing such documents, Nakor had a predisposition not to call attention to himself unless there was a reason to do so.

But the generals had ordered a bridge rebuilt across this tributary and a work gang was diligently doing just that. Nakor figured he would pose as a worker and when the bridge reached the opposite shore, he would simply vanish into the crowd on the other bank.

Unfortunately, the work was going more slowly than he had hoped, since the labor turned out to be slave labor and, as such, the workers were in no hurry. Also, he was now being closely guarded at night. The guards might not have noticed him when he arrived—if there was an extra slave in a squad, the guard would merely assume he had miscounted in the morning—but he would be certain to notice if there was one less.

Which meant Nakor would have to wait for exactly the right moment to vanish into the companies of mercenaries. He knew that once he was free of the guards watching the work gang he would have no trouble staying free, but he wished to create as ideal a moment as possible before he attempted it. A manhunt in the southern camp might prove amusing, but Nakor knew that he must share what he had learned with Calis and the others before too long, so that they could start planning their escape from this army and their eventual return to Krondor.

"That idiot" dropped his end of the plank before Nakor could move, and as a result he took more splinters in his shoulder. He was about to do one of his "tricks" in retaliation, a sting to the buttocks that would make the man think he had sat on a hornet, when a chill passed over him.

He glanced back and felt his chest tighten, for a Pantathian priest stood not ten feet away watching the construction, speaking quietly to a human officer. Nakor set down his end of the plank and hurried back for another, keeping his eyes down. Nakor had encountered the Pantathians and their handiwork before, while traveling with the man who was now Prince of Krondor, but he had never seen a living Pantathian that close. As he passed the creature he noticed a faint odor, and remembered having heard of this smell before: very reptilian, yet alien.

Nakor bent to pick up another plank and saw "that idiot" stumble over a rock. He lost his balance and took a half-step toward the Pantathian. The creature reacted, turning with a clawed hand sweeping out. The talons struck across "that idiot's chest, ripping his tunic as if they were knives. Deep cuts of crimson appeared as the man cried out. Then he went weak in the knees and collapsed, to lie twitching on the ground.

The human officer said to Nakor, "Get him out of here," and Nakor and another slave grabbed the fallen man. By the time they had moved him back to the slaves' compound, the man was dead. Nakor studied the face, frozen in death with eyes open, and watched closely. After a few minutes, he was certain he knew exactly what poison the Pantathian had on his claws. It was no natural venom, but something created by mixing several deadly plant toxins together, and Nakor found this revelation fascinating.

He was also fascinated by the Pantathian's need to demonstrate before the human officer his deadly ability to kill with a touch. There were politics here in the camp of the Emerald Queen that were not obvious to those far from the heart of power, and Nakor wished he had the time to try to uncover more about them. Any struggle in the enemy camp was good to know about, but unfortunately, he couldn't afford to spend the time insinuating himself where he could observe the byplays of power.

A guard said, "Drop him there," pointing to a garbage heap that would be hauled away by wagon at sundown and dumped at a fill a mile or so away from the river. Nakor did as he was bid, and the guard ordered the two slaves to return to work.

Nakor hurried down to the building site, but the Pantathian and the human officer were now gone. He felt a brief regret that he couldn't study the Serpent priest any longer, and even more regret that "that idiot" had been killed. The man had deserved to have his backside stung, but he hadn't deserved to die painfully as a poison shut down his lungs and heart.

Nakor worked until the noon meal. He sat on the bridge, now only a few yards from the other bank, dangling his feet above the water as he ate the tasteless gruel and hard bread to keep his strength up. All the while he ate, he wondered what Calis and the others were doing.

CALIS MOTIONED FOR the outriders on the right flank to keep an even line of sight, one man to the next, for a half mile. Signals from the closest man indicated the order was understood.

They had been riding since noon and still had no sign of anyone near the bank. Either the report of those tribesmen being nearby was in error, or they had left the area, or they were, as Praji had said, able to keep themselves from being seen.

Erik watched for any unexpected movement in the grass, but it was a breezy afternoon, and the tall grass moved like water. It would take eyes far better than his to see someone moving through this sheltering plain.

A short time later, Calis said, "If we don't find something within the next half hour, we should return. We'll be getting back to the ford in the dark as it is now."

A shout from an outrider, and everyone looked to the west. Erik used his hand to shade his eyes against the afternoon sunlight, and saw a rider frantically signaling from the base of a large mound. Calis motioned and the column turned toward the rider.

When they reached the base of the hillock, Erik could see it was covered in the same grass as the plains, making it look like nothing so much as an inverted shaggy bowl. Almost completely round, it was some distance from the next rise, the beginning of a series of hills leading toward the distant mountains.

"What is it?" asked Calis.

"Tracks and a cave, Captain," answered the outrider.

Praji and Vaja exchanged questioning looks, and dismounted. They led their horses close to the cave and inspected it. A short entrance, one a man could enter stooped over, led back into the gloom.

Calis glanced down. "Old tracks." Then he moved to the entrance and ran his hand over the stone edge of the cave. "This isn't natural," said Calis.

"Or if it is," said Praji, also running his hand along the wall, "someone's done some work on it to make it more sturdy. There's stonework under this dirt." He brushed away the dirt and revealed some fitted stones underneath.

"Sarakan," said Vaja.

"Maybe," conceded Praji.

"Sarakan?" asked Calis.

Praji remounted his horse and said, "It's an abandoned dwarven city in the Ratn'gary Mountains. All of it underground. Some humans moved in a few centuries back, some cult of lunatics, and they've died out. Now it just sits empty."

"People are always stumbling across entrances down near the Gulf," said Vaja, "and in the foothills near the Great South Forest."

Calis said, "Correct me if I'm wrong, but that's hundreds of miles from here."

"True," said Praji. "But the damn tunnels run everywhere." He pointed to the hillock. "That one could be connected somewhere over there"—he pointed at the distant mountains—"or it could simply go back a few hundred feet and stop. Depends on who built it, but it looks like one of the entrances to Sarakan."

Roo ventured, "Maybe it's built by the same dwarves, but it's a different city?"

"Maybe," said Praji. "It's been a long time since any dwarves lived anywhere but the mountains, and city folk don't linger on the Plain of Djams."

Calis said, "Could we use this as a depot? Leave some weapons and supplies here if we need to come down this side of the river?"

Praji said, "I wouldn't, Captain. If the Gilani are around here, they may be using this as a base."

Calis was silent for a moment; then he spoke loudly enough for the entire troop, except for the other outriders, to hear. "Mark this location in your minds. Check the distant landscapes. We may be very needful of finding this exact spot, soon. If we need to break from the camp, for any reason, or fight our way out, if you can't make straight for the city of Lanada, make for this mound. Those who do meet here, make your way to the south the best you can. The City of the Serpent River is your final goal, for one of our ships should be waiting there."

Erik looked around and then looked down at his mount. If he put her nose in line with two peaks in the distant mountains, the one that looked like a broken fang, and the other that looked like a clump of grapes, to his imagination, and kept the river at his back while keeping another distant peak off his left side, he thought he should be able to find his way back here.

After the men had taken their bearings, Calis turned to an outrider up on a distant hill who was watching. Calis made the arm signals to indicate they were turning back.

The man acknowledged the order, then turned and signaled an even more distant rider, while Calis gave the order to return to the host of the Emerald Queen.

18

★★

ESCAPE

NAKOR WAVED.

He had learned years ago that if you didn't want to be accosted by minor officials, look as if you know exactly what you're doing. The officer standing on the far end of the dock didn't recognize Nakor, as the Isalani knew he wouldn't. Slaves weren't people. One didn't take note of them.

And now he didn't look like a slave. He had ducked out of the slave pen the night before so that the morning and night head count would match. He had wandered around the camp, smiling and chatting, until he had reached the place where he had secreted his belongings when he had run off to play construction worker.

Then at dawn he had wandered back to the slave pens and fallen in a few yards behind the work gang. He had moved along the newly constructed bridge, past a guard who started to ask him something when Nakor patted him on the shoulder in a friendly fashion and said, "Good morning," leaving the guard scratching his chin.

Now he called to the officer, "Here, catch!" and threw him his bundle of bedroll and shoulder sack. The officer reacted without thought and caught the bundle, then set it down as if it were covered in bugs.

By then Nakor had jumped the five feet separating the end of the bridge and the south-shore foundation of rocks. He landed and stood up, saying, "I didn't want to take the chance of dropping the bundle in the water. There are important documents in it."

"Important . . . ?" asked the officer as Nakor picked up his bundle.

"Thank you. I must be getting those orders to the Captain."

The officer hesitated, which was his undoing, for in that moment, while he tried to frame his next question, Nakor slipped behind a party of horsemen riding past, and when they had moved on, the little man was nowhere in sight.

The officer stood peering this way and that, and failed to notice that a few feet away there were now seven sleeping mercenaries around a cold campfire where moments before there had been only six. Nakor lay motionless, listening for any sign of alarm.

He grinned as he lay there, his usual reaction to pulling off a good vanishing act. He found it amazing that most people never noticed what was going on right before their noses. He took a deep breath, closed his eyes, and started to doze.

Less than an hour later, he heard a voice and opened his eyes. One of the soldiers next to him was sitting up and yawning. Nakor turned over and saw that the officer he had flummoxed was standing with his back toward the camp.

Nakor rolled to his feet, said, "Good morning," to the still-half-asleep mercenary, and moved off down the trail toward where he hoped Calis was camped.

ERIK LOOKED UP from where he sat, a few feet away from Calis, de Loungville, and Foster, polishing his sword. They had returned to camp after nightfall, and Calis had gone to report to the officers' tent near the bridge while Erik and the others tended the horses. When he returned he showed no sign of how the meeting went, but Calis rarely showed anything that Erik could read as pleasure or irritation.

But now Erik saw a small betrayal of emotion as Calis rose with an expectant expression: Nakor was making his way across the narrow trail that had been worn by hooves and feet between the Eagles' camp and the one to the east.

The little man came trudging into view, with his seemingly ever-present grin in place. "Woof," he said, sitting down heavily on the ground next to Foster. "That was some doing, finding you. Lots of bird banners, and lots of red things, and most of these men"—he pointed in general at most of the other companies nearby—"don't care who's next to them. This is one very ignorant bunch."

Praji, who was lying back picking his teeth with a long sliver of wood, said, "They're not being paid to think."

"True."

"What did you discover?" asked Calis.

Nakor leaned forward and lowered his voice, so that Erik had to strain to overhear, though he and the others in his squad were trying hard to look as if they weren't. "I don't think it's such a good idea to talk about this here, but let's say that when I can tell you, you don't want to know what I saw."

"Yes I do," said Calis.

Nakor nodded. "I understand, but you'll understand what I mean when I tell you. Just let me say that if you have a plan for us to get out of here, tonight would be a very good time to do it. We don't need to stay any longer."

Calis said, "Well, now that we know where the ford is, we could try to slip across, or bluff our way and tell the patrol at the bank that we're going out on another sweep to the south."

Nakor opened his ever-present bag, slung over his shoulder, and said, "Maybe one of these passes would fool them."

Erik tried hard not to laugh at the expression on Foster's and de Loungville's faces. They looked at the documents, and de Loungville said, "I'm not an expert in reading this gibberish, but these look authentic."

"Oh, they are," said Nakor. "I stole them from Lord Fadawah's tent."

De Loungville said, "The Queen's Lord High General?"

"That's the man. He was busy and no one noticed, as I was playing the part of a slave. I thought one of these might do us some good. I wanted to poke around. There's something very funny about that general. He's not what he seems to be, and if I hadn't been in such a hurry to get my news to you, I would have stayed around to see just what this general really is."

Calis looked through the four documents. "This might do it. It's a vaguely worded order commanding all units to let the bearer pass. It doesn't say if the bearer will have a full company of more than a hundred men with him, but I think if we can keep our wits about us, it might work."

Praji stood. "Well, the day's half done, and if we're going to be convincing about a local patrol, we'd better be on our way now. Or did you want to wait until tomorrow morning?"

Calis glanced at Nakor, who shook his head slightly in the negative. "We leave now," said Calis.

Order was passed from man to man to act as if there was little urgency, but to get ready quickly to ride. If anyone in the other campsites took notice, Erik couldn't see. The surrounding companies seemed intent upon their own business. The coming and going of another troop of men seemed of little interest.

In less than an hour, Foster had the men in file, and Calis motioned for Erik's squad, the first in line, to fall in behind his own vanguard, Nakor, Praji, Vaja, Hatonis, and de Loungville. Foster would fall back and take command of the rear guard, the most experienced squad in the company. As Jadow Shati and Jerome Handy moved out of line, back to where Foster waited, Erik made a good-luck sign which Jadow returned, along with his broadest grin.

They rode northward, along the path to the road, where they paralleled the river until they came in sight of the bridge. "That's finishing up quickly," observed Praji.

"They have many men working on it," said Nakor. "I worked on it for a couple of days so I could get across."

Vaja said, "There're are ample fords nearby. Why all the bother?"

Nakor said, "The Queen doesn't want to get her feet wet."

Calis glanced at the little man, as did Erik. Nakor wasn't smiling.

They reached the guardpost and a stout sergeant came forward. "What's all this, then?"

Calis said, "Hello again, Sergeant."

Recognizing Calis from the night before, the sergeant said, "Going out again?"

"The generals weren't happy with my report. They think I didn't head far enough south. I'm going out until noon tomorrow, then I'll be back by morning the day after."

"No one said anything to me about your company crossing the river, Captain," said the sergeant, looking suspicious, "or anyone being out for more than a day."

Calis calmly held out the pass. "The General made up his mind just a short time ago. He gave me this rather than relying on a messenger getting to you before we were ready to leave."

The sergeant said, "Damn officers! We've got our orders, and then some captain of some company thinks he can get his drinking buddy to change the way we do things. Which of those strutting peacocks thinks he can just sign his name . . ." His voice trailed off and his eyes widened as he saw the name and seal at the bottom of the pass.

"If you want to send a messenger to General Fadawah to tell him that he's not observing procedures, and you want confirmation, we'll wait," said de Loungville. "I'd just as soon not have to go looking for the Gilani. Hell, I don't think the general will mind, Sergeant."

The sergeant quickly rolled up the pass and handed it back to Calis. "You may cross," he said, waving them past. He turned to the soldiers at the bank and shouted, "They're crossing to the other side!"

They waved back and resumed their bored poses while Calis walked his horse down to where they stood and into the water, taking it slowly and carefully.

Erik felt the back of his neck itch, as if someone behind would start shouting they were trying to escape, or someone else would be warning the sergeant that a pass had been stolen from the General's tent.

But they moved across the shallow ford in the river until the last company, with Corporal Foster the last man, had safely crossed. Then Calis motioned for them to pick up speed, and they all started moving south at a trot. Erik found himself fighting an unusually strong urge to dig his heels in and get his horse galloping. He wondered how many of the others felt the same way.

When they had moved some distance downriver, Calis ordered them to a canter and they rode at a good rate for another mile before he signaled for them to return to a trot. Nakor shouted, "You want me to tell you now?"

Calis said, "Yes, before you fall off and break your neck."

Nakor grinned. "It's bad. You remember our old friend the Lady Clovis?"

Calis nodded. Erik had no idea who she might be, but the darkening expression on Calis's face said he knew her. What surprised him was that de Loungville registered no recognition. But Praji said, "That bitch who was using Dahakon and the Overlord Valgash down at the City of the Serpent River way back when we first met?"

"That's her," said Nakor.

"She's the Emerald Queen?" asked Calis.

Nakor shook his head. "I wish it were so. Jorna, that's her real name, at least back when we were married—"

"What?" gaped Calis, and for the first time Erik saw him totally lose his composure.

"It's a long story. I'll tell you some other time. But when she was a girl she was vain, and when we were together she was always seeking ways to stay young forever."

"I think if we get out of this you're going to tell me every detail," said de Loungville, obviously as astonished as Calis.

"Anyway," said Nakor, motioning for him not to interrupt, "the girl had talent for tricks, what you call magic, and she left me when I wouldn't tell her secrets I didn't have, about staying young forever. She was using a different body when she was the Lady Clovis."

"A different body?" said Praji, now obviously confused. "How did you recognize her."

"When you know someone well, bodies don't matter," said Nakor.

"I guess," said Vaja, obviously amused by the entire conversation.

"Shut up," said Nakor. "This is serious. This woman made a bargain with the Pantathians to keep her young forever while she helped them. What she didn't know was they were using her. I warned her. I told her, 'They want more than you can ever give them,' and I was right. They've taken her."

"What do you mean?" asked Calis.

Nakor's expression turned grim. "What happened to your father, with the Armor of White and Gold."

"Yes?" said Calis, color draining from his face.

"It's happening again. Jorna, or Clovis, is wearing an emerald crown and it's changing her. She is becoming like your father."

Calis looked shaken and said nothing for a moment; then he turned to de

Loungville. "Tell Foster I want a rear guard to follow by fifteen minutes. I want to know if anyone tries to overtake us. If they encounter anyone, their fastest rider is to come find us, while the others are to lead whoever's coming away. We'll wait for a short time at the cave we found two days ago, then we'll strike straight for Lanada."

De Loungville said, "And if those who come after don't take the bait?"

"Make them take the bait," said Calis.

De Loungville nodded once, turned his horse, and rode to the end of the column. Erik looked back and saw Foster and six other men slow and then stop after de Loungville gave the order. They would wait a quarter hour, then start riding after Calis's company, hoping they would get the chance to catch up in a day or two.

IT WAS MIDMORNING the next day when someone at the rear of the column shouted, "Rider!"

Erik looked over his shoulder and saw Jadow Shati riding the life out of his horse. The animal was completely lathered, and from the huge extension of her nostrils, Erik could tell she couldn't catch her breath. She was blown out and ruined, he was certain. Jadow was familiar enough with horses to realize he was killing the mare, so Erik knew it could only mean trouble. He untied the cord that held his sword in its scabbard, as he did not need to be told that they were about to fight.

For in the distance, less than a mile behind Jadow, came a dust cloud. Erik saw the figures on the horizon, and before Jadow could get close enough to speak, Erik shouted, "It's the Saaur!"

De Loungville asked, "How can you tell?"

"The horses look too big for the distance behind Jadow."

Just then Jadow came within shouting range and cried out, "Captain! It's the lizard men! They are following."

Calis turned to de Loungville and said, "We stay in the saddle. Skirmish in two lines!"

De Loungville shouted, "You heard the Captain! I want the first fifty men dressed left on me!" That meant that the first fifty men in the column would line up on de Loungville's left arm, in a straight line. Erik was the man closest to de Loungville when he moved his horse around.

Jadow came reining in, his mount staggering as he leaped off. Calis shouted, "Where's Foster?"

Jadow shook his head. "They bought none of it. As soon as I took off, they followed me and ignored the corporal. The corporal turned around and hit them from the flank, buying me a head start, Captain, but . . ." He didn't have to say any more.

Erik thought of the big man, Jerome Handy, who had become something of a friend after being embarrassed by Sho Pi aboard the ship. He glanced to his right and saw Sho Pi, and nodded. Sho Pi nodded back, as if he understood what Erik was thinking.

Luis said, "Then we bleed lizards," under his breath, but loud enough for those near him to hear.

Erik drew his sword and put his reins between his teeth. He unlimbered his shield and made ready. He'd control his mount with his legs, but he kept the reins in his jaws in case he needed to yank them.

The Saaur's animals must be as incredibly strong as their riders, thought Erik, for if Jadow's mount was near death, the Saaur's looked merely tired. Yet the green-skinned warriors didn't pause once they saw the line of soldiers facing them.

"We don't scare them much," observed Nakor from behind Erik, who wouldn't take his eyes off the approaching riders.

Calis said, "When I give the order, I want bowfire; then the first rank will charge. The second rank will hold until I give the order."

The bowmen, all in the center of the second line, drew back their weapons, and de Loungville half muttered, "Wait for it!"

The Saaur bore down relentlessly, and as they approached, Erik started noticing details. Some wore feathers on their helms, while others had strange animals and birds on their shields. The horses were bay and chestnut, with some that were almost black, but while a few were near-white, he saw no buckskins or mottled colors. Erik wondered why he was fascinated by the fact of their being no pintos or buckskins. He fought down an unexpected urge to laugh.

Then Calis shouted, "Shoot!" and the forty archers in the second line let loose. The rain of shafts caused a half-dozen riders to fall, and several of the alien horses screamed. Then Calis shouted, "Charge!"

Erik dug his heels into his horse's flanks and with a shout and a powerful squeeze of his legs told the horse to gallop. He didn't look to see how the others were doing, but kept his focus on a Saaur with a metal crest topped with a horsehair fall atop his helm. The horsehair had been bleached and dyed a bright crimson, so it was an easy target for Erik.

Erik sensed more than saw when his own horse crashed into the larger animal. He was too intent on avoiding the blow aimed at his neck. The Saaur warrior used a large single-bladed ax, which meant he could bludgeon with it on the backswing, but cut only with a forward blow. Erik almost fell into the gap between the two animals after his own mount staggered away from the larger horse. Erik ducked under the looping blow, but recovered in time to deliver a punishing blow with his sword to the thigh of the Saaur.

He didn't see if the creature fell from the saddle or rode past, because he was too busy engaging another warrior who had just unhorsed one of Hatonis's clansmen. Erik charged him and got his sword point under the creature's shield before it could turn and face him, and the Saaur fell backwards, flipping completely over the rear of his horse.

Erik swore and reined his own horse away as the riderless alien horse lashed out with a foreleg. " 'Ware the mounts!" he cried. "They're trained to attack, too."

Erik moved to help Roo, who was attempting to work in tandem with Luis against one Saaur. He came up on the lizard man's blind side and delivered a killing blow to the back of the creature's helm. The Saaur fell over and the helm fell off, revealing an alien face, green and scaled, but covered in scarlet blood.

"Well, their blood's not green," shouted Biggo, riding by. "They're also dying right enough."

"So are we," said Roo, pointing. Biggo and Erik turned to see that while most of the Saaur had been unhorsed, for each one killed, one of their own was down as well.

Pushing back his helm, Biggo said, "We face them three to one, and still they take us out in equal numbers."

"Shoot," cried Calis, and the ten archers who remained to him started peppering the five remaining Saaur with arrows.

Jadow said, "Look!" and pointed into the distance.

"That's why they're so fearless," shouted de Loungville. "These are just the trail-breakers!"

Afar, a large column of dust rose into the sky, and even at this distance the rumble of hooves was thunderous. Erik didn't wait but set heels to the flanks of his horse and charged after the remaining Saaur, who were attempting to keep the humans engaged as long as possible until their companions could overtake them.

Biggo let out a whoop and charged after him. They rode full into the same Saaur, striking at him from both sides. Erik caught him on the sword arm, shattering bone and cutting deep into flesh, while Biggo hammered relentlessly at the creature's shield.

Soon it was quiet.

Calis said, "Ride for the cave! We'll stand there!"

Erik sucked a deep lungful of air and willed his tired horse to run. There was no choice. The alien horses were stronger and more powerful and had more endurance. They couldn't outrun them, it was clear, and at one to one, they couldn't outfight the Saaur in the open.

Erik hoped that the cave tunnel did lead somewhere, as Praji had claimed. For if it was only a cave in a hill, it would be a lonely place to die.

In ragged order, leaving the remounts to follow or wander, Calis's Crimson

Eagles, exhausted and sore from the short but furious fight, headed toward the distant hillock.

Nakor was among the first to reach it, and without much grace he half jumped, half fell from his horse. He grabbed a waterskin and a bag of rations, then struck her on the rump, yelling enough to send her running away as he ducked into the cave.

As Erik and the others began to dismount, he shouted, "There's a door! Come quick!"

"Strike a light!" commanded Calis, and de Loungville produced a special oil and motioned for someone to give him a torch. A bundle of them was fetched from the baggage along with a few other items the men would carry, but most of the baggage, food, and all the horses must be sacrificed.

De Loungville sprinkled the oil on a torch, then struck flint and steel to cause a spark. The oil caught and the torch was lit, and he ducked inside the cave.

Erik followed after, and had to duck-walk to pass below the low ceiling. After about ten yards, the ceiling rose and the corridor broadened, as the passage moved down into an underground cavern.

Erik looked for the door and discovered it was a huge round stone. It was nestled in a heavy iron and wooden frame, rigged so it could be rolled from its position to the right of the passage to block it. While a few strong men could use large wooden pegs set in the face to move it from inside this cave, those following after would have no handhold on the smooth surface, nor any way to gain enough leverage to move the massive rock.

When the last man was inside the cave, Erik, Biggo, and Jadow grabbed the wooden pegs and struggled to move the rock. Others insinuated themselves against the wall so they could push against the edge once it moved enough.

Slowly, protestingly, the rock budged and then with a grinding rumble moved as the sound of horsemen echoed through the entrance of the cave. Angry shouts in an alien language echoed down the hall as the grinding stone moved slowly to block their retreat.

Suddenly Erik felt resistance and knew that the Saaur on the other side had tried to prevent the closing. "Push!" he shouted, and another pair of hands moved below his, and he looked down to see Roo trying to add his strength to the task. The little man had slipped below and crawled on the floor to find a place from which he could help.

Nakor shouted, "Close your eyes!"

Erik was slow and was temporarily blinded by a sudden flash of light as Nakor lit something from de Loungville's torch and tossed it through the narrow space between the wall and the slowly moving rock door.

A scream and several shouts of rage answered, but the pressure on the door was released and it closed suddenly with a deep and final thud. Erik felt the shock in his shoulders as it slammed into the opposite wall.

His knees felt suddenly weak and he sat down on the cold cave floor. He heard Biggo laugh. "That was closer than I like."

Erik found himself laughing, too, and looked over at Jadow. "Foster and Jerome?"

Jadow shook his head. "They all died like men."

Calis said, "Bobby, light another torch so we can see where we're going."

"Do we have another torch?" asked the sergeant.

A voice in the dark said, "In the bundle here, Sergeant."

Calis said, "Biggo, while we're looking ahead, I want you and von Darkmoor to do an inventory. We've left most of what we had outside, but I want to see what we have here." He glanced around. "Though if there's not another way out, it really doesn't matter, does it?"

Without waiting for an answer, he moved off into the gloom as de Loung-ville lit a second torch, handed it to Luis, and moved after the Captain.

Nakor hurried to grab a few loose rocks and lay them between the stone and the floor. "Won't roll back very well if they do get a grip," he said with a grin.

Biggo turned and said, "All right, me darlings. You heard the Captain. Look around and tell ol' Biggo what you thieving rascals grabbed when you ran for your lives!"

Erik chuckled, but knew it was just relief at still being alive. He didn't know who else had noticed, but when he ran into the dark he had looked back over his shoulder and seen at least thirty of the hundred or more men who had left that morning lying dead on the ground. They had survived the first encounter of a long and bitter journey to come, and almost a third of them were already dead.

He put that thought from his mind and began looking to see what resources they had.

HOURS PASSED, AND there were faint sounds from the other side of the rock door, so they knew the Saaur were contriving ways to move the boulder and come after them. At one point Roo wondered aloud what they would do if some Saaur magician came along and used magic to open the door, and the anger that greeted the remark caused the wiry man to fall instantly silent. Erik couldn't remember a time when Roo had been shut up so quickly or effectively.

When Calis finally returned, Biggo said, "We've got food for four or five days, Captain. A few extra weapons, but mostly what each of us is carrying. We've got plenty of gold and gems, 'cause the sergeant there grabbed the pay sacks, and we've got a fair supply of bandages and herbs.

"But all our camp gear is gone, and a lot of us are going to be thirsty if we don't find water quickly."

Calis said, "The tunnel seems to head down gradually, and toward the foot-hills. I saw signs that someone's used this route not too long ago, maybe a month, but no more than that."

"Tribesmen?" asked Roo.

"Doesn't matter," said Praji, standing up. "Unless you're anxious to face that angry pack of lizards waiting out there"—he pointed to the door—"we go that way." He pointed into the gloom.

Calis said, "Everyone ready?"

No one said no, and Calis turned to de Loungville. "Get them into some sort of order, and let's start seeing where this passage leads."

De Loungville nodded once, then turned and gave the command. Once the men found their way to the positions they normally took while riding, a sense of the familiar surrounded Erik, as if following orders made the closeness of the tunnel and the gloom bearable.

Then Calis gave the word and they moved off into the darkness.

19

★★

DISCOVERY

A GONG SOUNDED.

It echoed off vast ceilings of carved and colored stone, ringing through the great hall, and the Warden turned. Miranda saw him regarding her with impassive features. But he made no threatening gesture as she approached.

She had been flying across the mountains since leaving the vast city known as the Necropolis, the City of the Dead Gods. Following the instructions given her by the fortune-teller in the Inn, she had returned to Midkemia and found her way back to Novindus, and from there to the Necropolis. Then she flew upward, guided by her arts, despite her fatigue, and she sought out this mythical place atop the mountains called the Pavilion of the Gods.

At last, when she had to use her powers to preserve air around her, she found what she sought, a splendid place atop a cloud, a vast series of halls and galleries that seemed created out of ice and crystal as well as stone and marble.

The clouds thinned, and she saw that the massive building stood atop the summit of the greatest mountain in the area, and in the center stood a single immense opening.

She floated through the clouds surrounding the Celestial City, moving through the door effortlessly. She felt a tingle as she passed through the spell that kept the freezing cold out and the air inside.

The man she had spied across the grand hall floated across the vast expanse of floor to meet her. She took a moment to study her surroundings. A vaulted ceiling was suspended nearly seventy flights of steps above his head, supported by twelve mighty columns of stone, each chosen for beauty. She quickly chose her own favorite, one fashioned of malachite, the green veins of polished stone that could capture the eyes for hours. The rose quartz was lovely, too, but something about the green stone spoke to her.

The floor of the hall was partitioned by some faint energy. Miranda used every trick of perception she had, and decided the fields were not barriers or traps but something closer to signatures, as if each area had a specific use or identity, but only noted for those able to sense those energy barriers. And in each area beings moved, humans from their outward appearance, but all wearing some of the strangest fashions she had ever seen.

The great windows were set with crystal panes so clear they seemed air frozen in an instant, and the snow fields outside reflected the afternoon sunlight on the peaks above, bathing the great hall in rose and golden hues. Those people moving across the vast floor threw long shadows, as jeweled, faceted globes threw soft white light across the hall, the source of that light having nothing to do with nature.

The approaching man glided through the air, standing regally as if being carried by a company of invisible bearers upon a heavy platform. He touched foot to the stone floor of the hall as Miranda gently touched down on the marble floor.

Several others nearby turned to observe the confrontation, though they remained silent. Miranda threw back her cloak's hood, shaking her dark hair as she glanced around the hall.

"Who comes to the Celestial City?"

With amusement she answered, "A fine lot of gods you are if you don't know who comes to your own palace to visit. I am called Miranda."

The Warden said, "None may invade the precinct of the gods without invitation."

Miranda grinned. "Odd. I'm here, aren't I?"

"None may invade without permission and live to leave," said the Warden.

"Well, consider me an uninvited guest, not an invader."

"What cause brings you to the Hall of the Gods?"

Miranda inspected the figure before her. Like the others who inhabited the hall, he wore an odd robe, tight-fitting across the shoulders, but billowing out below the arms, forming a perfect circle at the hem almost six feet in diameter. Miranda guessed there was a thin band of metal or heavy cord sewn into the hem. The sleeves were long, and also flared along the length, while the collar was stiff and high, surrounding the back of the head up to the ears, giving Miranda the impression that she spoke to a six-foot-tall doll fashioned from interlocking cones of paper, with a painted clay head stuck on the top. What a peculiar-looking character, she thought.

His face had olive-shaded skin darkened by years of exposure to bright sun, and his beard was as white as the snow outside. Eyes of pale blue regarded her from under white brows.

She glanced around the hall, wishing she had more time to study the place. Its grandeur was nothing less than breathtaking, yet somehow it was alien and as cold as the wind outside the great door. No mortal lacking great magic would find his way to this abode of the gods, for the clime was impossible. At least a hundred feet below the base of the plateau the air became too thin to breathe long and remain alive, and the temperature was constantly below freezing.

Most of the people were turned her way, and she noticed that each group seemed set off, isolated by the sense of separate areas she had detected upon entering, as if there was a zone on the floor they were confined to. After a moment, she was certain no one was leaving a given area to enter another.

"You limit the gods?" asked Miranda.

"They limit themselves, as they always have," came the answer. "Again I must ask, what cause brings you here?"

"I come because there are terrible forces gathering, and this world stands in jeopardy. I have visited with the Oracle of Aal, and she is ready to enter her breeding phase. Her vision will be lost to us. Those forces that march are committed to a course of action that will bring about the end of all we know, including this." She waved her hand, indicating the hall.

The Warden closed his eyes a moment, and Miranda knew something was being communicated; then he said, "Speak more."

"Of what?"

"Of what you hope to find here."

"I had hoped for some sense that the gods of Midkemia were ready to answer the threat to their very existence!" Her anger was poorly hidden, and contempt edged her words.

"These are but the aspects of the gods," answered the Warden, "those men and women who have, for reasons beyond our mortal understanding, been chosen to exist on the gods' behalf. They have come to live out their lives as mortal aspects of the gods, eyes and ears granting the gods mortal perspective on the world in which they abide."

Miranda nodded. "Then I would speak to one of these godly aspects, if you don't mind."

"I have nothing to say in the matter," came the answer. "I am but the Warden of the Celestial City. It is my task to keep those who abide here comfortable." He closed his eyes. "You may speak to whoever will answer."

Walking past the Warden, Miranda approached the area nearest the entrance, where a group of men and women stood surrounding one who loomed over them by a full head. All wore white, without a hint of color, and the woman at the center of the group had hair without hue. Her skin was also without pigmentation, but rather than possessing the look of an albino, she appeared to be of some alien race, with skin truly white in color. Those who surrounded her stepped aside, allowing Miranda to approach. At a respectful distance, Miranda bowed her head, then she said, "Sung, I plead for help."

The living incarnation of the goddess stared down at the young woman. Her eyes held mysteries Miranda could only begin to guess, but her face presented a kindly visage. Yet no answer was forthcoming. Miranda pressed on. "A great evil arises here, one that, unchecked, will release forces to rival even your own. I must seek aid!"

For a long moment the goddess studied Miranda; then with an economy of motion she indicated the woman should move to another area. "Seek one not yet come among us."

Miranda hurried to another quarter of the hall, in which an empty area stood ready, but unoccupied. Shifting her perceptions through each phase of sight she knew, Miranda searched for some hint of what she might find here.

A glyph shimmered in a spectrum of light beyond the ability of most men to see, yet Miranda saw it. She turned to discover the Warden had followed her, floating a foot above the stone floor.

"Who placed such a mark here?"

"One who recently visited, like you."

"What does the symbol mean?"

"It is the mark of Wodan-Hospur, one of the Lost Gods, whom we await."

"You await the return of gods lost during the Chaos Wars?" she asked in surprise.

"Everything is possible in the Hall of the Gods."

"What was the name of this man?"

"I may not say."

"I am seeking Pug of Stardock," said Miranda. "At the Inn, in the Hall of Worlds, I was told to come here."

The Warden shrugged. "Such matters are not my concern."

"Has he been here?"

"I may not say."

Miranda thought, then asked, "If you can say nothing else, where might I go next to find this man?"

The Warden hesitated. "It may be that you need to look at that place where you were misled."

Miranda said, "I thought as much." With a wave of her arm, she was gone, a faint popping sound the only indication of her having been there.

One of the people attending a nearby god turned and threw back his hood. He was short of stature, his eyes the color of dark walnut aged and stained, his beard as dark as that of a lad of twenty, but his manner and size did little to disguise the aura of power that surrounded him.

Stepping over to where the Warden waited, he said, "You've served your purpose." With a wave of his hand the figures in the hall vanished, leaving only a vast emptiness of rock and ice. Cold air rang in through the now unprotected opening and bit with enough harshness to make him gather his cloak tightly around him.

Glancing around to see that no trace of illusion remained, he was raising his hands to will himself to another place when a voice said, "Gods, it's cold without that illusion."

The man turned, and standing a yard away was the woman. "Pug of Stardock?"

The man nodded. "Neatly done, lady. There are few who could have seen through the ruse."

She smiled and something oddly familiar hinted at recognition, then was gone. "I didn't. But things just didn't feel right, and I thought if I could seem to have left, then perhaps I might learn something."

The man smiled. "You simply turned yourself invisible and made the proper noise."

The woman nodded. "You are Pug?"

The man said, "Yes, I am Pug of Stardock."

The woman's face took on an expression of concern, and again there was something hauntingly familiar about her. "Good. We must go. There is much to be done."

"What are you talking about?" asked Pug.

"Khaipur has fallen and Lanada is undone by treachery."

Pug nodded. "I know this. But for me to act too soon—"

"And the Pantathians counter your magic with their own. I know. But there is more here than a simple bashing of magics, like rams banging heads in the mountains." Her breath hung in the frigid air and she waited.

Pug said, "Before I presume to tell you there are forces at play beyond your knowledge, I suppose I should find out what you know."

He vanished.

"Damn," said Miranda. "I hate it when men do that."

PUG HAD TWO goblets of wine poured when Miranda popped into existence. "Why did you do that?"

"If you couldn't follow me, then telling you anything was pointless." Pug handed her a goblet. "There's something vaguely familiar about you," he observed.

Miranda took the wine and sat down on a divan opposite a writing desk; Pug pulled out the stool that went with the desk, and sat down.

"Where are we? Stardock?" She glanced around. The room was small and lacking any decoration. All she could see indicated that this was a library. Books lined every wall, save one narrow space that held a window, and besides the divan, desk, and chair, the room was devoid of furniture. A pair of lamps burned, one at each end of the room.

Pug nodded. "My quarters. No one can get in or out but myself, and no one expects me to visit, as no one has seen me here in twenty-five years."

Miranda looked around. "Why keep it so?"

"I made a major display of breaking off my ties here, after my wife died." He spoke of her death in a matter-of-fact tone, but Miranda could see a tiny tension around the corners of his eyes as he mentioned this. "If someone is to come looking for me, they'll look on Sorcerer's Isle. I've left enough people who work magic there that any spell designed to detect magic will be ringing like a dinner bell."

"And as magic is being practiced here every day, if you do decide to do some work, no one will notice." She sipped her wine and said, "Very neat. And this is very good."

"Is it?" asked Pug. He sipped. "Yes, it is. I wonder which . . ." He held up the bottle. "I have to ask Gathis if there is more of this in the cellar at Sorcerer's Isle when I return."

"Why all the misdirection?" asked Miranda.

"Why were you looking for me?"

"I asked you first."

Pug nodded. "Fair enough. The Pantathians are wary of me and my arts. They've discovered ways to neutralize me, so I make sure they and their agents can't find me."

"Neutralize you?" Her eyes narrowed. "I've run across snake magic before and there are smoking corpses to mark those battles. If you're as powerful as they say—"

Pug said, "There are more ways to stem attack than simply to meet it with more strength. What if I were to hold a child you love and put a dagger to her throat?"

Miranda said, "So if they don't know where you are, they can't threaten anyone you care about."

"Yes. Now, why are you looking for me?"

Miranda said, "The Oracle of Aal enters her birthing cycle and we lose her ability to help us. I have been asked—"

"By whom?" interrupted Pug.

"By some people who would rather not see this world end any time soon," she snapped. "I have been asked to help preserve the Lifestone—"

Pug stood. "How do you know of the Lifestone?"

Miranda said, "I am Keshian. Do you remember one who came to support the King's army at the battle?"

"Lord Abdur Rachmad Memo Hazara-Khan," answered Pug.

Miranda nodded. "It took years to penetrate the illusions and false trails, but after a while, those few who entered to speak to the Oracle and leave with whatever wisdom she gave them, even with that statue at Malac's Cross as the transfer point, even after decades, the truth was known."

"So you work for the Emperor?"

"Do you work for the King?" countered Miranda.

"Borric and I are something of cousins," said Pug, sipping at his wine again. "You beg the question."

"So I do." He set his goblet down. "Let's say that I'm somewhat less constricted in my loyalties than I used to be. Which is all beside the point. If you know anything of the Lifestone, you know that national interests are petty at this point. If the Valheru reawaken, we will all perish."

"Then you must help me," said Miranda. "If those foolish men I helped recruit for the Prince survive, we'll know who and what we face."

Pug sighed. "You, a Keshian, recruiting for the Prince?"

"It seemed the prudent thing to do to serve my real master's interests."

Pug only raised an eyebrow. "So which foolish men are these?"

"Calis leads them."

"Tomas's son," said Pug. "I haven't seen him since he was young; it must be twenty or more years."

"He's still young. And angry and confused."

"He's unique. There is no other creature like him in the universe. He's the product of a union that should not have borne fruit, and he will die someday, unique."

"And alone."

Pug nodded. "Who else?"

"A band of men condemned to die, none known to you. And Nakor the Isalani."

Pug smiled. "I miss his rambling brilliance. And his sense of fun."

Miranda said, "Fun is far from his mind these days, I fear. With Arutha's death, Nicholas becomes the hope for the Western Realm, the Kingdom, and the world. He has grudgingly adopted his father's plan, but he has little enthusiasm for it."

"What plan is this?"

She told him of the previous voyages to Novindus, and of the destruction endured by Calis and his men the last time. She told him of the plan to send men down to join with the conquering army, men who would return with the truth about what was facing them.

"Do you think," asked Pug after she finished, "that this is anything but a full-scale consolidation of all the armed might in Novindus, so that an attack can be launched across the sea to seize the Lifestone?"

"The Pantathians lack subtlety," answered Miranda, "but it could be someone is manipulating them the way they manipulated the moredhel during the Great Uprising."

Pug conceded that this was true. "But every indication is that they are seeking to put all Novindus under their sway, to create the largest army ever seen in this world, and from that it is just one logical step to assume they are going to throw that army at the Kingdom, perhaps sail right into Krondor harbor, then march across half the Kingdom to Sethanon." Pug was silent for a moment, then said, "I don't think anyone is using them in the sense you suggest. The Pantathians are too alien by other beings' standards, judging by everything I've seen.

"They have a view of the universe that is so warped it defies logic, but it is so ingrained in their very nature that they have not allowed more than two thousand years of observing the way in which the universe really works to sway them from their fanatic devotion to their unique view of things."

Miranda raised an eyebrow. "That's a little too analytical for me, Pug. I have encountered other fanatics, and reality doesn't seem to sway them much either." She waved off a comment he was about to make. "But I see your point. If they move for their own dark purposes in such numbers, then it's clear they risk all or nothing on this massive undertaking."

Pug shook his head no and sighed. "Not really. The damnable thing about all this is we can defeat them again, perhaps destroying every man and creature they send across the sea, but what does this gain us save wholesale ruin on our own shore?"

"We still don't know where they live," Miranda said.

Pug nodded yes. "We have only vague rumors. Up north, near the headwaters of the Serpent River, the Serpent Lake, down in the Great South Forest, somewhere deep in the heart of the Forest of Irabek. No one knows."

"You've looked?"

Pug nodded. "I've used every magic spell I could find or dream up and have traveled on foot across a great deal of that continent. The sad truth is they are either incredibly gifted in shielding themselves from sight, both magic and mundane, or they are doing something so obvious I'm not seeing it."

Miranda sipped her wine. After a moment she said, "That still leaves us with an army to defeat."

"More, I'm afraid."

"What?"

Pug said, "I believe that Calis is going to find something far more powerful at the heart of this particular campaign, and I can't tell you why." He went over to a bookshelf. "There are several tomes here that speak of doorways, pathways, and routes between different levels of reality."

"Like the Hall of Worlds?"

Pug shook his head no. "That place exists in the objective universe as we understand it, though it is somewhat of an artifact of creation, allowing those who travel the halls to exist beyond certain limits of that objective reality. Do you remember how real the Hall of the Gods looked?"

"Yes. A most convincing illusion."

"It was more than an illusion. I tapped into a higher level of reality, a higher-energy state for lack of a better description. A long time ago, I went into the city of the dead gods, and entered through a . . . seam, into the Hall of the Goddess of Death. I spoke to Lims-Kragma."

"Interesting," said Miranda.

Pug looked at her and saw she was not mocking him.

"It was really the Goddess of Death you spoke to?"

"That's the point I'm trying to make. There is no Goddess of Death, yet there is. There's the natural force of creation and the equally natural act of destruction. What breaks down a once-living being provides food for new life. We understand so little of these things," he said, showing a hint of frustration. "But these personifications, these gods and goddesses, they may be but a way in which we, who live in one state of reality, can interact with forces, beings, energy from another reality."

"Interesting theory," said Miranda.

"Actually, most of it is Nakor's."

"But what has this to do with all the murder about to be done?"

"Beings from these other states exist. I have faced the Dread, to name but one."

"Really?" she said, obviously impressed. "The stealers of life are not to be trifled with by all reports."

"That's the first clue I had." Pug's face grew animated as he said, "When I fought the Dread for the first time, I sensed a different rhythm, a different state to the energy of his being. When I bested him, I learned a few things.

"Over the years I've discovered other things. Living on Kelewan, the Tsurani homeworld, for a number of years gave me insights I never would have gained here on Midkemia.

"One thing I've discovered is that the Dread do not 'drink' the life of living beings on this world. They change the energies to a state they can use. The unfortunate side effect of that change is the death of the creature they touch."

"Such academic considerations are of little interest to those who die, I'm afraid."

"True, but you see, it's important. If they can do that, why can't forces we can't see in our normal frame of reference not be able to reach out and manipulate energy here in our world?"

"Where are we going with this?" asked Miranda, betraying impatience.

"What was the Lifestone like when you last visited the Oracle?" asked Pug.

"What do you mean?"

"Did it appear as it always did?"

"I don't know." Miranda looked puzzled. "It's the only time I've ever seen it."

"But there was something odd about it, wasn't there?"

Miranda shrugged. "I had a feeling . . ."

"That the Valheru trapped inside were somehow doing something."

Miranda had a faraway look. "Stirring. I think that's what I said. They were stirring more than usual."

"I fear they may have found a way to interact directly with someone or some group within the Pantathian community. Perhaps with this so-called Emerald Queen who now leads them."

"That's a chilling thought."

Pug said, "There is something few know. Have you heard of Macros the Black?"

Miranda said, "By reputation." Her tone was dry, and Pug assumed she didn't believe the inflated tales about the Black Sorcerer.

"Much of what he did was theatrics, but much was an order of magic beyond even my understanding today. He was able to do things with time that I can only speculate on, for one example."

Her eyes narrowed at that. "Time travel?"

"More. Tomas and I were trapped in a time well with him and we traveled to the dawn of time and returned. But he could use his mind and will across eons."

"How do you mean?"

"He used his skills and powers to fashion a relationship between Tomas, a boyhood friend of mine, and Ashen-Shugar—"

"The Valheru whose armor he wears!" supplied Miranda.

"It was never a simple case of an ancient magic lingering in a mystic suit of armor. Macros used that armor as a vehicle for his own manipulation of my friend, centuries later, so he could act as he did during the Riftwar."

"That wily bastard," muttered Miranda.

"What if Tomas's armor isn't the only vehicle for such manipulation?"

Miranda's eyes grew wide. "Is it possible?"

"Of course it's possible," said Pug. "The older I get, the more certain I become that there is very little that isn't possible."

Miranda stood up and began to pace the tiny room. "How would we know?"

"We wait for Calis to return, or somehow get word to us. When last I saw Nakor I asked him to travel with Calis if possible, for he is uniquely suited to spying out this sort of problem. I suggested the possibility I just spoke of to you more than three years ago. Now that you tell me he's gone with Calis, I am content to wait until they return. And we keep out of sight until then, so as not to provide the Pantathians with a target.

"I could protect myself for a while, as you can, I am sure, but constantly having to defend myself would prove wearisome and divert me from certain studies."

Miranda nodded. "What was that business of the clue and the rest, with the Hall of Worlds and the City of the Gods, all about, anyway?"

"I wanted a way to keep to myself and yet be found if someone with the wit and talent needed to find me. Had you gone prowling the Hall, asking questions on any number of worlds, well, you would have encountered difficulty."

"I was warned of your assassins," she countered.

"Who told you?"

"It was the gossip of the day at Honest John's."

Pug said, "The next time I hire someone for a quiet undertaking, I think I will avoid the Inn.

"Who directed you to Mustafa's?"

"Boldar Blood."

"When you left Mustafa, I went ahead to the mountains to wait for you. The simple trick of telling you to go somewhere else was my last trick." He smiled. "Had you not proved so agreeable a guest, I would have disposed of you up on those cold peaks so as to be as far from Stardock as possible when the Pantathians noticed the display."

Miranda gave him a sour expression. "Lacks subtlety."

"Perhaps, but time grows short and I have much work to do while I wait for Calis and Nakor."

"Can I be of help? Boldar Blood is waiting for me in an inn in LaMut if he can be of service."

"For now, send word to him to wait; let the mercenary enjoy Tabert's girls and ale," said Pug. "As for you, there are any number of tasks around here that I could use help with, if you don't mind."

"I won't cook," she said, "or mend your smallclothes."

Pug laughed. He was genuinely amused. "My, that's the first good laugh I've had in a long time." He shook his head. "Hardly. I can get all the dinner and laundry I require on Sorcerer's Isle. I inform Gathis, and when all is ready, I transport food in and linens out.

"No, I need you to start digging through a large part of a very old library, looking for clues."

"Clues to what?" asked Miranda, now obviously intrigued.

"Clues to where we may have to go to find someone if the need arises."

Cocking her head to one side, as if she already knew the answer, she said, "Looking for whom?"

Pug said, "If Calis brings me the news I fear most of all, we're going to have to find the only being I know of who can counter the sort of magic we'll face. We're going to have to try to once again locate Macros the Black."

20
★★
PASSAGE

CALIS SIGNALED.

Silently the men behind him halted in place and raised hands to warn the others farther down the line to stop. Since entering the tunnel two days before, they had adopted silent travel. All communication was done by hand gestures and noise was kept to a minimum.

While every man in Calis's company had been trained in such practices, the clansmen under Hatonis and the mercenaries hired by Praji had been a noisy bunch at first. They had learned quickly, however, and no longer needed constant reminders to keep silent.

Of the one hundred and eleven men who had left the rendezvous—the sixty-six men in Calis's command and the forty-five with Greylock, Praji, Vaja, and Hatonis—seventy-one had survived the clash with the Saaur above.

"Above" was how they now thought of the Plain of Djams. The tunnel had moved continuously down until Nakor estimated they were close to a quarter mile below the surface. At camp the night before he had whispered to Erik that someone had once badly wanted to trade on the plains above to have built such a long and deep passage; either that, or they had wanted their front door a very long, defensible distance from their home.

The tunnel had been a uniform size, varying only with an occasional outcropping of stone that was easier to move around than to dig through. Except for those minor deviations, the tunnel was a uniform seven feet in height, ten feet wide, and apparently endless.

At several points along the way larger areas had been dug out that might have served for rest areas or places to store provisions, but their original use could only be guessed at by those now passing.

Calis turned back to where Luis waited and motioned for him to come forward. Erik wondered at the choice until he saw Calis draw a dagger from his belt.

Beyond the Captain lay another opening, but Erik had the impression this was more than another widening in the tunnel. He sensed air movement and wondered if they had reached some portion of the abandoned underground city Praji had told of. He knew it was not possible that they had come far enough to enter the particular one Praji spoke of down in the south, but perhaps there was another such place up here, in the mountains.

Calis and Luis vanished into the gloom. The single torch was at the center of the column, and the light barely reached either end. Erik did not know how Calis did it; his vision must be inhuman, for the faint light that reached the head of the line barely gave Erik enough illumination to see de Loungville's back as he crouched, waiting. Erik hugged himself, for it was cold in the passage. All the men were chilled, but they endured it in silence.

Since losing Foster, de Loungville had been relegating tasks equally to Biggo and Erik that usually fell to the corporal. Erik was uncertain if this was any endorsement of his ability or simply a question of proximity; they were the two men de Loungville was most likely to find at his back when he turned around.

A few moments later, Calis and Luis returned, and Calis spoke in a hushed whisper, while Luis returned to his normal place in line. "It's a large gallery, and we're entering through a passage that empties into a ledge leading both downward and up—it's wide enough for three men to walk abreast, but there is no railing and it's a long way down, so pass the word that when we move out everyone should be cautious of the edge. I'm going to explore. You rest here for a half hour, and if I'm not back, that means follow the upward path."

De Loungville nodded and motioned for rest. Those behind him passed along the silent instruction and the men sat where they were. Erik shifted around until he found a relatively comfortable position resting against the cold stone, while the others did likewise.

He heard a faint scraping sound and realized de Loungville was counting knots in a thong. It was an old trick, moving your fingers along a piece of rope, twine, or leather, silently reciting a fixed ditty, one that had been practiced over and over until it was almost as exact as sand falling in a glass. De Loungville would move his fingers down a knot each time he finished the rhyme; when he reached the end of the thong, ten minutes would have passed. When he had used the thong three times, the half hour would be up.

Erik closed his eyes. He couldn't sleep, but he could relax as much as possible. Without thought he put his hands on his aching legs and felt them grow warm with the healing power he had learned from Nakor. As the rest of his body was chilled by the cold rocks, it was a welcome sensation.

Erik wondered how the rest of the villagers in Weanat were doing, and what would become of them when the Emerald Queen's army reached that area. There were so many invaders there was no chance they could lie low in the woods until they left. That host would strip the land of everything edible for five miles on both sides of the river. The only hope those villagers had would be to go up into the mountains and hide in the high valleys. Perhaps Kirzon and his people would help them. Erik doubted it; they would have barely enough food for the winter for themselves.

Then he wondered what his mother was doing. He had no idea what time it was back home—he didn't really know what time it was above; he thought it was midday. That probably meant it was the middle of the night back in Ravensburg. She was most likely asleep in her little room at the inn. Erik wondered if she knew he still lived. Her last news of him might have been that he had been condemned to die. Given the secrecy surrounding the mission and the chance of not surviving training, he suspected she thought him dead.

He sighed softly and wondered how she was, and Rosalyn and Milo and the others in the village. They seemed so far away and that life so alien, he could barely remember what it felt like to rise up every day with his only expectation being hard work at the forge.

Suddenly he felt a touch on his wrist and looked over to see de Loungville in the dim light signaling it was time to move out. Erik reached over and nudged the dozing Biggo, who nodded and nudged the man next in line.

Erik rose and moved out after the sergeant, who passed through the opening to the gallery, and turned right on the walkway, heading upward. In the deep darkness, Erik could only sense the size of the place, and he was about halfway around the circular path when the man holding the torch emerged from the side passage. Suddenly Erik could see the entire gallery and he involuntarily stepped back against the wall. The floor was lost in the gloom below, despite the torch light, as was the ceiling above. A faint draft of air rose up, and it carried a damp, stale odor.

Erik wished he hadn't known the pathway was so narrow and the fall so great, as now he walked with considerably more discomfort. He moved on, and followed de Loungville upward into the darkness.

AT SEVERAL POINTS along the way they encountered entrances to new tunnels, and they paused to see if Calis had marked any, indicating they should leave the upwardly spiraling path. They never saw any marks.

There were wide places, as if ledges had been carved into the rock of the mountain, to allow more comfortable movement, and places where the men could sit. Erik had no idea how long they had been following Calis, but he knew his legs hurt. The constant upward climb was taking its toll.

Suddenly they saw Calis ahead in the gloom. He said, "This area is deserted."

The men seemed to relax at that, and de Loungville said, "Praji, is this like that dwarven place you spoke of?"

"Not that I'd recognize," said the old mercenary. He was short of wind and obviously pleased to be halting, even if only for a few minutes. "Mind you, I have only tales, but it's been described to me several times by different people who've been there." He looked around. "This place . . . I don't know what it is."

Calis said, "There are dwarven mines back home and I've been through a couple. They have galleries and such, but this is something different. No dwarven hand built this place. This is no mine."

Erik heard Roo's voice coming from behind. "This looks like a city, Captain."

Erik turned and heard Calis say, "A city?"

Roo said, "Well, something like it. Those tunnels lead to other places, maybe. Sleeping quarters or places to store goods. But those wide places, if you noticed, are in a pattern: there's one for every two entrances along the way, and they're all of uniform size. I think they're like market areas."

"Then this would be some sort of central passage, like a boulevard in a city, only it moves up and down instead of north and south," said Biggo.

"Who would have built such a place?" asked Erik.

Calis said, "I don't know." He changed the subject. "We're about at ground level, so I'm inclined to start looking for a way out. I'm going to explore the next corridor we come to. I want the men to make camp at the next 'market' area we find."

"Is it sundown already?" asked de Loungville.

"I'd judge it an hour past," said Nakor from behind.

"More like two," answered Calis.

"How do you know?" blurted Roo.

Calis smiled in the dim light. "I'll be back before dawn."

With that he moved ahead, and the weary column of men followed after until they came to the next wide space on the trail, where they gladly settled in for a night's rest.

ERIK DISCOVERED HE had no sense of time in these caves. Calis had mentioned to de Loungville that it had been two and a half days of travel, which in his judgment accounted for a twenty-mile journey from the hillock to the foothills of the mountains, and then a gradual climb into the interior of a large peak. Erik felt as if it had been a lot farther, but he realized that so much of the trek had been up the spiral path inside this mountain.

Earlier that day, Calis had said he was convinced the entire region was deserted, but there was something in his voice that hinted to Erik there was more that he was not sharing. Despite Erik's constant pledge to himself not to seek trouble but to mind his own business, he couldn't help but wonder what it was that seemed to be lurking behind the Captain's words.

One fortunate result of Calis's exploration was his saying that he thought they were getting close to a way out of this maze of dark passages and tall caverns. At one point he had hesitated between two large tunnels, one angling down into the mountain, the other veering once again upward. Erik sensed Calis had wanted to take the other tunnel, the one heading deep into the heart of the mountains, but he kept them moving upward. Erik wondered what had drawn Calis to that other tunnel.

Late the next day, the soldier carrying the bundle of torches said they were running low. Calis acknowledged the report, saying nothing else.

Erik felt an unexpected stab of fear at the thought of being in these mines without light. They had been extinguishing the torches when they slept. On the first night he had awakened in total darkness and had to fight back the urge to shout in alarm. He had never awakened to so utter a blackness, and he had lain there listening in the dark. He realized he was not the only one awake, for he could hear the rapid breathing of men not able to sleep in such conditions, and the quiet weeping of one or two who felt terror so profound he could understand it even if he couldn't name it.

ANOTHER FITFUL NIGHT was spent in utter darkness, and then they resumed their march. At noon on the fifth day they broke for the midday meal, more dried rations. Water was a problem, as they had only two large skins and a handful of smaller ones, filled at an underground pool the morning before. But there was no sign of water anywhere nearby, and Calis ordered the men to drink as they had in the desert, one mouthful, no more.

As they were readying to move out, a distant clatter rang through the tunnel, as if someone had dislodged rocks. Calis motioned for everyone to stand still. After a while de Loungville whispered, "Rock slide?"

"Perhaps," answered the Captain. "But I need to be sure." He pointed up and toward the left. "If I am correct, somewhere up ahead you should come either to an opening that leads directly to the surface, showing you some light, or a big passage leading up and away to the left. Ignore any passages that clearly lead downward or off to the right." He smiled slightly. "You should be on the surface by the time I catch up with you. I will follow as soon as I am sure there is nothing behind us."

"Do you want a torch?" asked de Loungville.

"I can find my way without one. If we are being followed by the Saaur, I don't want any light to show them where I am if I get too close."

Erik wondered how he could find his way through the dark, and, even if he could, how he was willing to give up the torch's reassurance, scant as it was. Calis moved down the line, offering a quick tap on the shoulder or nod to each of the men as he passed them.

De Loungville motioned for hand signals only and indicated they should follow him. Erik discovered he was now second in line. He peered into the gloom, barely able to see ten feet beyond the sergeant into the murk, as the flickering torch in the middle of the line caused the shadows to dance. He fervently hoped that Calis was correct and they were getting close to getting out of these caves. They moved forward.

FAINT NOISES ECHOED through the passages as the torch burned low. De Loungville judged Calis had been gone for almost a half day. The men were tired, and it seemed an appropriate time for sleep.

Motioning for a halt, he whispered back, "How many torches?"

The answer came, "We have two after this one."

De Loungville swore. "If the Captain doesn't get back soon, we may be truly lost in the dark tomorrow, unless that passage he spoke of is nearby. Put out that torch and make sure you have everything needed to light it quickly if there's any trouble. I want two shifts, first four hours and second four; then we walk out of this gods-forsaken hole."

Erik knew he would be among those sleeping first, so he lay down and tried to get as comfortable as possible. Despite being tired to his bones, he just couldn't find it easy to sleep in the pitch darkness on rock.

He closed his eyes and heard muttering which told him that the torch had been extinguished; he was not alone in being troubled by the total absence of light.

He kept his eyes closed and turned his mind to pleasant thoughts. He wondered how the harvest at home this year had gone and how the grapes looked. He recalled the growers bragging about a record crop, but that was nothing unusual. You could usually tell if they were just talking to hear themselves talk or if they truly meant it by their manner. The more earnest they were that it was to be a great year, the more you could suppose it wouldn't be, but if they spoke of the harvest in a matter-of-fact, nearly indifferent way, it would be a great year.

He then wondered how the other young men and women in the village were. He thought about Gwen and regretted he hadn't gone to the orchard with her on the occasions he might have. Having a woman was a great deal more than he had imagined, and the memory of the whore's softness roused his flesh despite his fatigue. He thought of Rosalyn and found himself both fascinated and disturbed by remembering her without her clothing. He had seen her numerous times as a child bathing, but seeing her woman's breasts as she lay before the tree . . . He found the memory now oddly disturbing, as if there must be something wrong to think about how she looked as the result of a rape.

Erik tried to turn over and succeeded only in making himself less comfortable. Maybe he could talk to Nakor about this unsettling memory of Rosalyn; the funny man seemed to know a great deal and perhaps could tell Erik why he was suddenly aroused by such a repulsive memory.

Yet when he thought of that night the rage and anger were distant, and the murder seemed as if it happened to someone else. But those small firm breasts . . .

He groaned slightly and sat up, suddenly disoriented in the darkness. He started to berate himself for being as depraved as any man living when it struck him suddenly there was light coming from ahead in the tunnel. It was faint, but any light would be noticeable in the absolute gloom of the cavern.

He sensed more than saw the form of de Loungville before him and saw that the soldier who was to have been on duty had dozed off. He felt no anger for the man: remaining alert in total darkness was almost impossible. The sound of slow breathing everywhere told Erik he might be the only man remaining awake who was close enough to the head of the column to see the light.

He gently reached past de Loungville and nudged the sentry. The man came awake, saying, "What?"

De Loungville was awake an instant later and also whispered, "What?"

Before the sentry could say anything, Erik said, "Marc thought he saw light ahead, Sergeant. He was asking me if I saw it, too." Turning to the sentry, he said, "Yes, there is light up there."

De Loungville said, "Wake the others. Quietly. No torch. First six men come with me."

They crept forward, and after a few steps, Erik could see it was a moving light, coming from the left, from a passage that intersected the one in which they traveled fifty or so feet farther along. As they neared the passage, it was clear it was rapidly growing brighter, then suddenly de Loungville was motioning for everyone to hug the walls.

The sounds of movement preceded a figure who strode into view, passing through the intersection without a glance right or left. Erik gripped his sheathed sword hilt, ready to pull it free should the need arise.

The creature was a serpent man, dressed in a tunic and leggings rather than trousers, which allowed his short tail to swing freely.

Behind him came two more, larger and dressed in armor. Erik had had a good look at the Saaur, a better look than he would care to repeat, but these creatures were of a different stripe. The tallest of them was smaller than human by a head, and they were sinuous. Erik noticed they seemed slow and deliberate in their movement. He wondered if it might be the chill in the cavern that slowed them, for Nakor had said these creatures were cold-blooded.

Another pair of guards passed through, one glancing in their direction. Erik waited, but the creature moved on without comment or alarm. Erik could only reason that the creature's night vision had been harmed by the closeness of the torch before it, and that, hugging the walls, the humans were nearly invisible.

Another pair, then another, until a full dozen Pantathians walked by.

De Loungville motioned for the others to wait, then moved to where the light was quickly fading. He hurried back and whispered, "They're gone."

As the tunnel was plunged into darkness again, they reached the remaining column, now alert to the last man. Nakor, who had worked his way to the head of the line, said, "Serpent men, yes?"

"How'd you know?"

"I felt them" was his answer. "I feel a lot of strange things here. This is a bad place."

"I'll not argue that," said de Loungville. He let his breath out slowly, in frustration. Then he said, "I want us out of here as fast as we can get."

Erik found listening to his voice in pitch darkness only heightened his appreciation of the tone of frustration in the man's statement. Then de Loungville asked, "Which way do we go?"

Nakor whispered, "We move roughly to the southeast. I think we go the way the snake men came from, not follow after. I think they came from the surface and go somewhere deep within the mountain. We are high enough that we will find it cool, cold even, when we come out. Serpent people don't like the cold, so I think that would be the place they don't live."

"You think they live down under the mountain?"

"Could be," Nakor answered. "Hard to know, but they are here and we need to do many things before we start fighting again. If we die, then no one knows what's really going on, and that is bad."

De Loungville was silent. Erik found himself growing uncomfortable with the duration and at last said, "Sergeant?"

"Shut up," came the quick response. "I'm thinking."

Erik and the others stayed silent. Then at last de Loungville's voice cut through the darkness. "Greylock!" he called, his voice low but urgent.

From the rear a figure moved slowly forward, trying not to step on feet in the dark. At last a voice said, nearby, "Yes?"

"You're in charge. I expect you to get as many of this company out alive as you can."

The former officer said, "I will, Sergeant. I'd like Erik for my second."

De Loungville didn't hesitate. "Von Darkmoor, you act as sergeant for a while. Jadow, you're his corporal. All of you pay attention to whatever Nakor and Hatonis have to say.

"This is what you're going to do. I'm waiting here for Calis. I don't want to try to mark the passages we take in case more of those Pantathians come this way. Leave me one torch and I'll wait here until I decide the Captain's not coming back." There was a note of urgency and worry in his voice Erik had never heard before. He wondered if he would have noticed it had he been able to see de Loungville's face.

"Then I'll catch up with you," continued de Loungville.

"Now, here's what you do. When you reach the surface, get across the grasslands as best you can, and to the coast. Acquire horses or steal a boat, but somehow get back to the City of the Serpent River. *Trenchard's Revenge* is there or she's been sunk, for Nicholas gave orders that at least one ship would remain for us. Hatonis and his men will know the best route."

Hatonis, from the rear, spoke loudly enough for his voice to carry just to the front of the line. "There's an old trade route, overland from Ispar to the City of the Serpent River, through Maharta. It is rarely used anymore, but it should be passable on horseback."

De Loungville took a deep breath and said, "All right, light a torch and get out of here."

The man who had been harboring the torches lit a spark and soon the flame was going. Erik found he had to squint, which surprised him, given how far back down the line the light was. He turned and saw de Loungville; the sergeant had his usual mask of determination in place. Erik decided he wouldn't have noticed the sound of worry if he had been looking at the man.

Without saying anything, Erik reached out and quickly placed his hand on de Loungville's arm, gave a quick squeeze, and released it, the only gesture he could make without saying something.

The sergeant looked at him, giving him only a brief nod of acknowledgment, before Erik moved down the tunnel. Greylock reached the junction of the tunnels, peered both ways, then motioned for the men to follow to the left. Erik reached the junction and as he started to turn the corner, he fought down the urge to look back to where de Loungville waited.

If only the Captain were here, he said to himself silently. Where could Calis be?

CALIS HELD CLOSE to the wall as he stared in wide-eyed amazement. He and his father had spoken many times of what it would be like to confront their unusual heritage, a legacy of ancient magic, warped by the skill of Macros the Black, and used to bring to his human father the powers incarnate of the legendary Valheru.

Tomas had wooed and won the hand of Aglaranna, the Queen of the Elves, and had fathered Calis, impossible fruit of a union unique in history. Calis was young by the reckoning of the elven people, little more than a half century old.

By human consideration, he was a man of middle years, and by any measure, he had more than a dozen lifetimes' experience in watching the pain and madness of the creatures who lived on this world.

But nothing had prepared him to deal with the consequences of what he had chosen to investigate.

Elves possessed the ability to navigate by the dimmest light of the night, a single moon, or distant stars, but even dwarves were incapable of seeing in the utter blackness of underground tunnels. Yet they had other senses, and Calis, unlike his elven cousins, had traveled with dwarves enough in his youth to have learned some of their tricks: the sound of air moving, faint echoes upon the passage walls, counting turns and remembering distances. It was said that once upon a path, no dwarf could ever fail to retrace his steps. Calis possessed the same knack.

After leaving the company, he had moved back down to the vast gallery, the circular central hall of this city within a mountain. For that was what he was certain it had been, once in ancient days, a city beneath the mountains, as Roo had supposed. But the youth from Ravensburg had no idea what sort of city.

From what he had studied with Tathar and the other Spellweavers of Elvandar, Calis had suspected from the first that this was a city of elven construction rather than dwarven. But the elves who had built this place were as unlike Calis's people as they were unlike any other mortal race. Those elves had existed as slaves to the Valheru, and only by command of their ancient masters could such a place have come to be built by elven hands.

Once he had reached the gallery, Calis was convinced the sound he had heard had been nothing more than a distant rockfall. There were no signs of pursuit; still, he moved downward to make sure, passing the strange split in the tunnels that had called to him so strangely.

He had moved deep within the well of darkness, and when at last he could hear only his own breath and the pounding of his heart in his ear, he turned back. But as he approached that odd junction where he had hesitated the first time he had passed, at the head of the company, he again paused, sensing something ancient and compelling deep within the tunnel that moved downward.

It was a foolish risk, yet it was impossible for Calis to resist. He knew he should ensure the others got free, but he had faith in the cunning of de Loungville and the skills of Nakor.

And now he knew what had called him. There was something ancient at the heart of this hall. And he looked upon it with fear and astonishment.

He had taken the tunnel moving downward, following it through another gallery, smaller than the grand gallery they had climbed, yet large enough to have served as a small town. High above, a faint light shone down, so far away that the noon sun was but a pinpoint, yet that entrance, at the summit of some high mountain, told him his instinct was correct.

This ancient place had once been home to a Valheru, much as the great cavern below the Mac Mordain Cadal, the ancient dwarven mines in the Grey Tower Mountains, had been home to Ashen-Shugar, the Ruler of the Eagles' Reaches, the Valheru whose ancient spirit had come to possess his father and change his nature so profoundly.

Crossing a narrow stone bridge, he had come to a set of wooden doors large enough to admit a great dragon, and Calis knew that once they did, for the Dragon Lords kept their mighty mounts close at hand. In the door was a smaller portal, one used by servants in ages past.

He had moved a heavy iron handle, and to his surprise it opened a latch easily and without noise. The door had swung open on hinges recently well oiled, and Calis blinked his eyes as the sudden light threatened to blind him.

At the end of the long cavernous hall, a ledge overlooked a vast cavern ablaze with torchlight; and in the center of the cavern a village of mud huts, crude and without craft in their fashioning, was constructed around a series of cracks. Steam rose, heralding an underground source of heat, and at the center of the largest vent a heat shimmer danced in the air. As he had approached, Calis had been bewildered by the sudden rise in temperature. Where he had been feeling damp chill when he left the others, he was now sweating as much as he had been in the desert. The thermal vents showed that this Valheru hall was fashioned inside what had once been a volcano.

The air was pungent with the smell of decay and the stench of sulfur on the air. Calis felt his eyes burn at the sting of it as he looked down on the scene below.

Throughout the hall roamed serpent men, and at the center rear of the hall, on a high dais, a great throne rose against the wall. Upon that throne, where once sat a Dragon Lord, now sat one of their tribe, a creature of scales and claws, but its eyes were fixed upon space, for it was ages dead. The Pantathians nearest the motionless figure appeared to be priests, wearing vestments of green and black, and to the mummy of some ancient reptile king they paid homage.

Calis was no Spellweaver, but he felt the bite of magic in the air, and around the base of the throne he saw artifacts from eons past.

It was the presence of these items that caused him to suffer. He ached to march into the hall, brushing aside those creatures, and to mount those steps to the top of the dais, casting down this lesser creature, to take possession of the items of might that lay at its feet.

For Calis was certain these items were indeed relics of the Valheru. Never had his blood sung so, save once when his father had allowed him to hold the shield of white and gold he wore into battle.

Calis fought back such foolhardy urges and tried to make sense of the scene before him. It would be too easy to count this simply a Pantathian village, for there were too many strange things to account for; he wished Nakor was here—the little man's ability to see things clearly would have been invaluable.

As it was, Calis attempted to memorize every detail before him, drinking in the conflicting images and trying to record them in his mind without passing judgment on their significance, so as not to neglect an important detail through an error in judgment.

After a half hour, several human prisoners were brought into the hall. Most had the vacant-eyed look of those in shock or under some sort of spell or the effect of drugs, but one woman struggled against her chains. The priests ranged themselves in a line across the lowest step on the dais, and the centermost spread his hands, holding in one an emerald-topped staff.

He spoke in a hissing language unlike anything Calis had heard in his travels, and motioned to guards to take the prisoners and move them to another place. Calis wished for his bow, that he might kill this priest; then he wondered where such a violent rage came from.

Then the priest motioned for the first prisoner to be brought before the throne, and two guards moved to carry out the command. A series of ritual passes of the staff was punctuated by guttural croaks and deep hisses, and the emerald at the top of the staff began to glow brightly.

Death magic surged in the room as one of the guards held the first prisoner's head back, while another quickly struck with a long knife, cutting the head completely from the body. Calis held himself motionless, despite strong anger surging up within. The guard threw the head into a corner, and Calis followed its flight, watching as it landed with a wet thud among a pile of heads, some rotting, others now skulls, that sat behind the throne.

The two serpents holding the man's body lifted it, carried it to a recessed chamber, and tossed it down out of sight. The screeches of hunger that answered caused Calis to swallow hard.

The woman who seemed unfazed by the drugs started screaming, and Calis felt his nerves grow taut. He clutched his sword hilt and ached to charge this den of monsters. One by one the drugged prisoners were slaughtered, their heads tossed to the pile after dark magics seized their life energy, and the bodies were fed to the Pantathian young.

The woman screamed continuously as she crouched on the floor, her terror outracing her fatigue. At last she remained alone before the priests. The priest with the emerald-topped staff motioned for the guards to take the woman next and they lifted her up, ripping her tunic free, so she stood naked in front of the priest, who ignored the warm sticky puddle he stepped in as he walked through the pooling blood of the victims.

Calis saw the priest motion the guards to hold the woman fast, and he saw them force her to lie back, holding her down while the priest began to make more motions with the staff and prod her with the butt end while singing in his alien tongue.

Calis felt his throat tighten. He had encountered the Pantathians' evil sorcery before. They were able to use humans to create Pantathians who looked like humans. Calis had seen the results before and knew it was a powerful, black art being practiced below.

Calis was no student of magic, but he had some knowledge of it, and this next act was too vile for him to begin to understand. As the priest removed a long dagger from his robe and advanced upon the now shrieking woman, Calis looked away.

He judged himself too close to this place of dark magic for too long and moved backwards, slowly, into the gloom. A few paces up the passage, he turned, and hurried up the long tunnel. He quickly slipped through the door, closing it behind him, and paused a moment to let his senses start to adjust to the gloom.

As he paused, he considered what he had just seen. It was impossible to imagine what the Pantathians gained from the priest's slow torture of a human woman. He had no doubt that eventually the priest would kill the woman, and her head would join the others on the pile as her body went to nourish the young.

He wished for a moment that Nakor had been along, for the strange little man who claimed not to believe in magic seemed to know more about it than just about anyone Calis had met. He might make some sense of how this ritual torture and slaughter tied into what he feared might be occurring with the Emerald Queen and the Valheru artifacts of power.

Calis hurried through the darkness.

Without conscious thought, he started counting steps and measuring distances with his hearing, and he hoped that he'd find his company where he had left it.

DE LOUNGVILLE ALMOST leaped when Calis touched his arm. He spun around to hear a familiar voice ask, "Where is everyone else?"

"Captain!" de Loungville said. "I was about to say a brief prayer to Ruthia and a small testimonial to Lims-Kragma on your behalf, then get the hell out of here.

"Now I can sit down and die of a burst heart!"

"Sorry I startled you, but I couldn't tell who it was here in the dark, and it smelled like you but I wanted to be sure."

"Smelled like me . . . ?"

"It's been a while since you've had a bath, Bobby."

"You're no bunch of roses either, Calis."

"Have you a torch?"

To answer, De Loungville struck steel to flint and set a hot spark into the treated cotton wadding wrapped on a stick. The flame started modestly but spread quickly, and by the time de Loungville held it up, they were bathed in a pool of light.

"Call me mother, but you look a fright," said de Loungville. "What did you find down there?"

"I'll tell you when we've put some distance between us and it. Which way?"

"We found a passage used by some serpent men, so I put Greylock in charge and sent the men in the other direction, to the left."

"Good: that should mean they're on the surface by now. If we hurry, we can overtake them before they get too far down the hillside. We're a lot higher up than when we came in the tunnel, Bobby."

"And a lot farther from where we want to be than we were when we started," responded de Loungville.

"We'd better hurry. We have a long way to go." Softly Calis added, "And I fear not that much time to get there."

21

★★

ATTRITION

ERIK DUCKED.

A shower of darts flew through the air and bounced off his shield as he tried to keep low to the ground. Since leaving the cavern and moving down through the hills to the grasslands, Nakor and Sho Pi had both claimed they were being observed.

When they had finally reached an area of broken rocks, islands of limestone, shale, and granite that broke up pools of tall grass, a sudden attack of the Gilani had greeted them. Six men died in the first assault, which was barely driven back by the heroic efforts of those in the forefront.

Greylock had quickly organized the defense, and the struggle had gone on for nearly a half day. Two more men had died as they retreated up the hillside, looking for this defensive position. Praji and Vaja had moved to the front, and were in council with Greylock as Erik approached.

"I've got everyone situated as best I could, Owen. We're taking a beating."

"I know," came the calm reply. He looked at Praji and said, "Any idea why they hit us?"

Praji shrugged. "We're here and they're Gilani. They don't like anyone who isn't Gilani, and we're about to enter the grasslands. That's their range and they're trying to tell us to keep off."

"How'd the damn grass get so tall this time of year?" asked Greylock.

Vaja said, "There are some that grow in the winter and others in the summer, and they are all mixed in down there, is my guess."

Putting aside his frustration, Greylock asked, "Is there another way out of these mountains?"

Praji shrugged. "Your guess is as good as mine. Even if I knew exactly where we were, I've never traveled this way. Few men from the Eastlands have." He looked around. "I'm guessing if we could get over the ridge"—he pointed upward at the highest peaks of the mountains—"we might be able to make our way down to the Satpura River. Maybe make some rafts and get down to the coast near Chatisthan. Or we could move back up into the foothills, staying high enough so the Gilani don't come after us, and could head south, see if we can find a way to the river Dee and follow that down to Ispar, but I don't recommend that course."

"Why not?"

"That would take us through the Great South Forest. Not a lot of people get through there alive. Rumor has it that's where your Pantathians hole up, and it's where tigers that talk like men live. . . ." When Greylock looked at him with disbelief written on his face, he quickly added, "But that's only rumor."

A whizzing sound in the air warned them a scant second before another rain of darts pelted them. Erik tried to get his bulk below his shield. A shout and curse told him someone hadn't covered up quickly enough as darts rained off shields and the surrounding rocks.

"How bad are the wounded?" asked Greylock.

"The wounded aren't too bad," answered Erik. "One of the men has a dart in the leg, but it's down in the fleshy part of the calf—he can walk with help. A couple of broken arms, and Gregory of Tiburn dislocated his shoulder."

Greylock said, "Well, we can't outwait them here and find out how many of those damn darts they're carrying." In frustration he added, "Hell, we don't even know how many Gilani there are." The little men had swarmed over the front of the column, then vanished back into the grass when Calis's company had turned out to be willing to stand and make a fight of it. Since then they had been launching random flights of darts.

Looking around, Greylock said, "Erik, try to get back to the rear and start the men heading back up toward the cavern. We'll see if we can find another way down that won't bring us back into this hornets' nest."

Erik crouched as he moved along and twice had to flatten himself against the rocks to avoid missiles. The darts were rude things, but cleverly fashioned. Long reeds, little more than heavy grass stalks, were tied together in tight bundles until they were as rigid as arrows, and fitted with tips of sharpened glass or stone. The tied reeds were surprisingly strong, and they rained down with enough impact that they could punch through any unarmored part of the body. Praji had mentioned that the Gilani used a throwing stick, called an atlatl, to propel them in a high arc over their victims' heads, causing them to fall with great force. Erik would attest to their effectiveness.

He reached the end of the line and started the men moving back up once more. In less than ten minutes, Greylock, Praji, and Vaja came into view, the last of the forward element climbing upward.

Erik looked after and saw no sign of pursuit. "They don't seem anxious to come up here after us," he said.

Vaja said, "They're not stupid. They're little fellows. In an open fight we'd chew them up in less time than it takes to tell of it—but coming after us from tall grass, well, there's no one who can fight out there better than the Gilani."

Erik wouldn't argue that. "What has made them so hostile?"

Praji looked back. "Usually, they simply don't like strangers; they could be coming after us for the pure hell of it. Or maybe the Saaur are pushing them south and they're just mad."

Erik said, "But the Saaur who came after us couldn't have mounted enough of a force to clear out these grass-dwellers. They'd need an army as big as the one mustering on the Vedra to do that."

Vaja tapped Erik on the shoulder and pointed up the hill. Calis and de Loungville were hurrying downward to meet them.

When the Captain reached the men, Erik could see by more than one face in the company that many were relieved to see the Eagle of Krondor back among them. He retrieved his longbow from the man who held it for him and said, "Why are you climbing back up?"

Greylock quickly explained, and Calis said, "We can't get over the mountains. There's nothing like a pass up there I could see on the way down, and we can't risk going back into the cavern to see if there is a way through." He thought it best not to tell anyone of what he had seen until he compared notes with Nakor.

Turning to de Loungville, he said, "Send Sho Pi and Jadow ahead. Tell them to find us a trail heading south. If we can move along the face of these mountains, then down behind these Gilani so we can then cut across to Maharta, we still may get through this without too much more damage."

De Loungville nodded and went up the line to give the order to the men who would scout for them. "How's our water?" asked Calis.

"We're fine if we can find a source every day or two," answered Greylock. "We've got eight fewer men who need to drink than we did a couple of hours ago."

Calis nodded. "Praji, what's water like out there?"

"Might as well be a desert," came the answer. "The Plain of Djams has some streams and water holes, but if you don't know where they are you can wander by one, never see it through the grass, and die of thirst."

"Any birds you can follow?"

"A few, but damn me if I know what they look like," admitted the old mercenary. "If we get far enough to the south, the foothills along the coast are kinder. Lots of springs, lakes, and creeks, from what I've been told."

"South it is," said Calis.

Ignoring his own fatigue, he hurried past the men in line so he could take over his position at the head of the column.

Erik trudged upward, trying to be equally stoic as his legs burned with fatigue. Each step up the slope took its toll, and he was more than grateful when Calis at last ordered a rest.

Erik waited with anticipation as the waterskin was passed his way, and drank deeply. They had passed a pool on the way down, so there was no reason to stint right now.

As he handed the skin back he looked out at the distant plain and something caught his eyes. "What's that rippling movement in the distance?" he asked no one in particular.

Praji heard him and came down to where he stood. Squinting, he said, "My eyes aren't what they used to be." Turning to face up the slope, he called out, "Captain! You should take a look out there!" He pointed at the horizon.

Calis stared for long minutes, then said, "Gods above! It's the Saaur."

"But that's impossible," said de Loungville. "For that many to be marching, this far south . . ."

"There had to be a second army," finished Praji.

"No wonder those bastards were so determined to keep us away from that entrance to the mountains," said Vaja.

Calis said, "They must have been using the lower portions of the cavern as a staging area. So that's why our short friends in the grass are so out of sorts—they just got through having an army ride through their homes."

De Loungville said, "They mean to hit Lanada from the rear!"

After another minute, in which most of the men commented or swore, Calis said, "No, they move southeast. They're heading for Maharta."

Praji said, "If the Raj has sent his war elephants to fight with the Priest-King's army at Lanada, Maharta will be defended by the palace guards and mercenaries."

De Loungville swore. "The bastards weren't keen on having us serving them! They were just anxious to keep us from joining the other side." He almost spit.

Calis said, "How long before they reach the city?"

Praji said, "I only have a rough idea where the hell we are." He thought and said, "Maybe a week, ten days at the outside. If they don't waste their horses, two weeks."

"Can we get there before them?"

"No," came the flat answer. "If we had wings, certainly, or if we hacked our way through those Gilani and had fresh horses waiting for us on the other side, maybe, but if we keep going south, there's no way we can reach the city within a week of those lizard men."

"Can the city hold out for a week?"

"Maybe," answered Praji frankly. "It depends on how much chaos is going on due to the host that's got to be fleeing southward. With so many people trying to get in, they may already be under siege."

Erik said, "Can we get around them?"

Vaja said, "If we can get to Chatisthan, we might be able to find a ship that could take us up to the City of the Serpent River."

Calis said, "Too many maybes. We're going to strike for the coast, then we'll try for the City of the Serpent River." He called out to Hatonis, "Do you want to try for Chatisthan, or head overland to home?"

Hatonis shrugged, and grinned, looking youthful despite his grey hair. "One fight is pretty much the same as another, and if we don't fight the snakes at Maharta we're certainly going to have to fight them at our own door."

Calis nodded. "Let's go."

Erik saw the others get into line, and he slapped Roo on the shoulder as his boyhood friend walked past. Roo gave him a crooked smile that showed there was nothing to smile about, and Erik nodded in agreement. Erik waited until the last man had passed, then picked up the rear guard position. Suddenly he realized he had taken Foster's place in line without being told. He looked ahead to see if de Loungville was signaling or if another was coming to take his place, but when no word came down to give up the corporal's place, he continued along, returning his mind to the business at hand: staying alive.

PROVIDENCE SMILED UPON them, as they found a southern trail. It looked to be a miners' trail, for it was wider than any goat herder would have needed, and at several places along the way areas of bare rock proclaimed those workers who had hacked their way through the soil and stone to make it easy to get carts up and down the road.

For Calis's company it was as if at last they were running into some good luck. The men moved along swiftly, at a trot for a time, then a walk, the pace designed to cover the maximum distance by the end of each day.

The wounded were able to keep up, though the man with the injured leg was almost unconscious with pain and loss of blood by the end of the day. Nakor dressed his wound and told Calis that with him and Sho Pi working on it all night, the man would be slightly better each day.

They found water and were clearly able to increase their speed, as they moved quickly to a rising crest. A rumbling warned them as they climbed the rise; then as they topped the crest, in the distance they saw the falls.

De Loungville swore. They faced a gorge cut through the mountains; below them by a hundred feet a great fall of water cascaded into a small lake another two hundred feet below that. From there the river meandered southeast toward the ocean.

Ancient rocks marked where once a rope-and-wood suspension bridge had crossed the gap. Another pair of rock anchors rose up on the opposite side of the gorge.

"The Satpura River," said Praji. "Now I know exactly where we are."

"Where are we?" asked Calis.

"Dead east across the Plain of Djams lies Maharta," said Praji. Turning to Calis he said, "I don't know what sort of magic was in that tunnel, but we're one hell of a lot farther away from where we entered the grasslands than I thought."

"What do you mean?" said de Loungville. "We were fifty, sixty miles away from where we entered when we got to that big grotto."

"More like three hundred," answered Vaja. "It would take you a month on a good horse to get back to that mound out in the grass," he observed, "if you could get past the Gilani."

Nakor said, "It was a very good trick, then, for I felt nothing of it." He smiled as if this was a major feat. Then he grinned. "Bet it was as soon as we moved from the barrow. Bet you there is no tunnel there. It must be an illusion." He shook his head. "Now I really want to go back and look."

Calis said, "Some other time. How far to Maharta?"

Praji shrugged. "By caravan from Palamds to Port Grief, a month. No one goes from there to Maharta overland—they take a ship. But there is that old coast road, if you don't mind the bandits and other low-lifes that haunt it."

"Where's our best course?" asked Calis.

Praji rubbed his chin a moment. "I think we send Sho Pi and Jadow that way," he said, pointing down the slope near the gorge, "to see if there's a trail down nearby. If so, we take it. If we follow the river, we should be less than a week from Palamds. We can find a caravan or buy horses, and then we ride to Port Grief. From there a ship, and we're on our way to wherever you need to go."

"I need to get back to Krondor," said Calis, and several of the men nearby cheered when they heard that.

Nakor said, "No, first we must go to Maharta, then to Krondor."

"Why?" asked Calis.

"We haven't stopped to ask why the Emerald Queen is taking the river cities."

Vaja said, "Good question."

"Hatonis, Praji, you have any ideas?" asked Calis.

Hatonis said, "Conquest for its own purposes is not unknown in this land—for booty, to enlarge one's domain, for honor—but this simple taking of everything . . ." He shrugged.

Praji said, "If there was something I wanted in Maharta, and I couldn't trust to have those other cities at my back . . ."

Erik said, "Maybe it has to do with getting every sword under one banner?"

Calis looked at him for a long minute, then nodded. "They plan on bringing the biggest army in history against the Kingdom."

Then Roo said, "How are they planning on getting there?"

Nakor slowly grinned as Calis said, "What!"

Roo looked embarrassed as he repeated, "How are they planning on getting there? You needed two ships to get us here, with stores and all. They've got, what? A hundred thousand, two hundred thousand soldiers? And a lot of horses and equipment. Where are they going to get the ships?"

Hatonis said, "The shipbuilders at Maharta are the finest in Novindus. Only the shipwrights in the Pa'jkamaka Islands are their equal. Our clan has long purchased our ships in Maharta. It is the only shipyard that could possibly produce enough transports in a short time, perhaps in two years or so."

Calis said, "Then we must make a stop there."

Nakor said, "Yes. We must burn the shipyards."

Hatonis's eyes widened. "Burn . . . But the city will be under siege. They will have put hulks into the harbor mouth to keep the Emerald Queen's ships from sailing in, and it will be impossible to get within twenty miles of the city for the patrols on both sides."

"How long will it take to rebuild those yards if they're destroyed?" asked Calis.

Hatonis shrugged. "The yards are massive, and have been built up slowly over the last few centuries. It would take years to restore them. Lumber must be harvested up here and in the Sothu and Sumanu mountains and shipped downriver or carried in wagons. The great keels take a year or more to be cut and brought down, at great expense."

Nakor almost danced, he was so excited. "If we burn the yards, we get five, six, maybe as many as ten years before ships can be built here. Many, many things can happen in that time. This Emerald Queen, can she keep her host together that long? This I think unlikely."

Calis's eyes seem to light with the prospect. Then he fought back his enthusiasm and said, "Don't sell her short, Nakor."

Nakor nodded. The two had spoken at great length about what they had seen, and knew they were dealing with the most dangerous foe since the Tsurani invasion of the Riftwar. "I know, but men are men, and unless the Pantathian magic is so powerful as to make their hearts change, many of these soldiers of hers will forsake her banner without payment."

"Still," said Hatonis, "denying her the shipyards would be a major victory. My father ran the most successful trading consortium in the City of the Serpent River. We can send men to the Pa'jkamaka Islands and ensure they do not sell her ships. I will personally guarantee no shipwright in the City of the Serpent River will work on her behalf."

Calis said, "You know that after Maharta she will march on you? It's logical."

"I know we shall have to fight her. If we must, we can abandon the city and live again in the wild. We men of the clans were not always city men." Hatonis smiled a dark smile. "But many of her greenskins will die before that day comes."

Calis said, "Well, first things first. Jadow, Sho Pi, see if you can find us a way down from here."

The two men nodded and trotted back along the trail, looking for another way down.

"As long as we wait," said Nakor, opening his bag, "anyone want an orange?" He grinned as he pulled out a large one and stuck his thumb in, squirting juice on Praji and de Loungville.

THEY FOUND A trail down, a narrow rocky pathway as treacherous as the first one had been kind. Three men fell to their deaths when a ledge of stone, seemingly solid, had collapsed under their feet. Now the remaining sixty men huddled in a narrow defile, huddled around two campfires, vainly trying to withstand the cold as a sudden change in weather sent the temperature below freezing.

Calis and another three men had gone hunting, for the remaining rations were gone, but could only come back reporting no game was near. The company was too large, said Calis, and game was staying clear. He said he'd leave before first light and try to get as far down the trail as possible, to see if he could find a deer or other large game.

Praji said there were bison roaming the plains and many of them lived in the woodlands of the foothills. Calis said he'd keep that in mind.

Erik and Roo sat shoulder to shoulder, holding out their hands to the fire, while others huddled miserably as close together for warmth as they could.

The only exception was Calis, who stood a short distance away, unmindful of the chill.

Roo said, "Captain?"

Calis said, "Yes?"

"Why don't you tell us what's going on?"

De Loungville, from near the next fire, said, "Keep your mouth shut, Avery!"

Roo spoke through chattering teeth. "Hang me now and get it over with, why don't you? I'm too cold to mind." To the Captain he said, "You and Nakor have been thick as fleas on a beggar since you came back, sir, and, well, if we're going to be getting killed, I'd like to know what for before I close my eyes."

A few other men said, "Yes," and "That's right," before de Loungville's bellow silenced them.

"Next man opens his gob will find my boot in it! Understood?"

Calis said, "No, there's some justice in what he said." He looked at the men nearest him and said, "Many of you will not get home. You knew that when you were given reprieve from your sentence. Others of you are here because you're loyal to the Lion Clan or because you're old friends of Praji's. And some of you are just in the wrong place." He glanced at Greylock, who smiled a little at the last.

Calis knelt and went on, "I've told you some of what we face, and I've warned you that should this Emerald Queen prevail, this world as we know it ends."

The clansmen and Praji's mercenaries hadn't heard that, and several muttered disbelief. Hatonis silenced his own men, and Praji shouted, "He's telling the truth. Shut up and listen."

Calis said, "Long ago the Dragon Lords ruled this world. You may have heard legends of them, but they were not legends. They were real.

"When the men of the Kingdom fought the Tsurani a half century ago, a door was opened, a door between the worlds. The Dragon Lords, who had left this world ages ago, tried to use that door to return. Some very brave and resourceful men stopped them.

"But they're still out there." He pointed into the night sky, and several men looked up at the distant stars. "And they're still trying to get back."

Nakor suddenly spoke. "This woman, the Emerald Queen, she was once someone I knew, a long time ago. She is what you would call a sorceress, a magician. She made a pact with the serpent men and they promised her eternal youth. What she didn't know was that she would lose her soul, her spirit, and become something else."

Nakor continued, "There is very bad magic under that mountain."

Calis said, "You don't believe in magic."

Nakor smiled, but there was little humor in his expression. "Call it tricks, then, or spirit force or anything you like, but those serpent men, they use their powers in a very twisted way. They do evil things that no sane man would think to do, because they are not sane.

"These are not the creatures that mothers tell children of, to make them mind. These are very bad creatures who think that one of the Dragon Lords, named Alma-Lodaka, is a goddess. More, they think she is the mother of all creation, the Green Mother, the Emerald Lady of Serpents. She created them as servants, living decoration, nothing more, but they think they are her 'favorites,' like children she loves, and once they open a door for her return, she will elevate them to the status of demigods. They will never believe that if they do this terrible thing, this Alma-Lodaka will sweep them away along with everything else."

Nakor fell silent a moment, then said, "Calis makes no stories. If this woman, this Emerald Queen, is behaving as I think she is, then things are very bad. Calis, tell them of your father."

Calis nodded. "My father is called Tomas. He was a human boy as all here were. He came to own some artifacts of power, ancient armor and a golden

328 ★ RAYMOND E. FEIST

sword once the property of a Valheru, by name Ashen-Shugar. My father wore that armor and carried that sword through the Riftwar, against the Tsurani, and over the years he changed.

"My father is no longer human. He is something unique on this world, a human body changed by the spirit of the long-dead Dragon Lord who owned that armor and sword."

"Unique until now," said Nakor. "For this Emerald Queen may be another such as he."

The men muttered, and Calis said, "For reasons I only half understand, my father's nature is that of the human boy—"

Nakor interrupted again. "That is for another time. I know why, and these men don't need to." To the men he said, "It's simply true. Tomas is a man, with a human heart, despite his power. But this woman, this one who called herself Lady Clovis a long time ago—"

Hatonis said, "The Emerald Queen is Lady Clovis! It's been nearly twenty-five years since she fled the city with Valgasha and Dahakon."

Nakor shrugged. "It's her body."

"The point," continued Calis, "is that if the Pantathians are using their magic to do with this woman what others did with my father . . ."

Calis spoke briefly of how his father, a boy from the Far Coast, had come to wear ancient armor that magically gave him the memories and powers of one of the ancient Dragon Lords. "Nakor is convinced," he finished, "that this Emerald Queen is a mortal woman he once knew, with magic ability, but still much like you, who is undergoing a transformation much as my father did more than fifty years ago."

"Then another Dragon Lord may soon be among us," finished Nakor.

Biggo said, "Why can't your father settle her for once and for all—then we can all go home?"

Calis said, "There's more to this than two Dragon Lords facing off. More than I'm willing to tell." He glanced at Nakor, who nodded.

Nakor said, "She's not a Valheru yet." He nodded with certainty. "If she was, she'd come flying across the ocean on a dragon. She wouldn't need an army."

Calis said, "If you're completely through?"

Nakor grinned, but without any self-consciousness. "Probably not."

"In any event, someone must return to Krondor and tell Prince Nicholas what occurs here."

"What if only one of us gets back?" asked Luis. "What do we say?"

Calis was silent a moment, then told them, "You must say this: the Pantathians bring a host to take by force what they could not take before by guile. Leading them is one in the mantle of a Dragon Lord who may be able to seize the prize. Tomas and Pug must be warned."

He looked at the faces of the men, orange and yellow from the flicker of the firelight, all discomfort from the cold forgotten. "Just those three things. That will be ample warning.

"Now repeat them: the Pantathians bring a host to take by force what they could not take before by guile. . . ." The men repeated the sentence as if learning a lesson in school.

"Leading them is one in the mantle of a Dragon Lord who may be able to seize the prize." The men repeated that.

"Tomas and Pug must be warned." The company repeated that, too. "You may be asked a lot of other questions; answer truly and do not embellish or color your account. Truth is our only ally in this. But whatever else, you must remember these three things."

Nakor said, "Now, I will help you understand what each of those three things means, so even if you're too stupid to remember more than those three sentences, you might at least answer a question correctly."

A few of the men laughed, but most remained quiet.

Calis turned away and started down the hillside on his hunt, and he wondered silently if he could truly make any of them understand.

DAWN SAW SHIVERING men making their way down the trail, frost crunching beneath their boot heels. More than one man had a fever, and all were weak from hunger. Calis had been ahead of them for two days now, and no sign of game had been seen.

Thankfully, water wasn't a problem, but if they didn't find food soon, men would begin to die. Nakor's seemingly inexhaustible supply of oranges helped, but they would not be enough to keep the men alive in this climate. It was cold during the day, and colder at night, plunging below freezing. Without much body fat, through training and the rigors of travel, the men needed more substantial food. Already some were plagued by the stomach flux from eating too many oranges and nothing else.

Erik had never seen Roo look so pale, and he knew he must look the same. They were moving through fairly thick woodlands, devoid of color as the leaves of fall blanketed the ground.

De Loungville turned to signal a halt, when suddenly a shriek cut through the air and arrows came flying. "Defensive square!" shouted de Loungville.

Erik snapped his shield to the front, kneeling to cover as much of his body as possible while the other men in his squad did the same, forming a large square, roughly fifteen men to a side, ready to take the attack.

The brush and nearby piles of leaves exploded with the forms of the men who had been hiding there, and others came running from nearby hiding places. Erik saw the green armbands and shouted, "It's the snakes' men!"

Steel clashed and swords answered and Erik was suddenly swinging with all his might at a man wearing a full helm. He cleaved through the man's shield, his sword cutting deep into the left arm, then he was dodging a counterthrust as the man fell forward. Roo stepped behind him and took the attacker under the sword arm, killing him before he hit the ground.

Erik spun to his left and struck at another, while Roo turned to face one running at him full force. The second man leaped forward, smashing shield against shield, knocking the smaller Roo backwards.

In the hollow of the square, de Loungville, Greylock, and three other men formed a flying company, ready to plug any breech. De Loungville stepped forward and quickly killed the man on top of Roo, yanking him off and shouting, "Get back in line, Avery! You trying to avoid work?"

Roo rolled to his feet and shook off his dizziness, then half ran, half jumped back into place beside Erik. The battle hung close, with neither side taking the advantage, and Erik wondered how long he could keep this up, as weak from hunger as he was.

Then a shout, quickly followed by another, and men at the rear of the forward portion of the square saw attackers falling, struck from behind by arrows. Calis stood down the trail, quickly taking bead and letting fly, and before they knew someone was behind them, four attackers had fallen.

With the small pause on that one front, de Loungville shouted, "Charge them!" and led his five companions toward the strongest section of the attack.

The attackers were expecting anything but a counterattack, which threw them off balance. Seconds later, they were running for their lives.

Erik chased two men down a narrow pathway, overtaking one and striking him down from behind. The other swung to face him, raising his sword high, and Erik sought to take him with a quick thrust.

The man anticipated this, and Erik's head rang with the shock of a shield bash to the face. Red lights exploded in his vision and he staggered back, raising his shield in reflex.

Hours of training saved his life as an instant later a sword blow rang on the shield. Erik swung blindly, and felt his own sword strike his opponent's shield. His vision cleared in time to avoid another strike and the two men backed away a step, acknowledging that, in the other, each faced a dangerous opponent.

From somewhere behind, Erik heard de Loungville's voice cut through the woods: "I want a prisoner!"

Erik tried to shout, and found his mouth didn't work. He spat and felt a tooth wiggle. He tasted blood and felt his right eye burning as it began to blur with the blood running into it.

Gathering his wits, he shouted, "Over here!"

The man facing him, a large weatherbeaten figure of middle years, stood hesitating for a moment, then took another step backwards. "Over here!" Erik shouted again as he attacked the man, rushing him. The man stood to take the attack, but rather than strike an overhand blow, Erik ducked, threw his shoulder behind his shield, and bashed the man, hoping to knock him down.

The man staggered backwards, and Erik drew back his blade, then danced backwards as the other swordsman lashed out. Erik again yelled, "Over here," and circled to his right, attempting to cut off any avenue of escape.

The man tensed and Erik made ready to counter a blow, when suddenly the man let his sword fall from his hand. He quickly tossed down his shield and took off his helm, which he also threw to the ground.

Erik glanced behind and saw Calis drawing a bead on the man. Erik breathed hard. "Took you long enough."

Calis looked at Erik and smiled slightly. "It just seemed like a long time."

ONCE THE MAN had surrendered, he was affable enough. His name was Dawar, and he was originally from the city of Hamsa, but for the last seven years a member of a company called Nahoot's Grand Company.

Calis, de Loungville, and Greylock interviewed the man while Nakor and Sho Pi tended the wounded. Erik's wounds were superficial: a small cut to the forehead, a cut lip, some loose teeth, and lots of bruises. Sho Pi gave him some herbs to take and told him to sit with his hands over his face doing reiki for at least a half hour, and he might keep those teeth.

He sat on a rock with his hands over his face, elbows on knees, while others around him groaned in pain, those able to do reiki on their own wounds or being cared for by others.

Seventeen men had died in the battle; of the enemy, twenty-four. When Calis had struck from their rear, they had assumed another company was coming and it had broken them, otherwise it would have been worse.

Dawar said that a hundred men had lain in wait. Having spotted Calis passing the day before, a scout of Nahoot's had backtracked, seen the company coming down the trail above, and had returned in time for their captain to organize the ambush.

"Nothing personal," said Dawar. "It was orders. We got this trail and we was told to kill anyone comes this way. It's that simple."

"Who gave you the orders?" Erik heard Calis ask.

"Someone high up in the Queen's command. Maybe Fadawah himself. I don't know. Nahoot's not about to go around explaining everything, you see. He just tells us what to do and we do it."

Calis said, "So they're keeping their flanks covered."

"I guess. Things are pretty crazy and everyone's running around like chickens in a thunderstorm. We don't even know who's coming to relieve us."

"When are they due to relieve you?" said de Loungville.

Erik felt the heat from his hands healing him, otherwise he would loved to have removed them to see what was happening.

"Don't really know," said Dawar. "A couple more days, maybe a week.

We've been out here almost a month, and it's just about got the captain chewing his saddle."

Calis said, "Take him over there."

Erik heard Dawar say, "Captain, I'm wondering. Are you giving me a day, or are you going to offer me service?"

"Why?" asked Calis.

"Well, we're a hell of a long way from anywhere, that's all. My horse is down at the end of this trail, along with all my personals, and it's cold, as you may have noticed. I'd just as soon not be running from your men come sundown tomorrow."

Calis said, "Can we trust this one?"

It was Praji's voice Erik heard next. "As much as you can trust any of these mother-lovers. I know Nahoot by reputation. He's not one of the worst, but he's certainly far from one of the best."

"You'd fight against your own companions?"

"Much as any of you would. Rules of war. I've been given no bonus to die for lost causes." His voice dropped to a near mutter. "Hell, Captain, none of us have been paid in more than a month, and we're far from looting anything, unless it's nuts from squirrels."

There was a moment of silence before Calis said, "Guide us to where your former company is, and we'll give you your horse and turn you loose. No one will follow you as long as you head for Palamds."

"Sounds more than fair, Captain."

Erik heard the man being led away, then he heard de Loungville's voice, low but carrying. "Are you mad? There's still something like seventy or so swords down there."

"But they won't know we're coming at them," said Calis.

"Advantage of surprise?" said de Loungville, his tone one of disbelief.

"It's the only advantage we've got, Bobby," replied Calis. "We're out on our feet. We need rest and food. There's food down there, and horses. If we can take that company, we might even be able to get back to Maharta without interference."

"What are you thinking?" asked Greylock.

Calis said, "If things are as confused on this flank as he says, whoever comes to replace this Nahoot might not have any idea what he looks like. If we're waiting for them, in the agreed-upon place, wearing those green armbands . . ."

De Loungville groaned, and Erik was glad his hands covered his face, to hide the grimace he made.

ERIK WAITED. AHEAD, Calis, Sho Pi, Luis, and Jadow crept along, looking for the sentries they knew must be there. Calis held up his hand, motioned to his right, then handed his bow to Jadow. He tapped Sho Pi on the shoulder and pulled his dagger from his belt. Sho Pi laid his sword and shield on the ground, pulling his own knife. Luis had his out and Calis motioned for him to circle to the left. Calis pointed to Jadow, indicating he was to wait.

The three men, Calis and Sho Pi to the right, Luis to the left, circled out of sight into the evening gloom.

Three moons were out, the middle moon high in the sky, and the large and small moons rising. Erik knew it was only going to get brighter as the night progressed, so that the time right now offered their best cover.

A sudden sound of movement, then a low grunt cut through the night, and then silence. Erik waited for any sound of alarm, but none was forthcoming.

Then Calis was back, retrieving his bow and gesturing to the others to follow. Erik motioned to the line of men behind him and moved as silently as possible down the trail.

A few yards beyond where Calis and the others had stopped he found the dead guard, eyes staring vacantly skyward. He gave the man a quick glance, then got his mind back to the matters at hand.

His nose still hurt, but it was only a dull throb, and his lips were now puffy. His teeth wiggled when he touched them with his tongue, so he tried not to, but found himself constantly probing the loosened teeth. They had rested less than an hour, then Calis had abandoned the dead and left the wounded behind, and had ordered Dawar to show him where his former company's camp lay. Two of the walking wounded now guarded him back up the trail until after the coming fight.

Ahead they saw lights, and Erik wondered how many men there were to be so confident just hours after fleeing a battle. Then he could see movement and realized that they were anxious down there, for at least ten men stood watch around the camp.

But what astonished Erik the most was that no defenses had been erected. There were twenty four-man tents haphazardly scattered around the area, with a large bonfire in the center. The sound of horses carried through the night, and Erik judged a large picket line was situated somewhere on the other side of the camp.

Erik watched Calis, who signaled for him to approach. Erik moved to Calis's side, and the Captain whispered, "I want you to lead the first ten men behind you through the trees over there." He pointed to his right. "Circle around and get ready to hit them from the side.

"They're wary now, but after a few hours of nothing happening, they're going to relax. They may think we're running the other way or not coming down until morning." He glanced at the sky. "It's about four hours until midnight. Once you're in place, be alert but relax. I'm not going to hit them until most of them are asleep."

De Loungville said, "When you hear anything, come running hard. Hit them as fast as you can and numbers won't mean much. They'll be so confused they won't know what's out here in the dark, but only if you act at once."

Erik nodded, and moved back in line. He tapped the next ten men on the shoulder, starting with Roo, and motioned for them to follow him. Natombi, the former Keshian Legionary, grinned as they moved into the woods.

Erik was as quiet as he could be, but he was certain at any minute the alarm would sound. When he was approximately one-third of the way around the camp, he halted the men. A couple of sentries stood opposite their position, barely visible through the trees, but obviously more interested in talking to each other than in maintaining vigilance. Erik hoped Calis was right.

He motioned for the men to sit, indicating they should rest. He signaled Roo to take the first watch. Erik sat down and put his hands back over his face. He felt the warmth return to his hands and was glad he had been taught this healing. He decided he would hate to lose those teeth.

AT THE APPOINTED time, Calis shouted and launched his attack. The camp was slow to come around, as most of the men were asleep.

As they moved to repel the assault from one front, Erik and his ten men raced into their flank.

Erik was on a man coming from a tent before he had his pants on. The man died before he could pull a sword. Another was down before he could turn, then suddenly one faced him, astonishment on his face. He shouted, "They're behind us!"

Erik bashed as hard as he could with his sword and the man went down screaming. Natombi shouted some Keshian war cry, and Biggo let out a bellow to freeze the blood.

Men were scrambling from their low tents and Erik knocked several unconscious with the flat of his blade before they could gather their wits.

Then before he knew it, men were throwing helms, shields, and swords to the ground. De Loungville hurried along, commanding the prisoners be taken to the fire. Half-dressed, dazed, and dispirited, several of them swore openly when they saw how few attackers had routed them.

Erik glanced around, still suspecting treachery, but found only defeated men looking around in amazement. Of Calis's forty-three men, only thirty-seven had been fit for this fight, and they had almost bloodlessly captured nearly two times their own number.

Suddenly Erik felt like laughing. He tried to fight it, but couldn't. He let out a chuckle at first, then started laughing aloud. Then others in his company joined in, and soon there were cheers as Calis's Crimson Eagles had their first victory in a long time.

Calis moved through and said, "Get Nahoot over here."

A man among the captives said, "He's dead. You killed him up the trail yesterday."

"Why didn't Dawar tell us?" asked de Loungville.

"He didn't know, the bleeder. We carried Nahoot down here, and he died at supper. Gut wound. Messy."

"Who's leading?"

"I guess I am," said a man, stepping forward. "Name's Kelka."

"You the sergeant?" asked de Loungville.

"No, the corporal. Sergeant got his head split, too."

De Loungville said, "Well, that partially explains why there was nothing like a defense."

"Beggin' your pardon, Captain," said Kelka. "Are you going to offer us service?"

"Why?" asked Calis.

"Well, we haven't been paid in a while, and as we've got no captain and no sergeant . . . Hell, Captain, you kicked hell out of us with only half our number. I figure you've got to be better than anyone else we're likely to run into if you give us the day's grace."

"I'll think about it."

"Captain, if you don't mind, you going to take our tents?"

Calis shook his head. "Get back over there. I'll tell you what I'm going to do once I decide."

Calis motioned for de Loungville and said, "Get some food into the men, and send someone up the trail to lead the wounded and Dawar down here. I want everyone here by noon tomorrow." He motioned to the captives. "We'll figure out what to do with them in the morning."

Erik sat down, feeling his legs shake. It had been a very long day and he was exhausted, as he knew everyone else in the company was.

Then de Loungville's voice cut through the air. "What! Who told anyone to rest? We've got a camp to make ready!"

Men began to groan as de Loungville ordered, "I want a trench and breastwork dug, and I want stakes sharpened. Bring in the horses and stake them nearby. I want a full inventory of stores, and I want to know who's injured. Then, after we've got this camp in shape, maybe I'll think about letting you get some sleep."

Erik forced himself to stand, and as he moved, he wondered aloud, "Where are we going to find shovels?"

De Loungville shouted back, "Use your hands if you have to, von Darkmoor!"

22

★★

INFILTRATION

CALIS WHISPERED.

Erik couldn't hear the Captain's conversation, but he saw Praji and Greylock nodding agreement.

The prisoners had been moved to a small wash, where a handful of men could easily guard them. De Loungville was interviewing them, against what plan of the Captain's Erik had no idea.

The traditional head start for the losers who surrendered was a day before any hostilities would be resumed. Usually, according to Praji, those who cleared out were left alone, if they kept moving. Erik was lost in thought when Roo approached.

"How are the horses?" asked Roo.

"They're a little scrawny; the grass is poor this time of year and they've been kept too long in the same place. But otherwise they're fine. If we move them a couple of times over the next week, they should put some weight on, especially if I can find a place to shelter them at night from the wind. It's the cold takes weight off them as much as anything else. Their heavy coats are starting to come in, so they'll be all right."

Roo said, "What do you think the Captain has in mind?"

Erik said, "I don't really know. I find it strange he's talking about heading down for Port Grief loud enough so those prisoners can hear."

Roo grinned. "Not if that's where we want the Queen's army to look for us. What next?"

"We've got plenty to do," said Erik. "And we'd better get on it before de

Loungville comes back. He finds us loafing around and there'll be hell to pay."

Roo groaned. "I'm dying of hunger."

Suddenly Erik realized he hadn't eaten except for a quick mouthful the night before. "Let's grab something," he said, and Roo's expression brightened. "Then we'll get back to work." Roo's expression turned dark again, but he followed his friend.

They had done a complete inventory the night before and found that while Nahoot's men hadn't been paid in a while, they certainly were well provisioned. Erik and Roo made their way to the tent they shared with Luis and Biggo—Sho Pi and Natombi had moved in with Nakor and Jadow in another four-man tent—and found the other two sleeping inside. Half a loaf of trail bread, baked only a couple of days before, and a bowl of grain and nuts were sitting by the entrance, so Erik sat, let out a sigh, and picked up the bread. He tore it in half and gave a hunk to Roo, and then scooped up a handful of grain and nuts and started to eat.

The air was chilly, but the sun warm, and after eating, Erik felt drowsy. Looking at Luis and Biggo, he felt the urge to follow their example, but fought it off. There was still work to be done and he knew de Loungville would make it harder on them if he had to tell them.

Erik got up and woke Luis and Biggo. They saw Roo and Erik, and Biggo said, "It had better be good."

"It is," whispered Erik. "Come with me."

Luis looked at Erik with eyes made even more dangerous-looking by the dark circles underneath. As he rose, Erik asked softly, "Got your knives?"

Luis whispered, "Always," and whipped his dagger from his belt in a motion so swift it was almost unseen. "Are there some throats in need of cutting?"

Erik said, "Follow me."

He led them through the tents, moving quickly and pausing often to look around, as if to see if they were being observed. Erik moved to where the digging continued, as men made the quickly dug trench of the night before a deeper, wider barrier.

Reaching the work, he pointed to a stack of freshly cut dowels laying in a bundle and said, "Quickly, before they get loose! Those need to be sharpened and placed around the perimeter."

Roo and Biggo smiled and picked up a piece each as they pulled their belt knives, but Luis glowered. "You woke me for this?"

"Better I than de Loungville, isn't it?"

Luis stared hard at Erik a moment. For a second he held his knife point directed at Erik, then with a grunt he leaned over, picked up a dowel, and started to sharpen it.

Roo and Biggo laughed as Erik said, "That's good. I'm going to see that the horses are moved."

As he left, he looked over his shoulder at the men sharpening stakes. Anyone coming across that trench would have a difficult climb over the rampart because of the stakes; and once they broke camp, they could pack them away.

Erik moved to the other side of the large defensive square. He joined two men fashioning a drop gate out of wood cut from nearby trees. The lack of proper tools was making the job difficult, as they were basically having to cut the timber with the one ax Nahoot's company had carried, then trim the planks with knives and daggers. Erik would have given the small amount of gold in his purse for a proper drag plane and some iron working tools.

Erik knew a little about woodwork, so he suggested they carve some notches and dovetail the planks together as best they could, then lash the whole thing with cord. They could run it out when they needed from inside the compound. They wouldn't be able to break it down and carry it with them, as they had with the gate they had built at Weanat—that one had been lost with most of their other equipment outside the barrow up on the Plain of Djams.

Erik wondered about crossing the plain. Even though they were miles farther south than when they last encountered the Gilani, he knew that to encounter the diminutive warriors could spell the ruin of this mission. At the last he decided there were too many things to worry about, so he'd leave worrying to Calis and de Loungville while he just did the work that needed to be done.

After seeing the gate finished, he noticed the day was rapidly approaching noon. He ordered a couple of fires started and then decided to see if the watch had changed. He found the same men on duty since he had passed them at first light, so he went back into the tents and kicked some protesting men awake, telling them it was their turn on watch.

He was seeing that the mess was in order for the noon meal when de Loungville returned from interrogating Nahoot's men. De Loungville got off his mount and asked, "Is that parapet finished?"

Erik said, "About two hours ago."

"Stakes?"

"Being sharpened and placed now."

"The gate?"

"In place."

"Sally ramp?"

"It's being built—I doubt it will be much use, though; more than a single horse at a time and it might fall apart."

"Has anyone changed the watch?"

"I took care of that a few minutes ago."

"Where's the Captain?"

"Up talking to Greylock, Praji, Vaja, and Hatonis."

"Regular officer's country, eh?" asked de Loungville, taking a cup from near the cook's fire. He dipped it into a bubbling kettle, then blew on the contents before he finally took a sip of hot soup.

Erik said, "If you say so, Sergeant. I'm still new at this."

De Loungville surprised him with a grin, then drank his soup. Making a face, he said, "This needs some salt." He tossed the cup down and stated walking away. "If you need me for anything, I'll be with the Captain."

Erik turned to one of the men near the cookpot and said, "I wonder what that was about."

The man was named Samuel. He had served with one of the first groups taken from the gallows and had been around de Loungville for a long time. "Sergeant has his reasons for doing what he's doing." Then he paused. After a moment he added, "But it's the first real smile out of him since Foster died, Corporal."

Erik started to correct the man, as no one had named him corporal officially, but then thought if it made the men do what needed to be done that much quicker, he'd be better served by keeping his mouth shut. He only shrugged. As the food was almost ready, Erik decided it was time to get the men rotating through the mess, so the sentries could get a hot meal before the next watch.

ERIK OVERSAW THE distribution of horses to those men given one day's grace before being hunted down. Calis made an unusual offer to them: if they would ride directly for the river Dee, to the south, then follow it to the coast before making for either Chatisthan or Ispar, he would send no one after them. He warned them that if they followed him and his men to Port Grief, he would kill every one of them. He also paid a small bonus in gold. The men who were turned loose swore a mercenary's oath to do as bidden and were now getting ready to ride out of the camp.

What surprised Erik was that about twenty of Nahoot's men were being offered a place in the company. They were being kept apart from those trained by de Loungville by being put under Greylock and they would ride with Hatonis's clansmen, but having outsiders at this late juncture was a risk Erik was not sure he would be willing to take. Then again, he decided, that was probably why Calis was the Prince's Eagle of Krondor and he was only an acting corporal.

De Loungville came over and watched as Erik set up the sixty men leaving. They were being given the least desirable horses and knew it, but at least none of them were lame. They were allowed to carry a week's worth of rations and the gold Calis gave them, as well as their weapons. All other baggage and stores were remaining with Calis's company.

A half-dozen riders from Calis's company would shadow the men for a half day, then return. When all were mounted and ready, the order was given and the defeated mercenaries and their escort rode out.

Erik watched them leave, then asked, "Sergeant, why are we taking on those extra men?"

De Loungville said, "Captain's got his reasons. You just keep an eye on them to see they do as they're told, and don't worry why they're here. Just one thing: pass the word that no one is to talk about our previous set-to with the Saaur with those new men."

Erik nodded and walked off to pass word. When he reached the center of the compound, he saw that Greylock was passing out green armbands. Erik took one and said, "What is this?"

"As of this morning, we are now Nahoot's Grand Company." He motioned to where de Loungville was walking, inspecting the stores they'd won. "He's Nahoot. At least, the men who've joined us say Bobby looks the most like him of any of us here."

Erik said, "And Calis figures the Saaur might think we all look alike anyway?"

Greylock grinned. "Never thought you were stupid. Glad to see I was right." He put his hand on Erik's shoulder and walked him away from the men gathering to pick up their armbands. Lowering his voice, he said, "Nahoot's due to be relieved in the next few days. At least, that's what everyone thinks."

"So if we can pass ourselves off, then we can walk back into the Queen's camp and no one will look at us twice."

"Something like that. If those boys are to be believed, things are even crazier down here than they were up north of Lanada. There's a chance we might run into someone who might remember us from up there, but it's a slim one."

Greylock looked around to see who was nearby, then continued. "Seems Nahoot's boys were sent to find us."

"That a fact or a guess?" asked Erik.

"Guess, but probably a good one. The orders were to ride out to this road and keep a lookout for any company riding down out of the mountains that didn't have armbands and didn't know the password. I don't know who they were expecting to come down out of those mountains except us."

Erik said, "You're right. I wouldn't bet against its being us they were looking for."

Greylock shrugged. "Maybe they're concerned we saw something up in that maze of caves and galleries."

Erik said, "I saw enough to think it's not someplace I'm in a hurry to visit again."

Greylock grinned. "How are the horses?"

"Good. We've moved them and they're fattening up on fall grass. There's nothing here to ride that a noble back home would lose sleep over not owning, but for common mercenaries, they're a serviceable bunch."

"Pick me out a good one," Greylock said. "I've got to get back. We're setting new duty to get the new recruits out of our hair and then we're going to wait."

"Wait for what?"

"Replacements so we can head back to join in the assault on Maharta."

Erik shook his head. "We've got a funny way of fighting this war: helping the enemy take their objective."

Greylock shrugged. "Aside from the pain and dying, war can be a pretty funny business, Erik. I've read every written history of war I could get my hands on, and I know this: once a plan of battle is set loose, it takes on a life of its own. And once you make contact with the enemy, the plan has little meaning anymore. It's grab the moment so you can seize the day. Mostly it's hoping the other side makes a mistake before you do and getting lucky.

"Calis had a plan when we started out, but once he and Nakor found what they sought out at the Queen's camp, it's been tossed aside and now he's making it up as we go."

"So he's hoping the other side makes a mistake before we do and that we're going to get lucky?"

"Something like that."

"Then I'll say a prayer to Ruthia," said Erik as Greylock turned and walked away.

Erik thought about what he had seen so far and what he had done, and was forced to concede that Greylock was right. There was little of planning and cleverness in what Calis had done since making contact with the Queen's army, and a great deal of boldness and hoping for luck.

Putting aside such weighty considerations, Erik decided that as long as things were settling down to routine, he'd try to get some work done on his armor and weapons. He returned to his tent and found it empty, as his three bunkmates were off working on finishing the palisades. Erik unbuckled his sword, removed his helm, and stripped off his breastplate. He grabbed a rag and some oil he had liberated from stores and began to work on his armor. He frowned when he saw how corrosion was finding niches to take hold, and set to with a vengeance to expunge all imperfections from his breastplate.

A RIDER CAME speeding over the rise, pushing his lathered horse up the trail for all he was worth. Erik instantly turned and shouted, "Rider coming in!"

De Loungville had the men racing for weapons and taking up positions before the rider reached the gate. Recognizing the rider as one of their own, Erik motioned for the bridge to be run out. The moat and rampart camp had been turned into a first-rate base since Calis had run off Nahoot's company. They had found a wandering herd of bison down a ways in the woods, and some deer, as well as a good supply of nuts. With the food liberated from Nahoot's Grand Company, they were amply provisioned for the time being.

As the rider reached the bridge he reined in, dismounting as quickly as he could. He led the horse across the bridge, which flexed and creaked alarmingly, but which held better than Erik had expected. Shrinking the leather had helped, and it would serve, but it still made him nervous each time a horse was walked across.

The rider tossed the reins to Erik and ran past him to where de Loungville and Calis were approaching. "It's the greenskins," he shouted.

"Where?" asked de Loungville.

"Down the trail. It's a large patrol, maybe twenty of them. They don't seem to be in any hurry."

Calis thought for a moment. "Tell the men to stand down. I want us looking alert, but I don't want anything suspicious."

Erik passed the word as he led the rider's horse away. He found Luis on duty around the picket and told him to walk the horse for a while, to cool her out, then to rub her down and feed her.

He returned in time to see men back at their normal posts, but noticed that every man had a weapon close to hand and many looked on edge. As he walked by, he quietly said, "Take it easy," or "Relax. You'll know soon enough if there's going to be trouble."

Still, it was a painfully slow twenty minutes until the first of the Saaur hove into view. Erik studied them, for he had been too busy staying alive the last time he saw them mounted to study them carefully. Roo came to stand beside him and said, "That's some sight."

"Say what you will about the greenskins, but they know how to sit those impossible mounts of theirs."

The Saaur rode with long legs and easy seats, as if they had spent their lives on horseback. Each rider had a short bow slung across the back of his saddle, and Erik said a silent prayer that the company they had faced before had tried to charge them rather than stand off and shoot. Most of them carried round shields, made of hide over wood, marked with symbols alien to Erik. The leader wore a plume of horsehair dyed blue tied up in a large obsidian ring, affixed to a metal skullcap. The others wore simple metal helms that had large flaring sides and bar-nasals. When the last riders came into view, Erik quickly counted. There were twenty of them, followed by a baggage train of four more horses.

When they reached the camp, they halted and the leader shouted, "Where is Nahoot?"

His accent was thick and he tended to roar, but he could be understood. De Loungville, wearing a helm that covered his eyes, moved to the other side of the bridge. "What is it?" he shouted.

"What have you to report?"

Calis had thought on this and had instructed every man, save the new recruits from Nahoot's company, in what was coming next. "We were ambushed by some men trying to come down this road. We routed them and chased them back up into the mountains."

"What!" roared the Saaur leader. "You were told to send a messenger if you found any of those trying to leave the mountains."

"We sent one!" shouted de Loungville, trying his best to sound angry. "Are you claiming he never reached you?"

"I claim nothing, human," shouted the angry Saaur. "When did this happen?"

"Less than a week ago!"

"A week!" The Saaur shouted something in his own language and half his company started up the trail. The leader said, "We need provisions. You will leave and return to the host. I am not pleased."

"Well, you can bet I'm not pleased you went and lost my runner," shouted de Loungville. "I'm going to make sure General Fadawah hears of this!"

"And imps of the evening will come to have sex with you because you are so lovely," snapped back the officer. Erik suddenly relaxed. If the Saaur was going to fight, he wouldn't be trading insults with de Loungville while dismounting. Whoever this officer was, he had accepted that de Loungville was Nahoot and was content to trade insults with him while the two companies changed places.

"Any trouble with the Gilani?"

"No," grunted the Saaur officer. "Our riders have chased the little hairy humans back into the mountains to the north of here. The ride will be so quiet you may sleep in the saddle." He moved onto the bridge and his huge horse's weight made it creak alarmingly, but it held even if it did bow under the load. He led his animal into camp without noticing. Erik gave a silent prayer of thanks that it held. And he was pleased he wasn't going to be around to see if the bridge held after repeated Saaur use.

De Loungville shouted, "Break camp! I want every man mounted and ready to ride in ten minutes!"

Erik hurried, for like every man there, he knew the longer they were around the Saaur, the better the chance someone would let something slip that would start a fight. He hurried to his tent, with Roo beside him, and found Biggo and Luis already setting about breaking things down. "Roo," said Erik, "grab my kit. I'm going to keep an eye on Nahoot's men."

Roo spared Erik any barb about ducking work, and merely said, "I'll take care of it."

Erik moved to where the twenty men from Nahoot's company waited and saw they were muttering among themselves. Not giving them any chance to decide they might be better off turning Calis in to the Saaur, he shouted, "Get over to those horses and start bringing them up! I want the first six for the officers. Then start bringing them up to the first tent, then the second, and the third, until every other man has a mount. Then get your own gear together and get mounted. Understood!" His tone, as loud and ferocious as he could make it, imparted the proper message: the last wasn't a question, it was a command.

The twenty men moved quickly, several saying, "Yes, Corporal," as they half walked, half ran to the remounts.

De Loungville showed up less than a minute later and said, "Where are the newcomers?"

Erik pointed. "I've got them bringing up the horses for the others, and I'll keep an eye on them."

De Loungville nodded. "Good." He turned without another word and rejoined Calis and Greylock.

The Saaur commander was busy pulling a roll off the back of one of the baggage horses, and Erik turned to watch Nahoot's band. The twenty newcomers were hurrying with the mounts, doing their best to remain orderly, while around them the compound was abuzz with activity. Erik hurried to where his three tentmates were breaking down their equipment, and Roo threw him his bundle. "Did yours first," he said.

Erik smiled and said, "Thanks," as he grabbed his saddle and then ran back to where the newcomers were leading horses. He selected one and quickly tacked it up, then stowed his roll behind the saddle and mounted.

He rode briskly at a trot down the line, as the compound seemed to melt away. Tents were folded, somehow forced into the small packs that carried them, and stacked up to be tied on the back of a baggage animal. The palisades had already been cleared of stakes, which were now being stored away on a baggage horse. Men were in their saddles and getting in line before the last of the horses were brought up by Nahoot's men. The only things they were leaving behind for the Saaur were the moat, the bridge and gate, and some cookfires.

Erik watched as the Saaur camp went up. Ten large circular tents, fashioned from what looked like cane or wooden poles bent over into a semicircle, and covered with hide, were erected. They were so small that he wondered how the Saaur managed to get inside. He elected not to ask to see, and turned his attention to the last men.

The newcomers were ragged in getting themselves organized, but at last they were ready to ride. Erik moved aside as Calis gave the order to leave, and watched as the men rode past him. He also watched the Saaur commander keeping his eye on the departing humans.

There was something in those red and white eyes that seemed suspicious— at least, Erik thought that the case, but then suddenly the commander waved good-bye. Erik found his own hand raised in a parting gesture before he thought better of it. He turned his mount and took his place as last in line.

As he passed over the bridge they were leaving behind for the Saaur, he thought, "How odd. Like old friends bidding each other good journey."

★★

THEY PASSED DOWN from the foothills overlooking the Plain of Djams, entering grasslands patrolled by Saaur companies. Whatever else might have occupied the invaders, a company of mercenaries wearing emerald armbands riding calmly toward the heart of the army wasn't a cause for concern.

Several times they passed camps or signs of camps. Calis judged the Saaur and their allies were still sweeping the area regularly, perhaps to keep the Gilani at bay, or perhaps to guard against others seeking to hinder the southern conquest.

They rode for a week without incident until they came to their first major staging point, a motte-and-bailey construction large enough to house several hundred men and horses. A lookout in the tower high atop the motte called down and there was a squad of Saaur waiting for them at a checkpoint a hundred yards before the gate.

Without preamble, the lead Saaur shouted, "Orders?"

"We're to rejoin the host," said Calis evenly.

"What company?"

"Nahoot's Grand Company," answered de Loungville.

The lead Saaur fixed de Loungville with a steady gaze and said, "You look different."

Keeping his voice rough, de Loungville said, "You spend your evenings sitting up in those bloody damn hills chilling your backside for a while and see how different you look."

The Saaur tensed, as if this wasn't the answer he expected, but Dawar, one of the men from Nahoot's company, said, "Let us get by, Murtag. We don't have time for your games."

The Saaur turned and said, "You I know, Dawar. I should cleave you both for your bad manners."

Dawar said, "Then who would you have left to cheat at knucklebones?"

There was a long silence, then suddenly the Saaur named Murtag let out a bray that sounded like a leather thong being drawn through a drumhead. He said, "Pass, whoreson, but you must camp outside the moat. We are crowded inside. When you come to game tonight, bring plenty of gold."

After they had ridden away from the checkpoint, Erik urged his horse up to Dawar's side and said, "What was that noise?"

The mercenary shook his head and said, "That's their idea of laughter, if you can believe it. Murtag's a bully of sorts, but it's all bluster. Oh, he could cut you in two if he had a mind, but he'd rather have you trembling and pissing your pants, or insulting him back. It's the indifferent ones that get on his nerves. I've gambled with him enough to know. After he's had some drink, he's pretty good company, for a lizard. Knows some funny stories."

Erik smiled. "You've earned a bonus."

A calculating look crossed Dawar's face. "You and me should talk later, Corporal."

"After the horses are bedded," answered Erik.

Erik made his way quickly to where de Loungville and Calis rode, leaning over in his saddle so he could speak quietly to de Loungville. "I told Dawar he earned a bonus."

De Loungville said, "Then you can pay it."

Calis motioned for the company to fan out on the east side of the moat, near another company of men, who ignored their arrival. He turned his horse around and said, "What is it?"

"Young von Darkmoor here is giving away your money."

Erik explained and Calis said, "What's troubling you?"

"He was too quick and easy to bluff us past the Saaur. I don't trust him. I remember he was pretty quick to end the fight, as well, almost . . ."

"As if he wanted to be captured?" finished Calis.

De Loungville grinned, and Erik said, "What is it?"

"Those twenty we kept with us, Erik," answered Calis, "aren't the men we felt most able to trust."

De Loungville said, "They're the ones we most need to keep an eye on."

Erik sat back in his saddle and stared open-mouthed for a moment, then shook his head. "I'm an idiot."

"No," said Calis, "but you've a lot to learn about the less obvious side of warcraft. The twenty men we kept all had answers that came a bit too fast and easy for mercenaries. I think this Emerald Queen has agents sprinkled throughout her army. All twenty aren't agents, I'm sure, but I'm almost certain one or two are, maybe more. So we keep the most likely close by."

"Trusting bunch," offered de Loungville. "Now, look. You and a couple of men you trust, say Biggo and Jadow, keep close to those men, don't let too many of them off duty at any one time, and keep an eye on where they wander. If any of them head into that fortress, I want one of you along." He reached inside his tunic and pulled out a heavy purse. "We lost some gold on the baggage train, but I kept most of it." He opened the pouch and handed a dozen small coins to Erik. "Pass some of this around so that if any one of those twenty lads wants to step into the fort for a drink, you'll be the fellow to buy it for them. Understand?"

Erik nodded. "I'll make sure no more than four of them are free to cause trouble at a time." He turned his horse, put heels to its flanks, and rode back down toward the end of the line.

Calis said, "He's rounding out nicely."

De Loungville said, "Aw, he's still not nearly half mean enough, but I'll fix that."

Calis smiled slightly and turned back to oversee the making of the camp.

★★

ERIK WALKED THE perimeter of the camp, keeping an eye out for anything out of the ordinary. With the fortress at their back, Calis had ordered no rampart and trench dug. The men set up their tents quickly and saw to their stores, and began to settle in for the night.

As he moved along, Erik noticed that the eight men from Nahoot's company that he had put to guarding the remounts were at their posts, talking in pairs, but otherwise where they should be. Four others were bedded down, or at least had been ten minutes before when he had passed their tent. Jadow was watching that group. Four others were working commissary duty. That left four unaccounted for, and if Biggo was doing as ordered, he was close to them.

Erik found Roo in his tent, trying to get some sleep. "I thought you had duty?" said Erik, sitting down to pull off his boots.

"I traded with Luis. He wanted to go into the fortress and see if there were any whores."

The thought of women suddenly had Erik interested, so he stopped pulling off his boots. "Maybe I should check up."

Rolling over, Roo said sleepily, "You do that."

Erik quickly made his way to Calis's command tent, where he found Calis and de Loungville talking with Greylock, who had somehow found a pipe and tabac. Erik found the habit noxious, but had put up with it all his life; smoking was common enough in the taproom at the Inn of the Pintail, though it was discouraged when serious wine tasting was under way. For a moment, Erik wondered what had become of the fancy flint and steel lighter he had possessed back home.

"What?" asked de Loungville.

"I'm going into the fort," said Erik, "if that's all right. Luis is in there, and I think Biggo is there, too."

De Loungville nodded. "Keep alert," he said with a dismissive wave.

Erik walked up the damp hillock upon which the fortress had been erected, and made his way along the perimeter until he reached the gate. It was still open and the guards on duty were almost asleep. A pair of Saaur, one wearing what Erik took to be an officer's mark on his breastplate, were talking inside a hut at the gate, but they ignored him as he walked in.

De Loungville had called the fort a "classic" motte-and-bailey, and Erik was fascinated by its construction. An earthen hill had been raised up and a tower built high upon it. Around this hill and tower, a large open area, the bailey, had been left, with the buildings nestled against the wall, sheltered by it. Suddenly it struck Erik that this is the sort of construction Calis had undertaken at Weanat, but on a much more modest scale. This tower could house a half-dozen bowmen with little discomfort, on a platform thirty feet above the ground. A fifteen-foot-high log wall had been erected around a small village, complete with wooden rampart and earthen reinforcement. An army would have little trouble with such a fortress, but most single companies would have had more than enough trouble to take such a fortification.

Inside there were a half-dozen buildings, all made of wood and covered with daub made from dried mud and straw. Smaller wattle-and-daub huts had sprung up around the larger buildings, and a fair-sized town had evolved. Erik could see why the Saaur at the gate had ordered them to remain outside; it was quite close inside this fortress.

He heard laughing and moved toward what he assumed would be an inn, and once inside he knew he had been correct. The room was dingy with smoke and poor light, but the stench of ale, spilled wine, and human perspiration struck Erik like a blow. Suddenly he was terribly homesick and wished to be nowhere so much as back at the Inn of the Pintail. He pushed down the sudden surge of feeling and made his way to the bar.

The barkeep, a stout man with a florid complexion, said, "What'll be?"

"Got any good wine?" asked Erik.

The man raised an eyebrow—everyone else seemed to be drinking ale or fortified spirits—but he nodded and produced a dark bottle from beneath the counter. The cork was intact, so Erik hoped the bottle was fresh and not re-sealed. Old wine tasted like vinegar mixed with raisins, but you couldn't convince the average tavern keeper he couldn't just stick the cork back in at the end of a day and unseal it again the next and not have his customers complain.

The barman produced a cup and poured. Erik sipped. The wine was sweeter than he would have liked, but not as cloying as the dessert wines made to the north of Yabon. Still, it was acceptable and he paid and indicated the barkeep should leave the bottle.

He glanced around the room and saw Biggo on the far side, trying to look inconspicuous and failing mightily. He leaned against the wall, behind a table where five men gamed with two Saaur. The lizard men were too large for their chairs, but they hunkered down as best they could and seemed intent upon the game. Erik recognized the sound of knucklebones, as they called dice here, rattling across the table and the accompanying shouts of the winners and groans of the losers.

After a few minutes, Dawar stood up and left the game. He came over to Erik and said, "Got a minute?"

Erik motioned to the barkeep for another cup and filled it. Dawar sipped and made a face. "Nothing like the wine from the grand vineyards of home, is it?" he said.

"Where's home?" asked Erik.

Dawar said, "Far from here. Let's go outside for a minute."

Erik picked up the bottle and let Dawar lead him outside into the fresh, cold night air. The man looked one way, then the other, and signaled for Erik to follow him around the corner, into a dark place next to the wall, sheltered above by the palisades.

"Look, Corporal," began Dawar. "Let's have an end to the mummery. You're the company Nahoot was sent to keep from coming this way."

"What makes you think that?" said Erik. "You're the ones that jumped us."

"I wasn't born this morning," said the man with a grin. "I know your Captain's not your Captain, but the slender blond fellow is."

"What do you want?"

"A way to get rich," said Dawar, a greedy glint in his eye.

"How do you propose to do that?" said Erik, moving his hand slowly down to his sword.

"Look, I could maybe get myself a gold coin or two for telling Murtag you're not who you say you are, but that's a gold coin or two, and then I'm back looking for a company to join." He glanced around. "But I don't like what I'm seeing lately, with this grand conquest. Too many men dying for too little gold. There's not going to be much left of use to anyone if it keeps on, don't you see? So I'm thinking I might be a help to you and your captain, but I'll want more than wages and found."

"You'll get ample chance for loot when we take Maharta," Erik said noncommittally.

Dawar took a step forward, lowering his voice. "How long do you think you can keep this up? You lot are not like any company I've seen, and I've been around more than most. You talk funny and you have the look of . . . I don't know . . . some sort of soldiers, without the parade ground nonsense, but tough, like mercenaries. But whatever you are, you're not what you want people to think you are, and it ought to be worth something for me to stay quiet."

"So that's why you covered for us at the gate?"

"Sure. Most of us look alike to the Saaur and Murtag's pretty stupid—don't make that mistake about most Saaur—which is why he's stuck out here running this garrison and not with the main host. I figure I can turn you in any time, but I thought I'd first give you a chance to make me a better offer."

"I don't know," Erik said, holding his wine cup to his lips with his left hand, while his right moved to the hilt of his sword.

"Look, von Darkmoor, I'll stick with you until the end, if the pay's right. Now, why don't you talk this over with Captain Calis—"

Suddenly a figure loomed up behind Dawar in the darkness, and large hands reached around and gripped him by the shoulders. They jerked him around, and as he spun, they grabbed the back of his head and his chin and forced it in the opposite direction, and with a loud crack, his neck was broken.

Erik had his sword out as Biggo stepped forward. "We found a spy," he whispered.

"How could you be sure?" hissed Erik, his heart pounding as he returned his sword to the scabbard.

"I'm pretty sure no one's called you von Darkmoor since we met up with this lot, but I damn well know no man's called the Captain by name since then."

Erik nodded. Strict orders had been passed not to mention Calis by name. "How would he know who you were?"

Erik's heart sank. "I didn't even notice."

Biggo grinned in the faint light. "I won't tell." He picked up Dawar's body and hoisted it across his shoulder.

"What are we going to do with him?" asked Erik.

"Why, we're going to take him back to the camp. It wouldn't be the first drunk carried out of here by his friends, I'm certain."

Erik nodded, picked up the fallen wine cups and bottles, and motioned for Biggo to leave. Erik set the cups and empty bottle down next to the door and hurried after the large man.

For a tense moment Erik expected a challenge at the gate, but as Biggo had predicted, the guards thought nothing of one drunk cheerfully carrying another back to the camp.

THEY RODE OUT at first light. Erik had told de Loungville and Calis of the encounter with Dawar. They had disposed of the body down in a wash, not too far from their campsite, making sure it was fully hidden by rocks. There had been a brief discussion after that and Calis had said whatever they chose to do, they'd do it far from the Saaur and the other mercenaries.

The only attention they received as they got ready to depart was one Saaur warrior who came down to ask what they were doing. De Loungville merely repeated they had been ordered to rejoin the host and the warrior grunted and returned to the fortress.

As Calis had suggested, this fortress was as much for keeping deserters from heading south as it was to keep the main army's flanks free from attack.

At noon, while the men rested and ate trail rations, Calis told Erik to get five of the men from Nahoot's company and bring them over to where he waited with de Loungville. When they appeared, Calis said, "One of your companions, Dawar, got into a fight last night over a whore. Got his neck broken. I don't want to see any repeat of that stupidity."

All five men looked baffled, but nodded and left. Another group of five was brought up to Calis, then another. At last the final four men were fetched to Calis and he repeated the admonishment. Three of the men looked blank, but one of them tensed at news of Dawar's death and instantly Calis had his dagger out at the man's throat.

De Loungville said, "Take them away," to Erik as he and Calis, with Greylock, led the man away to be questioned.

As Erik escorted the two men back down the line, several of the men asked what was going on. Erik said, "We caught another spy."

A moment later a scream cut through the air, from behind a small rise some distance away. Erik looked over while the scream lingered, and when it ceased, he let out his breath.

Then it started up again, and Erik found every man looking off at the ridge. A few minutes later, de Loungville, Calis, and Greylock returned, all with grim expressions. De Loungville looked around and quietly said, "Get them mounted, Erik. We have a lot of ground to cover and little time to do it."

Erik turned. "You heard the sergeant! Mount up!"

Men scrambled and Erik found the sudden motion a release. The sound of the spy dying under torture had set his nerves on edge and made him angry. The sudden movement seemed to lift that anger from him, or at least give him a place to focus it.

Soon the column was moving, heading toward the main army of the Saur and the assault on Maharta.

23

★★

ONSLAUGHT

ERIK BLINKED.

Acrid smoke filled the air for miles, making it difficult to see any distance. Stinging wind carried the smell of charred wood and other less aromatic victims of the widespread fires.

Nakor rode back to where Erik brought up the rear. "Bad. Very bad," he commented.

Erik said, "I haven't seen a lot that wasn't bad in the last week."

They had been traveling for more than four weeks, heading across the plain toward the host surrounding Maharta. As they approached the site of battle, the area began to teem with all manner of passersby: patrols from the invading host, small companies of mercenaries who had decided to quit the city rather than fight—they tended to give Calis's company a wide berth, though two had chanced a parley. When it was clear that Calis wasn't interested in a fight, both companies had agreed to share a camp, and news.

The news was sobering. Lanada had fallen by treachery. No one was certain how, but someone had managed to convince the Priest-King to send his host north, leaving the city under the care of only a small company. The leader of that company had proved to be an agent for the Emerald Queen, and he had opened the gates of the city to a host of Saaur riding in from the southwest. The population had gone to sleep one night after a grand parade. The Priest-King's war elephants, with their razor-capped tusks and iron spikes ringing their legs, had lumbered out the gate, the howdahs on their backs filled with archers ready to rain death down on the invaders. At their side had marched the Royal Immortals, the Raj of Maharta's private army of drug-induced maniacs, each man capable of feats of strength and bravery no sane man could achieve. The Immortals had been promised great glory and a better life when reborn if they died in the service of the Raj.

The next morning the city was in the hands of the Saaur and the populace awoke to the sounds of wailing as the invaders turned each household out, herding everyone, to the last man, woman, and child, to the central plaza, to hear the Priest-King. He had been marched out under guard and had informed the citizenry that they were now subject to the rule of the Emerald Queen. He and his cadre of priests were taken back into the palace and never heard from again.

The host of Lanada that had been sent north to face an army already behind them returned under orders from the Priest-King's General of the Army, who handed over command to General Fadawah, then joined his lord in the palace. Rumors flew through the city, ranging from the Priest-King, his ministers and generals being quickly executed to them being eaten by the Saaur.

One thing was clear, this conquest was coming to a head. With Lanada's downfall a near certainty, General Fadawah had held back a token force at his position north of the city and sent the entire bulk of the host in a circling move around Lanada and down the far side of the river to Maharta. They had moved out only days after Calis's company had deserted.

The benefit to the Queen's army had been a swift strike south with almost no opposition. The detriment had been finding themselves on the wrong side of the river. Now the northern element from Lanada was moving down the main road between the two cities while engineers were throwing temporary bridges across the river some miles north of the mouth.

Erik looked at the blackened landscape; some locals had fired the dry winter grass to avoid being captured by the Saaur, he judged, for the brush fires had been started in several places. Only a cold rain had prevented a major conflagration on the plain.

Erik reflected on the cold weather and realized it was after midsummer back home. By the time they left Maharta, if they left Maharta, it would be nearly a year since he had fled Darkmoor.

One benefit to Calis's company from the swift mobilization of Fadawah's host southward was that most of the invading army was in the grip of turmoil and confusion. Moving closer to the front was surprisingly easy.

A day earlier an officer had tried to demand passes from Calis, who had said simply, "Nobody gave us anything on paper. We were told to move to the front."

The officer had been totally baffled and simply waved them past the checkpoint.

Now they were at the crest of a rise overlooking the river valley below, where the Vedra emptied into the Blue Sea. Erik squinted at the scene below.

Maharta was a city of white stone and plaster, bright in the summer sun, now reduced to grey by weeks of falling ash. It spread across two main islands, while several suburbs had arisen on smaller islands in the delta. The main city was surrounded by a high wall on the northwest, north, and northeast, while the remaining sections were flanked by river, harbor, or sea. Several estuaries and inlets provided a variety of anchorages in the deep channel of the river as well as along the coast. Sprinkled across numerous islands were villages, and on the western shore of the river, a large suburb with its own wall.

Nakor peered at the distant city. "Things move close to a finish."

"How can you tell?" asked Erik.

Nakor shrugged. "See the garrison on this side?"

Erik shook his head. "No. There's too much smoke."

Nakor pointed. "Look, there, at the river and sea, where they join in the delta. There were many bridges there—you can see blackened foundations where they were burned—and some villages on the smaller islands, but there, on this shore, there's a good-sized town, with its own wall."

Erik squinted against the smoke and fading sunlight and saw a spot of light grey against the darker water. Studying it, he thought it might be a walled town, but he couldn't be certain. "I think I see it."

"That is the western precinct of Maharta. It is still holding."

Erik said, "Your eyes must be as sharp as the Captain's."

"Maybe, but I think it's that I know what to look for."

"What are we going to do?" asked Erik.

"I don't know," said Nakor. "I think Calis knows, but then, maybe he doesn't. I do know that we need to be over there." He pointed at the far side of the river.

Erik looked at the massive host marshaled along the riverbank and said, "That seems to be everyone's problem, Nakor."

"What?"

"Being over there." Erik pointed northward and said, "They say there are bridges being built ten miles north of here. If so, why is everyone marshaled down here near the coast? They can't be thinking of swimming across, can they?"

"Difficult swim," Nakor admitted. "Doubt that's what they're going to do. But I expect they have a plan."

"A plan," Erik said, shaking his head dubiously as he remembered what Greylock had told him about battle plans and the realities of war. He sighed. "All we have to do is go through this army, cross the river, and get the defenders to open the gate for us."

"There's always a way," said the little man with a grin.

Erik again shook his head in uncertainty as the order to move down into the awaiting host was given, and suddenly he felt very much like a mouse invading a cat's lair.

IF THE OUTLYING fringes of the host were confused, the heart of the army was strictly under control. Calis noticed several heavily manned checkpoints and veered away from them, and twice had to improvise explanations for provost officers riding patrol. He claimed to be confused about which campsite he needed to locate, and said he was among those who were going to be first across.

Both times the officers assumed that no one would be lying to be the first across the river, so in both cases they merely waved Calis along. But as they skirted around the central position of the army, they got some sense of how things lay.

A large hill was central to the host, with the Queen's pavilion atop it. Around that tent were the officers' tents and rank upon rank of Saaur guard, with Pantathian combat troops arrayed behind them. Then came a series of tents used by Pantathian priests. The air was so thick with their magic it reeked, claimed Nakor. Then the bulk of the army radiated outward like spokes of a wheel.

De Loungville said, "It's a pity there's not another army lurking about in the grass nearby. These lads are so bound to conquer there's nothing remotely defensive about this place."

Erik knew little of warcraft, but after months of working hard to create defensible encampments, even he could see this: there were major flaws in the disposition of this army. "They must be planning on launching the attack soon," he observed.

"Why do you say that?" asked Calis.

"Greylock, what's that word you told me, for supply?"

"Logistics."

"That's the one. The logistics are all wrong. Look at where they've got their horses. Each company has them picketed nearby, but there's no easy way to get water to them from the river. This is going to be a mess in a day or two."

Calis nodded, but said nothing, as he looked around.

De Loungville said, "You're right. This host can't stay here another week without a major blowup. Either men are going to get sick, start fighting, or run out of food and have to eat their horses. They can't stay here much longer."

Calis said, "There," as he pointed.

Erik looked to see a narrow peninsula of sandy ground, near the river's edge, sheltered by tall grasses. They rode down a long incline, through some rocky gullies carved out by rain, and down to a sandy stretch, then back up a small rise, and at last reached the indicated area.

Erik jumped from his horse and knelt near the water's edge. He cupped some in his hand and found it brackish and salty. "They can't drink this."

"I know," said Calis. "Form a team and haul water down from upriver to give the horses something to drink." Looking around as the sun began to set, he said, "We're not staying here very long."

CAMP WAS QUICKLY made and Erik saw to it that the eighteen remaining men from Nahoot's company were always under surveillance. They were not certain exactly what had happened to Dawar and the other man, but they knew it had been fatal and it was clear they didn't wish to meet a similar fate. De Loungville had remarked there might be another agent among them, but if there was, Erik was forced to concede he was far more clever at disguising his nature, for not one of those men tried anything suspicious. Still, Erik billeted them closest to the river, with his own men and the horses on one side of them and the river on the other.

Roo came and found Erik as he was checking to see the horses were fit. "Captain wants you over there." He pointed to where Calis stood with de Loungville, Nakor, Greylock, and Hatonis.

Reaching the mound on which they stood, Erik heard Nakor saying, ". . . three times. I think there is something strange here."

Calis said. "That's a well-defended position—"

"No," interrupted Nakor. "Look closely. The walls are good, yes, but there is no way to bring in reinforcements, yet the man said they were facing fresh soldiers every time they assaulted the walls. Three times in one day."

De Loungville said, "Camp gossip."

"Maybe," said Nakor. "Maybe not. If true, then there is a way from that place"—he pointed toward the small western precinct of the city on this side of the river—"to over there." He then pointed to the distant lights of Maharta. "It might be why they tried so hard to take it last week. If not for a way in, why not leave it and let them starve?"

De Loungville scratched his chin. "Maybe they don't want trouble at their back."

"Bah!" said Nakor. "Does this army look like it's worried about trouble? This army *is* trouble. Trouble soon if they don't get across that river. Soon there'll be no food. Bad . . ." He turned to Erik. "What was that word?"

"Logistics."

"Bad logistics. Baggage train all strung out from here up to Lanada. Men pissing into the river upstream, and soon men downriver got belly flux and bad runs. Horse dung everywhere up to your knees. Men don't get food, men fight. It's simple. They take this precinct"—he made a diving motion—"and take tunnel under river, then up into city."

"There was that tunnel under the Serpent River before," conceded Calis.

Hatonis said, "But there's lots of bedrock under the City of the Serpent River. Our clans dug those tunnels over a period of two hundred years because of the storms of summer, the monsoons. You can't safely cross the bridges when the seas are high and the wind is that strong."

"They get big storms here in Maharta?" asked Nakor.

"Yes," admitted the clansman. "But I don't know what the ground around here is like."

"Doesn't matter," said Nakor. "A good builder, he'll find a way."

"Certainly a dwarf would know a way," said Greylock.

Calis showed a small flash of irritation. "Whatever. We take a risk of getting killed no matter what we do. That's not the point. It's wasteful getting killed to get into a city that has no way out, and we don't know there is a way out of the Western Precinct. We know that across the river is Maharta, and we don't know if there's a tunnel on this side."

"What if I go and find one?" said Nakor.

Calis shook his head. "I don't have any idea how you plan on getting in there, but the answer is no. I want every man ready to move out at midnight.

"Word's been passed there some sort of celebration on tonight. The Pantathians and Saaur are making some sort of battle magic, then tomorrow the northern elements are supposed to hit the city."

Nakor scratched his head. "There are some men building bridges north of the main camp, but they are not finished. Why this? And what tricks do the serpent men have to get this army across that river. They've been conjuring something all day long."

"I don't know," answered Calis, "but I plan on every man being on the other side when the sun's up." He turned to Erik. "That's your job. Those men from Nahoot's company."

Suddenly Erik's stomach tightened. He knew what Calis was about to say. "Yes?"

"Put them around the horses and give them this to drink." He handed Erik a large wineskin that sloshed. "Nakor's dosed it so they'll be unconscious for a while."

Erik felt himself grin as he took the skin. "For a minute . . ."

"If Nakor hadn't given me this drug, I would have told you to kill them," Calis finished. "Now see to it."

Erik turned away, again chilled and, for a reason he couldn't put any name to, feeling shame.

The camp rang with alien sounds, music from distant lands, screams of joy and pain, and laughter, swearing, and, most of all, drums.

Saaur warriors pounded on large wooden drums stretched with hide. The sound echoed across the river like thunder, and rang in the ears like the blood's own pulse. Bloody rites had concluded and now warriors readied themselves for the morning's battle.

Horns blared and bells rang, and on and on pounded the drums.

Hatonis and his men stood near the horses, and Erik quickly saw that all eighteen of Nahoot's men were unconscious. He knew that had any avoided the drug's effect he was to kill them.

Erik returned to Calis and reported, "All eighteen are truly asleep."

Praji said, "If they can sleep through that racket, they are indeed senseless men."

Calis stuck out his hand. "Good-bye, old friends."

First Praji, then Vaja, then Hatonis took it and shook. They and the eight remaining men from their companies would make their way up the river, trying to position themselves to get across the river over one of the northern bridges while the main band attacked. In the confusion of battle they were going to try to slip away and head east, making for the City of the Serpent River. Whatever occurred in the coming days, eventually the City of the Serpent River would have to face the Emerald Queen's might. Hatonis would ready the clans; once they had been nomads, like their cousins the Jeshandi, and if need be, they would roam the hills near the city again, striking at the host, then fleeing into the high forests. For Hatonis knew that this struggle would be settled far from his native city and more than mere strength of arms was needed.

The night was dark, as swift clouds from the ocean blew in to the shore, keeping the moons' light masked. Only those of especially good vision might notice someone moving along the river's edge from any distance away.

Nakor sniffed the air. "Rain coming, I think. Tomorrow, almost certainly."

Calis motioned and Erik turned and signaled the first company into the water. The plan was simple: swim across the swift-running but shallow delta to one of the tiny islands near the city wall and look for a way to climb the southern breakwater and slip along atop it into the greater harbor. They would still strike for the southernmost quarter of the harbor, the shipbuilders' estuary. That small firth fed off the main river and joined with the larger harbor, to form a natural launch point for ships. Calis had complete intelligence from agents who had been on this continent for years, but he knew little about the harbor beyond that. It had never occurred to anyone else that the Emerald Queen might need a navy until Roo brought it up.

After the burning of the shipbuilding facilities, the plan was still simple: steal a boat and sail up the coast to the City of the Serpent River. Erik thought, not for the first time, that simple didn't mean easy.

The water was chilly, but Erik quickly got used to it. The men had wrapped their swords, shields, and armor for quiet, and some of the men had abandoned their heavier arms so as to be able to swim better.

The path taken brought them perilously close to both a picket of the Emerald Queen's host and lookouts in the suburb fortification. Torches on the walls showed clearly that the ruckus from the Queen's camp had alerted the garrison that something was up. Erik hoped they were all watching the lights on the top of the hill and not the rocky shore below their walls.

Every man in the company was a competent swimmer. Those that hadn't had the knack had been trained at the camp outside of Krondor. But when they reached the distant spot that marked their first meeting point, a small sandy island in the mouth of the river, three men were missing. A quick head count showed thirty-two men on that island, exposed to view save for some tall grass and one lone tree. Calis signaled back into the water and Erik waited until everyone else was in before taking one look around for the three missing men, then he followed after the others.

The channel deepened and the current got stronger as they neared the city, and the water tasted saltier. A cough, sputter, and splash nearby were followed by a choking sound, and Erik knew someone else was in trouble. He swam toward the sound of splashing in the darkness, but as he reached the spot only silence met him. He glanced around in the gloom, then listened, and finally started swimming toward the distant shore.

Suddenly he skinned his knee and found he was clambering across an underwater islet. Then he was suddenly sucked downward and pulled back into a deeper, swifter current, and struggling to keep his head above water.

His armor weighed him down and Erik had to will himself to keep his head above water. He had trained for hours to swim with his sword and shield on his back, but nothing in training had prepared him for this nightmare of laboring through a wet inky darkness.

His chest burned and his arms felt leaden and he had to force himself to move forward. Lift one arm and throw it forward, and kick, lift the other and kick. He moved forward, with no idea how far he had come and how far he had left to go.

Then he heard a change in the sound before him and realized it was water lapping against rocks. More, he heard men quietly coughing, cursing, and blowing water from their noses. He lashed out with his last vestige of strength and hit a rock face first.

Red light exploded behind Erik's eyes, then collapsed into a ball that receded away from him in a tunnel of inky blackness.

Erik choked, spewed water from his mouth and nose, then vomited. He turned over and struck his head against a large rock. Roo's voice sounded in his ear. "Don't! You'll knock your wits out of your silly head again. Lie still!"

Erik hurt. His body felt like one large cramp and he had never felt so foul in his life. "You drank a lot of ocean," said Biggo, nearby. "If I hadn't been standing on the rock you swam into, I don't know if we'd have found you to pull you out."

"Thanks," said Erik weakly. His ears rang, and his face ached, and his nose hurt, and generally he wasn't certain he was glad to be alive.

Calis came and said, "Can you move?"

Erik stood, wobbly, and said, "Of course." As much as he might like to sit for a while, he knew that the alternative to moving was being left behind.

Erik looked around. Then his eyes narrowed and he counted. Thirteen men stood on the rocks. Looking at faces, he turned to Biggo and said, "Luis?"

"Out there," said Biggo, with an inclination of his head toward the river.

"Sweet gods," said Erik. Thirty-two men had gone into the river, and only thirteen had made it across.

Sho Pi was nearby and he said, "Perhaps some of them are washed up at different places on the shore."

Erik nodded. But he knew it was more likely they were swept out to sea or drowned in the river.

Erik saw they were out on the tip of the southern habor breakwater, a long finger of rocks built up to prevent tidal flow interfering with shipping in the harbor. Calis motioned and each man fell into line. They moved carefully along the heavy rocks piled high to form the breakwater. In the darkness the footing was dangerous. After about a half hour of moving slowly, they reached a flat road formed across the top of the stones. Nakor whispered, "They must pack dirt on it so they can bring more rocks out in wagons if they need to repair the breakwater after a storm."

Calis nodded and motioned for silence. He pointed to a tiny light in the distance. There was a small building located a few hundred yards ahead, where the stone breakwater turned into a proper jetty. It was certain to be defended.

Glancing toward the harbor mouth, Erik felt his stomach contract. "Captain!" he whispered.

"I've seen," came the answer.

Erik looked back and saw the others had followed his gaze and were now looking at the harbor. Three ships had been sunk in the harbor mouth, to ensure no raiders from the invading fleet could enter the harbor; and, nestled like chicks against a mother hen, a flotilla of ships hugged the docks. But none of them looked to be of shallow enough draft to get past the hulks blocking the harbor.

The pair of guards in the watch building were vigilantly watching across the river, so they were taken without knowing that Calis had slipped up behind. Using only his hands, Calis quickly disabled both men and lowered them to the floor of the hut.

Motioning for the men to gather around, Calis said, "The orders are simple.

"We wait until the sounds of battle in the morning. The Emerald Queen may try to slip some small boats around the jetty, so there may be a few defenders heading this way, but most of the city's army will be on the northern walls, protecting the landward side of the city. Then we move straight up this jetty, head off left toward the shipbuilders' estuary, and fire everything in sight. If anyone tries to stop you, kill him.

"Then we head back to the main docks, steal a boat of as shallow draft as we can find, and try to get out of this mess. If you can't get back to the harbor, try to get out of the city on the northeastern side, and make overland to the City of the Serpent River." He glanced from face to face. "It's every man for himself, lads. No one is to linger for a comrade. If no one gets back to Krondor, then this has all been for naught. If most of us are going to die, let's make it worth something."

Grim nods of agreement were the only reply he received. The men took what shelter they could around the small hut and waited.

ERIK SHIVERED. HE dozed, but the throbbing in his head made sleep impossible. He couldn't believe how tired he felt. And the throbbing in his nose drained him like no pain he had known before.

"It's broken," said Roo.

"What?" said Erik, turning and discovering his friend could be seen in the predawn gloom.

"Your nose. It's a mess. Want me to reset it?"

Erik knew he should say no, but he simply nodded. Roo had been through enough street fights to know what he was doing. Roo put his hands on either side of Erik's nose and, with a swift move, pushed the pieces into place.

The pain shot through Erik's head like hot iron spikes. His eyes watered and he thought he would faint; then suddenly the pain drained away. The throbbing that had bothered him all night lessened, and he felt as if his face might not fall off after all.

"Thanks," he said, wiping away tears.

A loud roar precluded any reply. It was as if the skies parted and a thousand dragons vented their rage. There came a hollow rush of sound like creation's largest waterfall echoing through a gorge, and a wind sprang up from the far shore.

"Oh, my!" said Nakor. "This is some trick!"

Across the river a giant light of brilliant white, edged in pale green, sprang up and arched across the river, slowly spreading and fanning out as it climbed into the sky. Men and Saaur riders moved tentatively upon it, then kicked their balky mounts forward. The horses moved slowly, following the rising bridge of light.

Nakor said, "Now we know why they massed near the mouth of the river across from Maharta—why no bridges. They're using the priests' spells to get the army across."

Calis said, "We leave now!"

He rose and moved down the jetty. They reached the main dock area without incident, ignored by those on the dock, who were transfixed by the sight of the rising bridge in the sky across the river. Erik forced himself to pay attention to his leader, and pushed more than one man after Calis.

They ran through a series of narrow streets, along a thin neck of land, between bodies of water. Erik had no sense of where he was, but he thought he might find his way back the way they had come.

Then they were moving left, down a major boulevard. A company of horsemen dashed past, dressed in white tunics and trousers, with red turbans and black vests. Another man similarly dressed reined in next to Calis a moment later and shouted, "Where are you going?"

"We have our orders!" Calis shouted back. "The estuary is at risk!"

The man seemed confused by the answer, but the incredible sight of a bridge of light rising across the river unnerved him enough that he accepted Calis's story and rode on.

They reached another street, which crossed the top of the one they were on, and Erik halted. Ahead was a dry dock. It loomed high into the sky, and upon it was the keel of a great ship pulled up for hull scraping. The wooden frame stretched back for what Erik judged a full four hundred feet, and the rear of the ship protruded out beyond that. He looked beyond it and saw the estuary, a mighty lake adjacent to the main harbor. The estuary was ringed by construction yards like this, forming a nearly perfect three-quarter circle around it. Either end was more than a quarter mile off.

De Loungville said, "Take some men and go that way." He pointed off to the right. "Go to the far end, and start burning everything in sight as you come back. Try to get back to the harbor. But remember, it's every man for himself!" At the last, he reached out and put his hand on Erik's arm and squeezed briefly, then he was off running to the left.

Erik said, "You three," indicating Roo, Sho Pi, and Nakor, the men nearest him, "come with me."

As he ran, his head thundered, and he tried to ignore the pain. His knees were wobbly, but his heart pounded and his nerves were taut, and after a few moments he felt his head clear a bit.

Riders came speeding past, heading back the way Erik's men had come. He barely got out of the way of one man, who seemed willing to ride him down rather than control his horse. The expression on the guard's face told Erik this was no movement of soldiers under order, but men put to flight by terror.

Glancing skyward, Erik couldn't blame the men. The bridge now reached a quarter of the way across the river, and upon it stood thousands of Saaur, their battle cries carrying across the distance like a thunder peal without end.

Erik rounded a bend and saw two shipyards beyond where he stood. To Sho Pi, the nearest man, he said, "Get down there and fire everything. Nakor, help him."

Erik grabbed Roo and moved to the hut before another gigantic cradle of wood. This one was empty. The door to the building was barred. He quickly made his way around it and found a single window. Looking in, he saw no signs of habitation. Using his shield, Erik smashed the window, and said, "Now put your size to good use." He boosted his small friend through the window.

Roo hurried and opened the door and Erik said, "Anything to burn?"

"Some parchment and a torch. Got any flint?"

Erik reached into his belt pouch and pulled out some flint. Roo took it and his dagger and struck a spark on the torch, then nursed a small fire into life.

When it was burning, he pushed it down into the pile of parchment, until it caught; then they hurried out of the hut. Erik led Roo down to the base of the cradle, and saw a pile of old wood scraps. He gathered them by the base and had Roo set them alight. They burned slowly, with dark smoke, but at last a good-sized fire was started.

Erik glanced around and saw a little smoke from the far end of the estuary, but no sign of any major fires. He motioned to Roo to come along and they made their way to the next establishment, and found it guarded by a shipbuilder and his family. Three men of middle years, as well as four sons in their teens, stood ready to fight. They were armed with hammers and pry bars.

"Stand aside," said Erik.

"What do you mean to do?" demanded the oldest man there.

"I hate saying this to any master of craft, but I'm putting the torch to your shop. That cradle and your tools go as well."

The man's eyes narrowed and he said, "Over my cold body."

Erik said, "Look, I do not want to fight you, but no one is going to build ships for the Emerald Queen. Do you understand?"

"Man, it's all I have!" said the builder.

Erik pointed with his sword to the distant bridge of white and green moving slowly toward them and said, "They will take all you have. They will rape your women and kill you, or make you slaves and force you to build ships for them, and they will sail them to my home and kill me and mine."

"What would you have us do?" the builder demanded, as much a plea as a challenge.

"Take a boat and sail away, friend," said Erik. "Get your sons and daughters and get away while you still have time. Go to the City of the Serpent River and hold there as long as you can, but if you don't leave now, I will kill you if I must."

Biggo and two other men came running up behind Erik, and the sight of five armed men proved too much for the shipbuilder. He nodded and said, "We need an hour."

Erik shook his head. "I can give you five minutes, then I start burning." He saw a small sailing boat anchored in the estuary. "Is that yours?"

"No, it's my neighbor's."

"Then steal it, and go."

Erik motioned for the men to spread out, and as Biggo passed, one of the sons shouted, "No, Father! I'll not let them burn our home!"

Before Biggo could turn, the young man struck him from behind with a pry bar, bringing it straight across the large man's neck. Erik cried, "No!" but was too late. The loud crack told him Biggo's neck had been broken.

Roo charged the young man, bashing him in the face with his shield, knocking him backwards into his brothers and uncles. The young man lost the pry bar, which clattered away across the stones, and Erik looked down at the motionless form of Biggo.

The shipwright and his family stood motionless as Roo stood over the boy, his sword poised to end his life. Erik stepped over and grabbed his friend, pulling him away. "Why?" he demanded, as he leaned over the now terrorized youth. Grabbing him by the tunic, he lifted him by main force with one arm, until he was nose to nose with him. "Tell me why!" he screamed into his face.

The boy's face contorted with terror. Then Erik heard a woman's voice say, "Don't hurt him."

Erik turned and saw a woman, who stood with tears streaming down her face. "He's my only son."

Erik shouted, "He killed my friend! Why shouldn't I kill him now?"

"He's all I have," said the woman.

Erik felt the anger drain away. He pushed the boy toward his mother and said, "Go." The boy took a half step, then Erik screamed, "Now!"

Turning to Roo, he said, "Burn it all!"

Roo carried a torch and hurried into the home of the family, who stood watching helplessly. Erik said, "Get to that boat and sail away. Otherwise you will all die."

The father nodded and led his band away, and Erik knelt by Biggo. Rolling the big man over, he saw his eyes wide. Suddenly he heard laughter and turned to find Nakor standing behind. "He looks surprised."

Erik suddenly heard himself laugh, for it was true. No anger, or pain, but amazement was etched on the face of the big man.

Erik stood. "I wonder if the Goddess of Death is everything Biggo expected her to be." Then he turned and saw Roo emerging from the building, smoke coming through the door after him.

"Come on," Erik said. "We're almost out of time."

Roo looked across the distant river and saw the bridge was now arching upward toward the midpoint of the river. Sounds of battle, screams and the clash of arms, rang from the north, and Erik knew the wall was likely breached or would be soon as the defenders ran in terror from the magic of the Emerald Queen and her army.

From the far end of the estuary, clouds of smoke rose, heralding the work done by Calis and his company. Sho Pi and two other men raced to the next building and set it ablaze, while Erik and Roo went down a series of stone steps to a low assembly point, a series of wooden sheds on a rocky point. These they quickly started burning. Nakor hurried ahead.

Reaching the quayside, they discovered the fire had spread to the other side of the street and was growing in strength. Erik ran along until he came to the next construction site and started setting fires.

As he moved back toward the main street, Erik noticed a flood of people running along, many carrying bundles, and he knew the enemy was somewhere inside the city. Roo tugged on Erik's sleeve and he said, "What?"

Roo pointed and said, "It's the Captain!"

Through the gathering press of men and women, Erik caught sight of Calis, Nakor, and de Loungville. Then they were swallowed up by the crowd.

"Head for the harbor!" Erik called out, in case any other of his band was nearby.

He and Roo made their way as best they could, Erik using his bulk and strength to push through the throng, Roo staying close behind him. He lost sight of the others.

Down a side street they overtook de Loungville. "Where's the Captain?" shouted Erik.

"Somewhere ahead up there."

Erik noticed de Loungville had picked up a cut to his arm, and had hastily wrapped it. "You all right?"

De Loungville said, "I'll live for the next few minutes."

"Where's everyone going?" shouted Roo.

"Same place we are," answered de Loungville. "The docks. The city's about to fall and everyone is going to be looking for a boat. We've just got to get one before anyone else."

Roo glanced over his shoulder. "At least we got the shipyards ablaze."

De Loungville said, "At least we did that."

Then it started to rain.

24

★★

ESCAPE

ERIK TURNED.

"The fires!"

"What do you expect us to do?" the sergeant asked as increasing numbers of people swarmed by him.

Suddenly Calis appeared, forcing his way back to where the two of them stood. Then Nakor and Sho Pi were at his side. "We have to go back!" shouted the little man.

"What can we do?" demanded de Loungville.

"We have to keep the fires burning," said Nakor. As if to taunt them, the rain increased in urgency, turning from a light sprinkle to a more insistent tattoo. "If we get them hot enough, only the worst storm will put them out."

Calis nodded. They started moving toward the fires, and Erik looked around for Roo. In the faint hope he could be heard over the din, Erik shouted in the King's Tongue, "Back to the estuary! Back to the fires!"

Whatever else might be taking place in the city, there was a full-scale riot brewing near the waterfront. Soldiers sent to keep order were joining in the general run for the ships. That the harbor mouth was now jammed by the hulks and only shallow-draft boats could manage to slip out seemed to be of no concern to the citizenry of Maharta.

Ships' crews tried their best to fend off citizens seeking a haven, and several captains raised sail to put some distance between the docks and their craft. A half-dozen horsemen rode furiously down the street, and men and women screamed as they attempted to get out of the way.

Erik shouted, "Get the horses!" and as the lead animal shied at the press of humanity before it, Erik leaped and took a hold on the arm of the rider, catching him off guard. Erik found surprising strength as he yanked the man from his saddle, given how beat-up he felt. With one crushing blow, he knocked the man unconscious, throwing him to the ground. It was probably a death sentence, as the crowd would trample the man, but Erik had no sympathy for someone who would ride down women and children to make good his own escape.

The horse's eyes were white with fear and its nostrils flared. It tried to back up and felt the horse behind, and without hesitation it kicked out. The flying hooves caught an innocent trader carrying his last half-dozen jars of valuable unguents, sending them flying through the air to smash on the stones as the stout man was knocked almost senseless. Erik spared a moment to grab the man and haul him to his feet with one hand while gripping hard on the horse's reins with the other. He shouted at the merchant, "Stay on your feet, man. If you fall, you die."

The man nodded, and Erik let him go, having no more time to spend. He mounted and saw that Calis and the others had followed his example, save for Nakor, who was being attacked by the one remaining rider. Erik kicked hard at the flank of his animal, and the frightened gelding leaped forward. Erik's sure hands guided him through the press to where Nakor struggled to avoid being skewered by a scimitar. Erik took out his own blade and with a single roundhouse blow took the rider out of his saddle.

Nakor sprang to the now-empty saddle and said, "Thank you. I grabbed the reins before I thought of how I was to get him to give up his horse."

Erik urged his animal past Nakor's and took off up the street after Calis and de Loungville. The two remaining riders seemed content to let them keep the horses as long as they were allowed to keep their own, and did not try to interfere with their passing.

The bulk of the horses parted the swarming mob that would have swept away men on foot. Once they were back on the street leading to the fires, the crowd thinned out. The rain was steady, and as they rounded a corner alongside the estuary, they saw the fires were beginning to abate.

Eric kept as close to the flames as possible, as there he had the least trouble passing the throng running through the street. The horse continued to shy from the flames, but Erik's firm seat and short reins kept the animal under control.

At the end of the estuary, where the first fire was set, the large ship's cradle and hull were almost completely intact, save for some scorching, and the once brisk fire was now guttering. Erik saw an abandoned house across the street and rode there. Leaping from the saddle, he swatted the horse on the rump, sending it away.

Running inside the house, Erik found furnishings turned every which way.

Looters, perhaps, thought Erik, or a family desperate to clear out their few valuables before the fire reached them. He grabbed a chair and ran across the broad street, to the top of the jetty that overlooked the fire and tossed the wooden chair into the flames below. He made several quick trips across the rainy street and every loose piece of furniture made its way into the fire. As Nakor predicted, once reaching a certain heat, the fire grew, despite the rain, which seemed to be leveling off at a steady drizzle rather than a serious downpour.

In the next house, Erik found more loose flammables and threw them into the growing fire. At last he felt certain the cradle and hull would stay alight, but as he looked down the quayside, his heart sank. His was the only fire burning strongly enough to withstand the rain, and there was only so much one man could do.

He hurried to the next fire, which was almost extinguished, and found a store across the street. The large wooden doors had been forced open, one hanging from a single hinge while the other lay on the street. Erik picked up the one door and carried it to the edge of the street overlooking the shipyard below. He tossed the wooden door as far as he could and it sailed down to land on the edge of the sputtering flames. If anything, it banked the fire even more.

Erik swore as he hurried back to the shop. The front of the store was almost intact; whoever had pried open the doors had taken one look and run off. The store was a chandlery, with nothing of value to a looter. Erik hurried through and in the rear he found yards of sail. More, he found sealing pitch in barrels. He quickly rolled one out through the ruined storefront, and across the street. There he picked up the barrel. He threw it so it landed squarely on the flames. The barrel struck with a satisfying crack and quickly the pitch began to burn. Erik took a step away and then a fountain of flame sprang skyward.

Nakor ran up and said, "What did you find? That was a good 'whoosh'!"

"Pitch," answered Erik. "Inside." He turned and the little man followed after. Nakor scurried around, looking at everything he could find. He came away with several smaller kegs and put them aside out front, then hurried inside. A moment later he came out, stooped over, pushing a barrel as Erik was returning from putting a second barrel on the flame.

Erik paused and turned to look at the western sky. The bridge of light was nearing the apex of its arc, the Saaur and mercenaries at the leading edge standing hundreds of feet above the water.

Nakor said, "Wish I had a trick, boy. If I could make that thing vanish"—he snapped his fingers—"that would be something, watching them all fall into the river."

Erik got another barrel and side by side they rolled them down the cobbles, toward the third builder's yard. "Why doesn't some magician around here think of that?" he asked, nearly panting from the exertion.

"Battle magic is difficult," said Nakor as he pushed the barrel along. "Magician has a trick. Another magician counters the trick. Third magician counters the second. Fourth magician tries to help the second. They're all standing around trying to best one another and the army comes along and chops them up. Very dangerous and not many magicians willing to try.

"Surprise is the thing." He paused as he reached the ramp leading down to the lower landing where the main building of the shipyard was ablaze, and let the barrel roll away with a guiding kick. "That trick there would be very easy to counter, if you gave a powerful magician the time to study it. Lots of Pantathians working together on that bridge. Lots of serpent priests concentrating together. Very difficult. Easy to disrupt. Like unraveling a bag. You pull the right thread at the seam, and it all falls apart." Erik looked at him expectantly. Nakor grinned. "I don't know how. But Pug of Stardock or maybe some Tsurani Great Ones could do it."

Erik closed his eyes a moment, then said, "Well, if they're not going to show up to help, I guess we have to do it ourselves. Come on!"

As they ran back toward the chandler's, Nakor continued, "But if Pug or some other powerful magician was to try, the Emerald Queen has even more magicians ready to burn him to a cinder if he . . ." He stopped. "I have an idea!"

Erik halted, gasping for breath. "What?"

"You go find the others. Tell them to steal a boat here, in the estuary. Don't wait. Leave now. Get out of the harbor fast. I'll take care of the fires!"

Erik said, "Nakor, how?"

"Tell you later. You gave me great idea! Now go! Leave soon!" The little man hurried back toward the chandler's, and Erik took a deep breath and turned. He willed his exhausted body into one more run and set off to look for Calis and the others.

AT THE FAR end of the estuary, Erik found Calis, de Loungville, and Sho Pi working hard at stoking a fire. Two dead guardsmen near by told him someone had objected.

The rain increased in tempo and Erik found himself soaked to the skin as he reached Calis. "Nakor says to get a boat and leave, now."

Calis said, "There's too much here left intact."

"He said to tell you he'd take care of it. He's thought up a great trick."

Instantly Calis dropped a long board he was about to toss on a sputtering bonfire and said, "Did you see any boats?"

Erik shook his head. "But I wasn't looking for any."

They hurried back up the road until they came to the first stone stairway leading down to a lower section of the docks, where some small fires still smoldered. The rain was starting to fall in earnest, a drenching downpour that obscured the mystic arch that now hung more than half the way between the opposite bank and the city.

Peering through the rain, Erik said, "There's something out there."

He pointed. Calis said, "It's capsized."

They moved along the edge of the estuary, and more than once thought they had seen something only to find an overturned hull or smashed bow. Then Sho Pi said, "There! Moored to a buoy!"

Calis tossed aside his weapons and dove in. Erik took a breath and leaped after him. He followed his Captain by the sound of splashing more than anything else. Each stroke threatened to be his last as fatigue and cold seemed to leech what little strength Erik had left.

But then he came alongside the craft. It was a fishing smack, with a deep center compartment half-filled with brine to keep the fish fresh. The single mast lay along the port gunnel, lashed in place. "Any small-boat sailors?" asked Calis.

Half falling as he pulled himself inside the boat, Erik said, "Just what I learned on the *Revenge*. I'm from the mountains, remember."

De Loungville peered inside the sail locker. "No sails, anyway." He reached down along the gunwale of the boat and found two pairs of oars.

Calis sat down and took one pair and fit them in the oarlocks, while de Loungville cut the boat free from the mooring buoy. By the time Calis had taken a third pull, de Loungville had unshipped the second set of oars and was pulling along in time with Calis.

Sho Pi found a rudder and tiller and set them up, while Erik sank deeper into the boat. He was soaked to his skin, battered, and exhausted, but he almost gave thanks for being able to simply sit and not have to move.

"Anyone see Roo?" asked Erik. "Or Jadow or Natombi?"

De Loungville shook his head. "Where's Biggo?"

"Dead," replied Erik.

Then de Loungville said, "Find a bucket. We're going to be swimming if we keep taking on water."

Erik looked around and in a bait box found a large wooden bucket. He stood there a moment, then asked, "What do I do?"

"Look for pools of water, fill the bucket, and pour it over the side," answered de Loungville. "It's called bailing."

Erik said, "Oh," and knelt. The boat had a bilge grate, and he saw water collecting under it. He moved the grate and dipped the bucket, and filled it half full.

Water wasn't coming in save for the rain, and he didn't have to work hard to keep the water contained in the bilge. Erik looked ahead.

A shallow flow out the south end of the estuary provided a direct course into the river's mouth. Calis shouted to Sho Pi, "Steer that way. The deeper channel for the big ships leads into the main harbor. This smack might be able to steer between the hulks in the harbor, but I don't want to chance it."

Erik said, "With the chaos in the harbor, we would be trading one mess for a bigger one."

De Loungville said, "Just keep bailing."

PUG SAT UP, as a strange keening filled the air. It was the dead of night at Stardock, and he had been asleep. He pulled on his robe as the door to his sleeping quarters was pushed open. Miranda, wearing a very short and sheer sleeping shift, said, "What is that?"

Pug said, "An alarm. I've established wards throughout Novindus, so I could keep track of what's going on down there without risking calling too much attention to myself." He waved his hand and the sound ceased. "The city of Maharta."

They had come to share a quiet sense of each other over the weeks Miranda had been staying with Pug. She found it amusing that so many of the "mysteries" surrounding him were really nothing more than sleight-of-hand.

When he "vanished," he was usually nearby, but keeping out of sight. He used a magical gate to leave Stardock and return to Sorcerer's Isle at will, and usually appeared there at night. Meals were waiting for him, as well as his laundry, much to Miranda's delight.

Pug regarded the dark eyes that studied him. "What do you intend to do?" she asked. "Go there?"

"No," said Pug. "There might be a trap. Come along. I've got something interesting to show you." He led her out of his personal quarters in the tower at the center of the keep of Stardock, and down the stairs.

"And why don't you put some clothes on? You're quite a distraction in that nothing you sleep in."

Miranda gave him a half-smile as she ducked into her own quarters, grabbed a dress, and slipped it over her head. Stockings, shoes, and the rest she'd worry about later.

She returned to the hall and followed Pug down the stairs. She had sensed over the weeks they had been together that Pug found her attractive, and on several occasions had wondered about him in a more personal way, but neither had broached the topic or acted upon it. She had slept alone in a room close to his every night since following him to Stardock.

A strange sort of trust had built up between them, for while Miranda refused to reveal much about herself, she had a quick mind and fast wit and the same dry sense of humor Pug had developed over the years. He had given her the run of the place, and she had been in most of the rooms, but not all. A few rooms were locked, and when she asked about them, he said there were things he was unwilling to share with anyone, and would change the subject.

He made a motion with his hand as he approached one such door, and it swung open without a touch. She understood the principles involved in the spell, but had sensed nothing of magic when she had investigated the door a month earlier.

Inside the room was a large assortment of scrying devices. A round object lay beneath a blue velvet cover, and as he removed this, she saw a perfect globe of crystal.

"This was a legacy from my teacher Kulgan, who died many years ago. It was fashioned by Althafain of Carse." She nodded in recognition of the name of the legendary artificer of magic items. As he passed his hand over it, the heart of crystal turned opaque, a milk-white cloud forming within the ball. With another pass of his hand, he brought a rosy glow to the cloud within the orb. "This device gave him the first hint I had some talent"—his voice fell low as he added—"a very long time ago."

"What can it do?"

"It's a sighting device, and the wonderful thing about it is that it is very subtle. Those being watched have to be very alert to sense its use." He sat on a stool and motioned for Miranda to sit nearby.

"The problem, though, is that what makes it subtle makes it very stupid. If you don't know what you're looking for, it's no help at all.

"Fortunately, I know where I placed each ward." He squinted a little, and Miranda felt magic turning and being adjusted as Pug said, "Let's see what is happening in Maharta. It must be midmorning there."

He focused his will, and the city of Maharta was revealed in the glass, as if viewed from the clouds by the birds. It lay in smoke and cloudy darkness.

"What tripped your ward?" asked Miranda.

"That's what I'm trying to . . . Here, I think."

The point of view in the glass shifted, and across the river he saw a bridge of light, and an army upon it. After viewing it for a moment, Pug closed his eyes.

He opened them again after a moment. "One thing about the Pantathians: there's little about them one might call refined. Unless I attacked them directly, there's no possible way they could know I was watching."

"Is Maharta going to fall?" asked Miranda.

"It appears that's the case," answered Pug.

"Calis?"

Pug said, "I'll try to find him."

Pug closed his eyes and the scene in the ball shifted, and as he opened them again, the colors swirling in the ball resolved themselves into an image. A small fishing boat, rowed by two men and holding two others, struggled through rough waters. Pug brought the image closer, and they could both see that the first man in the boat was Calis, pulling with his more than human strength against the choppy water.

Miranda sighed. "I suppose helping him is out of the question?"

"Difficult, without letting the Pantathians know where we are. A few I could deal with. Those guarding that bridge . . ."

"I know," she said.

Pug looked at Miranda. "You're fond of him, aren't you?"

"Calis?" She was silent for a while. "In a way. He's unique and I feel a . . . connection with him."

Pug sat back, his face a mask. "It's been a long time since I've felt that with anyone." Looking back into the ball, he said, "We could attempt—"

Suddenly there was a flash of orange light in the ball.

Miranda said, "What was that?"

"WHAT WAS THAT?" shouted de Loungville as orange light exploded at the docks.

They had been making steady headway against the running tide as they crossed the boundary of the estuary and entered the river proper. The winds were picking up and the rain increasing, to the point where Erik was bailing in earnest.

No one had spoken for a while. Despite their efforts to stoke the fires before leaving, the rain had been defeating them. Even the biggest fire was starting to diminish. And whatever Nakor's idea, it hadn't been manifested. Then a hum had sounded in the distance, followed a moment later by a bolt of white energy arcing down from the bridge to strike the center of the shipyard.

A huge ball of orange flame climbed into the air, followed by a rising column of black smoke. The sound of the explosion had hurt their ears even at this distance, and a moment later a hot gust of air struck them like a stinging blow.

"Keep rowing!" yelled Calis.

Erik bailed, but he looked over his shoulder, past Sho Pi, who also looked back. "Look!" shouted Sho Pi as a tiny dart of blue light rose from the docks and struck at the leading edge of the bridge of light.

Within seconds another massive bolt of energy rained down on the harbor, exploding buildings and sheds into flame. Two previously intact ships resting at anchor, waiting to be hauled out for repair, caught fire as flames touched their sails.

Now half the shipyard was aflame and hot enough, apparently, for the rain to have little impact. Calis and de Loungville pulled hard, and a few minutes later another blue bolt of light rose up and struck the bridge.

The third blast from above was as large as the first two combined, and fully half the waterfront was engulfed in fire. Suddenly de Loungville let out a harsh laugh. "Nakor!" he said.

Even Calis couldn't hide his astonishment.

Erik said, "But he said he didn't have any magic that would work against the bridge!"

De Loungville said, "But *they* don't know that!" He jutted his chin at the bridge, starting its descent toward Maharta. "Whatever he's doing, they think it's an attack, and they're doing our work for us! They're going to burn down half the city trying to fry the little maniac!"

Suddenly Erik started to laugh. He couldn't help himself. The image of the little man dashing madly from place to place, somehow avoiding the terrible destruction the Pantathians were throwing at him, was comic to consider.

"It's an illusion," said Sho Pi. "The serpent priests are so ready for combat, they don't trouble to look at what is only an illusion. They act as if it were real."

Another tiny blue bolt shot skyward and another thundering response answered, and more of the city's waterfront erupted in flame.

"Gods," said Erik in a half-whisper. "How's he going to get out of that?"

MIRANDA SQUINTED AGAINST the bright image in the ball. "What is going on?"

"Someone has the Pantathians convinced they're under attack, and they're spending a great deal of energy trying to destroy whoever it is."

"Can we help?"

Pug said, "There's enough going on that I think I can slip something in to make merry hell for this Emerald Queen." He closed his eyes and Miranda felt power flowing toward him. He moved his lips slightly, and, like music, the pitch of the energies in the room shifted.

Miranda sat back to watch, and to wait.

EACH TIME THE flames grew and Erik was convinced Nakor must finally be dead, another tiny blue bolt would strike the bridge, and another globe of hellfire would descend on the city. The entire waterfront was now ablaze, from the shipbuilders' estuary to the main harbor. As they took the river to the ocean, and rode the outgoing tide past the harbor mouth, they could see mighty ships burning at the dockside. Erik tried not to imagine Roo stuck on the docks in the midst of that fire and panic, trapped with no way to escape but to jump into the harbor.

As they steered clear of the rocks, they began to follow along the long breakwater they had used to enter the city. Movement caught Erik's eye and he said, "What's that over there?"

In the rain he could barely see, but Calis said, "Some of our men."

He told Sho Pi to move closer, but pulled up short of letting the boat get too close to the rocks. Eric looked and saw three of the men who had been lost in the river the night before. One looked seriously injured, and the other two waved frantically.

Calis stood and shouted, "You've got to swim. We can't risk coming any closer."

The men nodded and one slipped into the water. The other helped the injured man in, and the two aided him as he slowly swam to the boat.

One of the men was Jadow, and Erik was glad to see a familiar face. But of his own company, only Sho Pi was left. Roo and Luis were not with these men. Neither was Greylock.

As Calis sat down to start rowing once more, Erik heard something. It was faint and distant but familiar.

"Wait!" he said, looking down the breakwater.

In the distance, a tiny figure picked its way along the rocks. As it got closer, Erik felt a weight lift from his shoulders, for Roo was limping along toward them. "Hey!" he shouted, waving his hand above his head.

Erik stood and waved back. "We see you!" he shouted.

Roo came to the closest point he could, then jumped feet first into the water. He thrashed through the water and Erik was over the side before anyone could say anything.

Near exhaustion a moment before, he gained renewed strength from Roo's plight, and he struck out through the water as if he had all the strength he had ever possessed. Reaching the smaller man, he took him by the shirt and half carried, half dragged him back through the water.

He pushed Roo into the boat, pulled himself up half over the gunwales, and let the others pull him aboard. As he fell into the bottom of the boat, Erik said, "What kept you?"

"Some damn fool turned loose a horse that kicked me. Damn near broke my leg." He sat up. "I knew there was too much going on near the harbor, so I figured if any of you got out, you'd be coming this way. So here I am."

"Smart," said de Loungville as he and Calis began to row. "Now start bailing."

"What's bailing?" said Roo.

Erik pointed to the bucket in the bottom of the boat. "Take that, fill it there"—he pointed at the bilge—"then dump it over the side."

"I'm injured!" Roo protested.

Looking around the boat, where no man sat without a scar, Erik said, "My heart bleeds for you. Bail!"

"Natombi, Greylock?" asked Erik.

Roo said, "Natombi's dead. He was hit from behind by a soldier while trying to get past another. I haven't seen Greylock since we started back from the harbor."

De Loungville said, "Talk all you want, but start bailing!"

Roo muttered under his breath, but he dipped the bucket into the water gathering at the bottom of the boat and lifted it to dump it over the side.

POWER MANIFESTED IN the air and a singing sound caused every man to turn back toward the city. They had rowed for nearly an hour and were well clear of the harbor mouth, far enough away to have backed off the pace, and now they were turning northeast, making along the coast to the City of the Serpent River.

The bridge of light was close to touching down and armies were now upon it from end to end. But this strange keening, loud enough to cause the men in the boat to flinch, ranged over the landscape, and while they could see nothing of those on the bridge, Erik imagined it must be painful for those close to it.

Then the bridge was gone.

"What?" said Roo.

A thundering report sounded a moment later, and then a warm wind washed over them, rocking the smack against the roll of the sea. Sho Pi said, "Someone made the bridge go away."

De Loungville laughed. It was a dirty, unpleasant sound.

Erik looked at him and asked, "What?"

"I hope those Saaur on the bridge know how to swim."

Jadow, his broad grin lighting up his face in the gloom, said, "As high as that bridge was, man, I hope they know how to *fly.*"

Roo winced. "Must have been a few thousand of them up there."

"The more the better," said de Loungville. "Now, one of you lads needs to take over for me." Suddenly he was falling forward into the boat.

Roo and Sho Pi moved him, while Erik took his place. "He was wounded in the arm," said Erik.

Sho Pi examined him. "And in the side. He's lost a great deal of blood."

Jadow took the tiller and Calis said, "I mean to row until dawn, then we'll put in. That should put us ahead of most of those fleeing up the coast, and maybe we can find a place to lay up."

Sho Pi stood up. "Captain!"

"What?"

Pointing ahead, he said, "I think I see a ship."

Calis stopped rowing and turned to look. Looming up out of the late afternoon darkness, a white sail rose against dark thunderclouds.

"I hope they're friendly," said Roo.

After a moment, Calis turned, and there was no masking the broad grin on his face. "Thank the gods! It's the *Ranger!*"

"Oh, man, I'm going to kiss that Captain," said Jadow.

"Shut up," said Roo. "We want him to stop, not run away."

The others laughed. Then Calis said, "Start waving anything that will draw their attention."

The men stood and started waving swords, trying to catch the late afternoon sunlight, as faint as it was, and reflect it from the blade, or wave a shirt.

Then the ship started to turn and make its way toward them. After a seemingly endless time, it came close enough for a man in the bow to shout, "Is that you, Lord Calis?"

"Get some help down here! I've got injured men."

The ship slowed and sailors scrambled down and helped get the injured aboard. The smack was left to drift, and once they were all on deck, the Captain came forward and said, "Good to see you again."

Erik's eyes widened. "Highness," he said.

Nicholas, Prince of Krondor, said, "Here I'm just 'Admiral.'"

"How did you convince the King to let you come?" asked Calis.

"As soon as the *Ranger* returned with the intelligence you'd sent back, I just told Borric I was going. Erland's in Krondor with Patrick, acting as his son's Regent, so we're both where we want to be. I'll catch you up on court politics later. Right now let's get you below and into some dry clothing."

Calis nodded. "We need to get far from here. And there's much to speak of."

Nicholas called out, "Mr. Williams!"

"Aye, sir?"

"Turn us around and set as much sail as she'll carry. We're making for home!"

"Aye, aye, sir!" came the reply.

Erik was certain he heard relief in the first mate's voice. Sailors led Erik and the others below, and somewhere between then and the next morning, Erik passed out, and was undressed and put into a warm bunk by someone.

MIRANDA SAID, "You took a chance."

Pug smiled. "Not much of one, given the circumstances. All I did was irritate them, really. The city was already theirs."

"What next?"

"More waiting," said Pug, and for an instant she saw his chafing at the need to do so. "When the Queen is ready to make her next move, and she shows us how she is going to dispose of those things in her possession, then we'll know what we must do next."

Miranda stretched. "I'm thinking we need to travel."

"Where?"

"Somewhere warm and pleasant, with empty beaches. We've been locked up over these books for months now, and we're no closer to finding the key to the puzzle."

"There you are wrong, my dear," said Pug. "I've known what the key is for some time. The key is Macros the Black. The problem is where is the bloody lock?"

Miranda stood up and knelt next to him. Putting her arm around his shoulder in a familiar gesture, she said, "Why don't we worry about that some other time. I need a rest. You do as well."

Pug laughed. "I know just the place. Warm beaches, few distractions—if the cannibals don't notice you—and we can relax."

"Good," she said, kissing him lightly on the cheek. "I'll go get my things."

As she left the room, Pug sat back and pondered this strange woman. The light brush of her lips on his cheek was a small gesture, but the touch lingered and he knew it was an open invitation, if a demure one. He had not found time to become involved with any woman since his wife had died, nearly thirty years before. He had known lovers, but they had been companions or distractions. Miranda was possibly something else.

Suddenly he smiled and stood up as he considered that a lonely beach without distractions was the perfect place to begin unraveling her mysteries. The northern great archipelago would be lovely this time of the year, and there were far more deserted islands than populated ones.

As he returned to his own quarters, Pug felt a spring in his step he hadn't experienced since he was a boy, and suddenly he felt the troubles of the world were far away, at least for a little while.

ERIK LOOKED AT the whitecaps as the ship sped through the ocean. Roo had caught him up on the gossip: Prince Nicholas had come down from Krondor with the returning *Freeport Ranger* and had taken personal command of the situation. He had read the reports Calis had sent downriver from his first meeting with Hatonis, and had kept himself abreast of the enemy's movement. He had kept *Trenchard's Revenge* anchored at the City of the Serpent River and had come down the coast against the possibility of Calis and his men having to flee that way.

They had been anchored in the harbor at Maharta for a month when agents in the city got word to him of the coming blockading of the harbor. He had raised anchor and sailed out past a skiff full of city guards and an angry harbormaster, then sailed away from a pursuing cutter. He had stayed out to sea for a week, then returned to find the harbor mouth sealed.

Nicholas had then sailed up the coast for a day, keeping out of sight of the city against the possibility of enemy ships coming up the coast. When he had seen the smoke from the first battle, he had given the order to hug the coastline as closely as safely possible, to determine what was occurring on the land. He had been sailing toward the harbor for a better look when he'd spied the fishing smack carrying the last of Calis's party.

De Loungville came up on deck, his arm and ribs bandaged, and came to stand next to Erik. "How goes it?"

Erik shrugged. "Well enough. Everyone's resting. I'm still sore, but I'll live."

De Loungville said, "You did well back there."

"I did what I could," answered Erik. "What do we do next?"

"We?" said de Loungville. "Nothing. We're going home. It's back to the City of the Serpent River, give the Clan Chieftains what we know in case Hatonis and Praji don't get there, then we pick up *Trenchard's Revenge* and head back to Krondor.

"Once we're there, you're a free man."

Erik said nothing for a while until: "That's a strange thought."

"What's a strange thought?" asked Roo, limping as he came up beside them. He yawned. "Never thought I'd live to see the day I'd enjoy waking up on a ship."

"I was just saying," said Erik, "that the idea of being a free man is strange."

Roo said, "I can still feel the noose around my neck. I know it's not there, but I can feel it."

Erik nodded.

De Loungville said, "I was asking what you two were planning next."

Erik shrugged, but Roo said, "There's a merchant in Krondor who has an ugly daughter. I plan on marrying her and getting rich."

De Loungville laughed while Erik smiled and shook his head in disbelief. "Helmut Grindle," said Erik.

"That's the man," said Roo. "I've got a plan that will make me rich in a year, two at the outside."

"What's that?" said de Loungville.

"If I tell you, and you tell someone else, then there's no advantage, is there?"

De Loungville seemed genuinely amused as he said, "I guess not." He turned to Erik. "And what about you?"

Erik said, "I don't know. I'm going back to Ravensburg, to visit my mother. Then I don't know."

"I don't suppose it would hurt to let you boys know there's a bonus of gold in this for you."

Erik smiled and Roo's eyes lit up.

De Loungville said, "Enough for you to start up that smithy."

Erik said, "That seems like a faint dream."

De Loungville said, "Well, it's a long voyage, and you have a lot of time to think on it. But I have a suggestion."

"What?" asked Erik.

"This battle's just one of many, nothing more. We cut them and they're bleeding, but they're a long way from dead. Burning down the shipyards gained us a few years. Calis thinks maybe five, perhaps six, then the ships will start being built in earnest. Hatonis and the others will run a war, irregulars striking at the lumber trains as they caravan down the mountains and raiding the barges on the rivers; it'll slow them down, but sooner or later the ships will be built.

"We've got agents all through the area, and we'll burn a few of the ships and cause them general grief for a while, but sooner or later . . ."

"They will come," finished Erik.

"Across the Endless Sea, right into the Bitter Sea, and to the gates of Krondor." He waved back toward Maharta, out of sight but still fresh in their memory. "You think on that happening to the Prince's city."

"Not a pretty thought," admitted Roo.

"We've got a lot of work to do, Calis and I. And I could use a corporal."

Roo grinned and Erik said, "Corporal?"

"You've got a knack, son, even if you're not mean enough. Hell, Charlie Foster was a nice guy by anyone's measure before I got my hands on him. A couple of years with me and you'll be spitting cobbler's nails and pissing lightning!"

"Me in the army?"

De Loungville said, "Not just any army. Nicholas is going to give Calis a mandate, signed by the King. We're going to raise up an army the likes of which no man has seen before. We'll train them and drill them, and when we're done we'll have the finest fighting men in history."

Erik said, "I'm not sure."

"You think about it. It's an important job."

Erik said, "I'm a little soured on killing right now, Sergeant."

De Loungville's voice dropped and he spoke firmly but softly. "That's why it's important and that's why you're the right man for the job. We're going to train these men to stay alive."

He patted Erik once on the shoulder. "It's a long voyage. We'll have plenty of time to talk. I'm going to take a rest now."

Erik and Roo watched him leave and Roo said, "You're going to take the job, aren't you?"

"Probably," said Erik. "I don't know that I want to be a soldier the rest of my life, but I do seem to have the knack, and there's something about knowing where I belong that appeals to me, Roo. Back home I never felt that way. I was always 'the Baron's bastard,' or 'that crazy woman's son.'" He lapsed into silence a moment, then said, "In Calis's army I'd just be Corporal Erik." He smiled. "Besides, I have no ambitions to be rich like you."

"Then I'll get rich enough for the both of us."

Erik laughed and the two men stood quietly for a while, simply relishing the fact of having survived to be able to plan a future.

EPILOGUE

★★

REUNION

THE TRAVELER SQUINTED.

Atop a nearby hillock a figure sat, playing a thin reed pipe . . . badly.

The traveler leaned on a staff that compensated for his limp, due in the main to a nasty sword wound to the thigh that was only just now beginning to heal. He removed his hat and ran his fingers through his hair, and the figure on the hill started waving.

Owen limped closer and at last said, "Nakor?"

"Greylock!" said Nakor as he walked down the hill. The road was heavily traveled as thousands fled the invaders, making their way up the old coastal trading route toward the distant City of the Serpent River.

The two men embraced and Nakor said, "You didn't get out with the others?"

"I don't know who got out," he said, using his staff so he could ease himself to the ground. Nakor squatted next to him and put his pipe away in his ever-present shoulder sack.

"Most didn't," said Nakor. "I saw a boat and I think Calis was in it, pretty sure. And some others. Saw a ship, but they were too far away to see me."

"So someone's getting word back to the Prince in Krondor?"

"Pretty sure," said Nakor with a grin.

"What are you doing now?"

"I was practicing my flute and resting. I'm going to the City of the Serpent River."

"Mind if I walk with you?" asked Greylock. "I'm afraid I'm going to slow you down."

"That's all right," said Nakor. "I've got lots of time."

"What happened to you?" asked Greylock. "I got caught up in the crush when everyone was trying to get back to the estuary. I got a horse but got knocked off, then a guardsman swung at me with a sword before he ran off." He gestured to his leg. "I barely got out of the city when the citizens broke down the northeastern gate. Something happened to the invaders and there weren't a lot of them around for a while, so I got through. I hid for a couple of days, until the leg healed enough for me to limp along." He massaged his stiff leg. "Don't know what happened, back there, but something played fair havoc with their invasion."

"Pug of Stardock," said Nakor. "I think it was his trick. He dumped them all into the river. It was grand. I couldn't see much, though, as I was trying to keep from burning."

"You were responsible for all that in the city?"

"Most of it. A trick, really. Got the Pantathians to do the work for me."

"How did you get out of that holocaust?"

"I found that tunnel I told Calis about, the one that led to the western precinct. I got past some rubble and some guards, and when I reached the west side of the river, most of the defenders had fled."

Greylock said, "Ingenious." Then he said, "Wait a minute. If you were on the *other* side of the river, how did you . . ." Pulling himself up with the staff and a hand up from Nakor, Greylock said, "Why don't you tell me about it as we walk?"

Nakor grinned. "Good. If we hurry we may reach the City of the Serpent River before Calis and the others sail home."

"You sure they got out alive?"

"Ship I saw sail past a few days ago?" said Nakor with a grin, pointing out to sea. *"Freeport Ranger;* if that was Calis I saw in the boat, then they're alive, and they're heading that way." He pointed toward the northeast. "City of the Serpent River. They'll do some talking with the clan chiefs, make plans, do other things." They started walking. "If we don't dawdle, we might get there in time."

"Think we can steal some horses?" asked Greylock.

Nakor only grinned in reply as he dug into his sack and pulled out a large round object. "Want an orange?"